Fr...

Fear of Night and Darkn... ...
Underbelly, the BBC TV ...
prison system, was base... ...
The Scar. This success was followed by *The Butcher's Bill* and,
most recently, *Other People's Blood*.

FEAR OF NIGHT AND DARKNESS

'With his quartet of anti-establishment thrillers Frank Kippax
repudiates the form's usual conventions – the restoration of
the status quo, for example – and allows no voice of authority
to go unchallenged.

Everything in this chilling story is displaced and hollow:
modern village life is an empty shell; the police are supersti-
tious, backward and barely procedural; the press are caught
in a dilemma between reportage and exploitation. The
murdered, in the comfortable ignorance of their security,
are the logical targets of a resentful and brutal new underclass. The inevitability of (domestic) violence and terror,
given the present climate in Britain, is the true subject of the
novel.'
CHRIS PETIT, The Times

'Kippax shows an insider's grasp of how institutions like
press and police interact, but behind all this he portrays a
blinkered if not blind Establishment at odds with a disen-
franchised and terrifying underclass. Uncomfortable holiday
reading for complacent politicians.'
MATTHEW COADY, Guardian

'An eye-opener for anyone who thinks journalists are intru-
sive during a murder inquiry. This shows how they inter-
relate with police and how both use each other for their
own ends.'
KATHRYN BAILEY, Today

(further reviews overleaf)

'*Fear of Night and Darkness* is a chilling reminder that even in the developed world the thin veneer of civilisation is often ripped aside so casually. Frank Kippax's powerful and often shocking novel about a horrific crime reveals not only Britain's class divisions but the resulting tensions between two of society's central institutions: the press and the police.

As they cope with the after-effects of multiple murder, journalists and policemen, for different reasons, follow separate agendas. Here there is no right or wrong, good or bad, truth or lie. Employing the slogan "by any means necessary", society's moral guardians move ever closer to the barbarism of the people they fight. Kippax's book offers us a disturbing insight into a Britain where historical progress has suddenly stopped – dead.'

ROY GREENSLADE

OTHER PEOPLE'S BLOOD

'The tale of two young people whose life is shredded by the Troubles in Northern Ireland is all too credible. The exposure of lies, betrayals and hypocrisy – personal and political – is challenging.' *Belfast Telegraph*

'Kippax writes gutsily and conveys a strong understanding of the divisive passions that are destroying Belfast.' *Sunday Times*

'Full of steamy scenes, hatred, lust, snobbishness and all uncharitableness, it proceeds inexorably to its savage conclusion.' *Irish Independent*

'Blood and violence – and sex – there is in plenty, also some fine writing and a genuine feel for the reality of that poor, benighted part of the country.' *Sunday Press*

THE BUTCHER'S BILL

'Kippax unceremoniously kicks Winston Churchill off his pedestal and sniffs out a conspiracy surrounding Rudolf Hess's puzzling flight.'   *The Times*

'Was Hess killed by Winston Churchill? Kippax's book is a story of duplicity and hypocrisy on a massive scale. If true, then the reputations of leading politicians past and present are permanently besmirched.'   *Sunday Mail*

'Twists like a devil's maze . . . calculated to leave ageing colonels twitching and the rest of us open-mouthed . . . seems unlikely to endear him to the secret services.'   *Guardian*

THE SCAR – filmed as UNDERBELLY

'A thundering great novel. What's really amazing is how much he seems to know . . . what more could you want from a thriller? A cracking good read.'   *New Statesman & Society*

'Describes with unnerving prescience just what is going on inside our jails. The book is compelling for its vivid, racy narrative . . . it's also a serious attempt to use the thriller genre to analyse the forces in our society that have combined to create the prison crisis. Its exposure of the way that Whitehall manipulates the media has a chilling authenticity . . . it will appeal equally to conspiracy and cock-up theorists.'   *Guardian*

'Recalls the golden age of British investigative reporting: hard-hitting, crusading. Kippax displays a firm grasp of institutions and their traps, exposes expediency and self-interest masquerading as government, and reveals a Britain regressing to the dark days of Dickens.'   *The Times*

'Kippax develops a complex, ingenious plot at breakneck speed and has a sharp underdog's eye.'

JOHN MCVICAR, *Time Out*

FRANK KIPPAX

FEAR OF NIGHT
AND DARKNESS

HarperCollins*Publishers*

HarperCollins*Publishers*
77–85 Fulham Palace Road,
Hammersmith, London W6 8JB

This paperback edition 1994

1 3 5 7 9 8 6 4 2

First published in Great Britain by
HarperCollins*Publishers* 1993

ISBN 0 00 647617 1

Set in Meridien

Printed in Great Britain by
HarperCollinsManufacturing Glasgow

For Dhondy

Beware of willing judges.

Bertolt Brecht

ONE

In the heart of middle England, there are still places that most people who have never seen them might not believe exist. A quirk of planning, the downgrading of a major road, the building of a motorway to siphon off the traffic, and they are bypassed, isolated, lost. In the empty midland plains there are roads that still have cattle gates across them, there are pubs where passing trade is virtually unknown, in villages that essentially are forgotten. Rowsley is such a place, a lost oasis in a featureless green flat landscape, whose peace is shattered only by the intermittent crashing screams of US and Nato fighters as they train to keep the peace. On a blazing day in early summer, Rowsley can be so tranquil as to seem improbable.

It was, of course, not always like it is today. A solid group of red-brick houses, one strip of granite chips in melting tarmac, a few cars baking and shimmering under a huge blue sky, it has the air of a well-tended beehive. People come and go like bees, slowly, heavily, apparently at random. And very few of them. For the houses are replete, the honey in, the colony rich and rather idle. What workers live in Rowsley now are few and far between, the man who does the tiling, the odd labourer in a still-tied cottage, the rest of them retired. Their children, unable to afford new prices, moved out in the last decades, displaced by the professionals, many of whom commute to London via Northampton, Leicester, Market Harborough. What was once a working village full of neighbours, who in the country way rubbed along together, loved, married, fornicated, fought, is now a village of Good Neighbours, with stickers in their windows and on the telegraph poles to prove it. They do not know each other well, they do not care to, possibly, but they know a stranger when they see one. The nearest police are about three miles away; they are often called to check on those who linger, passing through.

Not that there is crime in Rowsley, it is many years since real crime ruffled the expensive calm. But travellers are a problem, minor and perceived as worse. Travellers, tinkers, gipsies, New Agers, call them what you will, those universal scourges of the modern rural dream with their sliding eyes, their dirty kids and their definition of lawful pickings as anything they can lift when backs are turned. The Good Neighbours when they do meet – at the annual fête, on the coffee circuit, after church, on the school run in the Volvos – often talk about the travellers, and wish they'd stay away. There is a general feeling that it's a growing problem, and that somebody should do something about it, soon. Nothing too drastic, naturally, nothing that would violate their human rights, but something definite. At the very least, it's said, the children of the village are entitled to be left in peace.

Apart from gipsies, and the occasional upset when farm labourers from other, less lucky villages go on a mobile drinking spree, Rowsley has no other public worries. The drains beside the old school house (now a charming conversion with five beds and three recep, lived in by a lovely young couple from Basildon) were troublesome until the council met its obligations, and Scullions' kennels caused untold acrimony before the health authorities closed them down on noise grounds, but apart from that . . . apart from that, probably nothing. Three hundred and fifty souls, or so, in one tight cluster and a few outlying farms, ex-farms, and mansions. Tucked away between the ancient London road and the newish motorway, but close to neither. A dozen miles from Leicester, but in another county. Well served for cities, towns, railways, theatres, shops and cinemas, if you have a car. All in all, a lovely place to live, an idyllic English country setting, a sort of dream. After all, not many people who had not been there had ever even heard of it.

One night three men who had, drove there in a van to do a robbery, and exact a small revenge. What they did must have caused a terrific noise – the noise of four people being put to death most savagely – but no one heard it. By the morning the men had gone, and by the afternoon the news was bursting far beyond the village boundaries. By the evening, this secret English place was firmly on the map.

*　　*　　*

Not all the rich of Rowsley were recent comers-in, as not all the comers-in displayed hostility to anything that might disturb their peace. Not far outside the village centre, up a winding track of well-laid and rollered gravel, was the house where Peter Wilmott lived. His father Simon had earned his money in the woollen trade in Leicester, making machinery to his own designs, then adapting and improving the fine new concepts that filtered out of Germany, and when he had made enough, he toured out from the city in a pony cart at weekends, searching for his ideal spot. Rowsley then was a tiny hamlet — although its heart was busier, placed as it was on a made route to London — and Simon and his wife Elizabeth had set their hearts on it. Brook Bank — like its name quite plain and unpretentious — had arisen slowly from the grasslands in the next eleven months, and cost the sum of one thousand and twenty-seven pounds and sevenpence. In one of its five bedrooms, seventy-eight years ago, their only son was born.

Peter Wilmott, to his father's quiet joy, was everything a son should be. As a child sturdy and courageous, as a young man hard-working and intelligent, and as a partner, diligent and far-seeing. He knew the business inside out by the time hostilities started, and by great good fortune had a 'good war' training younger men to understand the intricacies of weapons guidance systems. Among other things it taught him where the future lay, and in his father's dwindling years he began to diversify the firm from knitting and textile machinery into electronics, micro-engineering and, finally, computers. Both his parents died when he was forty-four, a personal tragedy compounded by the fact that he was still childless after seven years of marriage to a local farmer's daughter, Audrey. Two years later, at the age of thirty-seven, she delivered him their only child, a girl called Tessa.

Tessa, too, grew up strong and — as her mother liked to say — 'beautiful enough'. Clever enough, what was more, to go to Cambridge on a scholarship to study mathematics, a subject that she followed as an academic career until she met and fell in love with Damon Hegarty, a visiting mathematician who even at the age of twenty-six had seen the possibilities for his subject in the modern world, and could, he boasted, 'wrap any mainframe round his little finger in twenty minutes'. Surprisingly, Tessa's father reacted violently against the match, apparently on the sole grounds that Hegarty was 'named after some American writer chap, or something', but Damon was determined, and infinitely flexible. As well as the skills he would bring to the family business, he offered what to Peter was the ultimate in sacrifices – he would take the family name. Tessa, a feminist who was interested by this idea at first, later put her foot down hard. If Damon changed his name, she declared, she would not marry him. But neither would she change her own, and never would they change the firm's. Honour was satisfied, champagne was cracked, and the tiny church at Rowsley, two years after their first meeting, was filled to overflowing for the ceremony. The Good Neighbours, charmed and gratified to be invited by this distinguished if reclusive family, agreed it was a splendid match, despite the names question, and after six years nothing had changed to materially alter that general opinion. Except, of course, the matter of the babies. Where were the babies? Could Tessa Wilmott be cursed with her mother's problems with fertility?

But this weekend was too sunny for thought of curses. It was sunny and warm enough for the whole family to spend the day outside. The gardens of Brook Bank, over the decades, had been reformed and refined to give wonderful views in almost all directions, and to provide sun-traps at any hour of the day, whichever quarter the wind was blowing from. Peter Wilmott was sadly very frail now, with washed-out eyes set in skin that was loose and blotched with brown. Sitting in a stable wooden chair, his knees covered with a light blanket despite the heat, he had that morning looked at Tessa in her sundress of white poplin, and decided that she was filling out.

'Are you expecting, chick?' he asked. 'Are you going to make an old man happy before it's too late?'

Sitting next to him, Joyce Withers raised a thin, twisted hand in admonishment. Joyce was only sixty-two, but she had arthritis and could not walk without a frame, although she was Audrey's nurse and helper – a fact that caused the family some merriment from time to time.

'Peter. Don't be so bad. Leave the girl alone.'

Tessa, who was laying a shaded table for some lunch, glanced across the lawn towards the house, where Damon was uncorking vinho verdhe. Unseen by her father, she allowed her hand to brush her belly.

'It's never too late, Dad,' she grinned. 'Like it's never too early for a drink . . .'

It was just before midday.

About a hundred miles away, in a place called Moorside, in a road called Harding Lane, Ronnie Keegan lay on his back in bed and tried to keep his eyes open. The ceiling was a fawn colour – apricot, Eileen had named it – and it did not reflect what little light filtered through the curtains with any harshness. But Ronnie Keegan's eyes would not allow even that. They felt hard, like boiled stones, and they ached violently. His head hurt, also, except when he pressed his fingers fiercely into his temples. Worst of all, his mouth. The clichés rolled slowly through his brain: a tramdriver's glove; a coolie's jockstrap; the bottom of a birdcage. He settled for the one that fitted best, and muttered it: 'It tastes like shit.'

The bedroom window was open – it was the noise of a lorry grinding up the hill that had awoken him – and for a while he listened to the sounds outside. The next-door children playing in the garden, the intermittent barking of a dog, a radio somewhere playing pop. It was neither loud nor raucous, any of it, there were even cows calling gently across the road. Hung over as he was, he could still roll his luck round in his mind, examine it, wonder how long it would go on. It occurred to him that after tonight's work he would be putting something in, something substantial for the coffers, something that would open Eileen's eyes. It occurred to him that, somehow or other, he would have to keep it dark.

'Eileen!'

He shouted explosively, vibrating his skull in an agonising way. He leaned sideways, afraid he might be sick, the pattern in the carpet coming up to meet him. Control. Control. And no reply. Eileen had gone to see her mother, like he'd told her to. One day, undoubtedly, she'd decide not to come back.

Interested by this thought, Ronnie sank back into his pillow to turn it over better in his mind. He would miss the sex, she

13

worked hard at the sex however drunk he got, and he would miss the cachet of having such a classy bird. But in other ways it had gone on long enough, true love had a term on it, and surely, true love had run its course? She put up with plenty, he had no complaints in that department, but it was the way she took it, sometimes. So miserable, so much like her mother, that was it. Her mother, without the shadow of a doubt, was high-class poison.

In the beginning, the class had been the best thing. Ronnie was good-looking, sure, he could have his choice of women in the company he kept, the sort of woman he'd grown up with, but Eileen Thorpe was very different. She had the accent and the office job, the typing and the qualifications she had studied for. On top of that the car, a fully paid Fiesta, and the three-bedroom house on Harding Lane, not an estate. When he'd first seen that, Ronnie had not believed it, a girl of twenty-four with her own mortgage, something he had never contemplated. All her own work, too, she was not divorced or separated, she hadn't had a penny off her mum and dad for it. On top of that she'd slept with him the first night, and hadn't booted him out of the quiet, roomy house first thing next morning. A bit of rough, he'd thought – he'd still been on the roofing in those days – but she had kept him on. She fancied him like mad, she said, but she also liked him, reckoned he was great. They spent a lot of time in bed together in those early days, while she listened to his plans and dreams and didn't crack a smile. She'd believed in him.

The plans and dreams. Ronnie stared up at the ceiling, watching the patterns of the light, and wondered if he'd got it right this time. He must have done, he'd worked it over long enough, he'd polished up the details till they shone. They'd been at the final stages until five o'clock this morning, hadn't they, but they'd only really hit the hooch when they were satisfied they'd got it right. The drinking was a send-off, a good luck thing, even Boon had had too much, although he was the driver and a man of constant care. A good piss-up, then a good night's sleep. When Mick rang, they would have some liveners, then away.

'Tonight we'll all be rich,' said Ronnie, to see what it would sound like firm and loud. It sounded good, it brought a little tremor of anticipation. 'The old adrenalin,' said Ronnie. 'By Christ, it's going to be a good one.'

The phone rang, and he had it instantly.

'Hallo, Mick. You're fucking late as usual.'

TWO

Mrs Audrey Wilmott was the spryest of the old ones at Brook Bank, although she would tell anybody, with a touch of pride, that she could 'pop off' at any moment. She had a heart condition that had been established for many years, which occasionally laid her low for days on end. Now, standing at the open kitchen window with her daughter, she referred to it, obliquely.

'Look at them out there. Doesn't it depress you sometimes, darling?'

There was a note of sadness which surprised Tessa.

'What do you mean, Mum? They look wonderful.'

There was a long sweep of lawn between the house and the table where they'd lunched. The longish grass was blowing in the breeze.

'We're so decrepit,' replied her mother. 'Look at Dad, he's changed so drastically in the last two years.'

'But he's happy! He's slowing down a bit, but he's happy. Isn't he?'

Mrs Wilmott, aware that she had upset her daughter, turned a smiling face to her. She was sixty-nine, but her face was that of a much younger woman. All through her life she could have lied about her age by at least ten years, although she'd never bothered to.

'I'm being silly. It's the sunshine, the beauty of it all. It's such a lovely day.'

'Logic?'

'Logic. The sun's shining, the garden's wonderful, and Dad and Joyce look to me like two . . . I'm being silly. One too many glasses with my lunch. I've known them both so long, darling. I love them both so much. One day they're going to die.'

Tessa saw her father and Joyce Withers for a moment through her mother's eyes. They were bent, frail, both wrapped as if for winter. A cold hand touched her heart, and once again she touched her belly, a small, involuntary movement. Which her mother, sharp as a knife, noticed.

'You're pregnant, aren't you? Are you?'

Tessa nodded.

'It was going to be a surprise. Damon's sneaked champagne into the other fridge, everything. Why do you think we're having a dinner party on a Sunday night? Why do you think I paid heaven only knows how much for that asparagus?'

Her mother touched her arm.

'We may be decrepit,' she said, 'but we're not daft, you know. Tessa, I'm so pleased. I'm so happy for you. For all of us.'

'But the others don't know, do they? I thought Dad might have guessed.'

'I'm sure he hasn't. He just thinks it's because Damon's got to go away tomorrow. It's a mother's intuition.'

'But you are glad, aren't you? Really? I mean . . . intimations of mortality, and all that.'

Her mother said briskly: 'We all have to die, Tessa. Even your baby, one day. Dad's getting frail, he's wandering a bit, he's very old. The important thing is you're pregnant now, at last you're going to have a grandchild for us all. If Dad hangs on until it's born, I promise you he'll die happy. I promise you.'

The old man, across the lawn, raised a hand.

'He wants us,' Tessa said. 'He's waving. Oh Mum, I don't want any of you to die. I couldn't bear it.'

She turned and hugged her mother, who smiled into the fine dark curls, indulgently.

'Silly girl,' she said. 'I love you. Well done, Tess. Well done.'

Halfway down his second pint, Ronnie began to feel all right. They were in the Con Club, where the dark heavy curtains were always drawn, however bright the day outside. Open the curtains and the regulars began to moan, the snooker players muttered obscenities (you weren't allowed to swear out loud at table) and the lads on the dartboard went berserk. It was a very traditional club, with beer prices subsidised and the steward, Norman, mental. This lunchtime it was quietish, and cool, and dim, which suited Ronnie perfectly.

17

'You look terrible,' he said, with satisfaction. 'You look like a pile of turds without the class.'

Mick Renwick did not respond. Ronnie's insults, his 'witty strokes' did not amuse him, nor insult him, neither did they impress. At this time of the morning (that is, approaching two p.m.) not much got through to Mick. His head – to quote a social worker whose nose he'd broken once – was like a sealed container, full of smoke. The first task was to drink a pint of Guinness without spilling too much of it, so that he could come back to life again.

Ronnie, able to sip his bitter now that the first pint had hit the bottom floor, watched his friend in distaste and amazement. He was shaking, both hands clamped round the heavy pot to steady them, bringing his mouth towards the creamy head to suck the alcohol into it. The hands, although quite small, were hard and strong, as Ronnie knew, ingrained with slate dust, stone and brick from roofing work. The little finger on the right one was fluttering as he began to swallow noisily, as if it had no strength at all.

'You'll die, you will,' said Ronnie, as the last of the black fluid disappeared. 'It'll be a relief to me when you fall off a roof.'

Miraculously, though, the shakes were cured, as in some story from the Bible. Mick's pale face, almost waxen underneath the mop of dusty curls, was becoming lively, darker, full of fun. The eyes, dull and lifeless thirty seconds previously, began to sparkle.

'I've never fell off yet,' he said. 'If I did I'd bounce, I reckon. Anyway, you're the queer one. We supped enough last night to drown a horse. I don't know how your liver stands it.'

Ronnie, also, was cured. He smiled on his friend with gladness, all disgust and animosity gone.

'Youth, beauty and an iron will. You're a shagged-out old fart, that's your problem, mate. You can't do it any more, you're bolloxed.'

He raised his glass and tilted his head back far. The liquid cascaded down his open throat, cool and bitter, utterly divine. There was nothing in the world to touch it, not sex, not driving, anything. For a moment he forgot the purpose of the day, forgot the drive, the murderous intentions. For a moment he thought the afternoon and evening lay before him, for getting rat-arsed with his mates.

'You won't say that when the mayhem starts,' responded Mick, equably. 'You'll shout for shagged-out Mickie when they send the Army in.'

Ronnie closed his throat and licked his lips, the empty glass still in his hand. Don't say that, he thought. Don't wish problems on us, mate.

'Bollocks,' he said. 'There's no one they can call. One old geriatric and two withered-out old tarts. I don't know why I'm taking you, you're a bloody liability.'

'Experience,' said Mick. 'Some bugger who won't go soft when the wheels come off the bus. Talking of which, have you got the Vaseline? No point in doing it the hard way, is there?'

'You're bloody vile you are. You'd screw anything, you would. You'd screw your bleeding grannie.'

Mick grinned. His teeth were yellow and broken from his fights, like a terrier's or an ageing rat's.

'You dig her up, I'll do the business. Now go on, tightarse, bloody get them in.'

He would an'all, thought Ronnie, walking to the bar. I bet he would.

Even if Damon had not proved much good at fathering children, as the Good Neighbours sometimes whispered, he could not be faulted on the business side. Peter Wilmott recognised this, and within a year of his son-in-law's entering the firm, he was prepared, in his frank and open way, to acknowledge he'd been wrong. I was rich when Tessa trapped her man, he would laugh, but now I'm going to die a millionaire! It's me who was the stupid one, not my darling daughter.

Indeed, the family firm's steady rise began to look unstoppable when Damon took control. Peter, for several years, had played a backseat role, leaving the day-to-day running and much of the long-term planning to a board of trusted men. Damon said nothing of their trustiness, but saw huge holes very quickly in their strategies. His expertise was extraordinary, his grasp of business intuitively exact, and his foresight remarkable. He proved shortly that he had the ruthlessness as well. Within six months of taking up his post, he had targeted the

19

'dead wood' in both personnel and policy. Heads rolled and Peter did not argue. Within eleven months Damon was in full control, new avenues were being explored with Japanese-style vigour, and the profit graph was steepening. The mathematician with the quiet manner was something of a genius.

Tessa Wilmott was not surprised. Nor, despite her feminism, was she much upset about leaving her job. Cambridge was not the real world, she would say, nor mathematics anything other than a chimera, an ivory tower she was glad to run away from. The real world, for her, was a small house seven miles from Brook Bank, close to her beloved parents and close to the firm's headquarters where Damon worked. She tried actively to make babies – the couple's mutual lust enhanced by the possibility that each time might be the magic one – and did not panic when nothing seemed to happen. She knew her mother's record, she went to specialists early to be assured that there was nothing 'wrong', and she enjoyed the state of childlessness as much as she looked forward to the ending of it.

Nor did she vegetate. She allowed Damon to extend her basic knowledge of computers until she was more than competent enough to have run courses, which she contemplated for a month or two. But she loved peace, the isolation she could have in her small house while Damon was at work, and she did not fancy interlopers. If she wanted casual conversation she had the Chain and Harrow opposite, and rising young mums who were often lonely and always glad to chat. She began to dabble in programming, then in writing games. To her surprise she started making money from the royalties, building up a reputation among the cognoscenti for hard games that were noted for their humour. Not surprisingly, her 'fame' leaked out. There had been a chat on *Woman's Hour*, the offer of a book, most recently an extended interview with a young woman writer who was doing a big piece for one of the Sunday supplements. Tessa (unimpressed by her own 'vast cleverness') found it amusing and delightful.

But Damon had to be away a lot, and recently the meetings had been piling up. They had known for certain for nine days that she was pregnant, but they had wanted above everything to break the glad news properly. First a trip to Dublin, then he'd flown to Paris. He had come back late the night before, the Saturday, and he was due out to Frankfurt on the Monday morning. He had found Tessa in the Chain and Harrow, glowing with content, and she had worked it out. Mum and Dad and Joyce were expecting them in the morning, Sunday, and they would stay all day. She'd organised a lunchtime and an evening feast which they'd transport early, and Damon could get some champagne from the landlord (that sort of village, that sort of pub) to put on ice in the spare fridge in the garage apartment at Brook Bank. It was a window of opportunity, in the language of the circles that they moved in, and they would go for it. Then he could fly off to Frankfurt for three days, and she would wait and grow their baby for him, and everyone would be happy. They would *know*.

The phone call came at ten past three, when Dad and Joyce had both decided they would take a nap. Audrey took it, and waved to Damon from the drawing room window.

'It's Germany,' she said. 'A Mr Schulze.'

'Oh no,' said Damon. 'Coming.'

Five minutes later he returned. He would have liked to have talked to Tessa on her own, but they all knew business. He shook his head and made a face.

'Frankfurt. *Eine kleine Probleme*. I'm going to have to go tonight. I'm sorry.'

Nobody argued, they all knew business. But Tessa bit her lip.

'That's the Germans,' Damon said. 'We're meeting at six o'clock tomorrow. In the morning.'

'It's how they make their money, I suppose,' said Audrey.

'Oh dear,' said Tessa. 'It was meant to be so special, too, tonight.'

Damon took her hand.

'Excuse us for a moment everyone. We'll go and have a little talk.'

'Krauts,' said Peter, sadly.

THREE

After three pints in the Con Club, Mick Renwick would have loved a session, and Ronnie himself was sorely tempted. It wasn't that late, yet, and anyway, maybe it would count towards the alibi. After all, you wouldn't expect two pissed blokes to drive a hundred miles and back to do a job, would you?

'Just one more,' wheedled Mick. 'Christ, Ronnie, you sound like my old lady. I've only had the basic wetting of the throat.'

'No. Not today. For Christ's sake, you know the plan. Doggo's waiting.'

A shadow of dislike crossed Mick's face. Doggo Boon, to him, could go and stuff himself.

'You scared of him?' he said, playing on what he saw as Ronnie's weak spot. 'Is he the gaffer, then?'

Ronnie was stung, but he did not show it.

'I'm the gaffer and he's the wheels. We talked it through till five o'clock this morning, except you were too pissed to take it in. There's thirty grand on this, you twat, maybe fifty. There's shotguns, too.'

Mick digested this. He wanted a shotgun, he'd always wanted a shotgun, he did not quite know why. Except that there were some rats he knew, that he'd like to put to death. He continued to grumble only for the sake of it.

'Way you go on, you'd think I'd had too much. You've seen me on a roof with fifteen pints inside, did you ever see me fall? You're just a tightarse, cause it's your shout.'

Ronnie winked.

'That's right. Tight as a fish's whatsit. I was going to get some bottles to take out. Some cider and some Scotch. Anything else you'd like? Some crisps and peanuts? Or would that upset your stomach?'

Mick did not eat when he was drinking, it took up too much room. He grinned with ill grace.

'Get us a pint while you're waiting. Norman'll have to get the Scotch up from the cellar. Don't be a cunt all your life.'

The club was getting raucous now, now it was after closing time, but the crowd around the bar made room for Ronnie without interest. Ronnie was known there, but he liked to spread himself around the pubs and clubs, so he was not that well known. This was deliberate, part of what he called his long-term strategy, or his forward planning. As was, in fact, the reason they were drinking there today.

'Ronnie?' said Norman. 'Pint of blackstuff and a bitter?'

'Aye, go on. And a bottle of cider and some Scotch, for out. Can do?'

'Session, is it?'

On a whim, Ronnie changed his story just a little. He decided it was better if he and Mick were thought to be heading off in separate ways.

'Mick's off to Liverpool. See his mum or something, I dunno. Some sort of family do. I'm going home to fix the car. Probably end up sleeping off the cider in the garage.'

'Why not?' said Norman, without interest. 'One bitter. I'll fetch the Scotch up while the Guinness settles. How much cider? I've got the litre bottles.'

'Yeah, two litres. No, four. Cheers.'

To a man beside him, whom he knew by sight, he said: 'Bastard, intit? Working on a car weather like this. Waste of time.'

'Never mind, mate. Drink all that cider and you won't feel a thing. It's loony juice, is that.'

Ten minutes later, when they left, Ronnie felt smugly that he'd done a terrific job.

'Don't forget,' he told Mick, 'if any bugger asks, you're in the Pool tonight. A knees-up at your Mum's.'

'You should've been a fucking general,' Mick replied.

For once, Damon Hegarty's attitude caught his wife on a raw nerve. To her, it seemed he was more interested in the Frankfurt meeting than in their ruined celebration.

'I'll need to go home and pack,' he told her, as they walked into the kitchen. 'It's a nuisance, but I've got a feeling something good might come of it. Something terrific.'

Tessa's silence caused him to glance back. Her face was closed.

'Tessa? What's up?'

'What's *up*? Are you serious?'

'But . . . look, I know tonight was . . .' He realised the enormity of what he'd done, but could not think how to make amends. 'Tess,' he said. 'I'm sorry, honestly. I mean, there's nothing we can do, though, is there?'

The phone began to ring, two rooms away. Everybody else was still out in the garden.

'Well we can decide what to say, at least, can't we?' she exploded. 'We can decide whether to cancel the celebration, or not. How we should break the news.'

Damon was twitchy. A ringing telephone must be answered. It was an absolutely basic business tenet. She read his tortured face.

'Oh go and get the stupid phone! It's probably someone else who wants your time! It's probably some other stupid interference!'

His smile when he returned was carefully composed.

'It's for you. Janis Sanderson. Serves you right for giving her this number. Talking of stupid interference.'

Damon, as she swept out, got himself a glass of water. Outside the old ones still sat, and he felt a sudden pang. Selfishness, and guilt for it. When his wife returned he opened his hands in a quick, submissive gesture.

'OK, I admit it. I'm a selfish pig. Let's start again.'

Tessa laughed. 'That poor woman caught the earful, she must have wondered what had hit her. Unluckily for her, she wanted to come round. Wonderful timing!'

'On a Sunday? She's the journalist, yes? The colour supp?'

'Journalist, no. A "writer". No, I'm being unfair, that makes her sound an idiot and she's rather nice, in fact, she always sounds embarrassed when she says it. Did you know she only lives at Didwell?'

'I think so. I can't remember. I take it you said no?'

'Of course. She said she just wanted to check up on one or two things and she was going to Grayson's anyway to fetch some tack, but she understood. I blamed it all on you. I said we were having a family celebration on a Sunday because you'd mucked up last week, and now you've mucked this up as well by flying off to Germany and we'd had a row, so she's coming in the morning. I was most impressive, I sounded as if I hated you. I do hate you. Oh Damon.'

He moved across the kitchen and put his arms around her, in condolence and apology. Tessa squirmed so that she had her back to him, and pulled his hands down to feel her stomach.

'Dad said I was filling out,' she said. 'I'm not, am I? How can people tell? How can people guess so easily?'

'It's the maternal glow. I didn't used to believe in it before. There's something in your lips and eyes.'

She breathed in deeply and exhaled.

'Janis Sanderson didn't notice it when she interviewed me last week. Or the time before. It was one of her last questions, in fact. Were we planning on a family?'

'She should have asked around the village. Got the latest from the witches' coven. Why didn't she do it on the phone?'

'What?'

'These extra questions. Won't it be a nuisance, her coming round?'

'Not to you, you'll be away, you pig. No, she said she'd come first thing, I told her we were early risers, it won't take very long, she said.' She giggled. 'Maybe it's because she's a writer, not a journalist – she said she liked to see her subjects' faces. Maybe she's going to denounce me as a tax evader! A secret sex maniac!'

She wriggled back round face to face. She rubbed her forehead on his chin.

'It was nice conceiving, wasn't it?' she murmured. 'I'm sure I know exactly when we did.'

'Mm,' replied her husband.

Neither Ronnie nor Mick Renwick ever liked to walk, but today they had no option. Mick had last held a licence several years before, finally deciding after many fines and scattered weeks in Strangeways Jail that drinking was more to his taste than driving, anyway. As a roofer who could do stone as well as slate he was never short of transport, so for him the system worked. Ronnie liked to drive as well as drink, but part of his long-term planning was to keep his nose clean on essentials, so for sessions he either went by matemobile or used Eileen as his wheels. Driving was conspicuous, in any case, and on his home patch, Ronnie was well known. He had, in consequence, decided from the moment he had planned this hit that he would not use his own car, or even Eileen's, the brilliance of this stroke growing on him until it had reached almost talismanic significance. He had even stripped the valve-gear from his car, although there was nothing wrong with it, to make sure that no one would claim that he'd been mobile. For most jobs, Ronnie had observed, were pulled extremely close to home, and the police mind on the subject worked the same. If something big happened, the cops dragged in everyone in their local area, as if the motor car had never been invented, and nine out of ten times, they were right. In company sometimes Ronnie lectured his mates about it, privately assuring himself that they'd never learn, however. Ronnie did a lot of observation, a lot of thinking, and this key idea about the current job, this 'central tenet' as he called it, was characteristic of his forward planning. They'd drive two hundred miles or more, there and back, and they'd be in and out and gone again like a fox in a hencoop, like a thief in the night. It was a masterstroke.

Outside the Con Club, though, it was very hot. To Mick the masterstroke, and the thirst, were equally irksome and irrelevant.

'We must be mad,' he said. 'A day like this, to drive all that way with a streak of piss like Doggo. Let's just drink the stuff. We could put the whisky in the cider, do you like that? Great buzz.'

Ronnie was patient. He could read Mick Renwick like a book. Mick Renwick needed handling. Man management.

'When we've finished this,' he said, 'you'll be able to drink Scotch and cider out of the bellybutton of the fattest tart you've ever seen. They'll be queueing up.'

They shared the laugh, and Ronnie congratulated himself on defusing the trouble. The beer inside him was just the right amount. He felt warm and successful, he felt well towards the world. A tang of lust crossed his tongue. Whisky and cider would be all right.

'Come on, let's get up and meet him. You go up Turfpit, I'll go up Harding Lane. We're meeting him behind the cricket club.'

'Bleeding nonsense,' muttered Mick. 'Cloak and dagger shit.'

He did not argue, though, and Ronnie watched him go, still euphoric. He began to wonder, as he strode up Harding Lane towards his home, which he intended to be seen near, how the night would turn out. There'd be cash galore, that was one thing, and there'd be shotguns, too, although he'd more or less decided he did not want one afterwards, not at any price. He might use one for the executions, if it was the cleanest, safest way, but they'd decided the night before to leave the final method till they'd sussed the whole thing out. There'd been no arguments about the actual need to kill them, although in some respects he regretted that, because they were a bit pathetic, really, they were very old and brittle. They deserved it, though, no danger, they'd treated him like shit, the lot of them. The feasibility of masks had been brought up, but everyone had been unanimous on that: masks were stupid, they made you feel daft, and they were uncomfortable into the bargain. Why be uncomfortable, Mick had said, when you could knock them off instead? They were old, and they were rich bastards, and they certainly deserved it. But they would do it quick and clean, they'd all agreed on that, as well. No funny stuff, or torture, or sadistic practices. They were not animals. Although it did cross his mind, as he toiled up the hill, that Mick might change his mind, when faced with crumpet. Even geriatric crumpet.

Ronnie thought about their daughter. What a pity she would not be there. Tessa, the lady with the lamps. Now that would be a very different proposal . . .

He had reached the track across the top, and caught a flash of blue in one of the old turfpits, that he guessed was Doggo's latest van.

We'll come and we'll go, he thought, and no one'll know.

Brilliant.

FOUR

Ronnie's 'central tenet' – a high speed in-and-out in someone else's wheels – had led him almost inevitably to Harold 'Doggo' Boon. It was not that he knew him very well, or trusted him to do the business, except on hearsay, or ever saw him becoming an intimate of any sort, for none of that stuff mattered on a job like this. If they fucked up they were finished anyway, and if they pulled it off there was no way Doggo could grass on them. If it all went smoothly there'd be bodies everywhere and blood all up the walls. And just in case, he had another small trick up his sleeve, a custom-built insurance policy, which he'd keep there till the time came. In truth, though, he had few qualms about his wheelsman. Doggo came with form.

His name had been mentioned, quite appropriately, in a local graveyard where Ronnie had gone to split a quiet bottle on a Saturday with a man he knew called Scabbie. Scabbie was a con of considerable experience, who more or less divided up his life between his mother's house and Strangeways. When he was at home he drank, and to buy enough of it, when robbing was too much of a fag, he dug the graves at his local church. This was his insurance policy, because he saw himself as a bad man, a fallen lamb that God might yet consider saving, and it had the bonus of unlimited fresh air, something he missed when he was inside. He was a good gravedigger, although he had on more than one occasion been found unconscious in a fresh-dug hole just before its new occupant was due to take up residence, but he liked also to keep up with his trade. Primed by two large bottles of Strongbow and a quarter Scotch, he had recommended Doggo unreservedly, and given Ronnie a contact address, a pub in Huddersfield where he picked up messages.

'He's killed at least one man,' he added, earnestly, 'and he's as hard as arseholes, mate. On my father's grave, you'll be all right with Doggo.'

He stopped, seated on a mound of earth, his jean-clad legs

dangling into the hole that he was digging. A look of doubt had settled on his weatherbeaten face.

'Mind you,' he added, 'the bastard doesn't drink, so maybe you shouldn't trust him after all. He's a wizard with the cars, though. Magic.'

Ronnie had done a lot more homework before he'd picked his man, and the indicators were universally positive. The worst he ever heard was that Doggo was difficult to have a laugh with, the best that he was tight as death with information. When he finally got to meet him, Ronnie was almost nervous – until he saw a gangly nondescript with pimples and an enormous Adam's apple. And Doggo did drink, he was sitting in front of a pint of lager with the top well off. Within minutes Ronnie was relaxed, in charge again, expanding on the terrific hit that only he could lead them to, that only he could guarantee. When he left, the preliminaries had been done, and he told himself with confidence that Doggo was just another guy whose mates had talked him up sky-high. But a guy who knew the business, who'd done some proper jobs, and who was calm and steady for all he was only twenty-four or so. Ronnie realised, as he drove away, that he did not know, still, if he'd really killed a man. It wasn't something that you asked a bloke, was it? Not normally.

The feeling of the rightness of his choice grew steadily over the next three meetings. Each time they chose a different pub, each time Doggo turned up with different wheels. He showed no impatience at Ronnie's caginess about the details, and no excitement as the sums involved were gradually revealed. He accepted the rightness of not meeting Mick at first, and listened calmly as Ronnie introduced the element of violence that might be necessary.

'It's the ident thing,' said Ronnie. 'Me and Mick have talked it through. There's only one way to be sure I don't get recognised. Unless you've got another bright idea?'

'How long ago d'you work there? How many of them know you?'

'I quit months ago. I was the gardener. Well, general fucking dogsbody, you know rich bastards, they treated me like shit. I stuck it for six months or so, a bit more maybe. Then I told them where to stuff their job.'

29

Boon sipped his lager.

'How many in the house?'

'Old bastard and his two dried-up old shags. It's a piece of piss. They've got alarms but they're nothing, they're out the bloody ark. Tight, he is. Fucking millionaire.'

'They all are,' agreed Doggo. 'What about the neighbours? Village? Will anybody hear?'

They'd talked it round and round and inside out and backwards – Ronnie carefully giving no clues, no hints away as to what county it was in, let alone what area – and Doggo had never blinked at any of the implications. Ronnie, paranoid about this unnatural calm in bed beside a sleeping Eileen one night, conceived the chill notion that Doggo might take part in it, then claim he had not been told there would be violence, had been bumped into it by force of circumstance, and therefore was not guilty like the others were. Ronnie had hated him then, for an unknown quantity, not a comfortable old twat from way back, like Mick Renwick. He had had a brainwave, though, and got out of bed right there and then and rooted in the lumber room for the Instamatic camera that he'd once used to take filthy pictures of Eileen with, fuzzy shots of his foreshortened stomach and her blurred, ghostly face too close for proper focus, sucking at what could have been his prick. When he'd found it he'd returned, contented and aroused, and woken her to give her one, for old times' sake.

Mick, strangely, had been the major problem over Boon. Mick hated planning, and punctiliousness, and efficiency, and he showed it by undermining Ronnie, mocking at the endless worrying over details, which he said were forced on Ronnie by the new man, who clearly was the power now, the puller of the strings. Ronnie could handle it, and after the first get-together of the three of them, had taken Doggo off alone and laughed about it. Mick Renwick was all right, he'd said, he'd known him years, he was aces in tight corners. Doggo was uninterested rather than dubious, more or less indifferent.

'I'd say he was a drunken twat, if anyone asked me. If I didn't know you better I'd reckon you were crazy, having him along.'

For the moment, Ronnie decided to ignore that.

'He is a drunken twat,' he said. 'He'll drink anything, I've seen him drink brass polish. But the more he drinks the harder he gets, he's like a bleeding dynamo. He's killed blokes.'

The interest level in the angular, pointed face did not change.

'In my experience,' he said, 'twats who drink too much are dangerous twats. They make mistakes. They get caught out. They're asking for it. Would he talk?'

It was time for Ronnie to take umbrage. Maybe Mick was right about this kid, maybe he was too full of bullshit. He let his face suffuse with angry blood, leaning forward as he did so.

'Listen, twat,' he said. 'Are you suggesting I can't choose my men? If that's what you think, there's the door, OK? You can fuck off out of it.'

He had both hands on the table, his weight on them, his dark and handsome face thrust out pugnaciously. As usual they were in an empty pub, a lonely pub, not even the landlord or landlady at the bar to watch them. Whatever Doggo thought might happen next, he read the message so far. He put his drink down and moved his trunk back from the table, almost imperceptibly. Ronnie had learned about 'body language' from Eileen, who was into that sort of thing, he'd noted points while in the act of mocking her. He could tell that Doggo – the calm indifference of his thin face notwithstanding – was signalling submission to the leader of the pack.

Ronnie dropped backwards in his chair, spread his hands expansively, palms displayed. The dark, angry look became a sunny smile, perhaps a hint of ruefulness in it.

'OK, forget it. When you know me better you won't say that kind of thing, you won't even think it. Detail, that's my hallmark, right? Detail and planning. I wouldn't be surprised if you've heard that from someone else? What people say about me?'

Doggo did not answer, although there was, maybe, the faint ghost of a smile. Ronnie, after a moment, drained his glass.

'Listen. Let's seal it with a pint. Lager?'

Harold Boon had been drinking a slimline tonic water. If he demanded more, Ronnie told himself irrationally, there would be problems. If he refused a lager, he might have to seriously reconsider his fitness for the team. But Doggo nodded.

'Dash of lime,' he said. 'Thanks, Ron.'

Total submission, thought Ronnie with a glow. That'll do me fine.

In the garden at Brook Bank, the breeze had died away completely. Tessa and Damon, aware of passing time, tried almost consciously to make it pass more slowly. Damon was stretched out on a sun-lounger, while his wife sat languorously in a chair next to her mother. Peter and Joyce had gone into the house an hour or so before to have their naps.

'It's so lovely here,' said Audrey. 'Do you know, I almost prefer it now we haven't got a gardener. The grass is so lush on one's bare feet.'

'Until you step on a bee,' laughed Damon. 'Some of them are the size of bats this year.'

Tessa made a rueful face.

'What you're forgetting, Mum, is that I do most of it these days. That's fine when I've got the time to spare, but it can't go on for ever. There's so much of it.'

'Be fair. I do the flowers,' replied Audrey. 'Peter's done a fair amount as well, this last week or so. He's been good lately, hasn't he?'

No one answered. Peter had been 'good' in that his mind had been quite clear and sharp. Increasingly, these days, he had what Joyce had dubbed his 'fuzzy patches'.

Tessa sighed.

'Poor old Dad. It's hard to believe how quickly his memory's gone. A year ago his mind was like a razor. But he has been good.'

Audrey reached for her glass of orange juice.

'As long as he stays active I suppose it's not so bad. It would be unbearable for him if he became a sort of vegetable. All the time he can get about he doesn't need a brain like Einstein's, I suppose.'

There was another pause. It was an uncomfortable topic, and her mother's frankness about her father's failing mind embarrassed Tessa, as if it were some sort of disloyal act. Impossible to deny, though, that the blurs were becoming dominant.

Audrey said: 'It started as a joke, remember? Ageing, disability. How Joyce would have to go when she first had trouble with her legs? It's not so funny now.'

'Clouds across the sun,' said Damon. 'Why are we talking such gloomy talk? Tess and I have been thinking about it recently, Audrey. If it should ever become a real problem, we'll solve it in a flash.'

'What, come here to live? After the baby's born? That would be wonderful!'

Damon had been thinking more in terms of live-in nursing staff, not merely housekeepers and gardeners like they'd had over the past few years from time to time. He flashed a stricken glance at Tessa. To his surprise she did not appear too perturbed.

'It would save us having to go off home and get your stuff for Germany,' she said. 'That would be one thing.'

'I'm serious about it, darling,' put in Audrey. 'It's not as if you don't already, almost. What do you think?'

'It's rather sudden,' Damon mumbled.

'But hardly unexpected!' said his wife.

'Does that mean yes?'

'No, Mum, it doesn't! But it means we'll think about it. It does mean maybe, definitely. The house is going to be very small for three of us, no one could deny that.'

'Yes!' said Audrey, her eyes alight. 'Of course it will! Shall we tell Dad and Joyce? When we tell them that you're expecting?'

'Only that we're thinking of it. Only that. Mum, it's a big decision. Don't rush us, will you?'

As they drove out of the long drive twenty minutes afterwards, to fetch Damon's travel things, they were still discussing it. Even through the windscreen they were clearly animated, happy.

Janis Sanderson, passing in her bright red Renault 5, saw their expressions and was vaguely irritated by them. Some row, she thought, some family gathering. Too busy to talk to her for five minutes, but not too busy to swan about the countryside. She pressed her foot hard down, felt the turbo cut in meatily, and threw the car into a corner much too fast.

That was the way she liked it.

FIVE

That day, the weather was beautiful all over Britain, and indeed across Ireland, south and north. The people of Rowsley did Sunday things, baked in gardens, watched the children or the grandchildren splash in the plastic paddling pools, took their horses for slow walks from stream to stream and shade to shade. It was an airless day once the early breeze had died, and extremely peaceful. There were airliners, high and sonorous, but no military planes at all. Janis, racing her red car from Didwell to Grayson's stables, met few other cars beside Damon Hegarty's. She used the softened tarmac as a sex aid (so she told herself), got the car to glide, and skid, and almost frighten her.

Janis had had sex that afternoon, but it had not been very good. It had been al fresco, but Bren, her Welshman, had not been comfortable. The garden to her little house was private, but each little noise, be it a car, a baaing sheep, a distant cry, had been interpreted as someone coming – and not, as she had thought once, bitterly, her. For Bren was not the wild type, the type she craved and thought she might have landed at long last, Bren was a kind of . . . disappointment. Lying on the grass beneath him, feeling his firm, slim bottom moving like a lump of tensed-up wood, she had abandoned thoughts of careless rapture and bitten her lip to avoid more acid comments. Acid comments, in her life with Bren, were becoming much too frequent.

There was a bend approaching, the last one before the turn to Grayson's, and she concentrated on it. It was slightly devilish, with a little kink neatly twinned to a reverse camber at the apex. Coupled with a liquid surface it could be a bastard, Janis thought, pulling out to get the line with the turbo pressure still pushing at her back. At the precise-judged moment she dropped to third, matching the new revs to her road speed with perfection, accelerating hard as she swept through. The

34

exhilaration passed through her body, through her loins, consciously giving her more pleasure than she'd had with boring Bren. Back on the straight, braking, changing down, Janis's quick glance caught the muscles moving underneath the soft brown skin inside her thighs. Her skirt was short and high, and she felt that she looked marvellous.

'Too bad about the men,' she said aloud, as she turned down the lane to Grayson's. 'Why do I get stuck with all the wimps?'

When Ronnie reached the blue van, he saw that Mick had beaten him to it, which was not ideal. But they were not arguing, they were in a kind of harmony, each doing what he liked best. As he approached, Boon looked up from a map spread on the ground. Mick, on his back, did not look up at all. In one hand was a cider bottle, balanced on his hollow stomach. The other hand was deep inside his fly, scratching. Two portraits of contentment.

'OK, Doggo? Got it sorted yet?'

Saying it, Ronnie had a minor flash of pride – the general who knew how to delegate. Doggo was the wheelsman, so Doggo could decide the route. Ronnie had given him all the relevant co-ordinates to get them to within thirty miles or so of target, the last, vital, information to come when necessary. What a lovely phrase! Ronnie had to hear it spoken.

'Everything match up, mate? All the relevant co-ordinates accounted for? We ought to roll 'em soon.'

Mick made a noise that could have been derision. Doggo's thin lips curved.

'They'd need a tracker plane to follow this,' he said. 'They'd need radar.'

'They'd need someone to get the number of the van,' said Mick. He withdrew his hand from his flies, looking at the fingers with distaste. Doggo did not respond, even with a flicker.

Ronnie cleared his throat. It sounded nervous, although it was not meant to.

'That could happen, I guess. There's no way round that, is there? Don't mean nowt though.'

'Your van, is it?' Mick asked Boon. 'Registered in your name?'

Doggo got up from the grass, rubbing the knees of his pale check trousers. He said to Ronnie: 'Shut the pillock up, eh? He's getting on my tits.'

'Is it yours, then?' Mick had rolled onto his side, knees drawn up towards his stomach, cuddling the cider bottle. 'Go on, cuntie, tell us that it ain't.'

What Mick was after, Ronnie knew, was the reaction of any normal man. A kick in the stomach as he lay, with the hope of smashing the bottle into his flesh to seal the bargain. Mick would have ridden the blow to his iron muscles – tensed already as they were, undoubtedly – and jumped up with the shattered bottle neck, the funnel of brown glass, and driven it into the kicker's face. Boon, it would appear, was not a normal man.

'Hard,' he muttered. He stooped and picked the map up, began to fold it expertly into a book-sized oblong. 'He thinks he's hard, mate. Do you want a driver? What?'

He had his back to Mick, but Mick did not take the advantage. He lay flat on his back again, put the bottle on his chest and sucked from it, a docile little baby in its pram.

'Shut your mouth, Mick,' Ronnie said, in a tone of reason. 'Stop acting like a total pillock, eh?'

'Because if he doesn't shut his fucking bollocks,' continued Harold Boon, 'you can find another one. And another van. How quick could you do that, eh? A van that ain't on the computer, ain't got no engine number, ain't got no chassis number, with tax, insurance and an MOT? Eh? With documents to prove it. Eh? How long will that take you?'

'You are a cunt, Mick,' Ronnie added, equably. 'Honestly.'

And Mick Renwick rolled about the grass behind the cricket club roaring with delighted laughter.

When he awoke after his nap, Peter Wilmott felt less lively, less alert, than he had been before. He lay flat on his back on the broad bed that he still shared with his wife despite her frequent insomnia, aware that panic was gnawing at the edges of his consciousness, panic and a mild unhappiness. He looked at the ceiling, white with plaster mouldings, familiar, and he hardly recognised it. I am growing old, he thought, I am fading fast, perhaps I'm dying.

He wondered what day it was, telling himself angrily that he knew, if he only concentrated it would come back to him. He remembered that he had seen his daughter recently, and Damon – was it Damon? Yes, it was – and that something was due to happen on that front. He listened to the sounds of the outside world, the garden, through the open window, but they were few, and muted. No wind, although there had been breezes earlier, he was clear on that, at least. High pressure. There had been a big high pressure system, going on for days, the whole country had been basking in it. It was Sunday. It was Sunday afternoon and they had had a special lunch. Tessa and Damon were going to tell them something.

Thank God for that, thought Peter, I haven't lost it after all. How I wish that I still had insomnia like Audrey, I'd give my arm to be insomniac. The big old-fashioned alarm clock was clacking noisily by his head, part of the room, the bedroom furniture, nobody needed an alarm clock any more. He turned his head to see how long he'd slept, but could not remember when he'd come up for his lie-down. Hours, maybe. He could sleep for hours these days, twenty out of twenty-four unless somebody kept him awake. It was terrible, terrifying, his life would slip away. The next step would be a bed downstairs, like poor Joyce. The next step after that was fully paid-up death.

In her room somewhere below him, Joyce Withers had also awoken. Her bed was a single, and getting too much sleep would have been a luxury for her, a luxury she had not enjoyed for years. She contemplated the twinges in her joints and limbs, twinges dulled by drugs, with resigned distaste. Joyce was a religious woman, her faith in God the Father and his goodness bred into her, undimmed by anything she had encountered in this vale of tears. She was crippled now, at sixty-two years old, her walking frame gleaming beside her bed, a pulpit that she spent her standing hours in. And if any should doubt God's mercy, she had found the Wilmott family. Come as the carer, ended as the cared-for one. Joyce, consciously, clasped her twisted hands on her breastbone, close beneath her chin, and thanked her lord.

Joyce knew that she was lucky, and knew that she was strong. She came from a family of strong women, although her father had been born and died a rogue, and all of them except of course her mother had lived their lives as virgins. One sister, Alice, had been struck down with rheumatoid arthritis at the age of twelve, and had never grown beyond four feet eight inches tall. As she had aged she had shrunk and twisted, and by the time she was twenty was under four feet and bedridden. In the nursing home where she stayed until she died at forty-four she was in almost constant agony, growing smaller and more malformed as the years went by. She wrote short stories of a religious nature that she picked out on an electronic typewriter with a device strapped to her head, and which she submitted without ever revealing that she was a helpless cripple in case that fact should lead editors into dishonest kindnesses. When she sold one, as she did five times in all, she gave the money to the church. She lived and died, Joyce knew, a very happy woman.

Her younger sister, Grace, had killed herself at fifteen years, reason unknown, also by an act of will that Joyce, after a bitter struggle, came to see as inspirational. Grace, tall, calm, beautiful, had walked into a copse near to their house, and walked into a pond, up to her waist, her chest, her chin. Then she had stooped and drowned herself, holding herself under despite her reflexes, despite her bursting lungs. She had breathed in, anaesthetised herself (God is merciful), and died. After that their mother had not stayed long, although she had died of natural causes, during a bout of simple flu.

Her prayer finished, Joyce began the awkward ritual by which she rose and, panting, went slowly to her little bathroom for a wash. She heard a car draw up, crunching on the gravel, and knew it would be Damon and Tessa returning before the trip to Germany. Joyce cleaned her teeth, freshened up her face, raised a hand to pat her straight grey hair, wincing at the effort. Another hour before another pill. She smiled. Tessa and Damon brought such happiness.

Mick was asleep in the van, which everyone preferred. There had been another potential incident before they'd set off, because he'd said belligerently that if any twat had to sit on the floor pan and beat their piles to death, it sure as hell wasn't going to be him. Doggo, full of voiceless contempt, had left it to Ronnie to discover that there were back seats, too. Which

Mick had thought was really neat, unique, terrific, and colonised as his right, the whole folding benchseat to himself, plus some cider and the whisky bottle. It was a rear-seat conversion, Doggo told him after several times of asking, it was a kit, perfectly normal, he'd put it in himself. Mick, drunk but still lusting after trouble, asked him where he'd bought the kit and when, and how he'd paid, and bet it could be traced straight back to him. At which Ronnie had pushed him by his skinny arse into the seat and banged the front one down like the gate to a lion's cage – or a playpen. Within five minutes of bumping off the track and going up past Strinesdale, Mick was snoring.

'We could drop him off,' said Doggo, as they climbed up out of Delph on the A62. 'There's a couple of quarries off Lark Hill.'

Ronnie jumped. He had been thinking about other things. About blood, and death, and money.

'Eh? Come again.'

'We could drop him off. He's as pissed as a fart, he wouldn't even notice if we tipped him out. It's not a long walk home.'

Ronnie turned curiously. As he studied Doggo's pointy profile, the younger man slowly smiled. He was serious.

'Mind you, I suppose you're scared he'd open up his drunken trap? If we ditched him.'

Too bloody right he would, thought Ronnie. He'd track you down and cut your bollocks off, my friend. You just don't know.

'It's a possibility. Anyway – no change of plan, OK? We've talked this through in every pissing detail.'

'Mick says you changed your story. In the Con Club. He says they think he's gone to see his mam in Liverpool.'

'So?'

'I thought you were going back to your place, watch some dirty videos, fix the car. You're the one that don't like changing plans.'

'Listen, if I want to change the plan that's all right, right? I'm the boss, OK, I've got it all up here.' Ronnie tapped his head, relaxed, amused, a front to hide his upset at the challenge. Then he hardened his expression, to make it clear there'd be no argument. 'One less body to be linked to me,' he added.

'Would you trust the drunken twat? If the law came sniffing round? Detail, that's all. Detail.'

'I'm not arguing,' said Doggo. 'Just passing comments. Talking of bodies, though, that's the turn-off up ahead. If you think he'd talk we could always cut his throat.'

Ronnie's head snapped round despite himself. Doggo, aware, briefly curved his lips.

'Mark you,' he said, 'you do get couples up there shagging on a weekend afternoon. Be a shame to get spotted, wouldn't it?'

'Just fucking drive, why don't you?'

SIX

They held the ceremony in the summer house, where Tessa and her mother had laid a garden table with a cream cake and the glasses. Joyce and Peter were escorted over and told not to sit down until an announcement had been made. Audrey fussed about, pretending she was not privy to the secret, and squeaked as loud as need be when Damon appeared with the bottle of champagne.

'It's a toast,' said Tessa, 'a formal toast. I'll give you the cryptic version, and you can work it out. No prizes for the first one to the truth. To us. To all of us. To all *six* of us.'

Joyce looked as if she might explode. Her mouth dropped and her eyes went wide.

'Oh no,' she breathed. 'Oh Tessa, no!'

Peter, they had feared for. They had all noticed that the edge of his perceptiveness had gone. But he was galvanised.

'Well done!' he barked out, joyfully. 'Well done, Tessa, well done, my boy! Audrey? Haven't you guessed yet? Six of us!'

Audrey laughed.

'I'll be the first to drink,' she said. 'To all of us, and to the new addition. I just can't say how happy this has made me.'

She caught her daughter's eyes, however, as everybody drank, and her own were complicated, pleasure mixed with loss. Tessa moved to her and kissed her cheek.

'Thank you, Mum. For everything.' Louder, she said: 'Thank you everybody. Mum and Dad for being such great parents, Joyce for completing the big happy family, Damon for being everything I always wanted.'

Peter began to cough.

'This'll shut the devils in the village up!' he laughed. 'This'll show 'em! My boy, my boy . . . congratulations. And my heart-felt thanks.'

Later, when the cake was cut and eaten, Damon kissed Joyce and Audrey, shook hands with Peter, and prepared to go. Tessa walked him to the car, they checked his bag, they hugged each other.

'Come back soon,' she said. 'Silly Germans. I don't call it efficiency, to spoil our surprise.'

'It wasn't spoiled really, they all loved it. It was a tonic, in a way.'

'We'll have lots to talk about this evening. I bet the knitting needles are out before we go to bed. Poor Joyce, she used to love to knit. I bet she tries, as well. She never gives up, does she?'

The blank heat of the day was mellowing. The house, the lawns and gardens, were looking lovely. Damon moved his hands down onto her bottom, squeezing gently.

'And you've got a little me inside you. A little us. Tess, I'll think of that.'

He took her full mouth in his open one and enclosed her lips. Tessa darted her tongue momentarily inside.

'You may think of that as well,' she whispered.

In the last discussions, they had planned a route and they stuck to it. What people noticed could never be predicted, so the blue van was put about considerably. If it was reported in the aftermath, it would be reported from north, east, south and west of their destination. Not all the sightings could be accurate, so Mr Plod would discount all of them.

First they crossed to Huddersfield and took the Holmfirth road. They joined the M1 at Dodworth, then swung north east up the M18 until they crossed the A614, which they took south to Bawtry. After that they headed east, went south through Lincoln, then crossed the M1 between Nottingham and Derby and carried on west all the way to Stafford. It occurred to Ronnie that his dour companion − Mick having slept through most of this − might be thinking it was foolishness, although he had voiced no reservations during the planning stage. During the planning stage, Ronnie told himself as he wrestled with his small but nagging doubt, it had felt sensible, nay, bloody brilliant, and it probably still was. It was the element of day-tripping that might get to Doggo, though, cruising idly under clear blue skies, with no clear sense of urgency. For many miles he thought of ways to broach the subject, to talk it through, to get an 'in' behind those quick bright eyes. But in the end, he thought of nothing.

Just outside Cannock they passed a caravan in a lay-by that sold snacks, and decided it would soon be time to eat. Mick, as if by magic, had woken to the word and started belching horribly. Balls to eating, he said, he needed drink. He was bleary-eyed, belligerent, hung over. Ronnie pointed mildly to the whisky and the cider, but Mick demanded beer. Doggo, driving more slowly until the debate should be settled either way, listened with apparent uninterest. Ronnie thought that he could read the body language, though: Doggo was testing him again. Mick Renwick was an issue he must solve.

'Look,' he said, 'if you think we're stopping at a pub, you can forget it. We've talked it through till we're blue in the fucking face, mate. We don't go anywhere team-handed. When we eat, we buy the food and eat it in the van. We'll stop at an offie in a while and you can get some cans, OK? Otherwise — no.'

Mick farted loudly.

'I need a shit,' he said. 'Pull in quick, I'm going to shit myself.'

Doggo saw another lay-by and pulled in. There was a lorry at the other end, nobody else. Ronnie jumped out, pulled his front seat forward, and Mick stumbled by. He climbed the low wire fence and plunged into some bushes, noisily. Ronnie sat back in, staring at the truck. The curtains of the sleeper cab were closed. It seemed they were in luck.

'Mark you,' he said, as if continuing a conversation, 'if you want to shoot the prat when we've done the job, I'll pull the bleeding trigger for you. I don't often make mistakes, pal, but when I do I can admit it. That bastard's mental.'

This brought a smile from Doggo that Ronnie found some-how comforting. Complicity. Companionship. They sat and listened to the rattling of the diesel engine, staring straight ahead. It was passing through both their minds how sweet it would be just to put her into gear and go.

'With his trousers down,' said Doggo. 'Nice. What about these guns, though? Can we get to them first? That twat near me with a gun is something I can do without.'

Before he'd passed out after dawn that morning, Mick had banged on about the guns as usual. He had already demanded

43

first choice of the three that Ronnie said were in the house, plumping for a Remington pump-action that Peter Wilmott had been given by a US client in the sixties. Neither Ronnie nor Harold Boon liked firearms in the normal way – a passport to a longer sentence, Doggo had said – although both conceded that after the event they might prove useful to blast their way to freedom if they were stopped. That they could do this job without them had never been in doubt, even when Ronnie had raised the outside possibility that the geriatrics might have visitors on the night. They'd know as soon as they arrived, from the cars outside, and in the back of the van they would have rope in plenty, pickaxe handles, parcel tape for gags – enough to subdue, silence, kill or capture a dozen people if the need arose. Not new gear, either, nor bought in one place, recently – Ronnie thought of everything. Mick had been allowed his fantasy, and even allowed to add a hacksaw to the toolkit to cut them down to a carryable size, but neither of the others was much interested.

'He won't get near the guns,' said Ronnie. 'Not till I say so, anyway. They're in cabinets, and the cabinets are locked. Plus, the ammo's separate. Another cabinet, another key, another hiding place. Satisfied?'

Doggo grunted.

'Where is the bastard, anyway? D'you think he's fell in it and drowned?'

'Another thing,' said Ronnie. 'Once he gets inside he'll forget the guns till afterwards. I know Mick. He enjoys himself. He larks about. Then there's the booze. While he deals with the booze, we can be dealing with the cash. Do you get me?'

Complicity. Doggo turned his thin, beaked nose to Ronnie. His Adam's apple bobbed.

'Don't you think you ought to tell me where we're going, now we're nearly there?'

'Yeah, why not? It's called Rowsley. Ever heard of it?'

Doggo shook his head.

'I'm not surprised,' said Ronnie, with deep satisfaction. 'No bugger has. It's nowt, it's isolation-city. It makes a morgue look lively.'

'I can't hardly wait to shake it up,' said Harold Boon. 'Where is that dirty little toerag?'

SEVEN

The Good Neighbours were out in force that evening, and the smell of barbecues from a dozen gardens overlaid the scent of evening flowers and cooling tarmac that Janis Sanderson had hoped to savour on the terrace at the Hare and Hounds. She drank alone, but happily, conscious that Bren had been expecting her at Didwell for an hour or more. She drank a double gin with not much tonic, and wondered (satirically) if he had lit their barbecue. Next, the bastard would wear pyjamas in her bed.

Janis had a problem with her men, and she was getting old enough, at twenty-six, to take it out and look at it from time to time. She had been married once, at nineteen, and had known two days after arriving on her honeymoon that it had to stop. The reasons for the marriage had been little short of loopy – cool reporter from another town, open sports car, better with his dick than the others – and (the one thing she would not forgive herself) she'd known that it was loopy all along. She'd married out of shame, somehow, and fear. She'd started on the newspaper at eighteen, and the great shock had been not the job but her sudden, unexpected need for sex. Until that age she'd messed about with boys, but never needed to go the bundle, as it were. Then, in ten days she'd fallen for a junior reporter and gone into the flat Lincolnshire country and lost her virginity underneath an oak tree in the rain. It hadn't hurt, she hadn't come, and she'd loved it. In a month she'd left him – still without an orgasm – and switched over to the advertising side, and a bright red flash Toyota. Then back to the reporters' room, then Sammy from despatch, then Andrew Grice the area rep. She was getting a reputation as the office bike, she knew it and she minded. But she didn't want to stop.

Nor did the men who spread the seed and insults. They didn't want to stop because she was a sort of dreamboat to them – black shiny hair, good legs, good body, good fun, and undemanding. By the time she met Barry on a course in Nottingham where no one knew her, she felt she had to stay out of bed until the second night, to prove she was not addicted to casual sex – but when she did screw him she was bowled over. Although in theory he was not as experienced as she was (he'd only had one other partner), on the second time they did it something happened and she came, a fantastic combination of exhilaration and terror, because she thought she was in fact exploding. Barry also drove fast, like a raving lunatic, and got drunk a lot and sang and shouted and didn't give a stuff for anyone. Janis loved to be with him, loved to drive with him, loved to sleep with him, loved to come – which with the others, strangely, she never did.

Unfortunately, though, she still slept with them, as Barry lived and worked elsewhere and did not visit every weekend, and unfortunately, she knew she did not love him. She married him, almost, as a hedge against promiscuity, which increasingly upset and frightened her, and because he was the best in bed and best behind the wheel. Three days after coming back from her honeymoon, she slept with Andrew Grice by accident, and came. It was the most miserable evening of her adult life.

Not all her life, though. When she had been thirteen, Janis had seen a young man with a rifle and a combat jacket walk through the main street of the Suffolk village where her granny lived and shoot nine people, including her mother and her Uncle Malcolm. Janis thought sometimes that she had never recovered from that sight and never would, although she would not accept the therapy for long. At other times she thought that she was full of bullshit, and used it as an excuse for all the bad things in her life. In one of these brutal, honest periods she told Barry that she did not love him, and that she sometimes slept with other men. He punched her in the face so hard her smile was still not right, and kicked her out. Janis loved him for that, for that brutal act of honesty, and that worried her as well. She feared the other men she found would never measure up. Worse, she knew that had the makings, as analysis, of a self-fulfilling prophecy.

The fluid in the glass was melted ice, and Janis glanced yet again at her watch. Bren was nice, and kind, and loving (although she hoped he did not love her), and was becoming quite rapidly a royal pain. What's more, he was getting jealous of Clive Smith, the news editor, which irked her more obscurely. If Bren was a wimpy Welshman, Clive was a professional Northerner, all grit and crudity. What's more, he was pursuing her for reasons of the job rather than sexuality, which was insulting. He had lost her as a reporter the year before, and seemed determined to get her back. Janis, who had never been a natural in her own opinion, was determined not to go. She had switched to features, which she could just about bear to earn her wage, but her interests lay outside, in the wider world of magazines and the Sunday heavies. She saw herself as a writer and she dared to say so, knowing full well the contumely it brought down on her small, determined head. From Office Bike to Superego was the whisper, and she didn't give a stuff.

Janis went and got herself another gin, a single, plus more ice and a fresher slice of lemon. Damn Bren, she thought, she'd have to get him out without breaking his heart, poor lamb. If only he had been a better driver!

They went south to Birmingham where, in the teeming streets, Ronnie went and bought them fish and chips while Doggo picked up cans of strong lager for Mick to slake his thirst with. As they drove on they talked of vans and cars and jobs they'd done, although it was noticeable that Doggo avoided detail, indeed preferred to listen rather than to lead. Only on vehicles was he forthcoming, and the string of information he and Ronnie shared, on petrol, diesel, turbos, engine sizes, roadholding, soon drove Mick to grumbling, then to sleep again. He volunteered that he had served his time with Perkinses at Peterborough, then picked up tuning petrol engines with the father of a mate who'd done some racing. The way he talked, thought Ronnie, you'd never have known that he'd gone bent, or that he needed to for the money. What was it, booze, or tarts, or gambling, there must be something at his back. As they ate the miles in the comforting and throaty hum of the Peugeot diesel (it was the 1905cc, light, powerful and economical) Ronnie observed him cautiously, ticking off the possibilities. Booze was out, unless he had an iron will, because he could quite obviously take it or leave it alone. Women also seemed unlikely,

47

because unlike Mick (and himself to a lesser extent) he hardly mentioned them, and certainly did not go bananas at the sight of the black birds of Birmingham in their summer skimpies. Also (not to put too fine a point on it) he was fucking ugly. That left gambling. After trying out some gambits, silently, Ronnie went point blank.

'What about the gee-gees? Do you just like motor racing or do you do the horses, too?'

'Mug's game,' said Doggo Boon. 'Look at that. Big old Mack. I used to know a bloke had one of them. Forty-seven gears. Ridiculous.'

Ronnie watched the lorry sliding by on the other carriageway then let the diesel buzz replace conversation. It wasn't horses, it wasn't crumpet, maybe Doggo had nothing worthwhile in his head at all. It didn't matter much as long as he could do his job, and he was a good solid driver, no danger. Ronnie eased back in his seat and let the road and cars and scenery come rushing at him, roll over him and under and to his sides. He loved driving himself, but this was luxury, to sit here with a tin of spesh and a brilliant job in prospect and not a care in the wide world except maybe for Mick, who was curled up on his benchseat like a little baby now, moaning faintly, his hands buried deep into his thighs, and twitching now and then.

Even Mick was funny, on a job like this. Some time before, as they'd whooshed past a garage, he'd suggested they should go and buy some petrol, to burn down the place, destroy the evidence. Never mind that they'd been over it all before, never mind that it wasn't necessary because they weren't going to leave anything that anyone could trace to them even if they were ever thought of. But when Ronnie had pointed out that the only way anyone would know that anything was wrong was if some prat started a fire to alert people with smoke and flames, Mick had called himself every kind of fool.

'Correct, oh master,' he had said. 'I never thought of that. Tell me one other thing – why can't the Chinese make fucking fish and chips!'

Not a care in the world. But that was crazy, wasn't it? Three men in a van, screaming through the English countryside at nearly seventy, to a house where almost anything could happen. Ronnie took a mouthful of the strong, sweet beer and glowed.

'This is the life, eh?' he said to Doggo's profile. 'All this and thirty grand.'

It was beginning to get dark.

There was no barbecue at Brook Bank, although no one in the family had any objections to them on grounds of snobbery. It was one of the social changes, the little fads, that had passed them by, like the chance of buying garden shears in Boots, or pints of milk and pasties in every second garage on the road. Peter and Audrey could remember when the Hare and Hounds had served beer from wooden stillages in the kitchen, and when Tessa had invited them there to have a meal some years before, they had taken some convincing that a meal was possible in a public house. For the people of Brook Bank, dinner was a feet-under-table job, even when the fare was light and summery. Cooking out was the stuff of Yankee films, and farmyard pig-roasts done every ten years or so for charity.

After the announcement and the champagne, though, the very idea of a celebration dinner rapidly ran out of steam. With Damon gone there seemed little point in it, although the leg of lamb was still there to be cooked, and the fresh garden vegetables had already been prepared. Tessa and Audrey decided on a simple meal, with a bottle of Piesporter (light and floral, if strictly inappropriate) and some strawberries and cream to follow. Peter, after the excitement, had become a little vague, and in truth, there were only so many variations on the theme of new baby/surprise/delight that could be run through. At first, Tessa felt a slight depression clutch at her, but as the family settled to its time-worn evening rituals, she recognised it as a comfort, like envelopment in a warm old dressing gown.

The knitting did indeed come out, although at the level of pattern books and reminiscence rather than in any active way. When the sun faded completely they went into the house and put the electric fire on in the drawing room just to take the chill off, deciding unanimously that as Damon was not there to get the wood, a fire would be a ridiculous indulgence so mildly struck the evening air as it came in through the wide open windows. Joyce, on an inspiration, hobbled painfully into the study – refusing any offer of a substitute – to return with a bag of photo albums. There were Wilmott babies here to feast their eyes on, Wilmotts and relations, with little Tessa peering out through tousled curls 'like the spoilt brat' (she said) 'I must have been!'

At nine o'clock, although he'd said he would not, Damon rang them from the airport, where his flight had been slightly delayed, to ask about the evening. They had missed him, Tessa teased, but not a lot. It had been a perfect family evening, really, unhurried, full of peace. Inevitably, as they spoke, his flight was called at last.

'Oh well,' said Damon. 'Needs must when the devil drives. Look after him for us, won't you?'

'It's much more likely that he'll be a she, given my genes,' laughed Tessa. 'Goodbye, God bless, I'll see you soon, my darling.'

Trite formula, deeply felt. They were the last words that he ever heard her say.

EIGHT

The high pressure had been around so long, that the system was beginning to decay. There had been thunder in the south and west, and imperceptibly, soft whitish cloud was encroaching on the clear blue skies of daytime. At night the air showed a tendency to haze, with sudden, unexpected banks of mist. When it was fully dark on this night there were no stars visible, no moon to burn through the high murk. It was very dark, completely windless. When Ronnie – as part of his masterplan – stopped at a phone box on a lonely country road to make a phone call, the men left in the van could not make him out at twenty yards.

On the final stretch of motorway – M6 from Birmingham, then north on the M1 – the darkness had meant nothing, it was normal night-time, pierced by endless headlights. But east of the M1, in the hinterland, the van's main beam cut through the rural gloom as if through thick black treacle. Mick was awake, but no one spoke save Ronnie when he gave directions, and the atmosphere was almost palpable, an admixture of suppressed excitement, tension, chips and beer and cider, too many cigarettes. Mick's farts were coming faster, too, loud and vibrant despite the protests of the other two. The windows were almost closed, however, because they preferred the fug to sweet night air; it seemed more natural.

'We'll skirt the village, though it's dead by this time, usually,' said Ronnie. 'It's about a mile down here now. You never know, do you? Might meet some drunken yuppie coming from the Hare.'

He directed Doggo up a small lane between high trees, then down a narrower one half a mile along. At last they came to a clearing off the road. He pointed.

'There. The arse-end of nowhere, known to no one but me and a few selected shags.' He twisted suddenly to Mick. 'You'd be surprised at the number of them that do it in the wilds, mate. Little rich tarts out of their heads with boredom while Jeremy's down in London making TV shows. I've had some lovely fucks down here. Go on, Doggo – switch her off.'

Harold Boon turned off the engine, and for a few moments they just sat. He killed the lights as well.

'Fucking hell,' said Mick. 'It's so *dark*. Is it always like this in the country? It's fucking *horrible*.'

Doggo said: 'How far's the house? How can we be sure no one'll come along?'

His voice was slightly strained. Ronnie smiled to himself in the blackness. Was this a sign of nerves?

'Give over. I used to live here, didn't I? There's no one to come along in the first place, and if there was they wouldn't know the tracks in any case. This is part of it. We're on their land.'

'Christ, is this the garden?' Mick laughed and farted simultaneously. Ronnie pushed his door open and got out. The air was cool, and sweet, and still.

'Come here,' he said to Doggo. 'I'll show you. There's a gap just over there, we'll see the lights. Three hundred yards, that's all it is. We'll take our time, suss out which rooms they're in. We'd better get a move on, though, it's getting late. They might lock up. They might switch the alarm on, you never know.'

He did not turn as Boon came up behind him. The dark was amazing, to a city dweller. Even Ronnie, who had been amazed before, found it extraordinary.

'You can't believe it, can you? That it's the same country. Where's all the lights, the noise, the people? You can't believe it.'

Doggo said sardonically: 'Not even a Paki-shop on the corner. Not even a fucking corner.'

From behind them there was another raucous fart, and a hot, rich spreading smell.

'Oh for Christ's sake, Mick. You're an animal, you are.'

'Your fault for buying me them chips, weren't it? Oi, Ronnie, where's the torches?'

A dim glow blossomed around Ronnie's legs, a strong beam muffled in a cloth.

'That's all you're getting, right? No one'll see that while we're getting ready. Doggo, open up the back. Pick handles and the rope and tape. Grab that jemmy, just in case.'

Their lethargy was fading. Boon passed out the handles, and Mick took one and swung it viciously.

'Wheee!' he went, but quietly. 'Thunk!'

No one asked Ronnie 'just in case' of what. Now they were up to it they knew that there could well be little difficulties, and that they would solve them. Like the old alarm system, that possibly could be on. Ronnie knew which doors and windows were not covered and he knew where the master panel was, the key always *in situ*. But something would crop up, it always did. It was the challenges that made the job worthwhile.

'Christ,' said Mick, enthusiastically. 'You can make a mess with one of these darlings. D'you remember Charlie Seddon? He took that bloke's head right off with a pick handle. He were a barmpot, Charlie.'

Harold Boon had gone to the driver's door and was rooting in the glove compartment. Both Ronnie and Mick heard and identified the next sound, although they had not expected it. It was the childproof plastic lid of a pill bottle being twisted off. Oho, thought Ronnie, so that's the secret is it? Oho!

It was not a secret, exactly. Doggo upended the bottle in their sight, then proffered it. Mick jumped back as if invited to take poison.

'What is it? I don't take fucking drugs, mate!'

Doggo was amused. There was affection in his voice when he replied.

'You are a twat, Mick. Suit yourself. I've had a hard day's driving, haven't I? I can't afford to lose my licence drinking!'

Drugs culture had bypassed Mick completely. A cousin's son had made a good screw as a dealer at the university, he knew, and had been stabbed to death by the black bastards in Moss Side who had the trade in Manchester sewn up. Mick associated drugs with blacks, and students, and other such unpleasant types, and distrusted them. Ronnie had no such associations, but he also declined.

'Not my scene mate, ta. What are they? Uppers, downers, Ecstasy, Special K?'

'You name it,' Doggo replied, dismissively. You twat, thought

Ronnie, you think I don't know them, don't you? He caught himself at it, and smiled privately. He didn't know them, he'd tried drugs a couple of times and they'd only made him sick. Why be ashamed of that?

'They make me puke,' he said. 'The lot of 'em. Alcohol's my drug, Doggo.'

'Sex and violence, please,' said Mick. 'If you're taking orders!'

'They're good for that,' said Doggo. 'You want to try it.'

'Oi,' went Ronnie, sharply. 'For Christ's sake, Doggo, don't tempt him now. He's a shagged-out old fart with exploding bowels. Give him something new to try, and he'll fuck the whole thing up. He'll fuck you an' all, give him half a chance. Think about it. Now, for fuck sake, let's move, shall we? This is getting like a social workers' conference. Everyone got their gloves on?'

'I could kill a drink,' said Mick.

'There's a cellar waiting for you, son. And a cabinet of whiskies going back thirty year or more. All you've got to do is shift your fucking arse.'

'Makes sense to me,' said Doggo. 'Mick?'

'Lead me to it. Ronnie? Can I have a bleeding torch?'

'Not till we're in the house, you clumsy bastard.'

As if to prove his point, Mick slipped at the gap in the hedge, half disappearing into a dry ditch. They pulled him out in great hilarity, never forgetting to keep their voices down.

'Did you lock the van?' Mick panted, as they shoved him through the hole. 'There might be burglars about!'

'Tssch!' went Doggo, sharply. 'Lights!'

It silenced them. The target shone out at them, across the grassy slope. There were several lighted rooms, the squarish, solid house delineated in the utter blackness. Around them, in the hollow, wisps of pale, thin mist were gathering.

'When we've done it,' Ronnie said, 'we can get the van round to the door. If there's anything worth taking, besides the cash.'

No one answered. None of them had thought beforehand what they would feel like when it came to it, but all of them were receiving strongly now. Sensations, half-formed thoughts, vague emotions. To Ronnie, it seemed oddly unprofessional.

You're not afraid are you, he asked himself. This is it, the strike-back, and it's going to make you rich. This one'll put you on the map, mate, no danger. And anyway, they deserve what's coming to them, don't they? The bastards.

No, he was not afraid, and he knew Mick Renwick wouldn't be. Mick Renwick, after his own brief introspection, said chirpily: 'We could take the bodies to the morgue in it! The judge'd reckon that, aiding the police!'

Ronnie looked at Doggo's face and saw it pale and sweating, the redness of the pimples standing out. Maybe Doggo was scared, maybe that was another secret.

But Doggo grinned at him, a lop-sided, bright-eyed grin that showed long, crooked teeth.

'Booze is OK, but pills is best,' he said. His voice had risen a pitch or two. 'Come on, Ronnie, don't be an idle bastard. Let's go and have some fun.'

'What a good idea,' said Mick.

NINE

People who live in big, lonely houses pay a premium that is
beyond the extra their insurance companies demand. They pay
a premium in envy, which is hidden from them, normally,
and a premium in fear, which they have to hide, even from
themselves. The three inhabitants of Brook Bank had hidden
the anxiety for such long ages, that it had gone underground,
like a small, cold stream. Indeed, there had not been a burglary,
or any incident, since nineteen twenty-three. Deep down they
knew there was a possibility, but on the surface, it was more
or less forgotten.

Some people, when they visited the house for the first time,
looked at it from a burglar's perspective. Others shivered, involuntarily, at the awful vulnerability inherent in its defiant isolation. From the road, unless you knew of its existence, it was
hard to even guess at, near impossible to find. Two small grav-
elled tracks, unmarked, that twisted through a copse of English
woodland trees, separate by about a half a mile. The house,
red brick but mellow, stood in a gravel oblong, most of it in
front, overlooking lush, rolling lawns, hedged gardens, and an
orchard. But in all directions, the view ended in trees and
hedges, revealing only distant vistas of the same classic country-
side, green and timeless. Once in, a visitor was cut off from the
outside world completely, like the souls who lived there.

Tessa, now she lived away from Brook Bank, worried more
than she had done in the years of living there, nagging at her
parents occasionally to increase their security. It was she who
had instigated the fitting of the alarm system, when she'd gone
away to university, and her keen young belief that everything
was possible had been frustrated by her father's lackadaisical,
almost ironic, acceptance of her bullying. The result had been
an installation with more hope as a deterrent symbol than as an
actual means of calling for help or alerting anyone to anything.
There were bright-painted metal boxes on the outer walls

(faded now, of course), and bells that would ring merrily enough to frighten birds out of the eaves. Outside the grounds, though, no one would hear them, nor see the flashing blue lights that graced the main four corners. Peter and Audrey usually turned the system on at night, but by no means always. It was such a fag.

Such a waste of time as well, said Peter. It was only the travellers who were likely to come snooping, and only the new fools in the village who minded that. His family had never argued with the gipsies, and let them cart off any junk they fancied. If sometimes they had carted off some things more, a little extra that would be missed a few weeks later — well, so what? Even gipsies had to live, they were part of the country scene, like fieldmice in the butter when autumn came, like trees blown down across the drive. Last burglary — nineteen twenty-three. Call it luck, call it divine protection, he did not care. The main thing, he insisted, was a presence in the house, that was the only real deterrent. And as he and Audrey grew older, and Joyce less mobile, there was someone at home more frequently, almost constantly. Over the years, what's more, there had been live-in gardeners and housekeepers, quartered in the flat above the garages. It was not a problem, he used to say, if it should happen, *c'est la vie*. And in latter years: When your time comes, you must go!

This night, Tessa felt vaguely depressed, a product of the spoiled celebration, an awareness that Damon was very far away, a strange conjunction of being pregnant and alone. It was their frailness that was upsetting her, the frailness of their grasp on happiness, all of them. She was pregnant, and they were dying. It was a horrible equation. Tonight, for no reason more concrete than that, she was less sanguine than she usually was at her father's indifference.

Behind her, the old ones were preparing for their beds, the small domestic sounds failing to cheer her. She was standing at the open French windows, watching a fine pale mist gathering among the trees and hedges at the perimeter. Anyone could be in there, she thought, anyone could be watching us, waiting for the lights to all go off, waiting till they thought we were asleep. She turned herself away with anger, swinging the door as if to close and lock it. The night was fine, the air was sweet, she was being stupid, stupid. Her mother stood in the door-way, the empty Piesporter bottle in her hand, and their eyes met.

'Going to lock up, darling? Dad's already up. Leave some windows open, won't you? It's so airless.'

'Mum,' she said. 'We will move in. When the baby's born. Of course.'

Although delighted, Audrey was not fooled. There had to be a reason.

'That's wonderful. What does Damon think?'

'He doesn't know.'

'Of course.' Her mother laughed. 'Don't be hasty, Tessa. It's up to Damon, too. Or don't you feminists consult your men on anything any more?'

The tone was light, the intention not attack but satire. They understood each other very well.

'I might even change my name. To Mrs Hegarty.'

Now they were both laughing.

'You've got the blues, my girl. Don't have for our sakes. Just because Dad's going down, you don't have to get all dynastic. He might have ten years yet. More.'

All dynastic. It was true, it had been in her mind. In ten years time, or five, or twenty, they would be the family. The current generation.

'In any case, if you did decide to become a Hegarty, what price continuation then? I think it's pregnancy, my girl. You're not usually so easy to upset. Get an early night.'

She went out to the kitchen to make a drink for Peter, while Tessa walked moodily around the room, closing and catching windows, inwardly berating herself the while. She was being stupid, she was being ridiculous, she was being feeble. She'd never felt frightened in this house, in spite of everything. Her dad was right. The important thing was to have somebody in, that was the real deterrent, for how could a potential burglar know what opposition he might meet if he dared to come inside? She went and kissed Joyce goodnight, in her downstairs bedroom, then continued on her rounds, closing windows, checking.

What could we do if someone did come? she thought. She stepped out of the front door and stood quite still. The night was very black, without a star or breath of wind. She heard an owl hunting in the spinney, over to her left. If there was still mist rising, she could no longer make it out.

What could she do? Rush inside and slam the bolts and try and make a phone call? Press the so-called panic button and set off the bells no one would hear? She stared into the velvet blackness and prayed for peace of mind.

'Three old people without a shred of fear amongst them,' she said aloud. 'And one young idiot with the wibbles. Young-ish. God, I ought to be ashamed.'

She had seen a light. She was sure she had seen a light across the garden. A dim light that had flickered in the shrubs. Tessa turned backwards at the moment Joyce turned her bedside lamp off, darkening her window edge around the curtains. Was that it? Was it a reflection of some sort, a trick?

Tessa, in all her life, had never known fear. Nothing had ever happened to her to make her frightened. Now she began to lose her breath, she clenched her fists and stomach muscles, a numb paralysis was sweeping over her.

But why, she screamed, inwardly? Why are you afraid, there's nothing to be afraid of! Her tongue was swelling, it was cleaving to the roof of her mouth. She could not believe the whole sensation, its physicality, her total loss of reason or control.

There was another light in front of her, moving fast across the slope. Two lights! Her eyes were staring, she was gripped by disbelief. They'd sat there happily in their house for years, and all the time the wolves were prowling round outside! They were beset by wolves!

Tessa was going to run and scream. She was going to break her immobility and tear into the house and dial 999, screaming all the while. Dad had guns! There were kitchen knives! The wolves were coming!

It was not entirely a mad fantasy, the wolves. The men had seen her outside the front door in the light, and it had frozen them, as well. At first it had been a spill of light, a shaft that jumped towards them when they thought they were alone and safe, a block of brightness with a human shape in it. They had stopped, an audible gasp escaping from one of them. They had been still and silent for several long, tense seconds.

Then it had become a woman, then a woman Ronnie recognised.

'Fucking hell,' he said. 'Tessa Wilmott. Fucking hell.'

'A tart,' breathed little Mick. 'A lovely tart.'

'What about her old man?' said Doggo. 'Will he be here? We'd better fucking shift.'

'We better had,' Ronnie agreed. 'We better fucking had.'

He switched his muffled torch on to show the ground ahead.

'Come on,' he said. 'Let's go!'

'A torch!' said Mick. 'I need a fucking torch!'

Doggo switched his on and passed it over.

'You don't need eyes,' he said. 'You don't need eyes, you twat.'

Then, as Ronnie began to run towards the house, he threw his head back and made a strange noise, feral and appalling.

'Yip yip yip!' he went. 'Yip yip yip yip yip!'

The door slammed shut before the three men reached it, shut on Tessa's appalled, appalling screams.

But it was too late. Far, far too late.

The wolves were yipping as they kicked it open.

TEN

The process by which Janis Sanderson came to be the first person to enter Brook Bank on that Monday morning was something that troubled her for ever afterward. The milkman, Toby Barnton, had delivered two pints, and the postman had called in his Escort diesel van. The front door had been wide open – indeed it later transpired that the jamb was split – and the house had been in silence. But neither of them, as they swore on oath, had thought of anything untoward.

'I delivered on a Monday, Wednesday and Saturday,' Toby Barnton later said. 'My timing was not consistent, because Brook Bank was at the end of my round. There was usually a radio on, there was often someone there who'd say hello and pass the time of day. But sometimes there was no radio, and no one about. It didn't mean anything. Whatever happened, over the fifteen or sixteen years I delivered milk there, it had become ordinary. I had no expectations.'

When the postman, Michael Trask, had called, he'd seen the milk in the little holder with the order indicator. He'd brought two circulars – one governmental – and a bill. There was a table in the hallway – which was cavernous and dim – so he'd dropped the mail on that. The quietness had not struck him as significant, either. Maybe they were in the grounds – it was another pleasant morning – or in the bathrooms, anywhere. He was so used to a wide open door he did not see the damage.

Cars? He'd seen a small green one that he'd always assumed was Tessa Wilmott's – her husband drove a diesel Ford – but that was half to be expected. Peter Wilmott had an old saloon, possibly a Rover although he was no expert, but it was hardly used these days and kept in the big garage. Best place for it, Michael Trask had said – the old man's driving was no longer up to much, even on the empty country lanes around the village and Brook Bank. Tessa and her husband did all the necessary ferrying.

Janis Sanderson, anxious to get her article wrapped up, reached the house at 9.21 precisely. She was worried that this was an early time to call, despite Tessa's assurances the day before that they'd all be up and 'firing on six cylinders', and she had another little problem that was nagging her. Clive Smith, the news editor, had rung on Sunday night to offer her a 'sort of freebie' with 'no strings attached, sort of', and on an impulse she'd promised to consider it. It was not straight reporting, that was understood, but it was more news than features, probably – four days in Eastern Europe following the fortunes of a group of quasi-mercenaries from Northampton who had started off in Bosnia and now chased every bit of trouble they could find. It was the thought of revisiting old haunts that most appealed (Janis had spent a lot of time in the Balkans before the civil wars, a fact that Clive well knew), although the prospect of fencing dangerously with sex and sexuality also had a certain charm. For Clive was coming too, he said, and was 'quite frankly, going to try it on'. At the very least he hoped to show her she was wasting her time poncing about with arty-farty features when there was real reporting to be done.

Janis, knowing that Bren could hear her side of the conversation from outside the room, had suppressed her longing for a break from boredom, an adventure, and kept cool, calm and collected, promising nothing. But Bren's response – jealously inquisitive with a deepening of his current sulk – had confused her feelings further. Smith was an uncouth berk, whose attitude to what he called her 'little bits of writing' was arrogant and absurd. But he was a good news editor, who genuinely rated her ability in that field, despise it though she might. When Bren asked her, in his worst-case Cardiff whine, if she was going to go ('I s'pose that means you're going, doesn't it?' was what he actually said), she snapped.

'I don't know! I might, I might not, what does it matter?! Oh shut up, Bren, don't *start*!'

'I'm sorry, love, but I don't trust him, see? It's not your reporting that he's interested in, and well you know it. I don't trust him.'

Despite his wheedling technique, Janis had forced herself to leave that angle dangling. Her days of sleeping round the office were long gone, her days of any infidelity. Bren might have to go, but she wasn't planning to get rid of him by cuckoldry. Why tell him that, though? Why should she bother?

'Anyway,' he started up again, 'you don't need it, do you? You don't need Clive Bloody Smith to help you, you're not some bloody junior. You've got your articles, haven't you? You've got the *Sunday Times*.'

She had, she had the *Sunday Times* and a commission for the Tessa Wilmott interview. They could go and stuff themselves, the lot of them, she could get there on her own. As she swept up to Brook Bank in the morning, she was driven by a sense of urgency, a conscious need to get down to something solid, to get the thing completed and move on. Stuff Clive and his patronising attitudes, stuff Bren. If they thought that she was lost, or floundering, she'd have to show them, fast. Maybe it was she that should move out, not the Welsh whinger. Maybe it was time that she moved on.

Perhaps because she did not know the house, it struck Janis powerfully as somehow odd. Unlike the milkman or the post, she sensed loneliness even before she'd seen the open door. The house was bathed in light, its roof slates already shimmering with heat despite the earliness, and at one or two windows white lace curtains moved in the small breeze. For no reason she could pin down, Janis would have bet good money that the place was empty. In which, of course, she was not completely wrong.

She pulled the Renault to a halt, conscious of its embarrassingly sporty exhaust note in the seconds before she cut the engine and got out. The car fitted her exactly, compact and handy as they were, both with an air of well-controlled intent. Janis wore a red skirt that colour-matched the car, which she would lyingly have claimed was mere coincidence, and a plain white blouse. She reached into the Renault to bring out her bag, which contained among the usual things a pen and notebook and a small tape recorder. When she turned back to the house, nothing had altered, no one had come. There were birds singing in the trees, a tractor grumbling in the distance. No other noises.

Oh well, said Janis, to herself. She walked across the pale brown gravel, her sandals crunching, until she reached the concrete apron leading to the door. Instantly, she noticed that the jamb was split, indeed saw boot marks, black scuffs, on the paint. But the milk was there, and inside she could see letters on the table. Surely no one would have kicked in the door after these had come?

Her sense of dislocation grew. She listened, in the doorway, desiring fairly seriously to hear a sound, any sound at all. If there were people in a house, they made a noise. Taps running, footsteps, radio, the clinking of a cup. She pressed the bell and it buzzed noisily at the far side of the hall. She took her finger off, it stopped. The silence resumed. Complete silence.

What shall I do? she wondered. Standing there, she had a sense of interloping, intruding on something very private. But I'm just standing here, she thought. I'm here by invitation, to speak to Tessa Wilmott, and I'm just standing here, abandoned.

'Hallo!' She surprised herself. Less firmly, she repeated it. 'Hallo?'

There was mud on the hall carpet. She put things together in her mind, odd things and things that were not odd. The door was broken and had kick marks, but there were milk and letters. Someone had walked on the carpet with muddy shoes, but Tessa's car was parked outside, neat and untouched. Not one someone, either, her mind told her. As she looked, mud sprang up everywhere, it was all over the place, and there was grass mixed up in it. That was not one man's shoes, and what had they been doing? They'd been running everywhere.

Sickly, Janis saw a shiny thing obtruding through a door. Her mind leapt to guns, then away again. No, it was a walking stick, that sort of thing. It was aluminium, with a rubber end-stop. Just visible, lower down, was another one. Two walking sticks? A walking frame.

She had spoken to Tessa about her family. They were old, infirm. There were three of them, everybody knew that. Everybody knew about the Wilmotts, they were local celebrities. Celebrities who just happened to live almost like recluses. Who lived, in the main, alone.

A walking frame, sticking through a door, lying on its side. Mud on the floors, a broken door, milk and letters. Tessa's car.

I have to go and telephone the police, Janis heard her mind say, rationally. Something has happened here, there's been a

64

burglary or something. If I go into this house, I might find something that I can't handle. In any case, I have no right to go in. Something has happened.

She took one step, tentatively, across the threshold, then stopped. She had crossed the Rubicon.

Janis realised she was trembling, that her bag was now in both her hands, in front of her, the soft leather gripped like death.

She began to walk.

ELEVEN

In rural areas, few deliveries are daily any more. There was a general store in Rowsley until nineteen eighty-three, where one could purchase vegetables and processed meats and little more. The post office survived until nineteen eighty-seven, and old Mr Marchwood, whose family had baked on their own premises for a hundred and sixty years, clung on grimly until nineteen eighty-nine. He was closed down by a heady combination of what he called 'fruits of progress' – his only joke. The fact that new, young, rich people had moved in and thought his products quaint but overpriced, a series of public health inspections that praised his hygiene and insisted, naturally, that he install expensive new machinery to do a lesser job to EC standards, a 'fairer' business rating system that cut his profits to the bone. Finally, fed up and 'getting past it anyway', he sold the goodwill to a multiple, thanked the Good Neighbours with sweet irony for the petition they had raised to keep him producing the bread they did not buy, and went to live in Southsea, where he bought only packaged, pre-sliced bread. The multiple converted the bakery into two bijou cottages (with off-road parking where the flour store had been) and left the village to its fate. Within a week another small baker from the nearest town, clinging to the old ways more tenaciously than Fred Marchwood, had set up van deliveries, regular if not frequent. His wife, Ethel Bilton, drove the van, and there were just enough old people left to show a tiny profit. She came to Brook Bank every Monday, then on Wednesday and on Friday. She was two miles away as Janis set off across the hall.

Janis did not know why she was doing it. With every step she told herself that she was being mad, and her head was in a whirlwind of debate. She knew that it was mad for anyone to do it, but surely worse for her? Although she refused to let them leave her memory bank, the sight of death and blood were there, lurking just beneath her conscious vision. There was a young man with a gun and boots and camouflage, a man with a white straining face, there were broken people jerking in the gutter.

For some reason, she did not go to the door from which the metal tubes were poking. She got close to it, then moved off to the left, towards what turned out to be the kitchen. She stopped at the closed door and tried to catch her breath. You're mad, she told herself. You can't do this, you can't.

Angrily, she pushed the door, her mouth already preparing for a scream, a gasp, some necessary vocalisation. The kitchen was empty, and quite clean and normal. The floor was black and white, vinyl tiled, and the tiles were smeared with mud. There was a broken bottle beside the table, and a smell of brandy. The fridge door was open a small way. Burglars certainly, or intruders, but nothing too . . . Janis's eyes had strayed through the other doorway and she could see a foot. A woman's foot, with gathered nylon bunched above it. A thin ankle, not young, an older woman's foot. Janis stepped forward in a jerk, as if someone had plucked her by a rope around her neck. She stopped. Beyond the foot was something glossy, black or red. A pool of something horrible. Someone's blood.

She turned and stumbled, banging her hip against the formica kitchen table, her sandal splashing in the diminished pool of spirit. She caught sight of her face in a small mirror on the wall and jumped horribly. Her face was white and wild. She heard tyres on the gravel, the sound of an engine. She froze in utter terror, then ran through the kitchen, out into the hall, back to the front door. She was, as Mrs Bilton later put it, 'whiter than a ghost'.

Mrs Ethel Bilton was fifty-eight, and stout, and what older people still call 'sensible'. Despite the heat she was wearing a thick wool skirt, with zip-up dark suede ankle boots and white socks under them. On top of all she wore a white duster coat – the badge of bakery – covering her substantial bosom that was encased in yellow cotton. In her right hand she was carrying a plastic bag containing two wholemeal loaves and a cottage white, while balanced on her left she had a cardboard box of fresh cream éclairs. When she saw Janis – when she was confronted with her – she was disconcerted. But her expression did not change.

'What's up, love?' was all she said.

Janis shook her head. Relief and panic fought within her, mixed with a newer, less honourable emotion. She had not seen anything too terrible, but something terrible had taken place. Unaware that she had done so, she must have checked her watch. She was thinking deadlines.

Mrs Bilton had moved forward. She saw the broken door, and put her bag and package down. Her round face grew sharper.

'Has there been a break-in? Oh dear.'

Oh dear, thought Janis. Ye fucking gods! But she knew the woman was expressing concern. The woman stood four-square, she was like a bull. She was bracing her shoulders with determination. She was moving forward once more.

Janis stepped aside, faint and grateful.

'I'm afraid it's worse than that. I think they may have . . . I think there could have been a murder. Or something.'

'Dear God,' said Mrs Bilton. 'Are you sure?'

'No. But. D'you think you ought to? I mean, the police . . .'

Mrs Bilton and her duster coat were already well into the hall. The sense of gratitude in Janis grew.

'No point in doing anything till we know, is there? I'll have a look.'

Her line towards the bedroom door never deviated. She knew it was a bedroom, because she'd been in the house many times, upstairs and down. She usually had a cup of tea on a Monday, when she delivered, maybe shared a fancy with the family, a cake or pastry from the van. She pushed the door open, with a clatter from the walking frame, then stopped. Janis watched her broad back for perhaps ten seconds, before it moved. A long, long time.

Mrs Bilton backed out into the hallway, breathing hard.

'Call the police.' Her voice had changed, but not a great deal. 'She's dead. Old Joyce Withers. The rotten bastards.'

Although Janis still felt hollow and unstable, some of her colour was coming back. The women gazed at each other across the hall. It was all utterly bizarre.

So this is it, thought Janis. This is what it feels like if you're not a part of it. Not frightening, not corrosive or appalling, just weird, unreal.

'I saw another woman through the kitchen. A woman's foot. An older woman.'

Mrs Bilton put her hand up to her mouth, another oddness. It struck Janis like a movement from a film.

'Dear God,' she repeated. 'Tessa's car's outside. Dear God.'

But the body through the kitchen was Audrey. When she returned this time, the baker woman's face was subtly transformed. The sunburn, the weatherburn, hung on her skin like make-up, the skin itself drained bloodless from inside.

'You'd better go. You must go. You don't know what they've done to her.'

She put out a hand and gripped the newel post.

'It's Audrey. They've . . . Look, dear, go. Don't waste any longer.'

'I'll phone from here. If the phones . . . Perhaps I shouldn't touch anything? Look – I can't leave you on your own. Shall I . . . ?'

'You mustn't look. You can't come up with me. Phone the police.'

Mrs Bilton, hard, sickened, full of courage, began to climb the stairs. If there were two bodies already, Janis thought, why is she doing this? And she knew she wanted to be told all of it, the full story, before the police arrived.

The story. It was the sort of truth about yourself that you could never tell. Not to anyone, ever, ever. Hardly to yourself. But Janis was brave enough to admit it: there was a stain of excitement in the cocktail of emotions coursing through her blood, almost physical. It hadn't been her fault she'd stumbled on it, but she had. Two people dead so far, and the baker woman (must get her name, must *not* forget her name!) almost up the stairs. Mr Wilmott, the reclusive millionaire (was he a millionaire?) and possibly his daughter, Tessa. Suddenly, she hoped not. Oh Christ, oh Christ, she hoped not.

Or did she? She did not know, but she knew that shame had drenched her on the instant. For she noticed, this time, that she was staring at her watch, although she had not brought the face and hands, yet, into focus.

Upstairs, she heard a noise that was stomach-churning, a

cross between a scream and a deep groan, swallowed, choked, denied existence by its utterer.

The watch came into focus sharply. It was five to ten.

At ten o'clock, Ronnie Keegan was due in court. Outside, he chatted with his solicitor, a young woman called Maude Wimlock, showing her his teeth, almost flirting, although so far in their relationship she'd shown no sign of being interested. Perhaps it was because he'd pleaded guilty, last time round. Today he was only up for sentencing. Tactics that she wouldn't understand, would she? She couldn't.

Ronnie was tired, but it did not show that much. He was well turned out and personable, in a quiet suit that Eileen had chosen for him, off the peg but quite expensive, and a pale blue shirt and dark red tie. His shoes were leather, black, and polished, and in his hand he had a clean white handkerchief with which he dabbed his forehead. It was muggy outside the court, although the weather in the north was cooling, with a lot of high, thin cloud. Mainly, it was the excess alcohol in his blood, burning off. From time to time, Maude Wimlock had caught a whiff of something else behind the aftershave, which she recognised as last night's spirits. Her client had been drinking.

Indeed, her client had been drinking. What had her client not been doing? Although he tried to concentrate on what she had been telling him, his mind dwelt on other things, far away and seeming, somehow, long ago. Brandy, rum and whisky, some pills he'd swallowed, some things he'd done. The only part of Maude Wimlock he could relate to whole-heartedly was the top part of her breast, glimpsed periodically as she leant forward, nestled in crisp white cotton. That spoke to him, reminded him, became a component of the warm glow that still permeated him, his headache notwithstanding. Oh, the things they'd done, the times they'd had. Oh God, that breast and other breasts. Oh, marvellous.

A policeman that he knew walked past them, glancing appreciatively down the solicitor's blouse. He winked at Ronnie.

'Going down today then, Ronnie?'

Ronnie showed his teeth. White, strong, even.

'You never know your luck, do you?'

TWELVE

Mrs Ethel Bilton told the police five times what she had seen inside Brook Bank, each time becoming less certain of the exactness of her memory, but gradually becoming more coherent, to the point, indeed, of woodenness. It was typical of the police, she grew fond of saying later, that they asked her to repeat it all so many times, when they'd seen it all themselves, with their own eyes. What did they think she'd done? Rearranged the furniture? Laid out the corpses, what was left of them?

By this time, Mrs Bilton was able to view the whole thing fatalistically, as some of the people living in the wider area schooled themselves to do reasonably quickly. Otherwise, it would not have borne thinking about at all, the implications would have been too dreadful. Suddenly, the Good Neighbours were exposed, their vulnerability laid bare before them, the reasons why they had banded together to watch each other's houses brought sickeningly home. In the days and weeks after the outrage, salesmen of the very latest in security and alarm systems flocked to the village and the surrounding houses like any other scavengers for carrion, with open harping on the recent terror as their selling point. Many thousands of pounds changed hands – far more than had been shifted from the Brook Bank coffers to the pockets of the animals that Sunday night – and many thousand pounds worth of perfectly good equipment was thrown on the scrapheap and replaced. For many days and nights the peace of Rowsley was shattered frequently as the new, super-sensitive gear went off ad lib at any hour and for any reason or for none at all. But people, when they could sleep, slept easier, until the scare began to fade with memory. Before that, inevitably, at the younger, harder fringes, came the sick and dirty jokes.

The words 'beasts' and 'animals' and 'outrage' were first used by the police, at press conferences, and transmitted to an eager world. But Mrs Bilton needed little priming, to be fair, to feed such shorthand into her accounts. When she had returned to the front doorstep, to the waiting Janis, she had been hardly capable of speech. Her face was now quite whitened, her eyes staring out of livid rings. She was gasping, opening her mouth and closing it, as if pleading for sufficient air. Janis viewed her with a strange dispassion, feeling dislocated, fey, almost capable of floating from the ground she stood on.

'You poor thing,' she murmured, and immediately felt absurd. The banality of language struck her more forcibly than the woman's distress. It *was* absurd.

Mrs Bilton, obviously, was not going to notice such niceties of semantics and behaviour. She put out a hand to steady herself on the doorpost, then snapped it away as if burnt.

'Fingerprints,' she croaked. 'Oh Jesus, Jesus Christ. Oh, love.'

'Love.' They did not know each other's names. She had literally croaked, Janis had never heard a sound like it from a human mouth, and she wanted to fall into Janis's arms, collapse, be comforted. They did not know each other's names.

'They've cut them up,' said Mrs Bilton. 'They've bit her nipples off. They've stuck a brush up her. Mr Wilmott hasn't got a face at all.'

For a while, both women just stood rigidly. Mrs Bilton's eyes were staring hard at Janis, but she was not seeing her. Janis's brain rang with words and vile sensations. The pain was startlingly sexual, she had felt a discrete shock in her vagina, an electric twang of nerve or muscle. The reference to the nipples was worse, strangely, than the brush, although she guessed she knew quite clearly what that meant. But the banality of language carried through.

'Are they dead?' she said. 'I mean . . .'

Mrs Bilton, just conceivably, could have laughed. Or, Janis thought afterwards, punched her in the face, thrown up, anything. But she nodded, once, a very little nod.

'They're all dead. All four of them. Oh poor Tessa. Oh poor Tessa. Oh.'

'I'll phone. I can't use the one inside, it's evidence. Do you want to come?'

'They've pulled the phones out. I saw the wire. They've smashed things. There's a lot of blood. I'd better stay. I'd better stop here in case someone turns up. I couldn't bear it if some poor devil . . .' The muscles of her face rippled, her features altered, collapsed, rearranged themselves, reset. 'Saw all that,' she finished.

'But you can't stay here! You mustn't!'

The features had hardened, and the ruddy colour of the woman's real face, her normal, face-the-world face, was coming back.

'I can. I can't leave them alone. Hurry up though, won't you?'

Mild, polite, totally lunatic. The house reared above them, the windows shining in the sun. A white hand of lace waved through an open upstairs window.

Janis turned away.

'I won't be long. I'm Janis, by the way. Janis Sanderson.'

'Ethel Bilton.' The reply came automatically. 'Pleased to meet you.'

'Yes.'

Mrs Bilton told the exact truth only to her daughter, Linda. She couldn't tell it to the police because she'd touched things, covered poor Tessa up, which she knew from watching television was quite wrong. She couldn't tell it, either, because the constable who wrote down her first formal statement appeared to be illiterate, poring over a sheet of paper with a pencil which he actually licked from time to time, like the dunces in the village school she'd been to fifty years before. He took so long, she confessed to Linda, that the confusion of emotions she was feeling (although she did not express it quite like that) turned to frustration, then to anger.

'I thought, bugger me,' she said. 'If this is the best they can do, they'll never catch the bastards. They haven't got a prayer.'

The constable, with his stub of pencil, kept asking her to repeat things, and failed to understand plain English, as far as she could see. There was also no way, she told her daughter, that she was going to tell a man some of the details.

In a rush, she said to Linda: 'They'd even raped the old ones, love. I wouldn't have believed it if I hadn't seen it with these eyes. They'd took Joyce Withers' knickers down and there was stuff all on her legs. I nearly chucked up.'

She did not tell even Linda, she did not tell anyone, ever, her revulsion at the sight of Joyce's thighs, which were so thin, so withered, and so white. Or her pubic hair, which was also white, with a shocking stain of yellow round the business parts. So that's what we come to, thought Ethel Bilton, and felt ashamed and desolate, for herself and for her pointless, stupid thoughts. White pubic hair, stained with years of peeing – and although she did not look it, Joyce was not much older than herself, she knew. It was only after staring there that she'd stared at the congested, darkened face, which was also shaming. Joyce Withers had been strangled and her top teeth had come out.

'She must have messed herself as well,' said Mrs Bilton. 'There was this awful reek, and they'd used a sheet to wipe it up, one corner of it was . . .' She took a sip of tea, beginning to cry. Linda, a woman even more stolid than her mother, sat gazing at the unlighted gas fire, and far beyond.

Mrs Audrey Wilmott had been next, a woman Ethel had known for more than twenty years to pass the time of day with, and better than that in the years since Fred Marchwood had upped sticks. She was a lovely woman, open, without side, without the airs and graces that could so easily have been an adjunct of dwelling in the big house, and her riches. She was religious, quiet and refined, a respecter of herself and other people. Mrs Bilton had seen her almost naked, now, her body smeared with blood, her face bruised, her lips cut by her broken teeth, the evidence of sexual violation all too obvious. There was a look on Audrey Wilmott's face that she had been able only to glance at momentarily, but which she could still see clearly and knew she always would. A look of pain and terror etched so deeply it appeared to touch the bone.

'They say she died of a heart attack,' Mrs Bilton said to Linda. 'I say she died of fright.'

Outside there was the noise of cars, children shouting at the local school. They were in the flat above the bakery, some miles from Rowsley and Brook Bank. But Mrs Bilton, telling Linda almost everything, might just as well have been inside the house again.

'They always said she had a heart condition,' Linda said. 'It makes you think, doesn't it?'

74

Her mother's heart was upstairs now, or in her mouth as she reached the upper landing. She went by instinct first to Tessa's room, dragged there by fear of what she'd find, the need to know the very worst. For all she knew, both Tessa and her husband had been in the house; for all she knew, she'd find them dead together. The door was closed, and as she pushed at it, she was on the point of vomiting. The relief when she found that it was empty was for a moment giddying, although the contents had been thrown about or smashed. But the relief soon passed, and Mrs Bilton trod more soberly to old Peter Wilmott's door. Behind it lay the greatest horror.

'They'd put him on a chair,' she told her daughter. 'An easy chair, like he was sitting down to have a rest. But his face was mashed in, it was almost gone, there was blood and everything all down the front of his pyjamas. They must have done it with a hammer. His face was all smashed in.'

She drank more tea. The constable, when she'd told him, had asked her why she thought a hammer, had she any reason, any proof? The wild stupidity of the question, its massive irrelevance, had helped her carry on, had made the memory bearable. Her daughter Linda merely cringed, her shoulders hunching slightly. Mrs Bilton swallowed.

'They hadn't sat him down to have a rest. They'd sat him down to watch. They'd took off his pyjama trousers and put his hand . . .' She raised her head and looked straight at her daughter. 'His thing,' she said. 'They'd tried to make him hold his thing. A man of his age. Senile. Watching while they did that to his daughter. I hope to God he was already dead, that's all. I hope to God.'

But he was, she guessed, or when they bashed him he'd have ended up all over, wouldn't he? Not on the chair. They'd propped a corpse up to watch them do things to his daughter, what kind of people would do that? What kind of animals?

'She was lying on the bed, and they'd hit her head as well, her forehead was all lopsided. They'd strangled her, there was something round her neck, a nylon slip or something. Her legs had been pulled right open and they'd stuck a brush up her. Not a hairbrush, a dustpan brush, you know. Like that one.'

She indicated a brush with a chipped red wooden handle, beside the blue tiled hearth. 'I've got to tell you all this, love, I'm sorry. I've got to tell you.'

Linda moved her shoulders, a shrug of compliance. Shared misery hung upon them like a cloud. Her mother's lips made a wet noise as she opened them.

'The bristles were sticking out like a tail, there was blood on them, all over. They'd cut her stomach up, sort of slashed it. They'd done something terrible to her . . . bosoms. I think they'd . . .'

The nipples were torn off, torn or bitten, or cut. And on her neck, oddly, was a pink flannel and a bar of soap, the flannel folded, the soap resting in the square, symmetrical. Bunched at her feet had been a lightweight summer sheet, which Mrs Bilton, more or less involuntarily, had pulled up to cover her, right up to her neck, either for modesty or because she could not bear the sight. She had worried almost constantly that the police might somehow find out, and the worry had served to keep her mind off other things. She saw the sheet in her mind's eye, she could not get away from it, but her mind's eye did not probe beyond.

'Have you had a cry yet, Mum?' asked Linda. 'D'you want one of my sleeping pills? You ought to ask the doctor.'

'I don't need no doctor.' It came out sharply, so to soften it she touched her daughter's hand.

'Funny thing is, I'm sleeping all right,' she said. 'My mother always said I had no feelings, didn't she? But I've got some tears to get out yet, I reckon. I've got some tears to come.'

'I'll go and make another pot of tea,' said Linda.

Janis drove slowly off the gravel apron, as if in deference to what she left behind her, as if not to appear as flashy as her flashy motor car to the stolid, dumpy baker woman. Halfway down the driveway to the road she put on speed, and by the time she hit the tarmac she was going fast. The nearest phone she knew not actually in the village was more than a mile away, and everything seemed very urgent, at last. Somebody else might come.

She dialled 999, but before the operator had a chance to answer, she put the phone back on its cradle. She dialled her office number, and got put through to the newsdesk. Clive Smith picked up the telephone.

'Newsdesk.'

'Clive. Janis.'

'Well hallo! What can—'

'Shut up, I haven't even phoned the police, I feel an utter bastard. There's been a murder. Outside Rowsley, house called Brook Bank.'

'What! The Wilmotts' place? You're serious?'

'Four dead, at least. Mutilations. Someone went in and looked. The bread lady.'

There was a peculiar silence from the other end. Janis waited, her mouth bone dry.

'Clive, I've got to go. I've got to tell the cops. I'll ring you back.'

'Don't! Leave it for a while, do some snooping. Don't miss the opportunity.'

'You're mad!' she snapped. 'You're sick!'

'OK.' He did not try to argue. 'Janis, ring back immediately, OK? They'll take some time to get there, I'll have a think. Janis?'

'OK.'

'Janis, this is fantastic, this is big. Janis—'

Janis put the phone down. Her flesh was crawling.

THIRTEEN

By the time she had explained it to the police, in the sweltering heat of the phone box, Janis was soaked in sweat, with a badly churning stomach. It was reaction, she told herself, and also the weird impression she had got that the person at the other end had not known where Rowsley really was, let alone Brook Bank. He had also told her, peremptorily, to get back to the scene as fast as possible, to touch nothing, and to tell the other woman there to do the same. Whatever she'd expected, the attitude had come as something of a shock.

When she rang Clive back – after cooling down outside the box and mopping down her face and arms with tissues from the car – some steel had entered into her attitude. Not just towards the police, who had no right to tell her what to do, who had no right to come between her and a good old-fashioned scoop, but to her newsdesk and her paper, too. She'd stumbled on the story, and she had other irons in the fire. She was not about to play the dutiful reporter.

Clive's flattish northern voice was almost singing with excitement. Even if she'd tried to stop the flow she might not have succeeded.

'How quickly can you file? How certain are we of the numbers? You said four at least, is that the three old ones and someone else? The daughter? And her husband? Look, I've cleared the front page for the midday, and I can get two more pages on the next edition. I need copy in half an hour, just spout it and the subs'll knock it into shape. One photographer's on his way, and I'm sorting George out pronto, but if you can get into the house before the coppers, pick up everything, OK? Albums, happy-snaps, stuff from off the walls, just don't get caught, OK? Then I want interviews with everyone in a five-mile radius, village, all the farms and houses, plus the washer-woman. Jesus, Janis, we're going to scoop the world!'

She made her silence felt.

'Janis? You're not saying much. Well done, by the way. I always knew you had it in you, lass.'

Patronising sod, she thought. And ever ready with the *double entendre*, even under pressure. Quite honestly, she found his excitement catching, which she'd have to watch until she'd sorted out all her priorities.

'Clive,' she said, 'I'm not a reporter, I'm a feature writer. Despite your kind offer yesterday, I'm not about to change my mind.'

'Did I mention reporting! I'll get some legmen down immediately, I've got calls out dragging three off other jobs. I want background, Janis, atmosphere, a portrait of the village, The Day Fear Came.' A pause, infinitesimally timed. 'Plus the basic facts, you're not a total lemon. Weren't you doing a feature piece about Tessa? If she's dead, there'll be no one in the world with fresher information. Janis, this could be unique.'

Tension was flooding back into her stomach. Although she'd propped the phone box door open, her temperature began to rise. Clive Smith was going to really hate her soon.

'That piece is for the *Sunday Times*,' she said. 'I'm sorry, Clive, but—'

'Are you mad! Are you out of your tiny fucking mind!' Janis winced at the volume he achieved. She had a vision of him at the newsdesk, big, florid, in his shirtsleeves, dragging his fingers across his large pink balding dome. 'Look, you daft bitch, this is your own newspaper you're shitting on. The one that pays your fucking wages.'

She had to steel herself anew. She was contracted for a thousand words for the Sunday magazine, but she could see a lead in this, three thousand words and high-class pictures. It occurred to her, on the instant, that there must be a book as well, there had to be.

'OK, Clive, stop spitting feathers. I'll do the job, you know damn well I will, I'm just laying down benchmarks, right? Just don't try pushing me around, it doesn't work.'

His tone had changed. He sounded almost cheerful, and amused.

'I knew you were ambitious, love, but this is out the fucking window, this is. If you're prepared to make a twat of yourself for the sake of a crappy article in a colour supp that won't come out till three months time so be it, that's your funeral. If I was the editor I'd sack you, though, I just thought I'd let you know that. You're a toerag, love. Brass bound.'

'Fine,' said Janis. 'Nice to know the newsdesk's on my side.' Oh, and about that fuck you're after, she felt like saying – forget it.

'Run along then,' Clive Smith said. 'Do your little bits of writing while I get some real reporters down there. Here comes Tony now. He's been speaking to the cops. He's been telling them about it.'

'What!'

'Yeah, that would have pissed them off no end, wouldn't it? I wonder if he mentioned you by name?'

He hung up on her.

Back at Brook Bank, Janis was surprised to see a Panda car. It threw her badly, because she had come to a strange and difficult decision as she had driven from the phone box. She had decided that she would go into the house and see what the bread woman had seen. Her reasoning was complicated – too complicated for her to keep the strands of it clearly in her grasp – but it was something it seemed she had to do. She was losing her grip on the horror of the situation, it was beginning to be unreal to her, and she felt she had to confront the blood and violence head on, to see how much she'd changed, or if, and why. She was aware that her dominant image of the event was a young man with a rifle, in a street, and that was wrong. There was a Panda car, but no policeman, and no bread woman, either. Janis pulled up quietly and got out.

The house was unchanged. Silent, unseeing, spooky. The front door was open. Janis listened, hearing nothing. Instead of calling out, she padded to the doorway, listened further, then went in. She had reached the downstairs bedroom door, where the feet of the walking frame poked out, when she heard footsteps on the gravel. They stopped, then restarted, moving faster, running.

'Miss!' It was a deep voice, a country voice, a man's. Janis, heart in mouth, pushed the door with the side of her hand and stared in. She saw Joyce Withers lying on her back, her stomach and thighs and pubic hair, blood and fluids, and dark, congested face. There was a clattering of boots behind her.

'Miss! Oi, you! What are you doing there! Come away!'

Janis turned, taking in the fat policeman gratefully. A fat policeman, how traditional, what a lovely, tender cliché. He was enormous, bursting from his uniform, his brick-red face bathed in sweat. The image of Joyce Withers' face was wiped from her retina. The fat policeman was pretending to be angry.

'I'm sorry. I was looking for you. I'm confused and I got frightened. I'm sorry.'

Ethel Bilton appeared behind the constable, waxy but composed. She moved her face into something like a smile of recognition.

'It's her,' she said. 'The one that went to ring. He thinks you're the murderer,' she added, sardonically, to Janis.

The three of them stood there, hot, ludicrous. How could it all degenerate so quickly? Janis wondered. Why weren't they all in tears, rending their clothes, tearing their hair? It was like some bloody awful joke.

The large policeman, whose blond hair was plastered to his face in long wet strings, made a gesture of deep gloom.

'I wish you'd shut it, Ethel. I can't help it, about your bread. I can't let anybody go until the others come.' He included Janis in the conversation, that had clearly been wide-ranging. 'It'll be the gippoes, won't it? Sly bastards, if you'll excuse my French. They've been all over, recently.'

'Have they stolen anything?' asked Janis. Good God, she thought, a quote already. She began to visualise the front page.

Mick Renwick looked like a gipsy. Fat Marie, his current wife, stood in the bedroom doorway studying him, her bulk in balance, poised for flight if need be. Below she could hear the youngest of the children breaking up the television or something, screaming above its din. One good thing with Mick, you didn't have to keep them quiet while he slept. He didn't sleep, he went unconscious. You could have nailed a tent peg in his head.

He was naked, curled up like a baby, his hands between his thighs clutching his little tool. His face was brown, the long black hair sculpted round his ears by nature, not design. His nose was sharp, his features neat and foxy, his mouth full and sensuous and humorous. Oh yes, Mick could be funny when he wanted to, the bastard.

She wondered what he'd been up to, knowing that it had been no good. She'd heard him downstairs at four or five, crashing about, swearing, kicking things. She'd lain in the spare room with Seanie and Donna and the baby, praying he would not come and smack them up, which he might do if he'd forgotten it was on his instructions that she'd left their double free for him alone. But he had not, he had stumbled up the stairs and into bed and started snoring in fifteen seconds flat. You could stick a knife in him, you could beat his brains out with a hammer, easy.

His mouth was half open as he lay there, and his bottom lip was bruised and swollen. A fight, most probably. Across his back there were scratches that could have been done in anger or in passion. Fat Marie, catching the word as it rode through her mind, almost smiled. Two of her five were Mick's. Passion for Mick was a one-sided thing, no woman would have time to get worked up before he'd come and gone, unless it was a teenager who'd scratched because she'd thought it was what you had to do. For herself, she'd bitten off her nails even before she'd passed that stage.

On his side there was something that looked like dried blood, and there were cuts and bruises. On the floor were his clothes, jeans and tartan shirt, white socks (more black stains linked by grey, in fact) and slip-on shoes. There was stuff on them as well, every item, including the slip-ons. Blood or shit or anything, Fat Marie did not really care.

He breathed stertorously, twitching for a moment, rolling over to expose his little dick. All shrivelled, that was, but she did not look for long. In any case, his hand found it again and hid it. He liked to keep his hand upon his cock.

She hated him, did Fat Marie. She fucking hated him.

FOURTEEN

Nobody had ever heard of Rowsley, and suddenly it was on the map. Nobody had ever heard of Janis Sanderson, and suddenly . . . she lived in hope. Janis was working on instinct, fired maybe by the millstone-grit of Clive Smith's charm school attitudes, Manchester press division. Clive had worked in Manchester as a legman for the nationals, until new technology and proprietorial greed had blown away the second biggest corps of journalists in Britain, and he still hankered after those hard, dead days. 'Some day soon I'm going to tell the world,' he used to sing, 'about the Carving Game . . .' Janis, assessing her tame fat policeman almost subconsciously, told him that the woman's husband Damon had flown to Germany the afternoon before, most unexpectedly. She did not tell PC Gareth Page that she was a journalist, however.

When the main force came, they came in style. PC Page had told them on his radio what to expect, and they arrived down the gravel driveway from the road like the Seventh Cavalry, but caparisoned in white, fluorescent red, and flashing blue. There were three cars, heavy and squat, disgorging men in uniform and men in suits. There were two vans and a minibus, and a four-wheeled trailer behind a Land-Rover – this being a county, not a city, force – proclaiming in black stencils to be a mobile incident control unit. Just to confuse matters, three minutes before, a Mini Cooper and a Montego had screeched to a halt behind Janis's Renault, and a reporter and two photographers from her paper had scrambled out. Like the police they had got lost, and roared through Rowsley like some awful cavalcade of yuppie racers, scattering inhabitants. Two telephone complaints had been attempted by Good Neighbours, which had put the switchboard at headquarters into a total spin. Could these be the escaping criminals? Could it be an outbreak of coincidental joyriding? Could somebody explain?

Luckily for PC Page's subsequent career, he was a match for local paper men. For want of choice, Clive had had to let the chief photographer come out, a gentle man called George Thwaite, whose interests lay in improved colour techniques rather than snatch shots of blood, celebrities or crumpet, while the first man that he'd briefed was keen, but young and inexperienced, Pete Pond. The constable was fat but fast, and made it clear with an air of quiet charm that anyone who tried to sneak into the house would end up with a long lens down his throat. The reporter, as reporters do, made a beeline for his colleague, who eyed him coldly, as she might have done a rapist.

'Janis?'

'You don't know me,' she hissed angrily, from one side of her mouth. 'Get away, you fool.'

Tony Hester was not a fool, and turned away immediately, to watch the photographers taking pictures of the house exterior, the cars, the grounds, and Mrs Bilton and her bread-van. In moments, their tiny chance was gone. Twin-tone horns, the crunch of gravel, the flash of gleaming paint and lights between the trees.

'Fuck,' said Janis, quietly. 'Look, Tony, the whole world and his dog've seen that lot, the village'll be boiling with quotes and theories. I'll have to stay here for a while, I'm a witness. Get into the middle, and spread the word, take Pete. Ring Clive for me, I promised him some copy. The dead are Peter Wilmott and his wife, the home-help Joyce Witherspoon, I think, and Tessa Wilmott, 32, their daughter. She's a freelance computer programmer and games originator. She's married to Damon Hegarty – different name but definitely married – who runs her father's company, you know it, everybody knows it. Names and ages are in the cuttings, obviously, but Tessa's been on *Woman's Hour*, she's a local celeb, on the up and up. Oh, and the local bobby thinks it's gipsies. It's a good line to start with. They've been hanging round the place.'

Tony Hester had his eyebrows raised.

'Clive said you were a wanker. He needs his head examining.'

Janis grinned.

'I'd forgotten what it's like, that's all. Now bugger off, before they nab you. That lane leads to the road, too, they haven't worked it out yet.'

The police activity was instantaneous, enormous, and impressive. As Tony got into the Mini Cooper, a high-ranking uniform officer and two men in suits went into the front door of the house almost at a run, followed by a phalanx of lesser mortals who took up station around the door. Two other small contingents disappeared round the corners to the back, while policemen and a couple of policewomen began to unload gear from the vans and the mobile unit. Rolls of tape appeared, stakes and sledgehammers, screens and noticeboards. A concerted rush on the photographers, almost a charge, stopped their activities, and an angry-looking sergeant tried to prevent Tony from driving off. Tony, pretending bravely not to have seen the running officer, jinked round another group and got away. Pete Pond, catching his gesture, took a diagonal and caught him up a hundred feet away. Tony stopped just long enough to let him scramble in.

'Seal the entrance and the exit!' the sergeant bellowed. 'No one in and out at all! Nobody!'

Despite his staidness, old George Thwaite could fight his corner.

'We're press. You can't impound our cars.'

'I'll give you ten seconds to piss off, then,' snapped the sergeant. 'Hoi!' he added, as Janis opened her car door. 'Where are you off to? Aren't you the witness?'

Police were scurrying in and out of the front door like ants. One of them staggered to a bush and threw up noisily. Janis smiled, not too sweetly for fear of exacerbating the sergeant's rage.

'I'm from the *Clarion*. It's all right, I'll be back.'

'Like hell you will. Get out and stay out. I've a good mind to arrest you for obstruction.'

George and Janis exchanged smiles, nipping smartly into their respective cars. At the main road, she parked well onto the verge and went to the photographer's open window.

'Morning George, you've got some great shots, haven't you? I've given Tony some info for the captions. The bread lady's called Ethel Bilton, she went inside and saw the lot. I'll get an interview if I can, but I got her phone number off the breadvan, give it to Clive, will you? I've scribbled down some notes for him as well, can you make sure that he gets them?'

She handed across two pages from her notebook that she'd scribbled on before the police had come in droves.

'Do you recognise the cops who went in first?' she asked.

'Chief Inspector Charlie Altwick, Detective Super Arthur Patten, Detective Sergeant Rosser. I'd have preferred to get them coming out, but never mind. Patten's a hard sod, he'd probably have confiscated the film if he'd known.' He glanced at his watch. 'I'm off. Are you going back?'

Janis was torn. She dearly wanted to go and write, to hit the village with the awful news and get down their reactions. But if she played it right, there might be even better goodies at the house. In any case, she was a witness, and they knew.

'I better had. You know what bastards they can be. If they think I've pulled a fast one on them, they'll go spare.'

'They already do. They hate it when we get there first, it makes them feel like tail-end Charlies. They hate it when they can't control it all. I'd get back fast if I were you. Be humble.'

Janis watched him go, aware that she must find a lavatory soon, stricken for the moment by sharper pangs around the background discomfort in her guts. Her unexpected elation at the business of reporting faded at the thought of the next phase: interrogation by the lumpen intelligences of the constabulary. Even as a junior she had been startled by the lack of flair among the policemen she had rubbed shoulders with, the lack of style they showed in their enclosed and sexist world. Some reporters got on with them quite well, she knew, but then ... some reporters! Dredging her memories, as she walked back along the dark, shaded drive towards Brook Bank, she could not bring up one cop she had liked or been impressed by.

Things at the house had settled down. There was less scurrying, fewer officers visible, and two more cars. A photographer in black trousers and blue shirt was preparing his equipment on the bonnet of one of them, while two men were carrying square wooden boxes from the other to the house. The forensics, she presumed. Her fat constable was seated on a low wall with Mrs Bilton and two other uniforms. All three had notebooks out, and Ethel looked decidedly fed up. Then a tall, thin man in civvies broke away from a group by the incident unit and strode towards her, leading with a large and bony nose. Janis thought she recognised him.

'There you are,' he said. 'My God, you're lucky you came back, Sergeant Kemp was all for putting out a warrant.'

His manner was not unpleasant, but her irritation grew.

'Look,' she said, 'I'm busy. I'm on the *Clarion*, as you know. I didn't see much, I didn't go inside, and I know very little. If you want to ask some questions, would you mind very much doing it quite quickly? Please.'

He was amused by the way she held herself in check. He nodded, putting his hand out.

'Lance Rosser. Detective Sergeant. I think we've met.'

She was not disarmed, but she had to shake the hand.

'Although,' he continued, 'it seems unlikely I'd have forgotten, doesn't it?'

She looked into his face, not certain what he meant. His lips were thin, curved and predatory, and she guessed she knew. But Sergeant Rosser did not allow her time to get aerated. He pulled out a notebook, black and substantial, and flipped it open to a rubber band marking a page.

'You said that Damon Wilmott flew to Germany unexpectedly. Is that right? How do you know that?'

'His name is Damon Hegarty. They're married, but his name is Hegarty and hers was Wilmott.'

Sergeant Rosser made a small, sharp noise. He excused himself and went off to a car. The uniformed inspector and two other men were by it, and he talked to them. Janis saw one of the men pick up a radio handset from the dashboard. The thin detective strode back to her.

'Bloody plods. That fat bastard told me Wilmott. Did you know them, then?'

He was trying to draw her into his charmed circle, her and him against the sweaty constable and the other uniformed buffoons. Janis was not drawn.

'I'd met the wife. I was doing a profile, for the *Sunday Times*. I came round today to interview her.'

I'm venal too, she thought. Name dropping already. To this self-satisfied streak of piss. Sergeant Rosser, indeed, had raised his eyebrows.

'Not just a pretty face,' he said. 'Why do you think he did it?'

'What! Have you *been* in there!'

His eyes had narrowed.

'Yes, have you? You're blushing.'

She was, and she cursed herself for it. But whatever he'd intended by his approach, Sergeant Rosser was hardly gaining an ally by any of it.

'I'm hot,' she said. 'I'm fed up, and I'm probably pre-menstrual, OK?' She dropped that in routinely, she'd found it effective as a putdown. Lance Rosser did not twitch.

'You didn't answer me.'

'I've been in a little way. I felt the atmosphere. I listened to poor Mrs Bilton when she first came out. Are you seriously telling me you believe Tessa's *husband* could have done all that?'

'I'm seriously telling you nothing. Was he Irish? Was he a Mick? The name.'

'Was? Are you telling me he's dead, too?'

'I meant was he when you spoke to him. No, he's not dead, far as we know. We haven't traced him yet. Do you know where he went in Germany, or why?'

'Business. He wasn't Irish, but he was always off on business. Tessa was really . . .' She stopped. She realised that this was quite tendentious. But why should she try to hide the truth, even if she thought the police were mad. Irish! Ye gods, what had that to do with anything! 'I'm leading you to wrong conclusions,' she said. 'I'm feeding prejudices.'

Detective Sergeant Rosser was still quite calm.

'It seems to me that you're the one with prejudices, but let's leave that, OK? Tessa was really what? Pleased? Happy? Angry? Furious?'

'I was going to say pissed off, but I know policemen don't like to hear a woman swear.' He let it go, and Janis was ashamed. 'I'm sorry, that was childish. Tessa said he was always off on business, and sometimes it was quite infuriating. They'd organised a family celebration of some sort, and he'd had to drop everything and zoom off. I rang up yesterday. It had obviously caused an argument of some sort.'

'You see,' said the detective sergeant. 'You can do it when

you try. It's amazing how perspectives change when you spit out all the facts.'

Patronising guff again, but she was disinclined to get het up. She drew a breath and rubbed a hand across her eyes. She was exhausted.

'PC Page told me it was gipsies.' Something had just dawned on her. 'Is that why you asked me if Damon Hegarty was Irish? Don't you think that's just a little bit far-fetched, even for a policeman?'

He pretended not to know what she was on about, so she guessed that she'd been right. Damon had flown abroad to make an alibi, while his Irish tinker friends had come in by invitation to destroy his wife and in-laws. What a scenario!

'Anyway,' she said, 'it was tragically unlucky for her, if it was gipsies. Well, whoever did it. She doesn't live here, you know, she was just staying the night. They've got their own house about three miles away.'

'I know.' He nodded towards Tessa Wilmott's car. Two men were going over it, in their shirt sleeves. 'Police computer. I know your address as well. Didwell, nice place. Do you drink there, in the Ship?'

She did not reply, and Lance Rosser took out a cigarette packet, which he offered. When she declined he lit up and inhaled, deeply.

'I might be able to let you know some things,' he said. 'Angles. When we're a bit further on with the investigation. You could be the leader of the pack.'

'If you've finished with me, I've got my own investigating to do, thank you.' Christ, that came out pompous. Oh well, carry on. 'Unlike you, I have to work to deadlines.'

His face hardened.

'Some things the Boss won't want you to reveal,' he said. 'He'll be calling a press conference this afternoon, I shouldn't wonder. We don't want any idle speculation, do we?'

'That's your problem, I'm afraid. Or his. By this afternoon they'll be here in droves, won't they? Wall to wall hacks. I've got to get my stuff before the chequebooks come out.'

'You don't appear to understand,' he said. 'If I let you go before the Boss sees you I'll be skinned alive. You're a witness. You can't just walk away. Anyway, I want it down in writing in the end. Let's start again, shall we? There'll be plenty more you'll remember if we go over it a few more times.'

Janis was almost too tired for the battle, but only almost. There was a small smile on Rosser's bony face, a smile of premature confidence. It re-energised her.

'Look,' she said, 'I've told you what I know, and now I'm going. If you want to speak to me later, fair enough. If you want a written statement at the station try me this afternoon, when I've spoken to the office lawyer. But if you think you're going to stop me from leaving here to do my job, you're barking mad. I'm a journalist, I'm not a comfort blanket for the police.'

His eyes were glittering. In another situation, she thought he might have hit her.

'I could arrest you. For obstructing the police.'

'Bollocks. You'd be all over the front page. You'd get bigger headlines than your Super. What would Mr Patten say to that, I've heard that he's a hard bastard.'

'Wait there. I'll go and see.'

He turned on his heel and strode towards the house, fury evident in every bone and sinew. Christ, thought Janis, Patten must be hard if Rosser's scared enough to go and interrupt him. She glanced about. From the way Ethel Bilton was gesticulating, they were probably hanging on to her against her will, as well. But bread would keep. News wouldn't.

No one appeared to have realised she and the detective had been rowing. No one was taking any notice of her. Janis turned quietly away from them, walked quietly down the drive, wishing that the gravel did not crunch so brazenly. No one had challenged her when she rounded the first bend, but she saw a group of policemen where the driveway met the road, constructing a cordon out of fluorescent tape. Rather than argue with them, she pushed into the woods and took an angle that would bring her out well clear.

She did not want to make too many enemies in one day, did she?

FIFTEEN

Superintendent Patten was too steeped in vileness to respond to petty anger, so Rosser modified his stance as he approached. Patten was in the upstairs room of Peter Wilmott, in a jumble of men and flashing cameras. Wilmott's corpse was hidden now, so that he looked like an old armchair underneath a dustsheet, while Tessa was uncovered, her mutilated body open to the fingers, eyes and probes of the forensic scientists bent close down on her. The room was stifling, stinking of fresh human excrement, drying blood, chemicals and sweat. Lance Rosser's aftershave added a gruesome touch, a whiff of living decadence among the real corruption. In his hand, between two fingers and a plastic bag, Patten held a small domestic brush.

'Sir? One of the witnesses reckons she's got to leave. She's a journalist, she's mouthing off about deadlines.'

Superintendent Patten turned pale eyes on him. They were grey, intense. It was his unusual eyes, envious rivals had been heard to say, that had earned him his promotion. People remembered Arthur Patten, he looked keen and sharp and dangerous. He was only forty-one.

'That sounds pretty ghoulish. Have you spoken to her? Has she got anything we need to keep her for?'

'She gave me more about the husband. He's called Hegarty. He left unexpectedly yesterday afternoon, missed a family celebration, flew to Germany. After a ding-dong with his wife.'

The pale eyes moved to Tessa, on the bed. A man was probing in her mouth with long shining tweezers.

'Germany. Oh dear. Who told her this?'

'Sir?'

The superintendent walked to a folding table that had been set up by the bed. He laid the brush down carefully onto a sheet of plastic that had been prepared for it.

'Who told the journalist? Or did she overhear the row herself?'

'The wife told her. She was going to interview her for the *Sunday Times*, so she rang for an appointment.'

'And she told her there was a row? My God, it must have been a bad one. Unless they knew each other?'

'They'd certainly met before, sir. She called her Tessa. That's the sort of thing I want to ask her more about.'

'So we don't know exactly how bad the row was. Nor does she.'

'I don't think she knows much more, sir. She said the wife was getting dead pissed off. It was always happening, apparently. He's a businessman.'

'But yesterday he left unexpectedly. On a Sunday. What sort of business would make a man do that?'

Grimacing, Patten led Rosser from the bedroom. On the landing, both men filled their lungs.

'Mark you,' the superintendent said, 'if he did it on his own, he's Superman. He's indulged in a spot of burglary as well. He's had some shotguns, sawn the barrels off and left the scrapends in the drawing room, we found them underneath a coat. Drunk himself silly, there's empty bottles everywhere. Fucked his mother-in-law. Does it add up?'

You had to be careful, joking with the Boss, but Rosser assessed the risks as minimal. Jokes helped to ease the tension, that's what they always told themselves.

'Plenty of the lads would do that if they could, sir. Metaphorically, of course.'

Patten smiled tightly. It was widely held that his own mother-in-law had helped to wreck his marriage.

'Of course. It's a nuisance, though. A thorough-going bloody nuisance.'

'What, sir?'

'The journalist. Being a witness on the spot. There's nothing we can do, though, Lance. We've got men out already, house to house, so at least no one'll be able to say we read about it in the paper. Tentative, very tentative, that's the watchword.'

'Sir?'

'We haven't actually got any questions for them to ask, have we? So we've been reassuring, getting a general picture, anything suspicious seen, any prowlers in the area recently. I don't want it to look as if she knows more than we do when she gets into print. *Clarion*, is she?'

Rosser nodded.

'I told her there'd be a press conference, I presume there will be, sir? I warned her about too much speculation.'

Patten was thinking hard.

'Find out about the firm for me,' he said. 'Who the directors are, where they are, when we can talk to them. Before that, though, we'd better brief HQ. Give them a holding formula for when the jackals really come. I'll want an accurate list of the names, the ages, all the basic facts. Found dead, cause unknown, no details for fear of blowing vital evidence, you know the form. Do it now, get it to Bill Crane, tell him to give out nothing else before the conference, time to be announced. You'd better let the woman go, even if she does go shooting from the lip.'

'She knows more, sir,' said Rosser. 'She knows about the injuries, some of them, she knows about the rapes. She's spoken to the bread woman and I wouldn't be surprised if she hasn't done a bit of snooping in the house. I could arrest her.'

Patten looked sideways at him.

'Pretty, is she? Want to feel her collar?'

The sergeant laughed.

'Not her collar I had in mind, sir. She was the one in the red skirt when we arrived. Nice line in sweat. I actually thought it would be nice to cool her down a bit. In a cell. She's uppity.'

'Don't mess with them, they're trouble. I doubt if she'll cause us much pain, anyway, it's early days. If we need to, we can slap her later.'

'True.'

In her car, Janis headed for the Graysons'. She should have rung the newsdesk first to make sure that they had some early words, and to see if Clive wanted anything specific. She remembered her reporting days well enough to know that the first rule was to keep in touch, and she had heard Clive's flat, abrasive voice bawling people out enough times since for breaking it. Let him just try that with her, she thought, pleasantly grim. Before she rang him, before she did anything, she had to have the lavatory.

The Graysons' place, in any case, was as good as anywhere to start gathering reactions. It was a farm that specialised in horses, where Janis went from time to time to hack, and the family weren't the sort who'd be put out by her dropping in, however unexpectedly. They were a taciturn lot, the father and his son massive and watchful, the two daughters tall and thin and ugly, and her main contact – friend would have been too strong a word – was Margaret Grayson, whom she knew to be thirty-one. In her whipcords, tartan shirts and wellingtons, she could have been almost any age, from twenty-five to fifty. She knew everyone in the village and for miles around, and hardly ever mentioned them. The Graysons were not comers-in. The farm was a mile out of Rowsley, two miles from Brook Bank. Margaret knew Tessa Wilmott, also.

She even, to Janis's surprise, knew that Tessa had been murdered. As the Renault vibrated over the last lumpy setts into the yard, Margaret came slowly from the kitchen door. Uniquely, she was followed, by her sister Paula and her brother Tim. They did not hurry to her, but stood expectantly as she got out, towering above her, faces dark and curious.

'Look,' said Janis, put off her balance. 'I know I picked the gear up yesterday, but something's . . . Look, I'm sorry about this, but can I use your lavatory? It's pretty urgent.'

'Is it true?' asked Margaret. 'About the Wilmotts? Yes, of course you can. You know where it is.'

They moved slightly apart. Janis found it all acutely embarrassing. She ought to answer, but . . . She bent over, apologetically, to accentuate her plight. She damn near hobbled. Over her shoulder she said: 'Yes. Isn't it horrible? I . . .' Then, running out of things to say, she sped up, reached the door, gratefully disappeared.

When she emerged, the yard was empty, although she could see Margaret through the half-door of a stable. Janis walked across and entered the dim space, filled with the warm reek of horses and their urine.

'How did you know?' she asked. 'I went there this morning and I walked right into it. I spoke to her last night.'

Unexpectedly, she was wobbly again. Get a grip, she thought.

94

Pick on a reaction and stick to it. Her stomach, eased, was still not right.

Margaret rested her fork against a wooden rail.

'Everybody knows by now,' she said. 'The place is crawling with policemen. Poor Tessa. And the rest of them. Was it Damon, too?'

Janis was aware of movement behind her. The dark stable darkened further as Tim and Paula filled the door. They did not speak. They did not return her nervous smile.

'No, Damon was in Germany. He was called away. Look,' she said, impulsively, 'you know I'm a journalist. I'm not here to interview you, but I'll have to tell them what you say. I expect. To put it in the paper.'

'Fame at last,' Tim murmured.

'Do you mind? I mean – you don't have to tell me anything, I suppose.'

Margaret said: 'What's the odds? What does it matter, any more? It's them we're sorry for, no point worrying about us. There's talk of . . . filthy things.'

'Yes. The bread lady went in. Mrs Bilton. Do you know her?'

'Poor Ethel,' Paula said.

'She took it very well. God, that sounds awful. Look, honestly, I just don't know how to react to all this. Nothing like this has ever happened to me before. Remotely. Look, could I use your telephone? I've got to ring the office.'

'Use Dad's room,' said Tim. 'That's the quietest. They're bastards, aren't they? Are there any theories? The yuppies'll be shitting themselves.'

'Won't your father mind?' Janis was in awe of Mr Grayson, he was too much like a stallion for comfort. He had an edge of temper like a club.

'He's in the fields,' Margaret explained. 'He doesn't like all this. He shut his face up when we told him, and went out. He's known Peter and Audrey for forty years. Fifty, maybe. All their lives.'

'He feels the draught,' said Tim. 'We're more isolated than the Wilmotts were, in some ways. He was always telling Peter off for encouraging the gippoes, he hates gippoes, does our Dad.'

'Tim,' said Margaret, a slightly warning note. Janis searched their faces, hawklike, closed. Tim showed his teeth, a mirthless smile.

'We'll be questioned by the police for long enough, we might as well get practice. Dad hates gippoes because they're horse traders and so are we. It's a natural antipathy, it goes back centuries. You get on with them all right, you do some deals, then one night half your stock might disappear. They always blame the others, they're amorphous. The Irish blame the Romanies, the Romanies blame the diddicoys, everyone blames the tinkers. And as far as we can tell, us Gorgios, they're all the bloody same. Peter Wilmott used to give them jobs, let them take his scrap, park up their lorries sometimes. When they robbed him, he just laughed it off, part of country life. Our Dad hates that. We have to make our living from the land, unlike some people.'

It was the longest speech by far that Janis had heard any of the Graysons ever make. It had drained Tim. He turned away, his large shoulders rounded, and walked across the yard. Nobody spoke until he had disappeared behind a barn.

'How old is he?' asked Janis. 'If you don't mind me asking? I'll need it for the quotes.'

Margaret blinked.

'Thirty-six. D'you mean Dad? No.'

'Tim's thirty-five,' said Paula. 'He's not thirty-six till October.'

'Is he right about the gipsies, do you think?' asked Janis. The horsy faces were fixed and neutral. 'I think the police are working on those lines.'

'People pass through,' said Margaret. 'There've been the hippies in the last few years, what do they call them, New Agers, is it? The great unwashed. But not everybody would know the house was there, would they?'

'Or what was in it,' Paula added. 'Surely it wouldn't be a random crime? Surely not?'

When Janis had made her phone call, she found Margaret still inside the stable, forking soiled straw. She was excited, keyed up, anxious to get into the village. She'd spouted six hundred words to copy, straight off the top of her head, going on the gipsy line, and how outlying farm dwellers were 'feeling the draught'. Clive Smith had listened in to some of it, and spoken to her before and after she had done the story. His voice had been affectionate again — apparently the hard things he'd said were forgotten, or put on ice, at least.

'As to the manner born,' he said, 'terrific. Tony rang in with your basic info, plus a bit he'd picked up on his own. Then George swanned in with the early pics, they're magic. There's one of the bread woman with her head held in her hands that would make a Hitler weep. What now?'

'Vox pops in the village. The local vicar likes to make a meal of things, if I remember right. I'm going to try and get some works of Satan quotes.'

'Great. But don't forget the theories, will you? Every bastard in the village has a theory, see what they make of Damon going missing, too. Tony's digging dirt around the place, and Mary Faircloth's running down the members of the Wilmott board, then the workforce. According to Tony, the Rowsleyites are dead suspicious of Englishmen who can speak German. Especially Englishmen called Hegarty! Ring me in an hour, if you can.'

Janis came out on air. She was prepared to admit to herself that she felt better than she'd felt for ages, more alive, more sure of a direction. And at the back of everything, the old primeval buzz, was the knowledge she'd got Tessa in the bank. Tonight, when the first flush was dying down, she'd ring the *Sunday Times* and renegotiate. No she wouldn't, it was Monday. The Sunday journalist's day off.

She leaned through the top half of the door, waving at the tall figure in the contrasting gloom. Margaret moved towards the light.

'I'm off. I'm going to the village, thanks for your help. Is there anyone else there who knew the Wilmotts very well? Tessa in particular?'

'Not really. They didn't get out much. I have thought of one thing, though.'

She stopped, and Janis waited. Margaret was blinking in the sun, her long face vulnerable, shy.

'Yes?'

'There was a handyman. Some months back. He worked there with his wife, they lived in, there's a flat above the garages. They got kicked out after a while. Well, she ran off, or something, and he got the sack. He was a bastard, apparently, a con man. Good-looking, plausible, but a rogue. He used to beat her up.'

'The wife?'

'Well, not Tessa, obviously. Yes, I met him myself a few times. Jack the lad. Try in the pub. Try Monica.'

Something stirred in Janis's memory. A little light lit up.

'Was he a gipsy?'

'No, he was a northerner. Lancashire or Yorkshire, it all sounds the same to me. Although I think he had a sort of Irish name. I might remember it if you give me time.'

They stood unspeaking for some seconds. The memory nudged more strongly at Janis, it worried at her.

'No,' said Margaret, regretfully. 'I tell you what, though, Ronnie was his first name. Ronnie—' She balked, the surname in her throat. 'No, it won't come. Ronnie, though. I'm sure of it.'

And Janis had remembered.

SIXTEEN

Ronnie Keegan was fed up with British justice. British so-called fucking justice, as he called it to his solicitor, with crudeness delicately timed. He was bored, and so might Maude Wimlock be. She might reveal, in her boredom, that she liked talking dirty, you never knew, did you? Ronnie had many cards in his seducer's pack, and he had learned to play the 'bit of rough' one late but expertly, since Eileen, indeed, had dropped into his lap. Eileen had come as a surprise to Ronnie, and he was still not absolutely certain it had been a nice surprise, in the final analysis. Nice girls were OK – there was a certain thrill in making them do nasty things with dicks – but they could be a pain. Probably the best way with nice girls was to operate the Three F plan – find it, fuck it, and forget it. Maude Wimlock would be ace for that.

'Ten o'bloody clock,' he grumbled, looking at his watch. 'I even got here early. Now look at the fucking time. They'd only have themselves to blame if we pissed off.'

Maude gave a tired little smile. The bit of rough appeal, to be quite honest, didn't seem to cut much ice with her.

'They'd put out a warrant for your arrest, and an extra month on your sentence. Why be bored now, when you're going to have all the boredom you could wish for anyway?'

Ronnie wagged a finger at her in mock disapproval.

'You're meant to be on my side, you are. Don't tell me you want them to send me down?'

She made a small, impatient noise.

'You pleaded guilty, Ronnie. You have a record. Whatever you think I can do for you by being here, I can't. I have explained it all before.'

You'll do, he thought, you'll do. Before he spoke he made a rueful face.

'Sorry,' he said. 'You don't know me all that well. It's just the company, really, the support.' He grinned. 'Beneath this smooth exterior, there's just a frightened little boy!'

Her laugh at this was genuine, and her smile transformed her face. He showed his teeth, pleased with himself.

'Seriously, though. We sat up quite late about it, me and Eileen. I told her I'd go straight. It's a fucking worry all this, isn't it, to be quite honest? Sorry if I'm crude.'

'That's all right,' said Maude. 'I'm used to it.' She sighed. 'These surroundings don't help, do they? Do you know, it's places like this that would stop me being criminal, ever. I get paid to come here, and I'd give it all up just to stay away. Thank God it's sunny, anyway.'

They were outside the court, still, knowing the ushers would come and call. They were outside in the broken trees of the concrete mall, up to their ankles in the coke tins and McDonald's wrappers. At least the cooling breeze blew the smell away, the precinct smell that inside the court was like a sink school, only stronger, the smell of fellow criminals and their hangers-on.

Ronnie surveyed them with contempt, draped on the concrete plant tubs and low walls, waiting in the muggy warmth. Jesus fucking Christ, but they were pathetic. Men with thin faces and long hair, twisted mouths and drooping cigarettes, women with big knockers and big arses, short skirts ridden up unevenly showing the bruises on their thighs. Why were the men always so thin, he wondered, and the women all so fat? Why did the babies look as if they'd been roughly moulded out of dough?

Criminals. They were the dregs, the scum, the lowest of the low – he'd never be like that. They were animals.

The most interesting thing about yuppies, Janis felt, was how they were all exactly the same, and all thought they were completely different. Or to précis that, she thought, that they were all equally boring. The most interesting thing about yuppies – final version – is that they are boring. She was trying it as an intro to a story as yet unwritten, the story of a murder. She was trying to sort out in her mind how to turn her brutal, filthy murder into literature. Or, at least, journalistic writing of the highest order. Yo, she mocked herself – no shit.

Janis was perched on the bonnet of her Renault in the shadiest part of the car park of the Hare and Hounds. Only her bottom was touching metal, through her skirt and knickers, but it was burning her. She was flicking through a notebook, the names – in capitals, standing clearly out amid the shorthand – evoking images of young, concerned women that she'd spoken to, all of whom had responded just the same.

'Jesus,' Tony Hester had said to her. 'It's a shagger's paradise. D'you know, Janis, I've spoken to eleven wives, and not one of them's got a bloke who lives at home except at weekends or till very late at night. I think I'll come here for my holidays!'

Janis had smiled, but broadly, she had found the same. The ones she'd spoken to – loaded but alone, she summed them up as – had made her own vague discontentment, her inchoate feeling that her life was on a drip to nowhere, seem self-indulgent. Maybe the rat-race she was in threw up too many rats, but there was one thing worse in her experience – no rats at all. She realised that the events at Brook Bank had terrified them in a rather subtle way. Some appalling men had come and raped and murdered, and in their own homes, their pretty little cottages, there was no man resident to care. Or know. That was the worst of it. There was no man there to know.

Tony and Pete, the skinny young photographer, had had other preoccupations, naturally. Over a drink on the terrace where she'd sat the night before, they had gone over what they'd got so far, what they were after next, and how much cash they stood to make on it through the *Clarion*'s freelance pooling system, that had shot out words and pictures to all the nationals and agencies so far. Clive Smith, said Tony, was overjoyed with the way it had been going, but had warned them to get any other good leads wrapped up pretty quickly, before the Hungry Joes hit town. Janis had an interview lined up herself, she said, but she would not tell them who or what. When they had gone, she'd walked back to the Renault to think and wait. It was fifteen minutes before Monica Pagett, the landlady, turned up in her white Peugeot 504 estate. Janis followed her to the back door of the pub and smiled.

'Hallo,' she said. 'You may have seen me in the pub last night, but that's not why I'm here. Janis Sanderson. I'm with the *Clarion*. It's about the Brook Bank thing.'

Monica, a tall, angular blonde, put on an expression of concern.

'It's terrible, isn't it? Tessa and her husband used to come in from time to time, although I didn't know the old ones. It makes you think, though, doesn't it?'

It makes you think. If Janis had had a pound for every time she'd heard that said. She ought to work it into her piece somehow. It made you think.

Monica was lifting a cardboard case of tonics. Janis moved across to hold the door.

'I was up at Grayson's. Talking to Margaret, she's a friend of yours? She mentioned that you knew a man who worked up at Brook Bank. A handyman, she said. Ronnie something.'

Unexpectedly, Monica coloured slightly.

'Ronnie Keegan. What a bastard that man was.'

She nodded Janis through the kitchen door. As they entered the room from the outside, a hefty, florid man walked into it from the bar. The landlord.

'Just in time,' he said. 'It's just been on the radio, there'll be journalists and telly crews coming down like flies with any luck.' To Janis he added: 'You found her, then? It's an ill wind, isn't it?'

'Ted,' chided his wife. 'Don't be so mercenary. There's two more boxes of tonic in the car, and three of American dry. Make yourself useful.'

Ted winked at Janis.

'You understand, don't you, love, you're a reporter. It's bread and butter to you, this, but for us it's jam. You lot drink like fish, as well. Here comes Christmas!'

While Monica sorted out the mixers behind the bar, Janis went and sat in the saloon and waited with a gin and tonic. Ted was right, she thought. The pub was empty now, but when the hacks hit town it would be bonanza time. Four people dead, and they got in extra bottles. Ill wind indeed.

She had met this Ronnie Keegan, she was – for no sufficient reason – convinced of it. She'd met him on a chilly autumn dusk the year before when she'd been slightly drunk and rather in a state, having just run her car into a ditch in a dark back country lane she'd taken to avoid main roads and breath tests. She had been surprised to see a man emerge from nowhere, but too angry with herself to be afraid. She'd gone out driving, she recalled, after a row with Bren, and solaced herself by putting the car through its paces. Her miscalculation had been to power on too hard on gravel that was looser than expected, and the car – a Fiat Tipo that she'd never really liked – had bucked into the verge and bounced along the ditch on its left-hand front suspension.

The man had been tall and dark and handsome, casual and concerned. They had exchanged few words before he had got down onto the grass and started checking the suspension, leaving Janis feeling grateful but a little foolish, as she'd been swearing volubly and vilely when he'd turned up. Then he'd stood, brushing the knees of his crisply ironed jeans, and said he thought that it would be all right. Janis, rather quickly, had got in and started up, edging forward while he had pushed the front sideways and upwards to help it climb out of the ditch. That done, he'd asked her if she fancied going for a drink.

Janis, in the quiet pub, wondered if she could be right. The man had said he worked nearby, and he had had a northern accent, she was almost sure. But he was pleasant, quiet, not in the least bit pushy, as Margaret had seemed to say. When she had turned him down he'd merely smiled, she thought, although it was the vaguest memory. An unexpected helper on a stupid night. No, he could not be the same.

Monica appeared before her with a whisky, carrying a packet of cigarettes and a lighter. They sipped companionably, Monica wreathed in smoke, for a few moments. Funny, thought Janis. Last night we were customer and landlady, now we're allies. The complicity of the servants of the public appetite. Or another way – we're two whores, about to make a killing.

'Nah,' said Monica. 'Ronnie Keegan's not a murderer. He was a swine, but that doesn't mean he goes round cutting people into bits, does it? Is that true, by the way? That they mutilated them? There's some awful stories going round the village.'

Janis shook her head.

'I don't know any details. I've heard what you've heard, probably. This Ronnie. How was he a swine?'

Briefly, punctuating with her cigarette, Monica gave a run-down on the life and times of Ronnie Keegan. Plausible, could be fun, generous, a ladies' man. Also a fantasist, prone to believing that he owned Brook Bank, not just 'cleaned the lavatories', ever ready to hint of irons in the fire that lesser people could not hope to understand. In short, she ended, he was a dickhead, who'd caused a lot of trouble in the village. No one had been sorry when he'd gone. Well – no one publicly.

Janis sipped and waited. No one publicly. It hung in the air, dying to be expanded. Monica, finally, continued.

'His name was linked to me once, by the gossips, but it wasn't true,' she said. 'If it had been I wouldn't be here now, Ted would have cut my throat, or kicked me out, good luck to him. But a couple of the women, the young wives, you'd be surprised the sort that fell for his old chat. Posh girls, you know. Husbands working down in London, commuting every week, fair enough you expect some of them to get lonely. But you'd have thought they'd have known better with an oik like him, however charming he could be. You'd have to do a lot of digging before you'd get anyone to admit they had a broken heart, believe me, but I'm bloody sure there are some.'

Janis remembered the ironed jeans, the smart, pale jumper.

'An oik,' she said. 'Did he dress up rough? Was he like a handyman?'

Monica crushed out her cigarette in a big yellow Ricard ashtray. There were people coming into the pub, and she glanced across at them. Ted emerged from the back kitchen.

'I never saw him in a set of overalls,' she said. 'Even when he came to roof our outhouse, which is when the rumours started because Ted was up in Newcastle on a course. Airs and graces. People who didn't know used to take him for the local squire, he used to con them up and then we'd all have a laugh about it in the bar. When you got to know him, though, you didn't like him. I didn't, anyway. Maybe I'm just too fly.'

She stood, gathering up her cigarettes and empty glass. There was work to do.

'I'll come in later, Monica,' Janis said. 'My turn to get you one. Listen – Margaret Grayson said he used to beat his wife. That's why he got the sack, she said.'

'That's the theory. I don't think anybody knows for sure what happened. She buggered off, there's no argument about that, but as he never took her out I don't think anybody ever checked to see if she had bruises. My idea is that Tessa put the boot in, in the end, but you'd never catch her talking out of turn about the staff. He couldn't have lasted though, could he, with the woman gone? They were meant to be a team, the house, the gardens, the lot.'

'So she never came in here? He didn't keep her locked up, did he?'

'Nothing spectacular. He wasn't Bluebeard. He took her shopping in Harborough and Kettering and Leicester, and I guess they had nights out as well. But round here, socially, he stayed on his own. I think a lady on his arm might have cramped his style.'

'Was he good-looking?'

Monica took a cigarette and lighted it.

'If you like that kind of thing. Tall, black hair, bags of confidence. I suppose he was, until you got to know him. Not a murderer though, no way.'

So who was a murderer, thought Janis, as she went out to her car. Not someone anybody knew, ever. But someone had to do it, didn't they? Starting her engine, she was glad it was not her job to find out.

Power without responsibility, she quoted to herself. The prerogative of the harlot throughout the ages.

Mm – sounds good!

SEVENTEEN

The days when the police called press conferences to help the press are long gone, sadly. As long gone as the days when the press attended them to simply help the police. Nowadays most forces have an information officer, whose job, in part, is to advise on timing and control. Detective Superintendent Arthur Patten needed certain information to come out, but he did not want the press to know of any leads that he might later follow. Also, if possible, he wanted the *Clarion* to miss out on official quotes. He was angry with the *Clarion*.

He discussed the problem with Sergeant Rosser and with the information officer, Bill Crane. Between them they chose the time of four o'clock. It would give the early TV bulletins time to flesh out bare bones, ditto the radio stations, and it would give the national dailies an early start for them to run full pages in the morning based on legwork and some juicy quotes. 'House of Horror' was Rosser's contribution – obvious but extremely bankable – while Crane played around with 'charnel houses', 'death camp mutilations', and 'injuries reminiscent of the worst kind of serial killer.' Patten, who despised this sort of game but needed publicity to kick-start the investigation, chipped in on a minor key, with 'deeply dangerous men', 'animals who must on no account be approached,' and, simply, 'the beasts of Brook Bank.' Mutilation was a word that had already appeared, in the early editions of the *Clarion*, which was one reason Patten was so angry with them. The four o'clock call, it was hoped, might at least deny Janis Sanderson and her 'fellow reptiles' the benefit of official quotes for their main edition. As the information officer understood it, four thirty was their final deadline for any meaningful late stories, a time the conference would surely run beyond.

Janis and Tony knew of the bad odour they were in, because the editor, Simon Trapper, had been telephoned twice by the county's acting chief constable, Cyril Hetherington, for a bollocking he had passed immediately down the line to Clive Smith and the chief sub-editor, Ben Potter. The police objected to the fact that mutilation had been mentioned, and the speculation (villagers were quoted, and an unnamed constable) that gipsies or other travellers might have been involved. The fact of mutilation would make it easy for cranks and lunatics to claim they'd done the murders, it was said, while 'alerting a group of suspects so blatantly' was tantamount to contempt. Clive and Ben were unimpressed and said so, but Trapper, who as editor sat at the sharp end in terms of the local élite, had thrown his considerable weight about. He was not going to have his neck put on the block, he said, because some of his staff 'hankered for the values and the language of the gutter press'. That, relayed to Janis, had particularly hurt. The real reason, she knew, was because of the way her luck had panned out – first by being there at the very start, then by the repeated happenstance of beating the police to every interview. Both she and Tony had been in houses in the village when the heavy knock had come, and the frustration it had built up in the police had hardly been disguised. The hidden agenda was probably even worse: for unless the police had found some solid evidence at the house, Janis and Tony were up with them all the way, and might, indeed, have learned things they had not. 'Gutter press', to them, would seem a rather mild jibe.

The presentation at the conference was brave, but rather visibly empty. Chief Inspector Charlie Altwick and two other inspectors represented the uniforms, flanking Patten, Rosser and the information officer on a small raised platform. PC Crane immediately issued a 'straight-through information number, to be manned twenty-four hours a day', and gave a dispensation that they might smoke. But Patten, when he started talking, set the tone as downbeat, not trying very hard to disguise the fact that, so far, they knew little. The press contingent was excited and excitable, but not aggressive, listening politely while he outlined the bare bones, giving names and ages at dictation speed, although these details were by now well known. The causes of death could not be released until after post-mortems, he said, but gunshot wounds were not in evidence. However – among the items missing from Brook Bank were at least three shotguns, one of them a pump-action twelve-bore that was classified (and certificated) as a firearm, and extremely deadly. He revealed, also, that the barrels of the guns had been shortened by sawing with a hacksaw before they had been taken. Under no circumstances, he went on, deadpan, should any member of the public, for whatever reason, approach one of these men. 'One of these men,' quoted back a reporter. 'How many of them were there? Do you have descriptions?' Mr Patten, still deadpan, said that they had made 'intelligent conjectures' but that they were not yet firm enough to be made public. As soon as their deliberations had been concluded, 'you ladies and gentlemen will be the first to know.'

'How much was gone?' Exactly, we do not know. 'Did they take money, or other valuables?' Not antiques, certainly: clocks and ornaments had been untouched, except for smashing. 'Cash?' A wall safe had been opened, but not, apparently, forced. 'What, was it open?' Apparently it was. 'And the house? Had that been broken into?' It had, through the front door, which had been kicked.

Janis: 'But what about the other doors, and the windows? Were not some of them already open? Had any other entry been forced?'

Superintendent Patten turned his cold eyes on her for several seconds before making a reply. Then he said: 'For operational reasons, there are some facts we would regret disclosure of. Unfortunately, too many important pieces of information have slipped out, for one reason or another. We would like to appeal to you, all, to exercise restraint. So far, regrettably, there have been some lapses.'

To people in the know, all codes are readable. The other journalists looked at Janis eagerly, to see how she would handle the rebuke. She responded coolly.

'If a photographer reaches the scene of a crime before the police,' she said, 'I imagine you're not saying he shouldn't take a picture? I'm sure the editor of the *Clarion* wouldn't have printed anything that might give anything away.'

Chief Inspector Altwick's face had darkened visibly, but Patten remained calm.

'Four people have been cruelly and brutally murdered. Some of my officers – battle-hardened men, I do assure you – were shocked as they have never been before. I have been shocked.

Revolted, horrified. It is difficult to escape the conclusion that we are dealing with animals. That there were beasts in Brook Bank last night, not men. All I ask of you is that you do not appoint yourselves as judges of what is or is not evidence, or permissible, or desirable to transmit. I am confident that you do not wish to aid these men – these animals – but I beg you to consider that you may, through ignorance of the facts if not for any other reason. That is all.'

That was masterly, and Janis wisely kept her mouth shut. All around her men and women were scribbling, one or two holding up small recorders, not bothering with a back-up note. She thought the superintendent was playing his cards brilliantly, winding down towards an ending after a good, abrasive climax designed to cover up the fact that there were no facts, that he was whistling in the dark. She wondered if he'd heard of Ronnie Keegan yet, hoping – pettishly – that he had not. She wasn't going to tell him, anyway – let him whistle.

Superintendent Patten could be disarming, too. When the scribbling was over he held up one hand, palm upwards.

'Look,' he said. 'Ladies and gentlemen, we're all in this together, there is absolutely no sense in denying that. Out there somewhere, possibly not very far away, are some men who have wrought cruelty and murder on an almost medieval scale. To be quite frank, we have very little to go on, as yet. As yet we have no scientific evidence, no sightings, no hints of any sort as to who they were, these beasts, and whence they came. This will change, and it will change very rapidly, please God. In the meantime, please trust me to do my best, and trust my magnificent team, in whom I have the very highest confidence. You are responsible people, so I beg of you, consider what you write, and consider your first duty if any snippet of information should come your way, from whatever source. Now – if you will forgive me – we have work to do. Good afternoon.'

He stood, taking almost all of them by surprise, even his fellow officers behind their tables. Altwick responded first, then the others got to their feet. One of the reporters shouted: 'But the husband! Have you found him yet? Is he a suspect?'

Patten, who had turned towards the door, turned back. There was silence as he regarded them.

'Yes.' His voice was very low. 'Consider the husband. How

would he respond to all this? What would he feel if he saw lurid interviews and theories on the television or in a newspaper? I will repeat, ladies and gentlemen – you may speculate, I cannot stop you. But before you do – consider the husband.'

He had not answered the question but he left, followed by all the other officers save Sergeant Rosser and Bill Crane. After a moment of confused silence, someone in the front row said mildly: 'I guess we take that as no, do we . . . ?'

PC Crane, briskly, picked up a sheaf of papers.

'You've got the straight-through number. As soon as we have anything it'll be available. Thank you everyone. Come on! Chop chop! Deadlines, remember!'

It was a feeble jest, but they laughed politely. Early days, there'd be more to go on later in the evening, and they had some terrific quotes. As Janis waited for the door-crush to ease, Lance Rosser sidled up to her.

'You've upset the Boss, you know,' he said. 'I wouldn't push your luck if I were you.'

'Oh yes? What does he think I've done? Made up the facts?'

'He doesn't take kindly to people walking out on him. Nor do I. Then all that crap you put in the paper. Comfort to the enemy. You should have asked, you know.'

'And you'd have told me. That's not precisely been my experience of the police. Anyway, you're talking bullshit, nothing I wrote comforted any of the enemies, whoever they might be. You've got to know something before you can give anything away.'

He was very tall. He looked down at her past his chunky, bony nose, weighing something up. Janis waited.

'Suit yourself,' he said, at last. 'He's a bad man to cross, though, I'm giving you fair warning. There's still another way to play it, it's not too late. That invitation I made this morning. It might still be open. Just. There's nicer places than the Ship at Didwell.'

It had been a long day, hot and tiring. She had seen dead bodies, blood and filth. Now here was some insane policeman, propositioning her like some bloody office girl. Specifically, Janis did not know if she would laugh or be enraged. Then Tony Hester, who had gone into the corridor, came back in again, to speak to her.

'About that statement,' said Sergeant Rosser, cold and formal. 'We're going to need it soon. Have you spoken to the lawyer yet?'

'What?' said Janis. She remembered. Another piece of bullshit. 'Oh, no, no, I haven't. Is it urgent?'

'You know it's urgent, why ask? There's been a murder, you're a witness. I suggest, in fact, you do it now.'

His attitude was now hard policeman to a member of the public, obstructive and recalcitrant. Tony lifted an enquiring eyebrow, and Janis decided, on the spot.

'OK. Tony, you can cover all this, can't you? We've missed all but the fudge, in any case. I won't be long, I've got to give a statement.'

'Lucky you.' He grinned. 'See you in the Granby, yeah? I've got this idea Clive wants to get us a big drink.'

He went off down the corridor, flicking through his notebook, forming an intro with his lips. Janis smiled ironically at the detective.

'So here I am then, Sergeant. Take me!'

EIGHTEEN

It was five o'clock before Mick Renwick woke. He came round to the normal sounds of home – the TV fighting with the radio fighting with the screams and shouts of children – and he lay flat on the double bed, a sheet crumpled up across his calves, and wondered why he'd bothered. Full bladder, probably, the erection he was scratching was not to do with sex, although come to think of it, the night before had – ooh, a twinge. He had to have a piss.

Mick stood up feeling not unwell, and immediately felt much worse. His gorge rose so fast he had to blow his cheeks out to stop from throwing up, and he grabbed the bedhead to draw long, deep breaths. Simultaneously, a four-inch nail was inserted in his head, into the geometric top-point of his skull, and driven down. Mick gasped, wincing at the pain, all his tender parts contracting, cringing, all except his prick, which stood out from his small, thin body painfully, like an angry fishing rod. Oh you bastard, Mick thought, oh you bloody bastard. And the shakes began.

Once, long ago, Mick had thought he'd give up drinking. He'd woken in a ditch in Bedfordshire one night, pitch black and raining, and he'd not known where he was. That is, he'd known he was in a ditch, that much was obvious, if he'd slipped in there face downwards, he'd have drowned. But he had not known why he was, or how he'd got there, or who he'd been with and why. He was very cold, and the aching in his joints was almost as bad as the aching in his head. Also, he discovered, he had shit himself, the first time he'd ever done that, the presager of many. He'd decided, then and there, that he'd give up drink, or cut down drastically, a brave attempt and it had failed. He had got out of the ditch, and thrown away his underpants and cleaned himself with handfuls of wet grass, and walked along the lonely country road. Not far away he found the caravans, and remembered he'd been working with

112

a gang of Irishmen, some of whom, indeed, were lying in the mud beside the JCBs. At dawn they'd all awoken, made some tea, found Mick some whisky to revive him, and worked for six hours, all except him. Then at lunchtime they'd gone back to the pub and filled him up with Guinness – which he'd drunk forever after – and saved his life. In the afternoon, the foreman told him Work or get the sack, so Mick had worked. Mick liked the Irish. They were proper men.

Mick had always worked, and he despised people who didn't. He had failed to give up drinking, but he had watched the Irishmen, and trained. They had the great advantage, most of them, that they were big, but neither he nor they accepted that as an excuse. The trick was – the life was – to drink the Guinness and fill up with stodgy food, then fall down insensible to recharge the ould batteries. That way, you could work. You could hump stone, you could push barrowloads of wet concrete, you could dig, and shift, and haul. You could keep your end up, and you could show the foreman who was boss, the real boss. Anyone could give the orders, but the real men did the work. Mick suffered for his art, being so small, but he made it. He could work drunk, he could work hung over, he could work alongside pink elephants or little blue men in bowler hats. Being so small, though, the booze ate into him, destroyed him slowly. Or maybe it was just family luck. His father had died of drink, aged fifty-two, and like his father, Mick slipped into a pattern of vile irrationality, violent rage, when he was drinking. Even the biggest of the Irishmen grew wary of him, when he was on the hooch.

Into Mick's vision, now, swum the open bedroom door, and beyond it the top landing. A shaft of sunlight angled off a mirror, and despite the dust encrusted on it, pierced him with light. Mick had to close his eyes, crashing and stumbling towards the door, pushing the cot sideways with a squeak of castors. He reached the door and held the jamb, muttering beneath his breath, then launched himself into the bathroom, where, in the cabinet above the raw green of the washbasin, there was a half-bottle of whisky and an empty tub of Vick. He had dropped a bottle once, into the sink, and had smashed the bathroom up in his frenzy, hence the green suite, which Fat Marie had chosen and he'd plumbed in himself, after seven months. This time, no mistake. He sat, naked, on the lavatory to uncap the bottle, which he upended into his mouth with jerking hands. What a twat, he thought, that Ronnie Keegan, it was time to hunt the bastard down and kill the twat. Ronnie Keegan had never worked, properly, that was his trouble, he didn't understand the word. Ronnie Keegan lived in a world of dreams.

'Riches,' said Mick, out loud, 'beyond the dreams of Aberystwyth.' Whose joke had that been, Doggo's? Where was Doggo, what had they done with him? 'Thirty thousand smackers,' he went on, 'so we'll never have to work again. Guaranteed.'

The pain was fast receding, the shakes had gone, the old rough magic. Mick's sense of humour was his blessing, he could always see the funny side. And they'd had a lot of fun, and he'd got his gun, pump-action, beautiful, he wondered where the fuck he'd hidden it. He noticed things on his inner thighs, dried blood and slime, scratches. They had had a lot of fun.

'Riches,' he repeated. 'Poor old Doggo's face. Sick as a parrot. Thirty thousand quid.'

Never mind, there was always work. People always needed roofers, didn't they, especially on the moors.

'You've got to laugh though, haven't you?' he said.

Janis arrived at the Granby like a piece of chewed string. Any normal group of people, meeting after work for a chat, would have packed up and gone home long ago, but she knew she would find somebody. She wondered how journalists who weren't married to each other stayed married, the way they carried on. Then again, not many of them did.

At their normal table in the corner were Clive, Tony and Mary Faircloth. When they saw Janis, Clive and Tony whooped, waving her across. As she sat, Clive slid round the table and drew his mouth across her cheek to find her lips, but she did not oblige.

'Get off,' she said. 'You must be crazy going near my skin, I need a bath like I've never done before. I'm rancid.'

'He likes them dirty,' said Mary Faircloth, as if she knew. 'What d'you want, Janis? Big gin and tonic?'

'Gigantic. I've been in the nick for three hours. It's true, what everybody says, they're mad, they're mental, they make us look sane. I've just been interviewed by a policewoman who can't read and write. It's true!'

It almost was. She had been led to a yellow-painted room, high-walled and windowless, that smelled of something she could not quite identify, and frankly did not want to. Lance Rosser had shown her to a bare pine table and a plastic-covered chair, and asked her to wait. As she had sat on it, it had struck through her skirt as sticky, a sensation that had grown as she had shuffled to get comfortable. Left alone without an explanation, she had waited with increasing fury – five minutes, ten, fifteen. The room was hot and airless, and Janis was aware of how badly she had fared throughout the day. There was not an inch of flesh that was not covered in dried sweat, and the skin between her sandal thongs was smeared with lines of congealed dirt. The price of fame, she thought. I've earned my bylines this day, anyway.

She had decided, as the minutes had crawled by, that when Rosser returned he would get a mouthful of abuse. But Rosser did not return. After twenty-five minutes, the door opened and a woman constable came in, fairish, fattish, and twenty-two or three. She smiled tentatively, and sat down opposite, playing nervously with a pencil and a sheaf of paper. She explained that there had been a hold-up, and she had come to take a prelim statement. Would Janis tell her, please, in her own words, exactly what had happened, in what order. Janis, impatiently, had begun to talk immediately, and the WPC had gaped. First, she had said, apologetically, I need your name. Name and address, and age and occupation. Et cetera.

It must have been a joke, Janis decided. No, not a joke, a deliberate ploy to pay her back, to put her in her place. However slowly she told her story, however painstakingly she spelled it out, the policewoman got lost. Watching her, upside down, Janis realised that she could not spell the simplest of words. She could not hold her pencil properly, she used it like a blunt, blind chisel. After a while, her rage turned into pity, she thought the girl was being tortured, maybe, not her. At one point she offered to write it out herself, but the WPC got flustered, hurt, upset. After forty minutes, they had done two pages.

'No, honestly,' she told her elated colleagues, in the pub. 'I didn't know whether I should laugh or cry. I kept saying things – simple things – and she'd repeat them as she wrote them down, and get them wrong, completely wrong. And she could tell what I was thinking, and got nervous, and began to sweat. No, I mean *sweat*. I mean, I'm stinking, I've never been so filthy in my life, but she was stifling me, and she knew. Oh Christ, it was just *horrible*.'

They laughed and she laughed with them, but it had been awful at the time, demeaning and embarrassing, and terrible for both of them. Janis had modified her story, cut it down, simplified it, and helped the suffering policewoman all she could. At the end of it, when Rosser had breezed in as if on cue, she and the woman had shared a glance of complicit loathing, which she, at least, had made sure he did not miss.

'Finished?' he had jeered. 'Did you get that, Jean? Did you enjoy that, Janis? Now, I want to run through it again, if you don't mind? You don't mind do you, Janis? Jean, get us a cup of tea will you, darling? Sugar?'

'Jesus,' said Mary Faircloth, wide-eyed. 'What did you *do*? I'd have poked his bloody eyes out!'

'We did have words,' said Janis. 'But I didn't have much choice when it came to it. It makes good copy, any way. I'll pay him back, the bastard. I'll pay him back.'

'It sounds to me,' said Clive, 'like there's a man would like to fuck you.'

'Takes one to know one!' said Mary. 'It sounds to *me*, as if he's got as much chance as you have, too!'

Later, when Mary and Tony had gone off to homes, or meals, or other pubs, Clive asked her if she'd sleep with him that night. When challenged, he insisted it was not a clumsy pass, but a serious suggestion, a follow-on. He linked it, characteristically, to matters journalistic. The time for congratulations was well past, he said – she knew fine well how good she'd been. The time had come for her to accept the inevitable and come back on his team. Janis had brayed, cynically.

'Which team? The others have gone home! Or is this the team for bedroom Olympics?'

Clive's big, bland face still smiled.

'With me they're linked. There's nothing I can do about it, they're inextricable. I'd like to sleep with you, but I couldn't fancy somebody who couldn't do the biz! Where's Bren tonight?'

This was too much. Seduction was seduction, but discussing the domestic arrangements was uncouth. However, Janis decided to be nice about it, to laugh it off.

'Luckily, he's away. He's had to go to London for the firm. Big order on, or something.'

Clive's face was quizzical. He was much too smart to believe in simple luck. Bren worked for a firm that dealt in inks and colour agents, he knew. He also knew he was away at night occasionally.

'Luckily?'

'Luckily, Clive, because I'm a conscientious journalist, as you keep telling me. And I'm a feature writer, too. I've got about three background pieces to do tonight, and I want them in the computer before I retire to my bed. My chaste, lonely bed with crisp white sheets. Virginal. I'm sure you get the symbolism. Virginal on the ridiculous.'

'Ah well, Sally will be pleased.' He cocked an eyebrow. 'The current. She still likes me enough to want to see me sometimes.'

'Long may it continue. Look, seriously, I ought to go and start. And it's not for the *Sunday Times*.'

He grinned.

'Ah, I'm sorry about that, I was a little brusque. You'll ring them first thing, though? You'll be able to squeeze a bigger fee I should imagine.'

Their eyes met and held. Two cynics together. They smiled in unison, pleased with themselves.

'I've got a story,' Janis said. 'For you. It's not together yet, but I'll work on it tomorrow, and it's a goodie. I want to put it in the paper and see what it sparks off. Will you back me?'

'If it stands up. All the way. You tell me what it is, I'll tell you what I think.'

She shook her head.

'No. Might spoil the juju. I've got a feeling about this one. Tomorrow, though. I think you'll like it. Look – I'm going.'

She stood, contemplating his large, round, lively face. She liked him. She knew it.

'About that fuck,' he said. 'It needn't take very long.'

117

They both hooted, and she bent to kiss him, on the mouth. She did not linger, but there was intent.

'I'll see you in the morning.'

'Aye.'

Ronnie Keegan's Eileen received two phone calls that night, neither of which was much use to her. Mercifully, her mother did not ring. That would have been too much to handle.

The first came early, when she had been home for twenty minutes. It was Maude Wimlock, the solicitor, who was concerned and curious in probably equal measures. They had met two or three times, for complicated reasons. Ronnie thought, from time to time, that Eileen might be an asset in a court of law, him in a suit, her so clearly middle class and 'nice' – a winning combination. Even if it could not convince them of his innocence, it could affect the sentences, perhaps . . . Maude herself had noted the differences between them, and sought *rapport* with Eileen. Eileen, confused enough in the relationship, strove to avoid it.

'Hallo, it's Maude. Maude Wimlock. I wondered if there's anything I can do?'

Eileen felt no bitterness about the court case, only dull hurt. This was the third time that she'd stayed at work, it had become a method, a way to hold her head up with her colleagues. They read about him in the newspapers, of course, and they speculated about the relationship, but Eileen carried on as normal, quiet and efficient, too good-looking, by far, to be a victim. Eileen, in a way, was beautiful, chased by men wherever she had worked. The coolness, the distance, she had developed early in her life with Ronnie, when he had been prone to mark her face with bruises she could not really hide.

'There isn't, thanks. Thanks for asking, but I'll be all right.'

'We were expecting it, of course,' said Maude, 'but . . . well, you know.'

There was an awkward silence. Eileen knew all the details, because she had rung the court clerks' office in her lunch break. The rest was chatter, and she did not want to chat.

Maude said: 'Ronnie conducted himself very well in court. I was a bit worried at first, he seemed so . . . well, he said you'd had a drink or two, to soften the blow. His last chance for a little while to come!'

She finished on a rising note, inviting a shared rueful chuckle. The bastard didn't drink with me, thought Eileen, he sent me to my mother's. She wondered, in a little flash, if he had been with a woman. He had got home at some ungodly hour, two or three, and he had not seemed that drunk, he was certainly in a pleasant mood. Sweet smelling, too, as if he'd had a bath.

'Yes. I expect he'll miss the drinking more than me. If they had bars in prisons, people like Ronnie would never bother to come out. Crime problem solved.'

She had not meant it as a joke, but Maude seized the chance, her laughter tinkling down the phone.

'Seriously, though. I thought maybe we should meet up sometime, you know, socially? Have a drink, or chat, or something?'

'That would be nice.' The lack of conviction in Eileen's voice was absolute. 'Yes, maybe we should.'

At least Ronnie had rung her at her mother's, to tell her not to bother hurrying back – that was an act of courage, considering what her mother thought of him. He'd worked on the car but it was completely goosed, he'd said, so he'd gone out for a gargle, late. Pity he'd left the oily bits all across the kitchen table.

'Hallo, are you still there?' Eileen shook her head to clear it. Oh God, she was sick of this, she'd bloody had enough.

'Sorry. Look, I'd better go now. Thanks for ringing, but I'm all right, honestly. I'll ring you soon. Bye!'

She put the phone down. She stared around the living room, which was clean and well furnished and bright and nice. You bastard, Ronnie Keegan, you worthless bastard, why do I still love you?

The phone rang, and it was Mick. Eileen knew him only vaguely, and Fat Marie by sight and nickname. He'd been outside in cars and vans sometimes when Ronnie had done roofing jobs, a small, smiling man with black curls, said to be a demon drinker. Eileen had never seen him drunk.

He was drunk now, and incoherent. Basically, she could not understand a word he said. He mentioned Ronnie half a dozen times, asking if he'd managed it, and how long, and was he laughing when they took him down? He said something about a 'genius of the con' and riches beyond the dreams of something that wasn't avarice, but wasn't anything else she could decipher. She listened for about a minute, then said 'Goodbye' rather loudly, and banged the phone down. Then for a further while she willed it not to ring, then she went and put the kettle on. In the kitchen the radio was playing, they were talking about some murders down in the Midlands which were gruesome and unpleasant and which she found depressing, so she switched it off.

But she did love him, there was no point in denying it, although it had cost her most of her friends and, almost, her mother. Maybe if her mother didn't hate him so much, she might not be so defensive? But no, she did not think that that was it. She might have to leave him, though, she had done that before. The reunion had been such awful pain and pleasure.

Eileen drank her tea and stared out of the window at the cows. Perhaps she'd leave him this time.

NINETEEN

In journalistic terms, Superintendent Patten and his murder got a terrific show. The favoured headlines in the tabloids were variations on the bloodbath theme, with the sexual attacks and mutilation either in the intro paragraphs or just below. The heavier papers played it big – front page on all except the *Financial Times*, with the fact of Peter Wilmott's skill as an electronic innovator and entrepreneur masking the basic prurience of the approach. George Thwaite's and Pete Pond's early photos of the house and its surrounds – plus Ethel Bilton's 'face of horror' – appeared in almost all the papers, causing much rejoicing in the freelance pool and in the *Clarion*'s accounts department, while some of the less fussy gutter sheets went in for 'artists' drawings' to show what the 'brutally mistreated' bodies must have looked like – information that might have come from Mrs Bilton but in fact originated from one or more of the policemen who had been inside the house before the undertakers came.

While the others of the pack had been pleased enough to watch Janis take the flak at the press conference, they had quite naturally followed her line of theory and enquiry. The main area of speculation was Damon Hegarty, on eyeballing whom before the police scraped up the air fare several small fortunes had been spent. The hope had clearly been to track him down and spill some juicy ('tragic') details, then catch his appalled (or guilty!) reaction on camera for posterity. Unfortunately for the team that reached his hotel first, Damon had already heard the news, relayed to him via a director of the family firm. He had collapsed, been put on heavy sedatives by a German doctor, and was completely unreachable even by the cruellest methods of the desperate newshounds. The stories printed on the front pages reeked of legal circumspection, but the implications were all too clear. Janis, reading them, had a prickling at her scalp – excitement, envy, or disgust, who could tell? She couldn't.

The gipsies made a useful second band of possibility, with the added advantage that they were outside all known laws or human rules of libel, likelihood, or straightforward race abuse. Policemen beyond and above PC Gareth Page had been found who were prepared to give little anecdotes and saloon bar-type analyses about the nature of the beast, while the spectrum of opinion garnered in the village was narrow and steeped in vitriol. Superintendent Patten's stonewalling quotes were cited, but only as a foil to the unstated certainty that the travellers had done it, or if they hadn't it was only because someone else (no names, no pack-drill, Damon Hegarty) had got there first. In short, the jackals were spoiled for choice.

And Rowsley played its part, it must be said, with quiet gusto. The prettiest of the lonely wives appeared in little features, talking prettily about their fragile grip on confidence, and their terrors for their children. One or two of the absent husbands had hot-footed back from London to appear grim-faced and conscientious, agonising over whether they should move out the family, or give up working in the capital and take a major drop in salary, or what they should do. How they feared and suffered! How they lay awake and agonised in their pent-houses! Clive and his team gathered round the newsdesk to read out quotes and yell with laughter and no one found it odd at all. At police headquarters, two miles or so away, a similar suspicion of humans and their motives was corrosively at work. Both Superintendent Patten, in his way, and Janis Sanderson in hers, sometimes wondered what it did to them and other people, what it meant.

Sergeant Rosser, from the first, had little doubt as to the culprit, and spent much of his energy laying down the ground-bait for his boss. Indirectly or directly, it had to be Damon Hegarty's doing, and if they looked hard enough, they would find a motive that would stand up. To Lance, the sex angle was enough, although he knew Patten well enough not to give him that as undigested theory. In Lance's mind, anyone who travelled abroad a lot had opportunity, and anyone who had opportunity would take it, that was a matter of straightforward reason. When the news came through that Tessa Wilmott had been carrying a foetus of eight weeks or so, the theory faltered for an instant, then divided, seamlessly, like an amoeba. Either it was someone else's – jealousy leading to murder – or Damon was in love with someone else – sex-life complications forcing a bloody choice – or it was a question of inheritance. Lance Rosser made himself a note to investigate the wills, sure in advance that Damon would be better off materially with his wife dead, and probably even more so with his parents-in-law gone too. In both cases he was quite correct.

'Sure it's circumstantial,' he agreed with Patten as they mulled over what they had so far. 'But it smells good, sir, you've got to trust your instincts, haven't you? I'm running all the checks, I've contacted the family solicitors, but I think we've got to watch him, haven't we? We've got to watch him like a hawk.'

Patten, smoking a cigar, leaned back in his favourite office chair. The smoke rose thinly, to be stirred by the big, old-fashioned ceiling fan.

'The medicos say he's still virtually out of it. He's back in England but he's gone to Redlands Hospital. The private wing. I'm seeing him this afternoon, but I've been told not to expect too much to start with. He's not running, is he?'

Rosser made a strange noise of disgust.

'Tcheu. Convenient, isn't it? Sedatives, collapses, nursing homes. Would you do that, sir? Would I?'

Patten smoked. He got on well with Rosser as bagmen went, the acid in the sergeant's soul he found rather stimulating, but he was more wary of his 'instincts' than he usually let on. Rosser, he suspected, saw their relationship in TV series terms, probably casting himself as a more intelligent Sergeant Lewis, and his superior as a dimmer Morse. Patten did not look like Morse, being lighter in build and rather taller, and in his experience, drinking lots of country bitter merely made one fart. But he did allow his men to rattle on, and picked methodically at the best bits of their thoughts. He tapped his watch with his third finger, clear of the cigar.

'Come on, let's get to the incident room. First stuff should be in by now. I hear DC West got assaulted on a gipsy camp, daft bugger. Still, apparently they left the radio in his car. And the wheels on.'

Superintendent Patten had an open mind on Damon, although he did not think that Rosser was necessarily wrong. His first main assessment – theory, opinion, call it what you will – was that the thieves had had some inside knowledge, or preternatural luck. They had made a mess, but they had not turned the place inside out, which indicated that they'd known where things were – the safe, the gun cabinets – and they'd presumably known where the house was, what sort of resistance they might meet. By preliminary assessment, Joyce Withers and Audrey Wilmott had died before midnight, probably well before. To attack a house in the evening, before most people's bedtime, argued some sort of well-laid plan. Or deep stupidity, and luck. Unfortunately, such things could never be ruled out.

First reports had indicated, also, a marked lack of useful clues or pointers. There were alien fingerprints in plenty, but also glove marks. In the old days, gipsies would not have worn gloves, but nowadays burglars from whatever social stratum were afraid of the new sciences, and what they could do with infinitesimal bits. Also, the house was not meticulously cleaned or polished, so there were prints as good as new on furniture and door frames that probably had not been touched for months. No fingerprints, no footprints, no fibres, so far, that screamed out 'I am rare, I am significant'. So far, the fine-tooth combs of the forensic people had turned up very little. It was deeply depressing.

But if it had been Damon who had organised it, or set it up, or paid for it, had he not cared what they'd do to his wife? His pregnant wife? How much would a husband have to hate to allow such things to happen, or to even be a risk? A lot, thought Patten. But not an unimaginable lot. Did he know she was pregnant? he wondered. Eight weeks or so. He would have done, unless she'd kept it from him deliberately. He thought of Janis Sanderson, her statement and the supplementary sheets Rosser had got out of her. She'd talked of a family celebration. Maybe that was it. A celebration interrupted by the husband leaving unexpectedly for Germany so that a gang of hired thugs could come and kill his wife and in-laws. Was that hatred, or was it plainly unbelievable? It was a theory, one plank of a theory, that was all.

The trick, he told himself as he faced his team in the incident room and listened to Lance Rosser's lucid summing up of what they knew so far, was not to get bogged down, nor to make up one's mind too soon, to anything. As always, the investigation moved forwards by actions set by him and undertaken by his men (and woman, WDC Jenny Venner). This morning's actions so far, piled onto yesterday's and last night's, already constituted a fairly massive block of conjecture, possibilities, specifics. There were lines of enquiry emerging, people to be traced, physical items remembered by visitors to the house that might have gone astray. There was even a note about a certain Ronald Keegan and his wife or girlfriend Eileen, which would be followed up in due course. But still no clues, no solid, meaty lumps of physical reality they could get their teeth into.

The trick was not to get bogged down, but the possibilities of this case seemed endless. Premeditation, casual entry, a family who even welcomed gipsies, a hippy invasion of the area months before that could have led to New Age intelligence gathering of great sophistication – he knew full well that the latter-day long-hair brigade were not the dopes he'd hated as a teenager, nor so full of love and peace, however spurious. He wished there was a little spark, a chink of light, something to fire his enthusiasm for the hunt. Beginnings were always overwhelming, he told himself; but only half believed it.

This afternoon he would meet Damon Hegarty. It would be nice if it all fell into place. He caught himself at it, inventing simplicities. It was his turn to speak, Lance Rosser had his hand out, he was smiling.

'Right, gentlemen and Jenny,' said the sergeant. 'The Boss.'

Unlike a detective, or a national reporter, Janis did not have the luxury of being able to follow up one story, or indeed one 'action', until she was sure that she had got it right. On the *Clarion* there were pages to be filled about the Wilmott tragedy, and filled they had to be. She had stayed up half the night knocking her preliminary features into shape and sent them to the office through her modem. At seven she had woken Clive Smith from his sleep – she'd heard a woman grumbling beside him – and told him she was off to Rowsley to follow up her special. He had warned her not to take too long, and not to expect his thanks if the time was wasted. Ten minutes later she was off to speak to Margaret Grayson, who would be up and working. She milked her of every name that she could think of, every person who might know *anything* of Ronnie and his wife.

During the next three hours she toured the village and the outlying houses, crossing men from Patten's team as she had done the day before. She also crossed roving hacks, whom she avoided even more assiduously than she did the police, in case they somehow guessed what she was playing at. She did not speak to Monica at the pub, because that would quickly hit the grapevine, but she spoke to five other people who had known Ronnie. It occurred to her that Monica may already have mentioned his name and personality, but it had not surfaced so far in the morning papers, and she had the time advantage now. She could not hope to make the *Clarion*'s lunchtime editions, but she was determined she would get her story into the Final at the very least. That only left the radio and TV but she did not fear them much, they were too timid for such kite flying. In the gaps, she liaised with Mary Faircloth and Tony Hester, who were working the village, and checked in to Clive and the chief sub to confirm facts and alter emphases in the overnights. There would be features for the next morning on top of all this. She was working for her corn.

She hoped, of course she hoped, that one of the lovers supposed by Monica, one of the demure, corrupted housewives, would crack and spill the beans, would reveal something definitely suspicious. She hoped but did not believe it, and it did not happen. She gathered hints and some shocked looks, that indicated pretty clearly that her questions had hit home, but no confessions. Ronnie had been a lad, no question, and he'd treated Eileen badly, one could almost guarantee. But he hadn't gone round seducing wholesale, or in public places, and violence remained only hearsay. Janis returned to the office hopeful, but afraid. She wrote it up extremely rapidly, short, punchy, about three hundred words. She showed it to Clive and he sent her to the lawyer, Barry Newton. The arguments began immediately, and she knew that she would lose. It was a question, simply, of defamation, Newton explained. All she could say about Keegan and his wife was that they had worked for the Wilmotts for eight months or so, and that they had left. She could not say that he had got the sack, because she could not prove it. She could not say that his wife had left earlier, on her own, because that was hearsay. She could in no way nor under any circumstances hint that there might be a connection between them and the dreadful events of the weekend.

Janis was frustrated because she knew that he was right. She had gone in with a fixed idea, that was possibly the key to everything, but she could not stand it up. The young wives, if they had erred with Ronnie, would obviously not say, and would undoubtedly sue if they were smeared. The Good Neighbours, the older villagers, had closed ranks against all-comers, with most of them slamming their doors on anyone who might be press. The editor had already received twelve complaints about the *Clarion*'s coverage so far – coverage which had been straightforward, factual and sympathetic. People complained about and to the local press, because they knew it was a waste of time complaining to the nationals. The villagers were angry, sickened by the vileness that had torn their lives, and the plague of locusts that had descended in its aftermath.

'But we must put something in,' said Janis, her voice rasping with the reporter's archetypal outrage at the legal straitjacket. 'Whatever the law says, we've got a duty, surely? I honestly believe it's desperately important. Ronnie Keegan could be the man, I'm certain of it. If it turns out he is, and we've missed the opportunity, well . . . *oh*!'

They had moved into the editor's office, and the atmosphere was tense. Simon Trapper was not inclined to stick his neck out at the best of times. He began to shake his head, a negative.

Clive interrupted him.

'Simon, Janis is right you know, she's got to be. All right, the overall approach is wrong, if Barry says it's got to go, that's that. But we can get round it, if we can't get round it, what are we in business for? Most of all, what if some other bugger picks it up? They will, you know, they will.'

Janis nodded eagerly.

'As sure as God made little apples. People saw me nosing round the village, the rat-packers. They're staying in the pub, or drinking there. Monica Pagett's hardly a shrinking violet, either. Can you imagine the gutter rags holding back?'

127

Clive got in before Simon could.

'We're not the gutter rags though, are we? That's not the point. The point is Janis has scratched out something that is germane, suggestive, *useful*. It'll put a rocket underneath the police, for starters. People will side with us on that.'

The upshot was that Janis did a little dream piece. She rang up police HQ and asked for PC Crane and put to him one simple question: would former employees at the house be being traced as part of the investigation? Well yes, replied Bill Crane, they would he guessed, the recent ones in any case, if there were any. The normal thing would be to interview anybody who'd had connections with the place, in reason, did she have anything specific in her mind? No no, said Janis, just a thought – and got out of it a four-par box on the front page, enlivened with a fancy border: Brook Bank police in search for former staff. There were several posited, underneath her byline, including itinerants who might have cut the grass for cash, or done some weeding, but only one was named. 'Among those being sought is Ronald Keegan, who was employed as a live-in handyman and driver until about three months ago. He is thought to live in the North of England, possibly in the Manchester area.'

It was quick, and it was easy, and it owed almost nothing to the hours she had put in on the hoof. But at least it made the County Extra edition, plus the City and the City Final. Janis thought it was pathetic, a crying waste, but it had made its point.

By that evening, it had blown up in her face.

TWENTY

The power of a good news story is not always directly related to its size, although journalists who have flogged their guts out to produce a whimper are not the first to see that. Indeed, to those who did not know the code, the fancy border piece about the former Brook Bank staff was fairly uninteresting, if not meaningless. To those who did, however, it was a sort of dynamite. Sergeant Rosser, who was an avid follower of his own cases in the press, saw the County Extra at ten to four, when his eyes were drawn in to the box. It was the only change to the Wilmott spread on that edition.

He was alone in Arthur Patten's office, and had thrown his feet onto the Boss's desk to have a read and cigarette. He read the piece through once, then swung his feet back to the floor. That fucking Sanderson again! She was setting the agenda, she was holding them to ridicule, she was telling them in public what they should do. Rage flowed through him, rage and hatred, which he did not try to check. The Boss would go insane.

Rosser was a good detective, if not a very pleasant man. When he had calmed a little, he decided on some checks. The incident room confirmed what he had thought, that Ronald Keegan had been noted and would be followed up when his priority was reached. PC Crane, in the information office, admitted – although he hedged it carefully to cover any mistake he may have made – that Sanderson had been on. No, he said (with some relief) she had not mentioned Keegan. She had asked a general question about who would be investigated. I told her, said Bill Crane, that everybody would be, everybody who might help us, villagers, tradesmen, passers-by, employees, everyone, of course I did, it's standard, isn't it? Bill Crane, in Rosser's view, was an idle slob who wanted his fat arsehole kicking, because he clearly had not even seen the story, which surely was his job. He did not waste his breath on asking him.

129

Rosser put the phone down and lit another cigarette. The Boss was off at Redlands interviewing the prime suspect, which would give him time to find things out. He was a bit sore at Patten for not taking him, but he had this tendency not to let his best men get too close. No, that was not it, Rosser amended, he liked to give his best men independence, to do things off their own initiative. Rosser was tempted, momentarily, to ring the *Clarion* and make an appointment with Janis Sanderson somewhere, somewhere dark and isolated deep in the country-side, and give her a good fucking for her pains, then a beating with a great big stick to teach her to be more circumspect. But glancing through the piece again, he decided rather to follow her line up, to do it properly. Lance Rosser knew who'd done the murders, he absolutely knew, so he had no fears that he might come unstuck. What would be nice, though, would be to have the problem laid out neat and tidy for the Boss to look at on his return. What would be even nicer, would be to present him with its solution.

He rang the incident room and asked them for some files.

Down at Rowsley, in the Hare and Hounds, the rat-pack pored over the County Extra when it arrived by van, growing quite excited. They knew the code, and there was general agreement that Janis Sanderson had played a blinder. Most of the press men fancied her, but none of them resented her stand-offishness, that was her way and good luck to her. Some of them had found out from Monica who she'd been asking after, and followed it up a little way, but without too much excite-ment. So a guy had worked at Brook Bank and he'd been a little too flash by Rowsley standards. So who the fuck would not be, they laughed to themselves! And the cops certainly weren't taking any notice of him, were they?

Monica and Ted, who normally kept the old English opening hours, had responded to the press influx with foresight and enthusiasm. They'd started opening at eight a.m. for coffees and cooked breakfasts, served booze from eleven till eleven (and afterwards if the plods were still around, and friendly), and had opened up their own phone line to supplement the pay phone in the bar. Now, seeing the hubbub caused by the latest *Clarion*, Monica walked up to the drinkers and dropped in something she had genuinely forgotten when she'd talked to Janis.

'He came in with a gun once,' she said. 'A special one of some sort, he said old Wilmott couldn't have a licence because it was illegal. He said he was going to shoot some husbands, he was joking, it fired lots of bullets, or something.'

So far it had been a slow day for the hacks. Finding a fresh angle even on a crime so hideous is always difficult – indeed, the TV crews had packed up and gone that morning. Since lunchtime most of them had sat about drinking and pooling anecdotes, unfired by the idea of talking to yet more yokels or trying to pull strangely resistant bored young wives. Reporters, like policemen, can never fully understand why nobody will trust them. Monica's throwaway had them jumping up and down like yo-yos.

It was the pump-action shotgun, that had gone missing on the murder night, everyone knew that. There was a general surge towards the car park, that fizzled out before it had properly begun. The problem was, where to start? No point in going to the house, because the policemen guarding that were completely tight-lipped after early bollockings. Round the village, asking questions? To hear what? The sound of 'No comment!' shouted through a letter box? They settled down again, ordering more drinks. Monica's story first, in detail, then on the blower to Bill Crane. If Keegan was a gun freak, they would ask (and in their parlance, now, he had to be!) why had he not been mentioned, or arrested, even? Police incompetence, maybe? It was dazzling. Why stop at Crane, either, he was just the front, and not much good, to boot. Why not kick it up the line, go for the top, the jugular? Legal problems? Libel, defamation? Let the legal swine sort that out, that's what they were paid for, wasn't it?

Watches were checked for deadlines, and a swift euphoria set in. A toast was drunk to Janis, mocking but appreciative, because she, poor bitch, had been knocked down to four paragraphs by her dumb rag. But she'd given them their angle, she'd resurrected them for tomorrow's papers. And it was only five o'clock.

Absent friends!

*   *   *

It was nearer six when Superintendent Patten got back to HQ, by which time Lance Rosser was like a random powerhouse. He was watching through Patten's office window when his car pulled into the car park, and he noted that the Boss looked as shattered as he, Rosser, felt energised. The weather had broken down to a dull mugginess, hot, humid and exhausting. Patten stood beside the Ford Sierra wiping sweat from off his neck for quite a while before he squared his shoulders and looked up. Rosser felt triumphant, he allowed himself a great, wide smile. He'd send old Arthur's temperature rocketing!

Before he climbed to his office, Patten went to get himself a glass of water. He stood in the cloakroom sipping it, trying to recapture his lost energy. The interview with Hegarty had been long, difficult and inconclusive, interrupted three times by the doctor 'requesting' him to bring it to an end. Hegarty, to give him credit, had each time struggled on.

Was it an act, though? Patten had been put on his mettle by the picture of his patient drawn by the doctor, in advance. In his opinion, he said, Hegarty was by no means up to questioning, to the extent that damage might be done. Then, at the end of long, opulent corridors, Patten had been presented with a fit-looking man, in a quiet, airy room, fully clothed and completely rational. Why was he there, then? Why had he taken sedatives? He was a grown-up, for God's sake, and one, moreover, who lived by commerce. From the mysterious, British, roots of class, Arthur Patten felt mistrust grow, while all the time the doctor, by the self-same process, cast him ever deeper in the role of crass intruder, violater. Christ, thought Patten savagely, did they not realise, these people, that some men killed their wives? Forty-eight hours ago this man flew off to Germany, and his wife was buggered and abused and murdered. Either he was behind it, in which case sympathy was grotesquely out of place, or he must help urgently to hunt the culprits down. A little mental torture was hardly to be avoided, either way.

But when he spoke to Hegarty, he felt sympathy. The man was tall and thin, and there was something almost painful about the way he formed his words. In his first three sentences he apologised seven times, his whole body, in fact, embodied shame and self-disgust. He apologised for not being able to

132

grasp it as reality, for not being able to come to terms with having left the house, for not being able to approach the thing with proper rationality. It had been a bombshell, he said, and it was still exploding in him, multiple warheads were still going off. He had known his wife was pregnant, had the superintendent? Patten agreed he had and Damon took off his glasses to cover eyes that filled with tears.

Jesus, thought Patten. Grief. How do we ever live with it? How do we survive? He had to grip his psyche very firmly, go through his training and his experience, remind himself that men can lie, and cheat, and weep with cold-bloodedness that defies imagination. He had interviewed a woman once who had had her daughter's torso in a cardboard box beneath the table where she sat and tore her hair.

At the end of it, he was not sure. But as he said to Rosser, home at last in his own office, his third small cigar of the day alight: 'If he's our man, he's a damn fine actor. If we put him up in court in that state there wouldn't be a dry eye in the house.'

Which was not to say, his inner voice repeated, that Damon was not guilty. Away from him, his mind backtracked efficiently. Rosser, watching, timed his moment to toss across the *Clarion*, on which he'd ringed the fancy box in blue. Patten read in silence, turned up his pale eyes, shook his head.

'Where do they get them from?' he said, wearily. 'Where do they bloody find them?'

Rosser was only slightly disappointed. The fireworks would come later, when digestion was complete.

'The other rats have followed up, sir. Bill Crane was forced to do some graft for once, he's been going spare. Someone in the village told them Keegan went round threatening with a shotgun. The pump-action, that shouldn't have been there in the first place.'

'Wilmott had a firearms certificate,' said Patten, his voice still mild. 'Christ knows who recommended it, but they did. Was Keegan really toting it? Sounds like a load of balls to me.'

'Who knows, sir? It's what the journos think, which unfortunately for us is all that matters. They've been howling for more quotes and information.'

Patten pulled his tie off and sat down at his desk. He crushed out the cigar with more than half of it unsmoked. Thirst was the problem, not nicotine.

'She's a cheeky bitch and she's a bloody nuisance,' he said. 'This is just the sort of crap we do not need. It's just the sort of crap someone'll jump on to tell the world we're not doing our job. How much did Crane tell them?'

'Not much. I came down on him like a ton of wet cement. They were after addresses, how to contact the guy, all that crap. They got nowhere. In fact, Bill might have misled them just a tiny bit, I think. I think he mentioned Middlesbrough as a last known stamping ground. Or Newcastle, was it?'

Patten grunted.

'It says Manchester here. Is that correct?'

'It chimes in with what the lads have found so far. Big place, though. If the hacks even bother to try they'll never find him. My feeling is, they're not going to bother.'

That riled Patten. It smacked of idleness.

'Why? It's a bloody natural for those scum. Something to chuck at us, some half-arsed rumour that we can't deny because no bugger ever told us it. You don't seem to understand what we're playing with here, Rosser. Get on to Manchester police and see if they can find him for us, pronto. Because if we don't get him, those bastards will, and in my experience they won't take very long. Now get your finger out.'

Rosser noted with satisfaction the muscles in the Boss's cheeks. They were bunched beneath the skin, below his cheekbones. The Boss was getting mad.

Calmly, he said: 'I did do a little bit of digging actually, while you were out, sir. I might have salvaged a bit of something from the wreckage, in fact, I'm pretty sure I have. They won't find Keegan because they won't go looking for him. It won't come in the question.'

The eyes played over him but Patten, knowing he'd been had somehow, said nothing. As Rosser told him what it was he'd done and found, he demolished the remains of his cigar into the ashtray. When Rosser had finished, he let the silence hang for several seconds.

'Lance,' he said, at last, 'that is good. That is very good

indeed. Strangeways Prison, Manchester. That is very good indeed.'

'I thought you'd like it, sir.'

'So what we'll do now,' said Patten, 'is bring her in. Agreed?'

The sergeant's eyebrows rose perceptibly.

'What, arrest her, sir?'

Patten let out a bark of laughter.

'Nice idea, but no, just call her in.' He checked the wall clock. 'There'll be someone in her office, even if she isn't. Hold on, what's their office pub called? Still the Granby?'

Still the finger on the pulse, thought Rosser. He nodded an affirmative.

'Call all the others, too. You'll get them through the Hare and Hounds at Rowsley, they're probably in there at this time. Special press conference for seven thirty, on the dot. Get the woman here for half past six. Just her and me. Here. In this room.'

'It will be a pleasure, sir.'

TWENTY-ONE

Janis had been feeling pretty good when the call came, and – sitting in the Renault outside Police HQ – she was confident and in control, with just a tiny flutter in her stomach. Working on the free-phone principle, she had spent twenty minutes talking to the *Sunday Times*, negotiating some background pieces for the following weekend as well as agreeing provisionally on a full-scale profile of the people and events at Brook Bank as long as an early arrest did not come along and spoil everything. All told, it would make her well over one thousand pounds.

She locked the car and stood by it for a moment, smoothing down her skirt. Today she looked cool and efficient, not hot and rumpled, in a mid-calf cream skirt of calico and a white silk blouse. She still wore sandals, but her feet were clean, the nails varnished black to match those of her fingers. Keen, cool, efficient, she told herself. So what the hell had Patten called her in for?

At reception she was expected, and escorted straight to the office by a civilian auxiliary. She knocked, Patten answered, she walked in. He was alone, behind his desk, the window at his back. The roofs outside were somehow blurry, against the hazy, leaden sky. Patten was in his shirtsleeves, a ballpoint in his hand, his desk-top strewn with paperwork. He did not stand.

Janis knew about posers, what journalist with open eyes does not? She knew power games, and body language, and all the other nonsenses prattled by the gullible. She knew that Superintendent Arthur Patten was hoping to unnerve her, and she was relaxed. A sudden wave of happiness surprised her. She could handle anything.

'Did you know,' said Arthur Patten, 'that they forced a brush up Tessa Wilmott's vagina? And strangled her? And buggered her? And beat her head until the bones collapsed? Did you know that?'

She could handle that. The muscles in her stomach had contracted with a snap. He had not invited her to sit. It had become suddenly important, that.

'Did you know that the handle of this brush broke through her vaginal wall and displaced her uterus, Miss Sanderson? Did you know they had put it up her anus, bristles first? Did you know that Mrs Wilmott was carrying a child?'

Janis felt sick, her forehead covered in a sheen of sudden sweat. This is a policeman talking, not a monster. This is a policeman talking, the words repeated in her head, a policeman, a policeman, policemen could not do this sort of thing. She thought she was perhaps about to fall.

Her voice was faint.

'Why are you doing this to me? You have no right to tell me things like this.'

'Sit down,' invited Patten, amiably. 'Sit down and listen to some more. I'd hate to have you collapsing on my carpet.'

There was an easy chair and two uprights, tube-steel and plastic. She clutched the back of one of them and sat, back straight, head level, fighting nausea.

'I don't want to hear,' she said. 'I won't listen any more. You have no reason.'

'I'm telling you to make you stop and think,' said Patten, his voice still amiable. 'No listen – to make you stop and think what you are doing. I'm hunting for some animals who tortured a young woman mentally and sexually then killed her and her unborn child. Who made her father watch her, or arranged his corpse as if it was masturbating at the sight. I just want you to know that you're not helping me, that's all. You're impeding me. You're standing in my way.'

He was watching her expectantly, the small smile had never left his mouth. The enormity of what he'd done had left her bereft of speech, she wanted to refute him but she could not summon up the rage. She could only stare at him.

'You see,' he continued, 'you ignored all those pleas I made at the conference, didn't you? For restraint, and consultation, and sensitivity. You went bald-headed at the issue as if it was your concern and your concern alone. You published speculation that I begged you not to publish, you put in details that I begged no one to print. And now this.' He swept aside some papers and whipped the *Clarion* into view, her front page story marked up in blue crayon. 'The *Clarion* again. Our local paper. Blackening someone's character. Undermining us. Our *local* paper. You.'

'No!' said Janis. 'Not blackening! The lawyer cleared it! It's fact, the minimum of bare fact!'

Patten had a strong face, broad but with no fat on it. It registered contempt very efficiently.

'The lawyer cleared it. Oh, fine.'

The fury was beginning, hotly. She was leaning forward in her chair.

'Anyway,' she said, 'if we're talking character assassination, why me? If we're talking speculation, why pick on me and not the nationals? What about poor Damon Hegarty, the way he got mauled across the front pages, we didn't go in for that, we printed what you told us, less than what you told us! Come to think of it, whose idea was all that in the first place? Sergeant Rosser thinks the husband's implicated, doesn't he? D'you think he's been slow in pushing that line down our throats? Are you denying Rosser thinks the husband's implicated?'

Patten opened a packet of cigars. He took one halfway out, then put it back and closed the lid.

'Whatever Sergeant Rosser thinks or does not think, I know damn well he won't have talked to you about it,' he said, crisply. 'To you or any other journalist. Do you want to make a formal allegation?'

The dislike between them was almost palpable, like something solid in the air. Patten, finally, withdrew a cigar and tapped his nail with it.

'I wouldn't bother,' Janis said. 'Sergeant Rosser is a shit, the sort of caricature policeman who gives you a bad name. Now you're talking filth to me, browbeating me with things I have no desire and no need to hear, because you want to intimidate me, presumably. Why? Because I'm showing you all up? Because I'm showing you there might be other lines to follow? You accuse me of speculation over Ronnie Keegan, of undermining you, but it's the whole talk of the village, the man's a villain, a bully, he beat his wife up until she ran away! Everybody who knew him thinks he should be investigated, everyone except the police! Lance Rosser's not just a shit, that wouldn't be unusual for a policeman, would it? What gets up my nose is that he's an inefficient shit!'

She was elated with seized opportunities, points scored, although well aware that she had bent some facts quite blatantly. In that, she was unrepentant, she felt in command again, it was enough.

'He went into the pub once with a shotgun,' Patten said. 'Did you know that? He was going to kill someone.'

Janis jumped, she could not help herself. The superintendent's voice was calm and quiet, his colour normal. Janis swallowed.

'OK,' she admitted, finally. 'No, I didn't.'

'Do you honestly believe that we weren't on to him from the very first? Do you seriously think we're such total nincompoops? If you think that, Miss Sanderson, you're the caricature, not us.'

'Well then,' she said. She was struggling, both of them knew it, she was clutching straws. 'If you knew all that, how can I be blamed? When all I did was . . . tell the truth?'

Beneath contempt. Patten sparked a lighter, drew in deeply, exhaled. She watched him through the smoke.

'Keegan lives a long way away,' he said. 'Lancashire, not far from Manchester. That's unusual for a murder in this country, the distance. It also means it takes time to check things out. What you did, as you well know, was risk alerting him, and anybody else involved. We kept our mouths shut but you opened yours, you set out gaily to destroy a most delicate operation, you did something that could quite easily have led these monsters to escape. That is your achievement, Miss Sanderson, that is what your sense of responsibility adds up to.' He clicked the fingers of his left hand, the cigar held in his right. 'That.'

She had nothing sensible to say. She noticed he had damp patches underneath his arms, staining the white shirt. Possibly she had similar ones herself. Should she apologise over Ronnie Keegan? She had nothing sensible to say.

'Have you found him yet? At least the *Clarion* doesn't circulate as far as Manchester.'

'We have,' he said. 'You'd have thought with all that gunwaving, and wife-beating and so on, we'd have arrested him by now, wouldn't you? You'd have thought we'd be opening the champagne. Well it's circumstantial evidence, Miss Sanderson. It's a very useful illustration of its inherent dangers. It's a lesson you would be well advised to learn. He had an alibi.'

'Oh no,' said Janis. It was meant to be to herself, but it was audible, and she had the familiar sensation of language breaking down on her again. Louder, she added: 'Is it a very good one?'

'One of the best. He was in prison at the time. You can go now, Miss Sanderson. The press conference is in ten minutes, I imagine you'll bother to attend, although you know what I will say. I won't mention you by name, by the way, it will just be an announcement, I'm not a vindictive sort of man.'

Janis stood.

'Thank you,' she said. 'I'm sorry.'

Lance Rosser had 'screwed the Sanderson' with a series of quick calls, the last and luckiest to the CID at Oldham, where he guessed that Ronnie Keegan might be a well-known name. He identified himself by rank and force, without giving any hint at all as to what his enquiry was about. It was in fact a total piece of cake.

'Ronnie Keegan?' said the detective constable. 'That rings a bell. Hold on, sergeant.'

The man was new there, transferred a week before from outside the town, and he was lying. He covered the receiver and called over his shoulder, 'Someone asking for a Ronnie Keegan. Some Midlands bloke.'

'He can fucking have him,' someone shouted back. 'He's fucking welcome.'

'No he bloody can't,' said another. 'He's in Strangeways.'

'Oh aye,' said the new man. 'What for?'

'Receiving. Three months. They should chuck away the key.'

The new man, laughing, passed on the information, asking if there was more the sergeant needed. Lance Rosser, brimming with bonhomie, thanked him prettily and put down the phone.

That shows the bitch, he thought. Oh doesn't it!

TWENTY-TWO

Ronnie Keegan was in Strangeways, and he was enjoying it. He always did, to some extent, he saw it as a sort of refuge, a retreat. He liked the total idleness, the hours he was forced to spend lying on his back, doing nothing. It gave him time to plan, to regroup, to work out the next steps forward in his strategy. He also met old friends and had a laugh. As an old hand he had no trouble with the hardmen, either officers or inmates. And he usually got a good cell, with a reasonable companion.

Ronnie liked to think in systems, and he saw Strangeways as a very special one, that was valuable especially to him. Like other businessmen he had to go on courses, to refresh himself, recharge his batteries, but this time was a holiday, pure and simple. Strangeways was providing him with total cover for a crime the coppers would be very heavy on, and all he had to give it in return was to lie there, and eat the food, and give his body a well-earned rest from alcohol and sex. Not that he was without sex, naturally. He had some very vivid memories this time, to rerun. He watched them often in his private viewing room, with Mrs Hand and her five daughters as companions.

Even from the very start, listening to the details of the manhunt on the radio and seeing things on the television, Ronnie had had no significant qualms. He had gone over the events in the minutest detail, from lead-up, to execution, to aftermath, and each time he had found no flaw. He imagined that the cops would one day try and trace his whereabouts, but he doubted if they'd give it top priority. He'd left Brook Bank quite amicably – although he'd got the sack there hadn't been a row or anything – and Damon Hegarty had never known about the thing with Tessa, because, she'd said, there was no reason for her to trouble him with stuff like that. Ronnie chuckled. Haughty cow, at least she'd changed her mind on that, he'd

141

given her no option. But then again, she wasn't talking any more . . .

The point is, he told himself, even if they do follow up the lead, what do they find? Ronnie went to jail and stayed there, didn't he? Even if they worked the dates out (which he doubted, knowing the police) what would they think then? That a bloke who parted almost friends screamed down the night before a court case, killed four of them, and popped back home in time to put a suit on and get sent down at ten o'clock? Bollocks. And what would Eileen say?

Here Ronnie paused. What would Eileen say? He'd been in all day mending his car (and even if she'd rung him, which he'd forgot to ask, he wouldn't have heard it, would he, from inside the garage?), and in the evening he'd rung her (yes from home, of course from home) then gone out for a late drink with a friend who'd just come back from Liverpool, half pissed. He'd come home late, OK, but he'd come home clean, not too drunk, just so-so. Would they balk at that, would they give Eileen the third degree? Nah, never in the world. He couldn't see that, no way.

Then there was the backstop, good old Mick. He'd been in Liverpool half the evening, and he had witnesses to prove it. If the coppers did a follow-up and came to Mick they'd meet the old brick wall. Yes, he'd had a drink with Ronnie, at lunchtime in the Con Club, then they'd met up for a gargle at his place, later. When? Oh, midnight, well before, maybe. Who says so? Mrs Mick, Fat Marie, the Blob. Ronnie chuckled when he thought of that strange pair, Mick so tiny, like a walking mop, and Fat Marie a walking tub of lard. Beating her up, Mick said, was like kneading dough, and fucking her was something else. It was like a day by the sea, you could sit on the edge and dip your feet in it. Fat Marie, if it should ever come to it, would tell them exactly what Mick told the bitch to say, she'd had practice. But it would never come to it, would it? Why in God's name would they ever look for Mickie?

Which left only Harold Boon. Harold Boon the wildman, Harold Boon the weird. Where was Doggo, he wondered, where had that bastard gone?

Nowhere that should worry him. Never in the slightest. Not at all.

*   *   *

142

Janis Sanderson went to the funeral, wearing black. Her car was red, the day was hot again, and she guessed the whole thing would be a dreadful circus. In some ways, she felt, black was appropriate, a sort of mourning for herself, although later she was ashamed of that, appalled at her self-pity. But as she drove down the leafy country lanes towards Rowsley, it felt appropriate.

The night before, Janis had tried to tell Bren that he had to leave. She'd made the mistake of making love with him beforehand, and there had been a scene. Later he had left – although he'd returned before dawn – and she had fallen into a fitful doze. She had awoken suddenly, gripped by fear. It was the first night of a fear that soon became recurrent.

The sex was awful. Bren was a formal man in many ways, who signalled his intentions in advance. Janis, returning from the office miserable, had experienced a sinking feeling when she had seen the table laid, with a candle at each end and dishes ready to receive the halves of avocado. She had snapped at him immediately, hating the hurt that appeared on his long face. She had gone off for a shower, to be alone, but he had followed her – an annoying trick of his – and talked to her through the frosted plastic. He was worried, he said, because something seemed to have gone out of their relationship, did she agree? No, said Janis, not something – everything. Was that a joke, asked Bren, the Cardiff whine engulfing his would-be jokey tone. She had had to bite her lip.

Later, what natural tact he might have had overwhelmed by his desire to be loved, he had manoeuvred her onto the sofa and made clear his next intention. Janis had drunk Rioja with a quiet desperation, so she did not resist too hard. Not from desire, but from pity, maybe, regret that it was over. She had known for days, now, weeks possibly, that the latest great experiment had failed, and she was sorry for herself as well as him. They'd made good sex once, and there would still be comfort in it, mainly for poor Bren. She'd relaxed her thighs deliberately, allowing his hand to stroke slowly upwards until it met her pants, then wriggling abruptly to slip them off herself. Bren had covered her vagina and her hair with his big hand, entering her gently with his little finger. She looked at the mirror on the mantelpiece of the little cottage room, which, angled downwards, showed her leaning back into the cushions with spread legs, head on one side, gazing upwards and askance, with Bren's long back bent towards her, his head hanging on her shoulder, one hand inside her skirt. It was an interesting picture but it did not turn her on. Nothing about it turned her on.

Bren worked, patient and doglike, his left arm crooked around her neck, his hair touching her face. At first he whispered small endearments, but then he stopped. His fingers were long and skilful, she had once found them rather nifty, and he knew well which parts of her responded best. Tonight nothing responded, although she was wet enough for basic lubrication. Janis became strangely detached, as if her parts were made of glossy plasticine and his hands were moulding them, a not unpleasant sensation, but far from sexual. He did not know at first, but then he did, and a nervous sweat broke out on his brow. Janis, playing her part, had unbuckled and unzipped him and produced his penis, long and throbbing, with its narrow, pointed head (another thing she'd once found very nifty). Soon the head had softened, though, the purple glaze had dulled, and she discovered idly that she could bend it in the middle without it hardening at all. Suddenly, she became quite frightened, although irrationally, at what she was doing, what it meant to him. She swung herself sideways, seizing his working hand, catching sight of herself unintentionally in the mirror as she lay along the full length of the sofa, one leg up, the other crooked at the knee, right foot on the floor, her dark hair peeping from below her hem.

'Come in me quick!' she panted. 'Quickly! Bren!'

'But you're not ready. You're not interested.'

But his prick went like an arrow, with its pointed arrowhead, and he launched himself on and in her and came immediately, while Janis clutched the loose back of his shirt and groaned and murmured. She did not like to simulate orgasm, but you could not be a prig about these things, could you? The zip tab of his trousers dug into her thigh but she let it rest until he'd finished properly. Poor Bren.

'You didn't come, did you?'

'Of course I did. Only a little one, but very nice.'

He didn't believe her. He looked miserable. Later, drunk in bed, when she told him that she thought they needed to live apart to try it out, to let her get her head in order, to reclaim some lost space, he threw the so-called orgasm back at her, called her a liar and an insulting bitch. Janis, still sore at Patten for what he'd said to her, and how she'd lost the courage to fight back, saw red mist that turned to black, and beat him about the face and neck with incoherent fury, tempered, perhaps, by the knowledge he was not the man to strike her back, however much she goaded him. Bren was crying soon, which revolted her beyond belief and made her stride around the tiny bedroom, naked, bellowing with rage. So much so that someone banged on the party wall, something that had never happened in the years she'd lived there.

Silence had fallen, broken by Bren's erratic sniffling. He'd looked at her, also naked, kneeling bent-backed on the bed, steeped in tears and shame. She had stalked out to the bathroom, hard of heart, and Bren had gone, without another word.

I am a bitch, Janis had thought, lying on the broad bed alone. I am a hard and bloody bitch, what can I do though? I don't love him, though I've tried. I bet he's coming back in any case, the sod. He wouldn't have the guts to really go.

An hour later, maybe, she had awoken to a noise. She had been dreaming uncomfortably, and she was instantly alert, and she was terrified, a sensation that she had not had for years, a breathless certainty that there was someone in the house below, not Bren, someone who meant great harm to her. She lay rigid, open-mouthed, fists clenched, waiting for the footsteps to begin, the thing that dwelt below to climb up to her bed and murder her.

This is stupid, she told herself, this is insane. Call out, there's no one there. She was not breathing, her lungs were bursting with retained air, and she let it out slowly, making a faint moaning noise. She was sure that on the floor below her someone waited, and was going to come.

It was very odd, the rationality with which she contemplated this unknown. To be lying there, all alone, so certain that she was going to come to harm. She was choked with fear, but angry, with herself. Shut up Janis, she thought. Do something, you fool. Shout out. And as she lay there, thinking, it slowly drained away.

A coal brush, a dustpan brush, a grate brush, thrust up the vagina of Tessa Wilmott, was that it? Why did she care so little, now? Why were Tessa and her parents and the old companion such dim memories, figures in a balladic tragedy, so unreal? She'd known them, she'd laughed with Tessa, liked her. Why had she forgotten what she'd been like, how had she slipped away?

She had not gone to sleep again, and when Bren had come back she had cuddled him like a mother. In the morning she had dressed in black, and gone black-eyed to the funeral. To work, of course, that was the first reason, but also because she hoped to feel again, to suffer some sensation for the murdered people, to experience their lives and deaths as more than just components in a story.

But the funeral had been an awful farce.

146

TWENTY-THREE

The church at Rowsley is very small, and architecturally undistinguished. The idea that trendy churchmen are a late twentieth century phenomenon is sadly fallacious, and the blank green fields and faceless landscape of this part of the rural Midlands seem to have driven a succession of incumbents into the gentle madness of unbridled innovation. The church orchestra was disbanded years before Hardy's men of Mellstock got their quittance, and in 1903 the Reverend Abel Naylor employed the God-given destruction of the belfry in a lightning storm as a catalyst to pull the whole church down and replace it with a boxy modern structure, to which the Wilmott family, incidentally, heavily subscribed. The graveyard was cleaned up and regimented long before it became the fashion, and in the 1950s the old headstones were taken down and used to pave the field adjacent – that ten years later, under tarmac, became the 'most essential' car park. Today, for the Wilmotts' funeral, it came admirably into its own, although the TV scanners and mobile lighting rigs left hardly any room for actual cars. Most of the real mourners, though, were people from the village, the Good Neighbours, and they had walked. The rubberneckers from the towns and cities filled the roadsides with their vehicles, then spilled onto the verges where PC Page gave them parking tickets, while the press men naturally used the Hare and Hounds. In all there were four hundred people, probably, some sixty of whom may have known the Wilmotts and Miss Withers by sight.

Inside the church, before the hearses arrived, there was confusion. The vicar, a pleasant but unworldly man called Mason, had been put out at first by the appearance of the TV crews, then pleased and flattered by the attention, and the money, they had offered him to ease the inconvenience. They had argued persuasively for their need to have the space, playing on his naive belief (despite the evidence that their own presence

147

offered) that not *so* many people were likely to attend. When the sightseers started to arrive, mixed uneasily with Good Neighbours in various stages of mounting outrage, he began to panic, trying to sort out the 'sheep from the goats' at the church doorway. Several reporters simply refused to turn away, while a member of the public with a video camera actually swore at him in the porch. Consequently, when the cortège arrived the pathway to the church was a seething mass of people, whom the police then had to clear as discreetly as they could. The coffin bearers processed through the main door to find many people standing and gesticulating in the aisle, with the organist blasting *fortissimo* to try to hide the babble. Janis, to her relief, did not get inside, and retired to a corner of the razor-mown and featureless cemetery to observe and ponder on the tragic ineptitude of the English. A little later she spoke to one of the undertaker's men, whom she spotted smoking behind a bush. He was in his sixties, grey haired and dignified, and visibly upset. Nobody had expected anything like it, he said, and nobody had warned them, it was like a beargarden. She watched the faces of the real mourners as they left the church behind the coffins, Damon Hegarty, close family, ancient friends. They were white with shock and hurt, in a setting of the crazed and curious. Not a beargarden but a black charade, she thought.

But Janis, curiously, did not write it up like that, nor, she noticed, did the others. Last Farewell to House of Horror Victims was one of the headlines, a fair example of the general line. She contemplated putting in a paragraph or two, trying out resentment, regret, anger on the word processor before she scrapped the whole idea. The TV coverage that she saw also managed to be restrained, filming the crowds to make them look like decent onlookers, filled with sorrow and concern alone. Thus did the media project their own image as the nation's caring voice, a conspiracy too cosy and amorphous to be seriously complained about. She tried for distance in her piece, for cool appraisal of the vile crime and its human aftermath, and was revolted by the mawkishness she achieved. Some achievement, thought Janis. Some honesty. Some writer.

At the graveside, second only to family and close friends, came the police contingent, which also startled and disturbed her. Cyril Hetherington, acting chief constable and bull-necked scourge of anything he chose to disapprove of, was flanked by three more top rankers of the county force, and dignitaries of the police committee, there to represent the local government. Patten himself, somehow unreal in splendid full-dress uniform, with Chief Inspector Charlie Altwick, fat and rural in the heat. Why were they there? As a mark of respect because the Wilmotts had been so rich? As a token of intent, to show the killers would be hunted down, that justice would be done? As an interim apology, for having failed so signally, so far? All grist to her writer's mill, all discarded. Although she told herself that she would use it, sometime, somehow – soon.

In the Granby after work that night, she talked it out with Clive, after the others had gone off about their businesses. He had liked her coverage, but mocked her sense that she had missed the broader view.

'Pretentious crap,' he told her, 'no one gets it all in. People don't want complexity, anyway, they want a bit of tugging at the heart strings. A bit of terror, a bit of pity, then the old catharsis. All wrapped up in newspaper. Greek takeaway!'

He snorted at his joke, and Janis smiled. A new angle on the police presence had just occurred to her.

'Maybe they wanted to keep an eye on Damon,' she suggested. 'All those cops. My God, what if they'd arrested him!'

'Don't laugh,' said Clive. 'They do go to these things to observe, you know. There will have been undercover ones, as well, watching the crowds. Did you see his face?'

'Whose?'

'Hegarty's. That's what they'll have been studying, isn't it? He's still their number one, he's got to be.'

Janis sipped gin, moodily.

'He looked like a man whose pregnant wife was being tipped in a hole in the ground. Which is what he is. The whole thing's stalled, Clive, and I suspect they know it is. I'm stalled. I'm fed up with it. I'm going back to features, you've had me, mate.'

I haven't, said his eyes. Not yet. He did not voice the thought.

'Good piece in the *Sunday Times*. Are there more upcoming?'

'What can I do while nothing's happening? They want me, but they want me to hang fire. Get me another gin, you bugger. I'm sick of it.'

While he was away she contemplated her fingernails. It was true, all the old dissatisfaction had come back. Twenty-six years old, stuck out in the sticks, cooling in the embers of a dead relationship, watching a brilliant, appalling murder story decaying at her feet. It was dribbling away, her life, this wasn't what she wanted, not any of it.

Clive stood before her, large and bald and bland. Could you be bland, with those predatory eyes, that smile, that brain? He set down the two glasses and her mixer.

'What about your man?' he said. 'Have you given up on that?'

You cheeky sod, she thought. How did he know?

'What, Bren?'

'Not Bren, you fool, your grand obsession. The bloody gardener.'

She laughed.

'Ronnie Keegan. What do you mean, given up on him? He's out of it, as well you know. The best alibi I've ever heard, and I've still got a sore bum from all the kicking Patten gave me. What do you mean?'

'Well nothing, if you're sure. You fucking "writers" are all the same. Noses in the air, crying in your beer, and too idle to do the groundwork. Do you believe them?'

'Who?'

'The cops, you fucking idiot! Who else?'

'But they wouldn't lie, would they?'

'Not necessarily. Not as such. No, of course they wouldn't.'

He drank some bitter, his eyes above the rim alight with mild amusement. Janis shook her head, not knowing how to take it. He put his glass down.

'Go on,' she said.

'There's not a lot to say. Check it, that's all. If you still think Ronnie did it, or had a hand in it somehow, check it. They make mistakes, don't they? They're not infallible. If Ronnie was an Irishman, for fuck's sake, he'd be inside by now.'

'He is inside.'

'Yes, very funny. He's also got an Irish name, come to that, but you know damn well what I mean. Just because Arthur Patten's got penetrating eyes doesn't mean he's got a brain to match. They make more mistakes than they make right deductions, don't they? And when they've made one, they stick to it, through thick and fucking thin. So check it out. Get back to basics. You were a good reporter once, remember?'

'Not that again. Christ; Patten. What a bastard he turned out to be.'

'Aren't all the interesting ones? How is Bren, by the way?'

The smile had cracked his face. He filled the hole with bitter, lots of it. You're a bastard, too, thought Janis.

'OK,' she said, 'so how do you suggest I go about it, then? Have you got any names in . . . oh, of course you do.'

'Precisely. Not just Manchester, either. It's narrowed down to Oldham somewhere, isn't it, in which event I'd say Bill Stift's your man. If he doesn't know the case he'll find it out for you. Your round, little one. Feeling better now?'

'You drink too fast. You patronise, also.'

'But do you feel better, though? *La chasse!* The hunting instinct!'

She did, if truth be told. Why tell the truth, though.

'Nothing'll come of it,' she said. 'I've heard of long shots, but this is crazy.'

'I'll try one of my own,' Clive replied. 'You're about to tell me you're so grateful, you'll sleep with me tonight. Or is nothing going to come of this one, either?'

'I tried to kick him out last night,' she said. 'Shit, I shouldn't have said that. He didn't go, in any case. I didn't want him to, not really. I'm going to the bar.'

When she got home, at nearly midnight, she discovered Bren had gone. Not for good, there was a note explaining that he'd thought things over and agreed they ought to take a breathing space. He had taken some owed time, and was going down to Cardiff, if she would want to ring him, but he would not ring her, he thought she should relax. He would be back next week and he loved her, and hoped she still loved him.

Oh hell, Janis thought, Clive could have come back after all. Then she was ashamed, then she thought of Bren, eating fucking Welshcakes with his mam and sharing a good whine. God, she told herself, you really are an arsehole, Janis Sanderson, you are poisonous.

And very drunk. She fell into bed and turned off the bedside

151

light after arranging Clive's piece of paper by the phone. Some contact numbers, for the morning. Bill Stift.

Tonight she had no fear of fear at all.

TWENTY-FOUR

At 10.17 next morning, bolstered by a righteous sense of triumph, Janis rang police headquarters and asked for Superintendent Arthur Patten. Told that he was in a meeting, she sought for a connection with Sergeant Rosser, who, the switchboard said, was out. Janis, declining to talk to anybody else or give her name, hung up. Five minutes later she tried again, again demanding the detective superintendent. This time she gave her name. Rather to her surprise, his voice came on the line in seconds.

'Miss Sanderson? How can I help you?'

'Mr Patten? I've got some information that you ought to know. It's terribly important.'

She had expected him to be aggressive, a mode that she was well prepared to match. He sounded mild, concerned.

'Do you now? I liked your piece about the funeral last night. Considering the time you had to write it in, I thought it was remarkable.'

Wrong-footing her again. He must be trained in it. Janis growled silently in her throat.

'Thank you. But listen, really, this is urgent. I've got to see you.'

'What, now? It's pretty well impossible, I'm afraid. Could I pass you on to someone else?'

'No,' said Janis. Then she thought of Rosser. She'd like to grind the smile off that face. 'Well, Sergeant Rosser, I suppose.'

'He's out. I could see you in an hour, at a pinch. I have every confidence that you won't waste my time. What's it about?'

'I—' She bit her lip. 'It's not something I want to talk about on the phone. I'm in an office.'

'I understand. You'll come here, then? I'll tell them on the counter. Eleven thirty?'

'Yes.'

She walked back to the newsdesk to confer with Clive. They

had already sketched out how a story might go, and which edition they could hope to get it in. He gave her a mobile phone to cut delay.

'I must say I admire your guts,' he said. 'If only half the things you told me that he said to you are true! I can send Tony, if you'd rather.'

'Get knotted, Clive. I'm not a vindictive person, but I want to see this bastard squirm. He said quite clearly at the conference Keegan was in jail. Not once, but three times, the police had ruled him out.'

'I don't see how they're going to wriggle out of it, admittedly, but remember, keep it very, very simple. Make sure your recorder's running and put it to him straight, don't try to get your own back for the mauling he dished out to you.'

'I'll save that for the story. God, how I wish we had a proper lawyer, not just Barry. And an editor with guts, come to that.'

'The story will be short and sweet and factual, we've been through that half a dozen times. It's the effect it has that matters. For God's sake, you're meant to be professional, not a prima donna. Just put the facts to him, smile sweetly, and listen to him writhe. Then out, fast, and on that mobile phone. We'll fudge it for the first and run it on the second, so you can't afford to waste a second. And don't forget to ask him what they're going to do about it, formally. He won't answer, but it puts him on the spot. We can print his refusal as an act of record.'

Janis nodded, full of life and joy.

'D'you know,' she said, 'I think we've got him on the run. I think we're going to nail him, Clive.'

'Aye,' said Clive. 'And there's another possibility.'

'You're a gloomy sod,' she said. 'You're a boring northern pessimist.'

'Be careful of him, though, chuck. He's not a pushover, you know.'

Superintendent Patten was not a pushover and, it would appear, he liked to time his body blows. When Janis was shown in he was as nice as pie, as if they'd never had a row, not even clashed. He stood up from behind his desk, came round the side of it, and shook her hand. The windows were open, and he wore dark trousers and a crisp white shirt. Janis, somehow, felt under enormous pressure.

'Hallo,' he said, 'you're looking very summery. How much do they pay you in that job?'

She was still touching his hand. She withdrew self-consciously.

'Pay me? Do you really want to know?'

He laughed.

'I wouldn't be so rude. I just wondered if I could entice you to join the force. You never seem to stop investigating. I wonder what you've turned up now.'

She sat, although as usual Patten had not asked her to. She crossed her legs carefully, aware that her front-buttoned skirt could show more thigh than she intended.

'I've learned one lesson. I bring it to you first. Although I must admit I've got high hopes of it.'

Patten smiled charmingly and perched his bottom on his desk. His face was open, friendly, frank, amused. He delivered the first blow.

'Is it about an alibi? For Ronnie Keegan? Is it about the day he went to jail?'

Although she was not aware of it, Janis gaped like a fish. Then she swallowed, so noisily that it embarrassed her.

'Oh,' she said.

The smile was still in place on Patten's broad, rugged face, but it had acquired an element of steel.

'You must think we're crackers, Miss Sanderson,' he said. 'How do you see us, thumb up bum and mind in neutral all the time? Can you honestly have such a low opinion?'

'But you said he was in prison. You said he had an alibi. You told the press conference that he'd been ruled out.'

'He was ruled out. He is ruled out. Get it into your head, Miss Sanderson, that Ronald Keegan always will be ruled out, because he didn't do it. I don't know if it was actually said that he was physically inside at the time the murders were committed, it seems to me it's hardly relevant. Your theory, quite frankly, is ridiculous.'

'It was said. Are you saying that you authorised . . . a lie?'

The pressure build-up inside her was terrific. She could not believe she'd had the courage, or the stupidity. One did not

155

accuse senior police officers of lying. The superintendent merely looked at her, silent for some time.

'I wonder if you have a transcript to back that up,' he said. 'Quite frankly, I can't remember exactly what was said because it is a point of no importance. The man went to prison on that day, he was in court at ten o'clock or so, that was the point I made to you and that was reiterated in the conference. There are other reasons that he is not a suspect, other reasons beyond lack of motive, lack of presence within God knows how many miles. Other reasons that will be emerging very soon.'

Patten pulled out a file from underneath the papers on his desk. He did not have to look for it, the move was preplanned. He raised it, then let it drop.

'Apart from anything else, you do not know your man. How could you, all you've heard is village gossip. We follow up, Miss Sanderson, we take our investigating seriously. Keegan, who you say was involved in the vilest murder I have ever known, is not a violent man.'

Janis was fascinated by the file. A manila folder, new, with nothing written on it. She wet her lips.

'There was some violence,' she said. 'I found evidence that he was violent.'

'That is not evidence,' he said, 'that's gossip. I had the files faxed down, that is evidence. Keegan's record is as long as my arm. In all of it, there's not a hint of violence. He even gave himself up once, during a burglary, rather than resist.' He poked the manila folder with a finger. 'Psychiatrist's report, done two years ago for Leeds Crown Court. No, you may not see it, but I'll tell you what it says. Ronnie Keegan is not a violent man. Ronnie Keegan is not a murderer. Ronnie Keegan is not a suspect.'

There was a cheap point to be made, about the credence normally given to psychiatrists by the police, but she saw no point in making it. She knew that Patten had her beaten, and she knew he had another weapon up his sleeve, another reason for his supreme confidence. She saw no point in asking what that was, either, because that would play his game for him. Her best bet, now, was to warn Clive that there was something in the air, and that she was no longer the reporter most likely to be told about it. To put it mildly . . .

Patten had not finished with her, quite, although he had stood up and was reaching for his jacket.

'I have a meeting now,' he said, 'you'll have to go. I'd advise you to think very carefully about what you put into the paper about this, it could cost you very dear. Is that a tape recorder?'

Janis looked down, startled, to where the leather bag beside her on the carpet had gaped slightly. The tape recorder, running silently, was not visible.

'No, it's a telephone. Want to check?'

'God, the cash you people have to throw about. Is that the *Clarion*'s, or for the *Sunday Times*? A better class of prurience, very scholarly your piece last week, I thought. I suppose the rates are good?'

She stood up, hating him, but she did not answer. He held a hand out, showing her the door, careful not to come too close to her.

'Thank you for coming, by the way, and thank you for your information. Tell me, why have you got it in for Ronnie Keegan? If you don't mind me saying so, it smacks a little of obsession.'

She swept by him, still tight-lipped, and went down to the exit, and out into the street. In the Renault, she checked the time, and got a grip, and rang Clive to tell him the good news. She sounded devastated.

Clive was philosophical.

'You said it was a long shot didn't you, last night? It would have been a corker if it had come off, but never mind, I told you he's as hard as nails, that one. Maybe he's right, though, hasn't that occurred to you at all?'

It had, not once but often, and she still rejected it. Perhaps Patten was right, about her state of mind.

'Maybe,' she said. 'We'll have to wait and see. There's something in the air, Clive, and I think it's breaking soon.'

'Suits me,' said Clive. 'It can't be soon enough. We've got a hole to fill now, haven't we? On the front page . . .'

They got their front-page story, on the last editions, however much Patten and his men might have wished they had the power to exclude selected newspapers from the plums. From his viewpoint it was a plum, the sort of story that the flagging

157

Wilmott case was crying out for, with the added beauty that it undermined Janis's case with neat perfection. To Janis it was another coffin nail, an awful downer. Five days later, at the end of a brassbound dilly of a week, she found herself in bed with Clive, the night before Bren Hughes was due back home.

It was one, she told herself, for the record books.

TWENTY-FIVE

The story broke at one o'clock although the police, it soon emerged, had been working at it since the early hours. Bill Crane had lied throughout the morning's routine checks, but no one minded that, it was expected. The important thing was that here, at last, was action. Janis, to ease her troubled soul, had gone to have her hair done, then interviewed a woman for the features editor. If something broke, she had told Clive, she'd catch it later, she was sick of police triumphalism for the moment. Consequently, Tony Hester and Pete Pond had raced off to have the fun. Twenty miles into western Lincolnshire to see Rosser and his lads mop up the aftermath, then on a little tour. They saw some fighting and some broken heads, which made the trip worthwhile, but could only speculate on what had gone before.

What had happened, according to the police, was a fight the night before between some travellers and the hardmen from a funfair, which had simmered overnight and culminated in a dawn raid on the gipsy camp, the smashing of two caravans, three knifings – and the use of guns. The local police had gone in when some farmers had raised the alert, been set on by both factions, and had retired to regroup. At least five men had been seen fleeing in vans, and the traditional wall of silence had gone up. But firearms there had been in the gipsy camp, and Sergeant Rosser had known by eight a.m. From one o'clock onwards, when they let the news get out, the angle had been clear: who could seriously doubt that there was a connection with Brook Bank?

Janis could, but even Clive derided that as sour grapes. She walked back with her feature into a newsroom full of the scurry and excitement of a major blow-up, to be almost knocked over by the chief sub who was carrying a mock-up of the new front page. Clive grabbed her, thrust raw copy into her hands, told her in six sentences what was going on, and asked her for six hundred words of background and fresh quotes. Janis was bemused, then sceptical, and responded like a pro. Five minutes later she was at her terminal, clicking out the stuff. Deep down, she thought it stank.

Pete Pond and Tony, when they returned, had great tales to tell. Pete had lost one camera and had the start of a black eye, while Tony's Mini Cooper had lost a wing mirror and both wipers. They had followed convoys of police cars into several gipsy camps, and watched with fascinated glee the clashing of two sub-cultures. The camera, Pete said, had gone to a gipsy kid of only twelve or so, while the black eye had come from a policeman he had tried to photograph breaking the china in a caravan. DC West, who had been assaulted at a different camp the week before – a camp thirty miles away or more – had been noted as more brutal, in his act of vengeance, than his fellow law enforcers.

But the stories and the headlines were terrific. 'Gunshots at gipsy camp as Brook Bank police move in' was the *Clarion's* line, which went out with variations on radio and TV stations, local and national. By early evening the rat-pack was back, besieging campsites, fighting off furious young travellers, and failing to understand they could not be bought with cheques, however fat. In the cold light of morning, it transpired that six men had been arrested, with charges pending, but nobody would say what those charges might turn out to be. Superintendent Patten stonewalled at a midday press conference, refusing to confirm that firearms had been recovered, while stressing that they had been used. Were they the weapons stolen in the Brook Bank killings? That was only speculation. But were they shotguns? It was believed at least one shotgun had been discharged. Were the police confident that there was a link with the House of Horror? The police did not make such links, said Patten, but he could say that all manpower available was investigating this incident. He warned against two things: one, the glib assumption that gipsies and other travelling folk were any less law-abiding than other members of the public, and two (which almost contradicted it), any idea that collecting concrete evidence would be easy from this source. His team, however, were determined and experienced. Morale, he added, was riding very high.

Janis's – no secret from herself or anyone who knew her – was not. After two days of alarums and excursions on the story which apparently convinced everyone but her, she decided to try one more crazy long shot, one more gambit that she could have almost guaranteed would not come off. She got through to the CID and asked for DS Rosser. About that drink, she said, are you still interested? How about tonight? Lance Rosser, famous even in the police force for the thickness of his skin, did not bat an eyelid. Had he not been so dangerous, Janis thought, he could almost have been funny.

They met at a big, anonymous city pub called the Bull, which Janis deemed appropriate, although she kept the joke from him. He turned up in a sharkskin suit too sharp for his wages, driving a black Lancia. She dismissed the simple thought – graft, corruption – in favour of a more complicated one, that he probably spent every penny on such trappings and owed thousands to the bank. If he has a wife, she pondered, I bet she worries about the mortgage first, then where he puts his dick.

But it gave them a good opener, a lead-in to nice and friendly conversation. They talked about their motor cars, and what they could do, and relative brake horsepowers, which Janis enjoyed as much as he did, and found herself inferring from his long, hard hands that he was a good, fast driver. An attractive drinker, too, taking Islay malt with Malvern water as a chaser, with unflashy appreciation. God, what a mess I am, thought Janis also, an unexploded bomb, and covered a smile with her tumbler of gin and tonic. He noticed.

'Something I said?'

'Something I thought. One more of these and I'll be over the limit. I can't imagine it'll stop a policeman. Lucky.'

'One of the perks. Makes up for all the shit we have to eat. You're safe enough with me, though. When I think of doing you, it's not the breath-machine I've got in mind.'

He laughed, his ugly, raptor's face alight with confidence, challenging her to break the friendly mood.

'You're very rude,' she said. A token protest, only. 'I suppose that's a perk as well, that no one smacks your face?'

Rosser lit a cigarette, remembering apparently that she was not a smoker so would not want one.

'Talking of rudeness, the Boss tells me you think that I'm a shit. A caricature. The sort of cop that gives cops a bad name. That's rude, isn't it?'

'But you still came. Yes, that was rude. I . . . he knows how to get me mad, your Boss. Furious. But you still came for a drink.'

'And you don't apologise. You're a cheeky cow, Janis, I quite like that. We're adults, aren't we? Two grown-up people? So what are we doing here, in reality? What is it that you want from me? Don't say my body, I couldn't stand the strain. Not yet, anyway.'

She fished the slice of lemon from her drink and sucked it, giving him the benefit of the look. Then she put it back.

'OK. Damon Hegarty, let's say. The raid on those gipsy caravans, the guns. Ronnie Keegan. You said if I had a drink with you, you'd put me in the fast lane. Tell me what's happening with the case.'

They both sipped and swallowed. The pub was filling up, it was smoky, noisy, Janis felt unreal.

'Leave aside Keegan for the minute, Keegan's out of it, we checked him out. As to the raid — terrific. Six bodies in the cooler, and we'll find the ones that ran. You know all this. They're up in court tomorrow.'

'You had to get an extension from the magistrates for further questioning. They've been charged just with assault. Where are the guns? Where's the murder angle?'

'Come off it, love, you know the way it goes. The gunmen did a runner, that's hard luck, the flatfoots let them get away, the turnip-eaters. We keep this lot until we've got the evidence for the proper charges. You know the game.'

'But were there guns fired? In reality? A gun?'

Rosser was a tall man, with a large, hard frame. He was more frightening than Patten, he had much more potential violence. She knew that she was frightened of him.

'You're being stupid now,' he said. 'You're abusing privileges. Do you want another drink?'

It was another large one, which she needed more than ever. Or maybe not. Maybe she should take a cure. She noticed, as she poured in the tonic, that her fingers trembled slightly.

'Damon Hegarty? Has Patten crossed him off the list, yet? No one honestly believes it was him any more, do they, seriously?'

'Wait till you see the will. Amazing. Do you want to know a secret? Genuine?'

His face was deadpan, but she did not believe him.

'Go on.'

He laughed, knowing he'd lost her.

'You're too smart for your own good,' he said. 'I was going to tell you he had a tart in Germany. It's right about the will, though, I'd've killed my wife for half of it, his wife, anybody's. That's a story for you. Exclusive, it won't be made public yet awhile. If you mention it, it's strictly not from me.'

She was not interested in the will. Nor half-arsed information dribbled out like that. She let it show.

'So Damon's in the frame still. And Keegan?'

'Oh get out of here! D'you think the Boss tells you stuff just to waste his breath? We checked him out, the boys up there all know him like a wayward fucking child, he's a twat, a prat, a blowhard. Even the trick cyclists say he is, and you know how purblind they are. Leave it off.'

'When did Patten know you'd got the date wrong? For Keegan going into Strangeways?'

'We didn't get the date wrong, it was a slight misunderstanding, that's all. Soon enough to hit you with it like a brick! The Boss was chuffed to death with that. It's a hard old world, love, isn't it? The Boss got the impression, incidentally, that you'd like to get a shufti at that report, is that right?'

There was something in his eyes as he leaned over that was specific and well known.

'Is that why you're here?' she said. 'Is that why you agreed to come? That's rather blatant, Lance.'

'Blatant? I didn't say a word!'

He knew, again, that he had lost her. No matter, he didn't fancy her that much. It had been a case of getting even, mainly.

'We're grown-up people, as I said before. But I'm not all bad, Janis. There's nothing in it that you'd like, there's nothing in it that would fit your nutty theory, I'll tell you that for free. You've got the wrong monkey, why can't you just accept that, you're barking in the dark, you're stupid.'

He said it with a casual contempt that she found crushing. He'd assumed there might be point in 'bribing' her with information, and when she'd turned him down he had not cared a jot. She was of no great interest, neither her body nor her intellect. Janis, somehow mortified, certainly confused, failed to recognise the knowing calculation. Rosser, satisfied, got up.

'I can't waste any more time, anyway,' he said. 'Drive carefully. There are some bastards in the police, you know!'

Janis, on reflection, left the Renault in the car park till the morning. She took a taxi home.

The night in bed with Clive was not so bad as waking in the morning. She had been so drunk that when she did so, she was honestly surprised to find somebody there beside her. She had slept long enough with Bren to know instantaneously that the body was not his, but for a second or two she had no idea exactly who it was. Then she did. Oh God, she thought. Oh Christ.

In the old days, in a peculiar sort of way, it had been part of the fun of sleeping around. To wake up and guess whose the shape was, underneath the duvet, to try and summon up a name before they woke. Some sort of fun that must have been, she told herself sourly. She'd grown out of all that shit, so what had happened now? Clive, beside her, looked like a pale blue hummock, just a bald spot and some wisps of blondish hair peeping from the covers. She remembered his pale fat body, and his drooping drunken cock. They'd laughed about it, she remembered that much, but had they . . . yes, they had. They'd got it in at last. Well, if you want a proper go, she thought, if you're feeling frisky now it's morning, you're at the wrong address. She was angry with him, and angry at herself. She looked at the alarm clock. Ten past eight. It only needed Bren to have driven up from Cardiff early to avoid the traffic, the sort of boring thing he did. That would just about put the lid on it.

She eased herself out of bed without waking Clive, put on a dressing gown, and breakfasted on instant coffee and four aspirin. When he got up she went back upstairs to the lavatory, then had a shower. Dressed, she returned for toast. He was sitting in his shirt, his naked bottom spread across a kitchen chair.

'Look,' said Janis, 'use a little tact, can't you? Get your trousers on and piss off home. If I seduced you last night I apologise. It doesn't represent a permanent commitment. Please don't mention it to anybody else.'

'That's a bit unfair. I'm insulted.'

'Tough. I don't know you well enough, quite frankly, to take the risk.'

'I meant the seducing. I thought that I seduced *you*. By force of charm and personality. And my performing willy.'

'Did it perform?' But Janis laughed. He was all right, this fat git, he wouldn't tell anyone and he wouldn't expect a thing. Maybe that was why she'd gone to bed with him.

'You were marvellous,' she said. 'That's just so you don't demand another go, to improve your standing. Rating, I mean. No jokes, Clive, my head hurts too much.'

She'd driven home the night before, breath-tests or not. So had Clive, his car was parked slap-bang outside the door. Ten minutes later he drove off to the office, and Janis sat at the kitchen table wondering what to do.

Bren was coming back today, and she didn't think she could stand it. She was so tired, so sick of everything, not just him. So sick of men who tried to get to bed with her, sick of men who managed it, sick of herself, sick of the drinking and the long shots that did not come off. She reached for the telephone to dial train enquiries. She'd told Clive she would be late, he was going to pass the message on to features.

Well they'd have to wait. They'd have to wait a damned long time. She wasn't going in.

TWENTY-SIX

Although she was one of her oldest friends, Janis, like everybody else, needed an appointment to see Professor Hilary Swale. After checking on the London train times she rang her in her office, then tried the TV Centre at Wood Lane. Several people fielded her, but Janis persevered, wielding her name like a club until someone passed it on. The warmth and richness of Professor Swale's voice startled her, as it always did on the telephone. It seemed too fulsome to be sincere. But with her, Janis was completely confident, there was not the slightest element of insincerity. The call lasted half a minute, and a lunch date was arranged. Janis left a note for Bren and shut the house up with relief. Time to move.

Professor Swale, in a quiet way, was big time. Janis met her in the foyer, watching from a distance as the sycophants fluttered round. She was a large woman, aged fifty-eight, and she dressed to emphasise her robustness, her power. Her producer and some lesser minions clustered round proprietorially, evidently put out that she was lunching with a mere mortal outside the magic circle, who – when they saw Janis – looked like a lightweight into the bargain. For it was an oddity of their relationship that Professor Swale inevitably made Janis feel small, causing a sudden draining of her independent confidence, that showed. It was only the eyes, so clear, so calm, so glad to see her, that remade her public shell. Hilary Swale took Janis's hand, held it, then touched her almost tenderly. The sycophants, somehow, were diminished.

'Don't you find me awful, Janis?' she asked. 'I've become a media personality, an unreal thing, a projecting screen for other people's egos. Why have you come all this way to see me? I'm no longer worth the bother.'

It was not true, and everybody knew it. They drew back disconsolately as the two women walked out into the sun, as if without her they were at some kind of loss. A taxi moved forward as she put up her hand, and soon they were ensconced in a quiet French restaurant, cool and elegant. To Janis, it was a satisfaction in itself, a subtle balm. The woman opposite had not even asked her why.

But why should she? Hilary Swale was a professor of psychiatry who combined pre-eminence in her field with a 'common touch' that inspired love outside the confines of her profession and possibly hatred within it. She had always known the art of empathy (some colleagues might say 'had the knack'), and appeared to many of her patients to understand their suffering as if she could see inside their skulls. She had come into Janis's life in the aftermath of the killings in the Suffolk street, and talked to her for so many hours and so many times, that the teenage girl had come to believe in some secret way that the pain was truly shared, as was the burden. Janis knew, and so did she, that when the time was right she would tell everything.

The thing they revelled in, both women, was that Hilary was a guru of the real world, not merely the ethereal. It was she, in fact, who had guided Janis into journalism, recognising a certain 'vicious literalism' (as she described it) that might have been implanted on the 'village afternoon', a residue of savagery vicariously experienced through eyes she could not close, and she who had told Janis quite bluntly that everything in life should be used for furtherance if it had no other purpose than for self-corrosion. As her own career had branched off into the 'media tangent,' she had discussed it excitedly with Janis, comparing notes on the most unlikely (for a psychiatry professor) angles. Professor Swale – ugly, unmarried, formidable – had an amazing zest for life.

She also had a sharp intelligence and a mighty talent to communicate, that had made her into a household name and rather rich. At one time she had had two books in the bestseller lists, and her programme had rapidly turned an off-the-wall idea into something popular and influential. On it, politicians and other self-important people jostled to reveal dark secrets about themselves, while imagining they were increasing their lovability and gaining respect. Thus was she lauded by the mighty, while maintaining a bedrock of good sense and integrity visible to the rest. She always held that Janis, even as an adolescent, had been too sensible to really need her help, nor did most other people who went to bare their souls to therapists and analysts of every kind. In her experience, she suggested, it was the healers who were crazy, for taking themselves too seriously. Janis, like many other people she had saved, indulged this point of view rather than argue.

When Janis did explain, she listened carefully, filling her mouth methodically with large quantities of pork fillet and good red wine. Janis told her about the murders, and knowing Tessa Wilmott slightly, and her strong desire to go and see the dead. She told what Ethel Bilton had said about the mutilations, and the way Superintendent Patten had tried to horrify her with the details into some kind of submission. She tried to delineate the deadness that had come over her afterwards, the callous sense that the whole thing mattered only as a story, the way she'd hoped the funeral would shake her into pain. Quite honestly, she said, she treated it in some ways as an antidote, and it had let her down. She was flat, jaded, boring, rootless, lost.

'An antidote. That's interesting, an antidote to what? How's your sex life, how's that man, what was his name, Gatling was it?'

'Gatling? Do you mean Bren?'

'Some sort of gun, I knew it,' said Hilary, with an obscure smirk. 'Well of course he was no use to you, I've never met a bigger wimp. Have you started sleeping round again, or thinking of it?'

'Thinking of it, yes. Well no, thinking of not sleeping with anyone at all, actually. Although come to that, I did sleep with the news editor last night.'

'That could be construed as getting on! No? Job satisfaction? Infidelity, pure and simple?'

'It was a mistake, that's the simple part. But there's no harm done, I think. He's nice, is Clive. Not my type at all really. Large and fat and cynical.'

'Sounds like one for me. Sounds as if you need a cynic, though, all this nonsense about not caring, not feeling for the murderees. What do you expect a journalist to do, cry herself to sleep? Good word that, by the way. Murderee. Do you like it? Martin Amis.'

The waiter was hovering. Hilary drained her glass and ordered another bottle, 'encore une bouteille' with an execrable accent. Janis's hangover was fading nicely.

'What I'm really worried about,' she said, 'Is this feeling that I'm out of joint, out of kilter, out of step. I've got this feeling that I know who did the murder, and everybody thinks I'm bonkers or obsessed. The police just hate me, I suppose. It's understandable.'

She explained it all to Hilary, about the evidence and the alibis, the gipsies, Damon Hegarty and Ronnie Keegan. Even as she said it, it sounded sensible to her, although she could recognise that her theory was by far the weakest, which she added as a rider at the end. She also told about the psychiatrist's report, which 'good old Sergeant Rosser' had offered her in part exchange for sex.

'Good lord, what an exciting life you journalists do have,' laughed Hilary. 'I thought that boredom was your problem, not galloping excess. I see what you mean about the police, though, there do seem to be some problems of esteem.'

'There are. Rosser thinks I ought to screw him because he'd like me to and I'm only a reporter after all, and his boss appears to reckon I've got some sort of morbid interest which boils down to money. I did a piece in the *Sunday Times*, an analytic piece, and it made his flesh creep, you could tell. My straightforward weepie on the funeral – which left no cliché unturned, I must confess it – well, surprise surprise, he loved it.'

'And have you got a morbid interest?' She sat back in her chair, while Janis thought.

'Yes. Or maybe no. Quite honestly, Hilary, I don't know, but I am afraid. I mean, seen from one point of view it would be stupid if I *weren't* interested, wouldn't it? It's a bloody murder, an archetypal act, that I just happen to be involved in, from the bottom up. It's crying out for understanding, it's demanding to be analysed, dissected, understood. Exploited also, that's the problem, isn't it? I can tell you that I want to be a writer, not a journalist, without fearing that you'll mock me for it, but that's a terribly rare luxury, believe me. I think that I can learn something by digging in the murk, delving into the awful things that happened, and I think I can put them down in print and help other people understand, as well. Which must be worth it, surely? Which must be valid?'

The waiter was back, pouring wine. Hilary let him finish before replying.

'It's what I do,' she said. 'Except that my judgements are instant and upfront. And facile, as befits the medium and most of my subjects. No one accuses me of exploitation.'

'But you don't anatomise murderers and their victims. Even I can smell the scent of opportunism, it's that what worries me.'

'Exposing the slug-like brains of politicians is every bit as gruesome, don't ever doubt it. And probably more lucrative. That's opportunism. As to supposed validity, you'll be accused of all sorts, there are always people waiting to shout off about voyeurism, and profiting from others' misery and so on. There are always people with axes to grind, too, your superintendent springs to mind, however pure he thinks his motives are. But you've been there, you had Suffolk, you've probably got something that still needs working out.'

'An unnatural interest,' said Janis, flatly. 'But doesn't that make Arthur Patten right?'

Professor Swale had finished her pork fillet, but not her eating. She looked purposefully into the wings for service.

'Let's forget the word unnatural in your case, it's completely meaningless. So what are we left with? A policeman's sneer. I'd have to have him on the couch to find out what his motive was for that, and that's not likely, is it? Shall we try for the report?'

'I'm sorry?' Janis did not understand.

'It's not something on the menu, dear. Do you want me to get the report? Of course you do. An even better plan – why don't you go and speak to him? Your Ronnie Whatsisname. What do you fancy, cheese or pudding? Or both, I'm having both.'

Janis thought about it while they ordered. Contacts, and pulling strings, and possibilities. Hilary told her she was serious, and how she would go about it. She was sure that it would not be difficult.

'Stay in town tonight,' she said, 'and I'll bet we have the psychiatrist's report before I take you out to dinner. Listen –

if you are right, and he did it, there really would be possibilities if you'd already struck up some rapport, wouldn't there? Writing, naturally, not mere journalism! I'm mocking now, just like the others, but it is a point, you know what I think about wasted opportunities, it could make a book, and cash as well. There's a man I know, a total shit but extremely useful, who'd publish you, I'm sure. He's an MP. Stay in town.'

Janis had had no plans for going back, so that was easy. Suddenly she saw new vistas opening before her, she had a wild notion that she'd ring the *Sunday Times*, give up her *Clarion* job, sign a megadollar contract for the crime blockbuster of the century. She realised she was getting drunk again, and wanted to get drunker.

'Hilary, you're wonderful,' she said.

TWENTY-SEVEN

Mick Renwick was a nice bloke, and a good father to the little kids. When he was all right, he treated all of them like a father, even the ones that weren't his own. He wiped their noses or their arses without fear or favour, or promise of reward, and at the pub he'd buy them crisps and lemonade until it came out of their pores. Never mind the noise, the way they messed the carpet up, the broken telly knobs, that was the way with children wasn't it, he didn't care. He didn't even hit them very hard.

But when he wasn't right, he could get vicious with them, too. He'd broken Billy's arm on one occasion, just picking him up off the floor by it and shaking him about. He'd knocked out half of Donna's teeth, and blacked the baby's eye for pissing on his leg. Once, in a better mood, he'd pissed on the baby, lying in its cot, he'd almost drowned it through the slats. But that was different, that was for a laugh (not that Fat Marie had felt like testing him by laughing). When he was serious, he could get quite cruel.

Marie Conway – Mrs Renwick, as the social workers called her – had learned a wide variety of techniques in her twenty-eight years of life, the main one being not to worry. When she'd been younger, and not so fat, she had worried about men, from the way her father beat her mother up, to the way her first ever boyfriend bit her on the neck until he drew blood to claim her for his own. But three years later, with one baby and another on the way, she had realised that this was what life was all about. If she was pretty she got thumped for being looked at by other men, and when she was pregnant she got thumped for being ugly, a gross cow. By the time she was twenty-one – one toddler, one baby – she was more than eleven stone and called Fat Marie by everyone except her mother, who didn't speak to her at all. And Fat Marie, if nothing else, did not appear to worry.

For one period, from age twenty-three until just before she met Mick Renwick, Fat Marie was almost happy. She had the two kids, Donna and Billy, and she had not seen their father for a good two years. She'd had a few more blokes on a basis that she much preferred – anywhere but in her house – and she'd had another baby, which had been stillborn, then little Seanie. Then for three months she'd had another live-in bloke, and he'd been worse than any of them, he used to beat her black and blue, using her big tits for a punchbag until he'd got framed up by a bad policeman and gone to jail for five, during which, miraculously, he had died. I'm staying on my own, she told her mother – who was speaking to her again – I'm not ever going to have another feller. Chance would be a fine thing, quipped Mum, you're like a fucking bus, our kid, enormous. Then along came little Mickie, who loved a laugh and big fat women, and that was that. The good times, admittedly, were good. But there weren't so many of them, when you reckoned up.

But why was Mick so bad these days, she wondered, sitting in the bath matching the bruises to the blows. Why had he taken to chasing her out into the street, involving the neighbours and terrorising the kids? Why did he go out every night and come back completely arseholed, practically beside himself with rage? How long could it go on before he killed someone?

Fat Marie, moving in the water, had a funny thought that it was his conscience pricking him, because he had already, hadn't he? But Mickie didn't have a conscience, not one that you could count on. Much more likely to be a fear of getting caught.

She could hear him in the bedroom next to her, snoring the afternoon away. The kids were at school, the toddler and the baby both asleep, and he was sleeping off the dinnertime booze, the guilty conscience not keeping him awake, not so's you'd notice. When he awoke he'd be feeling vile, and the lot of them would have to jump or run. She thought about the story, the trip to Liverpool, the drinks downstairs with Ronnie Keegan, the way he'd come to bed at two a.m. and fucked her – 'Yes, full sexual intercourse took place, since you've got the cheek to ask!' She almost laughed. If she was ever questioned she'd feel like mentioning how hard to tell it was, his little dick was such a little thing, but he might well have done! Then when they'd gone, she'd get beaten up some more.

Maybe I'll turn him in, thought Fat Marie. Maybe he'll die, choke to death on drunken vomit like her uncle did. Maybe he'll get cancer.

No, none of these things. None of them.

Janis and Professor Swale did not go out that night, they stayed in and talked and planned. The house was in a quiet street in Bayswater, an amazing house for a lone woman, three storeys and a basement floor, with gardens front and rear and a garage in a mews that would probably have sold at fifty thousand on its own. Hilary liked to give big parties, and had many, many friends, so the whole enormous house was decorated, each room its own motif and colour scheme, each floor its bright and modern bathroom. Janis was shown her room, then went to have a shower, which became instead a long soak in a bath with a glass of Perrier and a twist of lime. When she returned downstairs, the fax machine was humming and Hilary called her cheerily into her office. She waved some glossy sheets, showing her big strong teeth.

'*Voilà*. The superintendent's secret!'

The report, to Janis, did not yield much, containing yards of what she saw as psychobabble, interspersed with tables of responses to standard tests. Hilary, annoyingly, left her to it while she went and bathed and changed, to see what she could make of it as a layman. Janis, more naturally a journalist, went through for quotes or soundbites, always hoping for the six-word phrase that would unlock a personality. What emerged most strongly, though, was a hedging of all bets. The doctor who had talked to Ronnie reiterated several times that his subject had problems with the truth, and wondered, in a memorable sentence, if he perhaps had Welsh or Irish blood that might account for the streak of optimistic fantasy with which he viewed his life and (largely negative) achievements. Naked racism, thought Janis, and right off-beam to boot. Bren Hughes was a 'mystic Celt', and a whingeing, pessimistic swine! Ronnie Keegan, despite his name, and origins in the north, came across more like a London wideboy, or a spiv.

On violence, however, there did appear to be a basis for the Patten view. The whole report was spattered with disapproving references to other 'villains' who 'went in for it', and there were a couple of sentimental passages about old ladies and the need to bring back hanging for people who harmed them, as well as for child molesters. The biographical stuff, while a trifle inconsistent, did return several times to Keegan's childhood with his 'Nan' in Middleton, the 'only human being who had ever cared for him'. Apart from Nan, indeed, his childhood appeared a pretty bleak one: abandoned by his father, beaten by a succession of 'step-fathers', and finally abandoned by his mother too, in Cleethorpes of all places. Taken to the beach, bought a toffee-apple, and left. Janis, despite herself, snorted. True or fantasy, it was quite funny, in a way. Quite funny. She let her mind wander over it, pictured the scene, a little boy on a crowded beach, probably in the rain, if she knew Cleethorpes, looking for his mum, who'd got back in the car or train or coach and fucked off home. No, it wasn't very funny after all. He had been nine. After that it had been children's homes, two years back with Mum on Hathershaw Estate, then Nan. Then his record had begun.

'But not for violence,' she said to Hilary, who had come back bathed and glowing in a gigantic kaftan. 'He's never been convicted for it and he bangs on about it quite a fair amount. Protests too much, yethinks?'

Professor Swale flicked through the sheets, looking for a point she'd spotted earlier.

'The conclusions are a nonsense, where is it now, no matter. What the Irish would call a ballix, if you'll pardon the expression. He's not protesting about violence, he's indulging in a process I once called "feeding Freud". Did you read that book?'

'Of course I did. Very amusing. Isn't that when they tried to strike you off?'

'There's no machinery to cover such a case, fortunately. They hate jokes, though. They hate the Jung at heart.'

'Hilary.'

The women laughed, and Hilary tossed the fax sheets across her desk. She was in a great humour.

'OK, let's be serious. The whole thing reeks of Keegan

175

spouting stuff he knows they want to hear. Not just my esteemed colleague, but the courts as well. The criminal as victim, the criminal as decent bloke, the criminal – above all – as a seeker of salvation. "Look at me, I've had a shitty life, but I can rise above it. I'm not like other law-breakers, I'm not a thug, an animal, you owe me one more chance. And one more, when this one fails to do the trick. And one more." I'll make a prediction for you.'

'Yes?'

'If you get to speak to him about this case, he'll bring the subject up, he'll mention animals. It's funny, isn't it? People have been behaving like animals for so long in these situations it must be much more likely they're behaving just like humans. It wouldn't look so good in a headline, though! Killers were like humans, say police! The upshot is, from that report, that Ronnie Keegan could be an animal with the best of them. The childhood bit's almost classic, come to that, even if he thought it made him out to be as harmless as a fly. Whatever the law and order brigade believe, almost all poor sods who do this sort of thing have been destroyed as children. Sorry, not poor sods – these animals.'

They looked at each other, sobered for a moment. The men inside Brook Bank that night had been like savage beasts. But children were destroyed in other ways.

'He can't be stupid, can he, manipulating his own reports? He's got intelligence, or cunning. Do you think there is a value in trying to find out? Writing a book about it? It's a genuine question, Hilary.'

'The genuine answer is that I don't know. But what a stupid, crazy answer! Hilary Swale, professor of psychiatry and wealthy populist – if I'm not genuine I'm an utter charlatan, a moral tart, myself. No, you go ahead Janis, follow the question where it leads you, see what you can find. I want to know as well, quite frankly. But do you think it's safe? Do you see any danger in it, to yourself?'

'Aside from the "unnatural interest"? Yes, I do. But let's stick to the mechanics first, shall we? How I go about it, how I get to see him. Until I know I can, I'm not even going to wonder what I might say to him. After all, I've got to bring up a murder no one's remotely suggested he had anything to do

176

with! That's danger, for a kick off! He might tear me limb from
limb. Worse, he might slap a writ on me!'

Hilary touched the telephone.

'It's not exactly what I had in mind,' she said. 'Look, Buster
Crabbe. That's the publisher I mentioned, the MP. Apart from
the commercial aspect, he's the man to pull the strings for us,
because he shadows on home affairs, prisons, things like that.
As I understand it, one has to be invited in to see a prisoner,
you can't just turn up on visiting day and start the third degree.
I've laid a little poison down, from the office. He's pretty keen.'

'Why? What did you tell him?'

The laugh was deep and rich.

'You're a woman, dear. I told you, he's a shit. If I didn't have
entire confidence in you, I wouldn't let you in the same street
as him. You have been warned.'

'I'd better ring up Bren,' Janis replied. 'God, what a strange
non sequitur!'

TWENTY-EIGHT

The Right Honourable Donald Crabbe, MP, had been famously dubbed Buster by an 'honourable friend opposite' who compared his debating skills (most unfairly) to those of a headless corpse. This was a reference, Janis learned, to a Royal Navy frogman who had disappeared in the murky waters of Portsmouth Harbour while spying out the secrets of some Russian warships on a friendly visit, and whose body had indeed turned up, sans head, some time afterwards. It seemed to her more apt as a description of his general personality than of his technique in Parliament, of which she knew nothing, for she found him devious, rotten, and at first distinctly slimy. And those, she joked to Hilary, were just his good points!

Their first meeting took place next day, and involved another restaurant, another good meal, and another bout of serious lunchtime drinking. Janis, as a journalist, knew how to hold her liquor, but she started with a tonic water, straight, and tried to keep her glass emptier than Buster Crabbe would have wanted it. From the moment she saw his hot brown eyes she knew that he would try to get her into bed, and she knew him as the type who would use any method, however low or hackneyed, to achieve it. Her hangover was now into its third or fourth day (who was counting?) so there was another motive for her caution. She did not want her liver to explode.

On the other hand, she began to find him, after a while and much to her discomfiture, rather refreshing. As a medium-sized fish in a rather small pond, she had long ago decided that the 'personalities' who ran her part of the Midlands were not personalities at all, but moderately successful mediocrities. Crabbe, she soon decided, was not many things. He was not nice, he was not brilliant, he was emphatically not a man you'd tell a secret to. But he was not mediocre, either, nor was he dull. Laughing at him, with him, gasping at his scurrility and his bile, she began to get an inkling of the danger. The man, for God's sake, could almost be *attractive*.

To other women, there was no doubt of it, he was. He was tall, and lean and horsy, with that long thin structure to his head that was almost a living caricature of the ancient English aristocracy. His face was brown and haughty, his black hair slicked thinly to his skull. There was something military in his bearing, and he wore cavalry trousers and tweed jackets, superbly tailored in Savile Row. His shoes were glowing with deep polish, his shirts were winter quality and of a quiet, noble check. There could have been a regiment at his beck and call, or a mighty charger tethered outside the restaurant in New Bond Street. There certainly could have been a gaggle of young fillies, which was how she actually heard him refer to some girls who passed outside. In fact he'd been in publishing all his life, had never been to war or in the services, and had been married no fewer than five times. All his wives had brought money to the match, and parted from it considerably poorer. This much, and plenty more, she'd had from Hilary.

'Now,' he said, fixing Janis with a penetrating eye. 'I've heard a lot about you and your proposition. Sell it to me in six sentences.'

She shook her head.

'I certainly will not. I'm sure you know the outline of it already. If you're interested, say so. If you think you're going to steamroller me, I'll go.'

'Good lord, a fighter, now that is a treat! Hilary said you'd be prepared to go in and hang on, the British bulldog thing. What we publishers most fear, you know, is people who screw us with a proposition, then can't deliver it. I'm going to like you, Janis.'

Yes, boiled or fried, she thought – or maybe without the dressing. But she smiled and nodded, and listened to him talking 'generally, of course, only generally' about the money that could still be made with 'the right product'. Mass murder, luckily, was always a growth area, the public's maw for bloody detail was insatiable, with the more and fouler the sex the better. They might be talking – and the gaze was sideways, and more shrewd – they *might* be talking of six figures, in advance.

179

Six figures, that's a hundred thousand upwards, thought Janis, in a reverie of her own. Jesus, can he mean that? A girl could be seduced . . .

She did not think so, though. Quite honestly, she did not even believe him. Buster Crabbe had been one of Professor Swale's most celebrated soul-barers, talking with terrifying frankness of the messy businesses of life and love and marriage. After the first of his divorces, which his wife had instigated, he had been the prime mover and the 'injured party' in all the others, a way, he laughingly agreed, of getting in the first – crucial – financial blow. He had no children, which he said was his decision only, and a tactic, and came fairly close to accepting that he had married them for their money, every one. Although, as Hilary had pointed out, they had all been rather beautiful.

'I am not much liked by men,' he was telling Janis, when her mind came back on line. 'They appear to think I'm out to steal their mistresses, of whom there are many in the House of Commons, as you must know. That makes it easier for me to operate, because their dislike blinds them. I'm the Opposition expert on crime and general mayhem, did Hilary explain? Not only can I move this project on, but I can have some fun with it, we both can. So tell me, now, just what it is you've got? How can we turn it into something sexy? And make a packet for us both?'

As Janis told him, Crabbe made no attempt to hide his prejudices and enthusiasms. When she demurred about her Ronnie Keegan theory – that that was all it was, and full of evidential holes – he pooh-poohed vigorously and insisted she have faith in her own intuition. The police had been in chaos for at least two decades, he said, and showed no signs of getting out of it. They were corrupt, self-serving, inefficient, and had the backing of a judiciary in blinkers and a succession of Home Secretaries who had been third-raters to a man. They worked by pressure, not by logic, they were a prey to political doubts and influences, they clutched at straws and called them theories, and thought every decision infallibly correct as long as it might lead to the conclusion of a case. Did she doubt that? Had she studied recent history? Had she never heard of—?

Janis, laughing, interrupted him.

'Yes, yes, yes,' she said, amused to find herself defending the police, 'but that doesn't mean they couldn't still be right! It could just as easily be their gipsies, or even someone hired by the husband. They seem pretty happy with the evidence so far!'

'Then let us test it!' cried Crabbe, bringing down a large, strong hand and rattling cutlery. The restaurant was large and their table chosen for discretion, but other diners glanced at them. Smiling, he lowered his voice. 'Then let us put it to the test. See Keegan, start digging seriously, see his friends, his wife, his enemies, his associates. The first time you held up anything they said to scrutiny, you found that it was wrong. You'd better go and test the rest of it.'

'OK, that's fine by me. There's just one little problem, though – the money. I'm a working woman, journalist on a paper. This hundred thousand plus – if I got some of it up front, I could take time off. Well, I could quit, in fact. The point is, if I'm going to do the digging, I'm going to need the time. They're not likely to give me leave at their expense.'

A look appeared that she did not like. A cunning look, oddly hungry.

'I could let you have some. I recognise the need. I agree that this needs moving fast.'

'What do you mean by "let me have"? As an advance?'

'Well naturally that will be it ultimately. I think we've got a fantastic product here, Janis, the potential is enormous. But in the first instance, I suppose, a loan would be the easiest. I'm not a shark, there won't be any interest. Let's say five thousand, shall we? To start.'

He had modified the look, but she was no fonder of it. Janis hardened her heart against temptation.

'No,' she said. 'I think we've got a fantastic product, too – or no product at all, if it doesn't turn out the way I want it to. I'll tell you what I'll do, I'll finance myself as best I can, I'll get the time off somehow. And as soon as I stand something up, something really concrete, you can pay me an advance. Not five thousand, either, we'll go straight into the silly money, please! How does that grab at you?'

He did not argue. He refilled her glass.

'You're a tough-minded young lady, aren't you? I do like that. You'll be threatening to find another publisher if I'm not careful.'

'I shouldn't think so. If you play fair. Anyway, you have your uses, don't you? I'll need permissions, rules bending, that sort of thing. I need to speak to Ronnie Keegan. Maybe two sentences from him and it'll be all off, I'll be shown up for a fool.'

'Never in the world.' Crabbe checked his watch. 'Listen, I have a little flat not far from here. Half flat, half office, I find it rather useful. When we're finished, why don't we pop round there and make some calls?'

Janis thought of Hilary and all the early warnings.

'OK,' she said.

It could be argued, that the pressure on Superintendent Patten had already started. It was to do, as much as anything, with the raising of false hopes. That, and an as yet not fully formed distaste that Damon Hegarty should be among the list of suspects, at whatever level. The deeper that sank in, in certain circles, the more distasteful it began to seem, the more impossible that it could be even contemplated. It was a matter of connections.

Patten was at his desk when the first hint came, in a phone call from the top. He was poring over the photographs of the victims, glossy and heart-rendingly obscene. Much as he wanted to, he had not lit a cigar.

'Patten? Hetherington.'

'Sir?'

The acting chief constable was an irascible man, whose great weight appeared sometimes to frustrate him. He was not comfortable with it as some big people are, but moved awkwardly, especially in spaces that he felt confining. He did, however, believe his size made him important, and possibly cleverer than the normal run. He thought police procedures were too rigid, but could be circumvented by applied intelligence.

'How close are we to charges?' he demanded. 'There are people breathing down my neck.'

There were six men in custody already, remanded for a week. Patten recognised the technique, he was being manoeuvred into statements of the obvious. For the moment he decided to oblige.

'We've got six of them inside already, sir. Every force in Britain's on the lookout, including Northern Ireland. With luck there could be new arrests at any time.'

'You know what I mean, Patten, I mean real charges. These six men come up in court again in two days time. Are you expecting the magistrates to refuse them bail again on what they've heard so far? I wouldn't, if I was on the bench.'

'We could beef up the charges, sir. If you insisted. We've got a GBH now, offensive weapons, assault on three or four police officers. I have to say the legal department doesn't think it's necessary.'

'Why not?'

'The case we made out on their first appearance was more than adequate. No fixed abodes, danger of absconding. We propose to tell them this time that more serious charges are in the pipeline. Which is true.'

Hetherington's breathing was stertorous.

'Well is it, Superintendent? Frankly, that's what worries me. From my reading of the case, you haven't got a scrap of evidence that links them to Brook Bank. Not a scrap. Frankly, I think it's time you had.'

Patten cast his mind over the hours of taped interviews he'd listened to. In the nature of things, he suspected, there would have been other interviews, longer and less scrupulous, that Rosser would probably have categorised as 'necessarily unofficial'. If these had yielded anything, he would have known.

'We're working on it, sir. I'm confident we'll make the linkage soon. In the meantime, I'm confident the magistrates know some of the things we're up against with these people.' Even if you don't, he added, to himself.

The acting chief constable was in a delicate position, Patten knew. In one way a case like this could make his confirmation in the post a mere formality. Equally, if it went wrong, he would have to be politically adept in the extreme to win the permanence he coveted. The last chief constable had retired unexpectedly (on 'ill health' grounds) amid a fog of rumour. Hetherington, he guessed, was suffering.

Down the telephone came a heavy sigh.

'How many men have you got working on this, Superintendent? Don't tell me, I know. Gipsies are difficult, you don't have to spell that out, but you must appreciate my problems, also. They're liars, they stick together, perjuring themselves is second nature, I know it isn't easy. But in my considered opinion, you have men enough and more to make this stick. You could take every caravan in this county apart and put it back together again, twice over. Have you done that?'

Metaphorically, he had. He had also, metaphorically, harried endless columns of Bedford TKs and Ford Cargoes as they'd slipped like wraiths across the borders. In reality, such things were more or less impossible.

'The geography hasn't helped,' he said. 'Three counties within spitting distance. Naturally, I'm getting full co-operation. Naturally, I'd rather we could do the job ourselves.'

Shift the blame, rehearse the problems, procedural niceties beyond their full control. Let Hetherington pick up on it, give him ammunition for his own fights, subtle ammunition. The sigh this time was friendlier, more full of understanding.

'You mean the way these devils move around? They would do, wouldn't they? Listen, if you have anything specific, any incidences of obstructive behaviour from other forces, however minor, let me know, I'll take it up immediately, at the highest level, at chief constable level, that's my job. My God, Patten, we've got to move this on, and fast. I promise you, I won't let procedure stand in your way.'

The voice had become enthusiastic. Patten thanked him, and was rewarded with 'Good man!' Do all promotions lead to bastardy? he wondered. Do only pompous dickheads make it to the top? A photograph caught his eye as he put the phone back on its cradle, a close-up of Joyce Withers' pubic area. Yes, he thought. A typical chief constable.

He was still studying the photographs when Lance Rosser knocked on his door and entered. Indeed, he looked at them obsessively, sometimes for hours at a time, because he had a feeling, hardly articulated, that there must be a key in them, that somehow they would yield up a sudden, glaring, truth. Rosser took up station on the opposite side of his desk, silently flicking round two prints of Tessa Wilmott so that he could see them. One showed the full length of her, prostrate, with the soap and flannel on her upper chest, the bristles of the brush protruding grotesquely.

'Wash and brush up,' he suggested. 'I've got something for you, Boss.'

'You're vile,' responded Patten. 'What is it?'

He noticed for the first time that Rosser was carrying a heavy-duty plastic bag. He cleared the desk so that its contents could be viewed. Carefully, the detective sergeant extracted something covered in lighter plastic. It was some sort of ancient gun.

'It's a fowling piece, sir. They've already dusted it. Eighty or ninety years old. Still lethal.'

Excitement churned in Patten's stomach.

'But the barrel's been sawn off. Christ, what a botch-up.'

'That's tinkers for you. If they'd ever fired it, they'd have blown themselves to buggery. We found it in a caravan. Woman and three brats. "Me man's away, sorr, but shure, and he'll be back again."'

Patten rolled it over, gingerly. Prints were clearly visible in the dusting powder.

'Go on, then. You're not crazy. Tell me why I should be interested.'

The thin-lipped smile cut the ugly face almost in half.

'Because Damon Hegarty's identified it, hasn't he? It was in the old stable, on two nails above the door. For years and years and years. It's from Brook Bank.'

Superintendent Patten stretched his back, and filled his lungs, and sighed.

'Thank you, God,' he said.

TWENTY-NINE

Ronnie Keegan wanted money. Which was not, as Clive Smith argued, the reaction of a guilty man to the idea of being interviewed by a journalist. Terror, yes, outright refusal, but surely not to ask for cash?

'But he doesn't know what it's in aid of,' Janis said. 'My motives aren't as plain to everyone as they are to you and me. He just thinks I'm a journalist from the *Sunday Times* doing an article about crime and criminals. Murder never passed my lips.'

'Still seems pretty bold to me, if he did do Brook Bank. Or stupid.'

'Or conceited. Reading between the lines, his solicitor seems to be implying that he's got a fairly high opinion of himself. She gave me the impression he's the sort of bloke who'd do it in the end to get his picture in the paper. Yes, a she. Maude Wimlock.'

They were sitting in the garden of a country pub, not far from Didwell, as it happened. Not a pub she'd drunk in before. Not a pub that Bren might turn up at. Clive swallowed beer.

'Conceit.' He appeared to ponder it, as a notion. 'The *Sunday Times*. The poor old *Clarion* doesn't get a look-in, even in your fantasies. Are you really going to leave us?'

Janis was brisk.

'Don't be so stupid, Clive. I'll leave the *Clarion* if I have to, which means if I can find a better way of making cash. You came here because you didn't fancy Fleet Street after Manchester, and the rural idyll suits you. I've had the rural idyll up to here. I want some grime. And anyway, I'm asking for time off, aren't I, not a fucking reference! Grow up.'

The big bland face broke into a grin. A couple with two children sitting nearby were less entranced by the bad language. They moved.

'They should have waited for my response,' Clive said. 'I'll

186

give you time off if you'll sleep with me again. You can have three months!'

'Three months would be wonderful, but I'll make do with one. But you're not serious?'

'About the sex? Three French kisses and a feel of bum gets you the month. You drive a vicious bargain, missus.'

'Shut up and talk sense. Can I have it, honestly? Please? If it really is the *Sunday Times* that rankles, I promise I won't do any articles for them beyond what I've already agreed to do. Unless they offer money, naturally.'

'Of course.'

What really rankled, though, was not the *Sunday Times*, but the Balkan trip. Clive had pencilled in a date that he could get away, but it was in the next three weeks.

'Anyway,' he said, 'I can't pay you for a buckshee month, you know I can't. Especially if it all comes good and you piss off completely to become a famous author. Talking of coming good, the Balkan trip might have given me the chance. To make up for the last time.'

She regarded him with amused affection.

'I wasn't wanting paying, you buffoon. I just want four weeks off. And you're crazy. Bren's back.'

'And you're sitting here avoiding him. So how about it? I give you four weeks off — no pay, that's a bonus! — and you give me your body in some sleaze hotel in Bosnia. Sounds miraculous!'

'It sounds like prostitution and extortion, Clive. Blackmail, as well.'

'It's bargaining. It's trade. Anyway, we're prostitutes. We're journalists. Anyway, you don't have to sleep with me and you know it, you're not that sort of girl. You'll sleep with me if you want to, no other reason. All jokes aside.'

The man mountain. Large, pale, freckly. He wiped a line of perspiration from between his eyebrows and she pictured him naked, strangely attractive, considering all things. Wasn't sex peculiar?

'The dates won't fit,' she said, 'but if you could alter them? No, that's no good, what if this thing really does take off? What I'm saying is that, in principle, I've got no objection. No, I'd like to. But this comes first, Clive. This is serious.'

187

'Your Big Chance.'

'I said serious. Yes, my big chance. You know what I think about round here. You know the way I'm feeling. I want to get away, to do something. I feel as if I'm haemorrhaging, Clive, bleeding to death, but slowly. It's horrible. Do you understand?'

He understood. She could see it in his eyes. Janis reached across and touched his hand, his big, pale paw.

'When I'm rich,' she said, 'I'll take you away from all this.'

'When do you start?'

With Bren, Janis had been neither so desperate, nor so combative. On her return from London he had been waiting for her, and he had done his best to 'make things right'. The fridge was full of good food from their favourite deli in Leicester, there was red wine in the rack and two bottles of cheapo champagne ready to be popped. He asked how she'd been, but not exactly where or why, and made no reference to Cardiff beyond saying his mother had been fine and sent regards. His tactic, clearly, was to pretend that nothing untoward had happened. When she mentioned the night she'd 'disappeared' he smiled (despite her good intentions she had never rung him), and when she talked about following her trail to Manchester he made a joke of it.

'How exotic. Don't forget to pack your best bikini.'

That night, in bed, they had made love, but Janis had not been sure about things, and it showed. Afterwards she had lain awake for several hours, her thoughts a jumble. If things went on like this he'd have to go, no question – but if the other thing took off . . . Well, perhaps her jaded life was not all to do with Bren, who was at least domesticated and quite reasonable, unlike some men she'd lived with. For the present she decided, unilaterally, that everything should go on ice. Until, at least, he started up the Cardiff whine . . .

She had given Maude Wimlock the number of a mobile she had borrowed from the office (with Clive's connivance) to keep her actual whereabouts hazy, and Maude phoned her on it three days later, just as she was about to ring to speak to her. Ronnie was now talking three hundred, she said (his starting price had been five) but she thought he might go down to two.

Janis – who had borrowed from the bank to cover the next month – found herself wondering whose side Maude was on, but thanked her warmly and suggested adding fifty. Then Maude asked about seeking permissions, and could she help?

'No, that's all right, thanks. We've got people working on that from this end, as Ronnie's only one of many. We don't anticipate any problem getting into any of the jails. Listen – about his wife. He has got one, hasn't he? Do you know her, by any chance?'

Silence down the line. Janis held her breath.

'I do. But I don't see . . . well, she's a pretty private sort of person, actually.'

Oh yeah, thought Janis. Wife of a petty criminal, probably a murderer. Scared to put her nose above the parapet, more like.

'Yes, I can understand that. Perhaps I'd better leave it. Does she work, d'you know?'

'Oh yes, she's with the council. I could have a word with her, perhaps? She's home by five, I think.'

'No,' said Janis, 'I've put you to enough bother already, I can't tell you how grateful I am. If it all comes off you'll get a mention in the article, I promise you. It won't be advertising, but it shouldn't do any harm, should it?'

'That sounds great, thanks. Are you quite sure about Eileen?'

'Eileen? That's Mrs Keegan?'

'Eileen Thorpe. She's not actually his wife, they never married.'

'Very wise! No, I'll forget her for the moment. Look, I won't be on this number from now on, so I'll ring you later or tomorrow. As soon as Ronnie says OK, I'll do the rest. And thanks again for everything you've done.'

'It's been a pleasure, honestly. Goodbye.'

Janis checked her watch, and walked up to the newsdesk, where Clive was going through the diary with a black marker. She tapped the desk-top with her knuckles.

'I'm off. Where's the best place to stay in Oldham? Except with relatives of yours.'

'Cheeky sod. I don't have relatives in the home of the tubular bandage, I come from Wigan, in the Patak's pickle belt. Strange-ways, incidentally, is in Salford, which is virtually joined to

Manchester centre, which is lousy with hotels, which is a much better bet than Oldham, any time. D'you want me to ring one up for you, or can you manage to walk into one all by yourself? God, you intrepid reporters. Keep in touch.'

An hour later she was belting up the motorway at eighty, doing mental calculations as she drove. By the quickest roads, at night, it would have been utterly simple, she thought. Even within the law you must be able to do the major roads from Oldham in two and a half, or maybe less. Then down the back routes to Rowsley, what, another twenty minutes if you knew the way? Why were the police so adamant that people didn't do these things?

She came off at the road for Huddersfield, threaded through the urban sprawl, and climbed out on the A62 across the Pennines. Getting lost in Oldham, she was redirected up another climbing road, which her map showed her joined the M62 across to Leeds and the M1. So there was Rowsley, direct from Moorside, quick, fantastic. If she did that route, at night, and really hammered it, she reckoned she'd make door to door in just no time at all. If she left at eight o'clock, say—

Out of the corner of her eye, Janis saw Harding Lane and screeched round for it. It was not yet four o'clock, she had a good hour before Eileen Thorpe got home from work. Careless and elated, she drove up until she spotted the right number, and parked just past it. Outside there was a smart blue Fiesta, but nothing in the short driveway leading to the yellow garage door. She wanted a good nosey round, get the feel of it, see what sort of man this Keegan was, and how he lived. She was a bit surprised at how much green there was all round, fields and cows, they were almost in the country. The house was pleasant, too, a neat brick semi.

Janis got out of her car and walked back down the hill to get a closer look. She was actually standing on the drive when she got the biggest surprise of all. A wicket gate beside the garage opened and a young woman emerged. She was smart and young and rather beautiful.

'Yes? Were you coming here?'

Oh shit. No point in denying it, she'd seen her. She'd know her in the future. Fuck.

'Er. Eileen, is it? Mrs Keegan? I'm Janis Sanderson.'

A look passed across Eileen's face, a shadow of distaste, or pain.

'I'm Eileen Thorpe,' she said.

THIRTY

Janis, to her shame, had not legislated for a chance encounter. She had compartmented Eileen, stuck a label round her neck marked later. It was Ronnie she was after first, a Ronnie who might easily be suspicious. She had no idea when – or if – the two of them would speak, but the cat would be out of the bag with a vengeance if Eileen came to Ronnie with a tale of a mysterious journalist poking through the dustbins. Also, it would look as if she'd been double-crossing Maude Wimlock.

She was much more thrown, however, by the sight and sound of her, and the surroundings. Janis realised that she had been working on assumptions that would not have been out of place on the pages of the gutter press. Ronnie Keegan, in her mind, was probably a monster, processed by her memory of his normality into some sort of charismatic escaper from the lower depths. But she knew he beat his wife, and she knew he had convictions as a petty criminal, so she had expected something pretty concrete of Eileen. Something pale, and crushed, and hopeless, something drab. 'She's with the council,' Maude had said. Entirely unconsciously, Janis had placed her in a nylon overall, cleaning lavatories.

'Look,' she said. 'You don't know me, and you can tell me to go away if you want, I won't be offended. But I've come up all the way from London, so I'd like the chance to talk if possible. To explain myself.'

'What's it about? I mean – you're not selling anything, are you?'

Janis laughed.

'Only an idea. I'm from the *Sunday Times*, actually. I'm doing an article about prisons.' The look of pain again. 'Well, prisoners, more specifically. And their wives. And women.'

Eileen's face appeared to have become marginally paler. She was wearing make-up, with a pale pink shade of lipstick. The end of her tongue showed briefly.

'Stand by your man,' she said. It was flat, neither a question nor a statement, nor obviously the line from a song. Then she blew air out from between pursed lips. 'I don't think I want to talk about it, thanks.'

'It won't take very long,' Janis put in quickly. 'I'm seeing Ronnie later, it's been agreed. If you prefer it, I could come back after I've spoken to him in . . .'

She stopped. A woman was coming down the hill with a toddler and a baby in a buggy. A brisk wind was blowing a plastic windmill tied to the handle. When she had passed, Eileen had backed through the wicket gate, but held it open.

'Strangeways,' she said. 'He'll be out soon, though, won't he? Then you'll see if I really am "standing by my man". Would you still be interested, if I did a bunk? Would that still fit in with your ideas? Romantic crap.'

Her eyes had taken on a hardness, glittering with what might have been unshed tears. Or might not, Janis conceded. She moved forward, very carefully, as if approaching a dangerous dog. She could hear a big dog barking, close. She wondered if it was behind the semi, waiting to be released, to spring.

'I would. To me it seems much more valid, actually. I mean – why should anyone put up with it? Well, just as valid.'

The vapidity of it was overwhelming. She realised that Eileen Thorpe was very tense, the muscles in her face rigid. Otherwise, thought Janis, she'd throw me out.

'Can I come in and chat? I promise at the end of it I won't publish anything that you don't want me to. Just have a chat, for starters?'

And she was in. Eileen turned, walked into the garden, held the wicket wide. As Janis passed her she gave a little shiver, then closed the gate. The garden was small and neat, mainly lawn but with a border, reasonably well tended. Eileen gestured to the kitchen door.

'Go in. I'll make a cup of tea. Go in there, find a place. It's chaos. Gin bottle on the table, the housewife's friend. Maybe you'd prefer one? You're a journalist, I'm a wreck. Look, I've changed my mind, will you go away now? Just sod off? Please?'

They faced each other in the kitchen, Eileen's chest heaving, her hands clenched, her eyes bright and hard with anguish.

Janis held her breath, afraid that Eileen might collapse, or cry. She felt a shit, a heartless intruder. Christ, she thought, I'll never make a journalist, this is pain. She did not move, however.

After a few moments, Eileen took the kettle to the tap, and Janis walked through to the front room. It was indeed in chaos, with cardboard boxes strewn about, some half-filled to match half-empty shelves. There was one uncluttered easy chair, facing a TV and video down a corridor of mess, with a dirty dinner plate on the carpet at its side. Beside that was gin, as promised, and a supermarket carton of tonic water bottles, several of them empty. Three glasses, one on its side. She heard Eileen behind her.

'It wouldn't suit the *Sunday Times*,' she said. 'Room with a view, or whatever they call it. I was going home to Mum, except that if I do he'll take the house, won't he? It's my house, but I put his name on it, God, that pleased her! Look, there's a good chair underneath those curtains, clear a space. Do you take sugar, because there isn't any. Make yourself at home, relax. I took the afternoon off work to sort things out. This is the result! Marvellous.'

In the kitchen, listening to the kettle begin to grumble, Eileen pressed her forehead to the wall and rehearsed the story of her life, for publication. I'm twenty-seven years old, she said, and I was brought up by a nice mum and dad, an only child and probably spoilt rotten. But I worked hard at comprehensive, and I went to sixth form college, and I got my A-levels and I learned about computers. I worked for a solicitor, then an insurance agent, then I tried a season as a courier but I didn't like the greasy men and the cockroachy hotels. I liked men to be a lot of fun, and clean, and handsome, and to drive cars, and I didn't like them to wear suits or work in offices or have spots like most of them who went for me at work did. I liked to go to discos, and down to Manchester to clubs, and have a really good time, dancing till I almost dropped. My father said it was terrible, but he trusted me until the day he died, and he was right to. I never slept around, although I wasn't a virgin, don't be silly, and I went out with boys, then men, for long periods at a time. Then I met Ronnie.

The kettle had boiled, and switched itself off. Eileen found the teapot, which had two teabags in that had grown mould. She balanced them on the pedal bin, full to bursting, and rinsed the teapot out. Then I met Ronnie. What a disaster that had been.

'He was nice at first,' she told Janis, as they drank their tea. 'Well obviously, or I wouldn't have gone out with him. I was back at a solicitor's then, which I found quite boring, frankly, and I thought I'd got in a rut. I'd bought this house, and it needed the roof fixing, and Ronnie came along with a firm I'd got out of the paper. You know builders, don't you? He was good-looking in a macho sort of way, tight jeans and no shirt on and a hairy chest. There was a chap in the solicitor's called Derek who wanted me to marry him, and that did the trick I think, no contest. I got the roof done half price and Ronnie moved in under it. He was a ferocious drinker, and a ferocious everything else to match. My mother hated him, and after about a year he hit me and she found out and tried to call the police, which was a bad mistake, you know how young girls are. No, that's not fair on Mum, she didn't drive me to it, I was already there. In love. Honestly and truly for the first time, and the last, I hope. I even loved him when he broke my teeth.'

Without even glancing up, she put her thumb and forefinger into her mouth, pulling down and forward on her front teeth, which slipped out on a plate. She held them there a second, like an exhibit in a court, then pushed them back.

'Gin bottle.' She smiled, entirely to herself. 'I was drinking like a fish then, to keep up with him. I didn't get drunk, though, not stupid drunk like him and his mates. I just used to giggle and get happy, then maybe go to sleep or sometimes get sick. He pushed the bottle in my mouth to wake me up, he said, because they were playing poker and they wanted food and I'd passed out on the sofa. One of the others drove me to the infirmary, because Ronnie wouldn't, he had a winning streak. I could have left him then, couldn't I? My own fault.'

Like many people talking to a stranger, Eileen, once she'd started, seemed to find it a relief. The art, as Janis knew, was not to intrude, and to apply the sympathy like a balm. The art of being rueful, but alert. She waited seconds before posing her question, although she had been itching for the opportunity.

'Did you?' she said. 'Did you leave him, ever?'

She knew the answer – one of the answers – and she ached to casually drop in Brook Bank. She could not, of course, it would have been ridiculous, as ridiculous as it was to hope that Eileen might. But she willed herself to be receptive, she emanated warm concern. Eileen, indeed, appeared to have slipped deeper into self-absorption.

'He left me a lot,' she said. 'Always the same reason, prison. Thieving, burglary, receiving stolen goods. Never very long, because it was never very serious. He's a funny bloke, is Ronnie, he used to say he was doing it for me, for us, he had this sort of dream, this hankering for a better life, you had to like him, really. He was an orphan, you know, he had a terrible childhood, just lousy children's homes. Anyway, I did get fed up once, said he'd have to go, I was selling up and going back to Mum, and he said he'd had this great idea, to take us to the country to work on this estate, get away from all the urban crap, him as a sort of chauffeur and gardener and oddjobs with me as housekeeper. I said "get stuffed", actually, I wasn't scrubbing any floors, but we drove down one day and saw the people and the place and it was actually dead good. That's when I did leave him though, in the end, because it didn't last long, it was a disaster, the whole thing was . . .'

The tape recorder whirred, and Janis ached. Eileen glanced at her, as if having a minor struggle of her own. She's going to tell me, thought Janis. She willed her, tell me, Eileen, tell me!

'What went wrong?' she asked. So calm, so neutral. 'Did Ronnie steal something?'

Eileen looked down at her cup of tea, that must be almost cold by now. She slowly shook her head.

'There's no reason I shouldn't tell you, but it's just so weird, one of those horrible coincidences that happen. The house we worked at was in . . . well, you'll have read about it, there were some awful murders there last month, five, six weeks ago. Brook Bank, at Rowsley. That was where we worked.'

The sympathy in Janis's face was tinged with shock.

'Oh no! How awful for you! But . . . but surely . . . ?'

Their eyes met. Eileen shook her head.

'No, of course not, we'd left months before. It just makes the thing more horrible, that's all, thinking about it. I was quite happy there at first, and then I've never been so miserable, it's a really lonely place, deep in the country. The woman there, the young one that got killed, Tessa, she was very sympathetic to me, but I couldn't stay. Ronnie had been going with some-one in the village and he'd started hitting me quite badly. I had the house, I had my Mum. It's pathetic really, isn't it? The way we run back to our Mum? You won't mention this will you? You won't put it in? You did promise.'

'Of course. Of course not. How awful for you, though, what an awful thing.'

But she had mentioned it. She would not have done so if she'd had a shadow of a doubt about her lover, would she? Another thing she ached to follow up. But Eileen had dropped her eyes. She made a gesture with her free hand, small, helpless.

'I felt terrific when I got away from him,' she said. 'And better when I got him back. Which he said he'd totally reform, and I believed him, or at least I agreed to let him try, inside my head. He hasn't hit me much since then, but they caught up with him for some receiving and he pleaded guilty, which he swore meant he was making a new start and he's back in Strangeways and he's coming out soon and I've got sick of it, and along you come just when I'm packing up. Stand by your man, eh? And before you ask the obvious, I don't know if I love him, or if I'm scared. Scared what he'd do if I ran off again. I'd have to leave the house, and then he'd have it, wouldn't he? And he'd follow me to my Mum's, he's not scared of her. Probably, the stupid fact is that I love him. Probably.'

What Janis wanted to say was, 'is he a violent man?' By which she meant over and above a little bit of wife-beating. By which she meant: 'Would he come and seize you at your mother's, and drag you home? And what about those guns that he had access to at the Wilmotts' house? Is he a killer, do you think?' But of course she could not ask those things, there was no way to start. She leaned forward and switched off the recorder, with a serious, sympathetic, rueful look.

'You poor thing,' she said.

Not far away from Harding Lane, on the edge of Noonsun, Mick Renwick lay in wait for Fat Marie. He was drunk, and

197

even to himself, his mind seemed clouded. From the outside, his face was curtained, darkened, closed down, as if his skull was a cave that had been vacated. Only, maybe not: from the deadened eyes there was a flicker now and then, as if a beast had moved in, a beast that peered out intermittently, a beast in pain.

Noonsun was a sorry sight, in some ways not dissimilar to Mick. Half of the buildings were vacant, the high windows blind, the lower ones shuttered off with plyboard and nails. Those that had inhabitants were even bleaker, their dereliction a comment on the lives of those within. Mick, though tiny, was bent over at a corner of the street, facing down the hill. The wind was strong and warm, but he bent into it as though it were mid-winter. It was a peculiar, almost crippled, stance.

Thirty years ago, Noonsun was a tiny hamlet, huddled in a fold that was the only protected area on a huge open sweep of northeast-facing moor. It was tiny because the elements had for centuries dictated thus – come from the fold, warmed by the midday sun, and we will torture you. Thirty years ago the architects and planners and the council decreed that there would be a large estate built, of wonderful new maisonettes and flats, cheap and cheerful, to drain the pus out of the older slums. The views were lovely, so the windows would be big. The times were hard and getting harder, so the materials would be cheap. The public health statistics were important for the image of the town, so there would be no polluting open fires, nor even any gas mains laid – electricity was clean, and easy to cut off. The place was built, the poor were hoiked out of their inner city lairs, and the winters came (as might have been expected). Within five years Noonsun was a sink, a wreck, an eyesore, a disaster. People like Mick Renwick and Fat Marie lived there.

Fat Marie was waddling up the hill. Through his blurry eyes, Mick could see her coming like a pale pink blancmange on sticky-outy legs, a stance she had developed to ease the rubbing of her inner thighs. She was pushing a buggy, leaning into the uphill push, the front wheels lifting rhythmically as she applied her weight. The toddler clutched a handle of the buggy, the baby lay in it, the other children ranged around, fighting, shouting, ignoring their fat mum. Mick was going to kill her when she came close enough, he was sure of that.

Mick was having nightmares now. He kept seeing Fat Marie with Doggo pissing in her face. He kept seeing the space between her thighs engulfing objects, a gun barrel, Doggo's foot, a brush. He kept on waking, sweating alcohol, finding her awake beside him, looking at him dangerously, her eyes like small black currants in a white bag pudding, currants filled with hatred and despair, which then turned into mirrors in a powder compact puffed with white. He kept having pains in his head as if he had been axed, whisky pains that only whisky could relieve. He kept punching her, every time he saw her, everywhere.

Neither Fat Marie nor any of the children noticed him until they were only feet away. Then little Seanie – little Sean, the faithless, betraying bastard – gave a fearful yell and pointed, his eyes and mouth grotesquely open, his face a parody of television fear. He screamed and ran, knocking into Donna, who smacked him in the face and turned herself and fled, followed by Billy, who went with a frightened sneer. Mick rushed out from behind his corner as if projected and drove his fist into Fat Marie, while chopping downwards at the baby with an open palm and kicking at the toddler who fell over, screeching. Two old ladies, bent by nature as Mick was bent by whatever was inside him, stopped at another corner for a moment, looking sad. Fat Marie fell backwards, her open legs rising, her head landing on the pavement with a crack. Mick hit the baby once again, spinning round the buggy till it teetered on the kerb but did not fall, then drove kicks into the thighs before him, trying to penetrate to the hated cunt which Marie, instinctively, had locked off in flesh a split second after the first blow had bitten home. He fell over her, knocking the toddler right into the road, banging his own face heavily on the tarmac, drawing blood. Fat Marie, in one movement, indescribable, miraculous, regained her feet, her balance and her toddler, spun the buggy downhill and fled, crying hard but not aloud, the only quiet one in the family. The family. Ye Gods! The two old ladies, judging they were safe, had resumed their vigil, and their old, lined, Oldham faces said it all.

Little Mick lay in the gutter for a while, blood bubbling from one nostril, pain throbbing through the tooth he'd landed on.

He wondered why he did all this.

THIRTY-ONE

Although she had not expected miracles, Janis's first meeting with Ronnie left her anxious and perplexed. Although it was short and rather formal, as she told Hilary Swale on her hotel telephone afterwards, it had shaken her confidence quite badly. Why? asked Hilary. Because he did not strike me as a murderer, Janis replied. And – in case that sounded ridiculously silly and naive – because his girlfriend didn't have the vaguest inkling. Surely, if it were possible at all, Eileen would have had suspicions?

But the good people of Weimar, Hilary responded, always claimed they knew not about Buchenwald. I have been there, and I believe them. Strange things happen, Janis – who knows what humans can divine?

But there were other things that had worried Janis, things she did not want to mention for embarrassment. All in all, it had left her feeling rather stupid. When the call ended she ran a deep, hot bath and lay in it with a massive gin and tonic for ages, staring at the misty bathroom tiles. The hotel was an old-fashioned one, nice and solid. Amid the steam and dripping walls, at least, she was quite safe.

In fact, she had felt quite stupid from the off. The huge reality of Strangeways Prison, as she had stepped out in front of it from her taxi, had been overwhelming and impressive. On television, she had seen it burning, seen that elemental penis-tower rising through the Salford dawn day after day as the rioters of 1990 had made their mark on history, and had assumed that afterwards – and after all the millions spent on it – it would be new, and soft, and civilised. As the old black cab had rattled off into the appalling wasteland stretching back to Manchester, she had stood beneath the wall and been somehow ashamed.

Inside the jail, Ronnie had preened himself for hours in anticipation, still hardly able to believe his luck. A high-class tart coming to visit – out of hours – and for money, too! Maude Wimlock had agreed, without enthusiasm, that it was a 'golden opportunity' (he did not say for what) and he had spent even longer working up his story, tidying the pieces, and fabricating juicy morsels that he thought this 'lady of the press' would like to hear. The *Sunday Times*. He'd never read it, but it was one of the heavy ones, that he did know. The sociological angle, then. The deprived childhood, the victim of society, all that social-work crapola. He wondered if she'd like some sex abuse, but it was one branch of crime that he had little first-hand knowledge of at all. Now *self*-abuse! He discussed it with his cell mate and they had a real good laugh.

The tart, when he was let into the room by the prison officer, who told her solicitously that he would be just outside the door throughout the interview, was more than just high class, she was excellent. She was wearing black (her funeral dress, in fact), and she had dark tights on, too. Probably, he thought, she wanted to keep it prim and formal, so as not to inflame any lags who caught a glimpse of her. Some fucking hopes. His eyes flashed from her lovely face to her swelling tits to the angle of her legs and body as she sat, an angle that he couldn't get enough of, that he loved, that drew his eyes back time and time again. Ronnie – only at her invitation – sat down himself and leaned luxuriously back, luxuriating in the blood that rushed into the vessels of his cock and scrotum, engorging, sensitising. There was a big smile on his face, contrasting with her circumspection. He brought it down, diminished it, because this was, of course, a very serious business. I wonder if she fucks, he thought. *Sunday Times*, you probably need a university degree. She'd be a great one for a wanking session, though. To that, she'd agreed already, had she but known it.

Janis thought she recognised him, and wished she hadn't tried, inhibited by the logjam in her head. If this man was a monster, where were his horns? If this man was a stupid petty criminal, why was he so lively, so alive? This man beat Eileen Thorpe, that much she did know, but even Eileen said she loved him, probably. Where was the sense in all of it? How could she find out? What would she ask?

Ronnie pulled himself up. He could read the confusion in her face, the anxiety, and guessed a reason for it. He guessed she found him coming on too strong, emanating sex too openly, behaving like some stud in some Yankee film. He straightened in the chair, the last louche vestiges of smile were wiped away, his clear bold eyes took on a look of frankness. She preferred it, admittedly, but it did not really help. There was a brick wall of enormity to cross, a higher brick wall than the jail's itself. Was this man a murderer, a savage beast?

'I've met you, haven't I?' she asked. Eileen had told her about Brook Bank, so she had her cover if she should need it . . . but no, oh Christ, it was much too early, far too soon. 'No, I'm raving, you must look like someone else.'

'Met me?' said Ronnie. (I wouldn't think so, love, I wouldn't have forgot a pair like that.) 'I can't recall it, but I've been around. I don't spend all my time in jail, you know.'

It was a nice, small joke and it got her on the track. She asked him questions about his times in jails, and his multiple convictions, and his life. He answered carefully, quietly, with no wild improbables, no lurid fantasy. He said that he was married, but did not expect his wife to wait for him forever, that was not reasonable, was it? His eyes jumped slightly when she revealed that she had met Eileen, and he asked her shrewdly, after she'd explained the circumstances, if she thought Eileen would wait. Janis answered that it would only be three weeks or so, wouldn't it, and Ronnie, even more shrewdly, repeated the question. Whatever else you are, thought Janis, you are not a fool. She said she thought she would, that she was sure of it.

'I hope she waits, poor Eileen,' Ronnie said. 'She's had a lot to put up with, hasn't she? I've told my brief, this time I'm going straight. I pleaded guilty to this lot, you know? Receiving. I probably would have got off if I'd fought. If you see Eileen again you could ask her, would you mind? Tell her that I'd like it if she did.'

This time she had half an hour only, and he was palpably, almost ludicrously, on his best behaviour. But he hoped she would return, he said, because they could get down to the nitty-gritty, she could write a book about the life he'd had, she should get her money's worth! And when the end came, rather abruptly, the prison officer and the prisoner exchanged a look of such complicity that she felt naked, like a crab without a shell. It was not a sexual stripping, she was open rather to two hungry aliens, two men who understood something she could not even guess at. But there was something sexual in the way that Ronnie projected himself when he stood. He was tall and whippy, quietly self-confident in blue and grey. Against the flat matt wall, surrounded by the faint, unpleasant noise of prison and enveloped in a faint, unpleasant smell, he threw some kind of charge at her, some magnetism.

Afterwards, to Hilary, Janis did not mention this. I must at some stage, she told herself, or it will do me harm. But face to face, not on the telephone. On the telephone they discussed more concrete anxieties, about guilt and innocence, Buster Crabbe, what would happen next.

That night, she had the fear again. She awoke convulsively, almost exploding from the double bed, her back arched, her fists clenched, her elbows thrust out from her.

She had heard a noise, and seen the door ease open, and seen Ronnie Keegan enter, with his awful, handsome smile. In his hand had been a brush.

Janis lay spreadeagled on the hotel bed, sweat pouring from her rigid body, panting.

Oh Christ, she thought, I'm frightened in the dark.

Oh Christ.

THIRTY-TWO

Buster Crabbe, because Janis had made him promise, made no references to the Brook Bank case in public or in Parliament. Behind the scenes, however, it delighted him to turn the screws. His overall intention was to goad the people with responsibility by playing on their fears of their incompetence – in law and order terms an easy game. His theory – deeply held if deeply cynical – was that those in power could not begin to understand any criminality which did not chime with theirs, that is, an unthinking corruption of the fact of wealth and privilege. Therefore, their only answer was to wave an ever bigger stick at people stupid enough to want to burgle terraced houses, beat up old ladies for their empty handbags, or rape and murder people they did not even know. Concomitantly, although they paid lip-service to the police force and its excellence, they held it privately to be an army of ill-educated louts, whose fault it was alone that crime had run out of control. It was a doctrine Crabbe had polished over several years, and used before to brilliant effect.

The first to feel his cattle goad had been the Home Secretary, who, naturally, had hardly twitched before he'd passed it to his junior. Crabbe's line had been a normal one for him, the application of a few facts embedded in a base of disheartening speculation and a hint of dark secrets that would soon mature into a major problem. The police had made a pig's ear of the Brook Bank case, he said, and the shit was going to hit the fan. When asked about the nature of the shit he tapped his nose, and when asked about the timescale said 'rather soon'. Pressed for details – 'You might consider, Donald, that you have a duty in this case' – Crabbe said: 'Ask Cyril Hetherington. Acting chief constable down there at the moment, surely you know that much? Disaster. Utter fool. Ask him if he's nailed the gippoes yet. Ask him why he's hounding that poor young fellow Hegarty. Disgraceful.'

Perhaps the oddest thing of all, in Crabbe's doctrine, was that despite the quasi-democratic structure of the police, the officers who made it to the very top were a remarkable reflection of their administrative masters. They rose, he held, because they were of like mind (and often background), and made use of the same rungs and handholds. True it was that his implied attack on Hetherington, passing quickly downwards from Home Office to area to county, electrified a class of people who could not accept that they were blameworthy, but thought they knew a man who was. And much as Cyril Hetherington hated outside interference, much as he thought politicians who attacked the police the lowest of the low, much as he wished that men like Buster Crabbe could recognise the appalling pressure the force was operating under in a case like this – he had to pile the pressure on himself. It was Arthur Patten, inevitably, who bore the brunt.

The saddest irony in this was that the other natural source of irrelevant and unfair pressure, the press, had for the moment more or less forgotten the whole thing, time, inevitably, having turned up many other items of overwhelming public importance to be picked and harried at for their brief moment. Even in the *Clarion* the case was dormant, a circumstance which Patten assumed without much interest might be connected to Janis's apparent dropping out of view. It was a breathing space only, as Rosser said, because the press would come back down on them like 'ten tons of turds' when something concrete happened. In the meantime, wouldn't you just know it, the bite came from on high.

What infuriated Rosser – and Patten to a less extent – was that the ones who piled it on would never say what their dissatisfaction was. Hetherington was not directly the mouthpiece, but they were made to realise something had to happen soon, or something would give. Coincidentally (coincidentally!), a whisper began to go around that Patten was the wrong man for the job, too young, too inexperienced, and probably not hard enough. Rosser, at this time, was still intensely loyal, and Patten was not paranoid, but they both knew that there were wheels within wheels in any large police force, and that covering one's back was not sustainable for an extended length of time. Patten was aware he needed something more, and soon. Or at least to be going somewhere, definite and fast.

In one hot argument − not face to face but on the telephone at least − Patten offered to go through everything his team had come up with so far, which would, he insisted, allay all Hetherington's fears. The acting chief constable refused, angrily, on the grounds that he did not want to interfere at an operational level, by which he meant, in Patten's firm opinion, that he planned to keep sufficient distance. 'If we fuck up,' he told Lance Rosser, 'he can say he never knew exactly what we were up to, and if he'd known, of course, he would have put us right. He's as difficult to pin down as Bernie Smith.'

Rosser laughed, but his face was grim.

'He's a fat bastard, sir,' he said. 'He'll want the credit when we don't fuck up, an' all. We're not going to fuck up, Boss. I think we're getting close to Bernie now.'

Bernie Smith was the tinker whose caravan had housed the Brook Bank gun, and Rosser's statement had an element of wishful thinking. Teams of detectives had ranged far and wide to run down Bernie, but there had been no actual sightings yet. That he was Irish seemed hardly in any doubt, so it seemed a fair assumption that he might have tried to get back there, although the travellers who could be made to talk at all said that this was not their way. But there were many 'seems', many 'assumptions'. It was not even established fact that his name was Bernie Smith, and if it was . . . well, Smith, for Godsake! There was nothing in his caravan bearing his name, no driving licence, birth certificates for the children, social security documents, anything. For feckless, idle, money-scrounging bastards (and who in the police would question that, if they were talking tinkers?) Bernie Smith's lot took precious little off the State, unless they drew by magic.

The gipsy element had its plus side, though. Despite a 'level of policing' that made the normal PACE infringements look positively benign, no travellers had complained, because they knew no one would listen, because nobody cared. They fought back in their sneaky, offhand way when caravans were searched, illegally and by force, often by stepping up child-damage to police cars and other property, but largely, everything was seen as being normal. Rosser and his colleagues revelled in it, in a minor way. They could do detecting properly, as they saw it, and nobody kicked up. They went in, they did the job, they left. No complaints, nothing in the papers, invisibility. Unfortunately no Bernie Smith, as well. Or any of the other men who had disappeared. But that would change.

One thing that Patten never got from on high, of course, was anything specific to help him with his enquiries. He did get one specific hindrance, however, which he managed to convert to leverage. It was conveyed to him, after a constant drip of pressure by the local establishment élite, that Damon Hegarty was no longer a candidate for investigation. No evidence against him had been found (ran the argument) nor was there any reason in the world to think he would have perpetrated such a deed. Patten, having watched him closely and talked to him on three occasions, tended to agree. His alibis for the times of death were cast-iron, naturally, and the conspiracy idea was improbable in the extreme. Patten saw a man still suffering, occasionally distraught, every inch a grieving widower. Nevertheless, he pretended outrage (which Rosser felt in fact), and achieved as quid pro quo for such 'unwarranted interference' more money and more men, to institute a new search, a leaf-by-leaf, grassblade-by-grassblade going over of ground already covered, in the fields and woods and ditches all around Brook Bank, in the gipsy camps and their environs in a radius of many, many miles. He and Rosser visited the individual searches, occasionally taking a part. The teams were harangued, encouraged, made competitive, rejigged. Tony Hester and George Thwaite, out to do a 'booster' pic and story, were promised that no stone was being left unturned.

'We've even got search warrants out on snail shells,' Sergeant Rosser quipped. 'Given long enough we'll find something, that's guaranteed.'

A self-fulfilling prophecy.

Janis, for her peace of mind, had to get back some certainty in her life. As even Donald Crabbe, MP, could not talk her into Strangeways every day (his representations had of necessity been super-subtle and low key), she decided to go home to Didwell to recharge her batteries. She wondered, as she roared the little Renault down the M1, if being with Bren Hughes was what she was thinking of, but decided before reaching him that it was not. Instead, she did a somewhat crazy thing – and half an hour later phoned Clive Smith from a country pub she knew, twelve miles from Didwell, called The Crooked Billet. Janis had always liked the significance in some pub names, and this was perfect. A crooked billet for a bent enterprise. She booked in for the night, a double room.

She did not tell Clive this directly, but invited him out for a meal. Clive asked no questions, but thought his thoughts, and took the opportunity of checking the register while Janis was in the ladies before they went into the restaurant part. She was not the sort to use a false name, naturally, and there she was, as large as life. To the girl who came back to reception at that moment, Clive merely winked. But he drank without inhibition, and when Janis remarked on it, and the problem of drink-driving, suggested saucily that he should book a room for them, to stay the night. Janis did not give herself away yet, but the few doubts that she had were dwindling. By closing time nothing had been said, but all assumed. As Clive followed Janis up the stairs the girl on reception got a different wink.

This time both of them had drunk quite freely, to a point they each regarded as an optimum. They had talked throughout the evening of the case, with Clive filling her in on the latest police moves, and Janis telling him about Ronnie and hinting at some of her doubts. Clive, bless his socks, had asked her what the hell she had expected, and told her to get back up there and do some rooting. What about his friends? His muckers in the criminal fraternity? The pubs around his home? He gathered from her looks that he had hit some targets, but they both took it as therapy, not criticism – she was far away from home with little back-up. As he closed the bedroom door they were still talking, which struck them at the same moment, and struck them dumb. Then they moved into an embrace that was remarkably relaxed, as if they'd done this sort of thing together a dozen times before, instead of once, an utter failure.

'Do you want to undress me?' Janis asked. 'Last time you took twenty minutes and nearly broke my arm. That was just to get my jacket off.'

'Undress yourself, you lazy bitch,' Clive replied. 'What d'you think I am, your body-slave?'

They undressed themselves, standing and sitting side by side in amicable quiet in the large, old-fashioned room. Janis, in the bad old days, had grown sickened by this sort of thing, casual stripping with an almost unknown man, but this released no fears or even qualms for her, quite the opposite. She dropped her clothes happily to the floor – one blouse, one skirt, one bra, her pants, two shoes – then leaned back on the pillow to watch the show.

'God, you're fat,' she said. 'Why do I fancy you so much?'

He was fat. But apparently, it did not inhibit him at all. He had taken off his tie and shirt first, then unbuckled his trousers and thrust them down over his hips. He was wearing boxer shorts, ridiculous ones, with Popeye and Bluto on them, punching out each other's lights to win fair Olive Oyl. Through the front of them, she was pleased to see, his penis was already protruding, not fully hard, but unbending with a purpose that struck her as pure luxury.

'That's nice,' she said, 'but aren't you going to take them off? Faint heart never won fair lady, ask old Popeye.'

'Socks first, don't you think? Never trust a man who leaves his socks on during intercourse, you don't know what he's got to hide.'

'Two feet?' suggested Janis. 'That would be all right!'

Clive pulled off his socks, then slid the Popeye shorts down like a stripper, stepping out of them then lifting them on one foot to be flicked into a corner of the room. He was pale and gingery, with orange pubic hair and little elsewhere on his body. His prick was hard now, and he walked forward to the bed with it. Janis changed position on the instant, came up onto her knees, leaned forward, took it in her hand and slid its head into her mouth. Clive, his own mouth open, groaned.

'But I have to take it out,' he murmured, leaning down towards her head with his, 'otherwise I'll come immediately, and that would be a bad mistake, Janis, a *baaad* mistake.'

He took her by the neck, one palm on each side, and eased her backwards till her lips released him, glistening with saliva and as sleek and hard as aubergine. Janis's eyes had taken on a dulled and sleepy, druggy look, and she helped him move her body backwards till she lay full out. The bed sagged and creaked as Clive put his knee onto it, shifting her around him so that he could lie on his left side, facing her, turning her to face him, half encircling her small body with his large, pale, fat one. The contrast, in both their eyes, was wonderful, his whiteness setting off her brown, his bulk making her small slimness almost fragile. Janis held his cock again, but carefully, and Clive covered her black, crisp, curly pubic hair with his gigantic hand. His third finger bore down gently, sliding beside her clitoris, and she moved herself against it, very slowly, making the pressure all her own, until she had to move her upper leg along the top of his, up towards his hip, opening the soft gap wider as he spread his gently moving hand.

Clive was very big and Janis rather small, so they manoeuvred themselves very carefully – but never speaking – until his penis was engulfed in the hot wet opening of her vagina. Then, moving very, very slightly, they enfolded each other in their arms, their ankles embracing also, breathing each other's air and touching tongues and lips, but very softly. They did not do much else for quite some time, lay breathing, only an inch of him inside her, while the sensations grew, and changed, diminished, altered, grew again. Then slowly, slowly she took all of him inside her, twisting her body at the waist so that her back was on the bed, raising her left hand to take her nipple between her first and second fingers, teasing and rolling it as she teased and rolled his penis with her internal muscles. Clive put his hand between them, stroked her vulva and her saturated hair, touching himself from time to time, moving himself off hotspots of sensation that were set to make him come, hard inside her, his stomach soft around and over her belly and her hips.

To Janis, coming was like a kettle slowly rising to the boil on a metal hob. Deep inside sensations spread, running through flesh become electric until they reached the outer part of her and fused in Clive's electric hair. She pulled him over onto her, feeling his heavy flesh fall and join with hers, the warm sweat of his chest slide across her small and flattened breasts. She felt him rise upon his toes somehow, lighten himself, and drive the last few millimetres softly hard inside her, the large, pulsating root of him pulling up her lips, dragging each hair, it seemed, upwards with his own. Then he hovered, weightless, as he pulsed into her, and Janis's muscles beat rhythmically

211

with his. She stretched her legs out, arched her back, tore her shoulders open, expelled all air from her lungs.

Then, in a blink, they were a heap of relaxed flesh, wet and gasping, blowing noisily into each other's faces.

'Yum yum,' said Clive. 'Fuck me. Yum yum.'

I needed that, thought Janis. I knew there was something I was lacking, and that was it.

'You're such a fat git, too,' she said, affectionately. She pulled a hank of damp hair off his forehead, out of his eyes. 'Sweaty, fat, obnoxious. I must be crazy.'

'I only agreed to it to get you back on course,' said Clive. 'You've got work to do, remember? Now you've had your fun you've got to concentrate, OK?'

Janis went to sleep unsure if he was joking. She went to sleep in seconds. She did not give a damn.

THIRTY-THREE

The next time she saw Ronnie Keegan, Janis knew she had to seize the opportunity. In the intervening days she had done her digging, assuaged some of her doubts, and – most of all – convinced herself that there was no alternative. Her case was still extremely rickety, but unless she made the leap and gauged his reaction to it, she was going nowhere. As she was conducted down the hot and noisy corridor to the interview, her heart was fluttering, her breathing shallow. What does it matter? she asked herself. If I'm wrong I'm wrong – no book, that's all. But it mattered terribly.

After her night with Clive, Janis had gone home to Didwell genuinely wondering how she would respond to Bren. She told herself, driving with uncharacteristic sedateness down the country lanes, that the 'fling' was probably what she'd needed, and that she'd now be over it – whatever 'it' was. When they'd awoken in the morning, they had not made love again, although she'd still found the mountain of pale flesh beside her quite attractive. Clive had had other considerations – it was late, and he was hungry, and he had no way to shave before going to the office. Janis had tried to tease him about his lack of romance, but he'd not reacted well. Good sex, it would appear, was for the night before: the morning after, it was always work. Hungry as he was, he skipped breakfast; so did she. She would at least catch Bren that way, if he was going working, and that was worth doing fast, before she lost her courage and resolve. If I don't like him, she told herself, if it's still over, I mustn't piss about. Sleeping with Clive was a test-run, maybe, to see if Bren still had to go. But Bren had gone to work, a trip to Nottingham, and his note said he would be back that evening. She dickered as to whether she should go north again, but it was Friday so she had a long, luxurious bath, an enormous breakfast, and a sleep. Then she did some gardening.

The weekend was not bad. Bren was pleased to see her, and had brought back a bottle of champagne just in case she had turned up. He asked her questions and did not mind when she gave scrappy answers, and was quite witty about the boredom and sameness of his week. He avoided whining (even a whining tone) and hardly mentioned Cardiff or his mother. They went to bed quite early and quite drunk and made love quite nicely, Janis thought. His pointed cock was interestingly different from Clive's fat, blunt one, although she realised afterwards that it was the difference that was interesting, not the cock, which saddened her slightly. But she kept her mind off the fat man reasonably well, and came through actuality, not thought-transference, she believed. Wrapped round the long, lean body for a sleepless hour, she did not know if she was happy or dissatisfied, or what she ought to do. When she drove back north on Monday morning nothing was resolved, but Bren clearly thought his sacking had been shelved. It was raining, so Janis could concentrate on keeping up her average in bad conditions. To everything else, her mind was blank.

Ronnie, when he was brought into the room, greeted her with a pleasure that disoriented her still further. In her mind, she had receded him almost forcibly, placed him on a fitting level for a criminal, a suspect, or a monster. He swung in easily, reminding her of a businessman at a conference about to greet a valued associate. Both he and the officer accompanying him were lean, and tall, and bronzed. Of the two of them, the officer was the less at ease, if anything.

'Janis,' he said, 'how nice of you to come! Raining outside? That's Manchester for you. Would you believe I miss it?'

As on the first time, they were left alone, although the door was slightly open and the officer was outside. Janis had worn less formal clothing than before, and was sitting with her legs crossed, waiting. Her handbag had been checked but left to her, and she had a notebook open on her knee, her Bic in hand. To her annoyance, though, her mouth dried slightly. As Ronnie looked at her, almost stared, she had to lick her lips.

'Hot in here,' he said. 'It always is. Never mind, not long now. Are you going to meet me afterwards? Is that the plan? Or are you going to wrap it up inside?'

Janis struggled to retain her supposed advantage. The interviewer's power over the subject. It was not a question that she wanted to answer, yet, not even to herself. There were certain dangers inherent in it, much too close.

'Nothing's settled yet. Quite honestly, in terms of the article, I haven't got much out of you so far.'

He nodded, quite relaxed.

'You've only got to ask, love. You call the shots. But I can promise you, you'd get some good material. A night out on the town with Ronnie Keegan!'

Janis saw an opportunity and went for it, hoping she would not go off half-cock.

'What about your friends? Now that would make an angle, a night out with Ronnie and his friends! Quite honestly, I was hoping you could help me in that area.'

She thought she saw a tension come into his face. Ronnie, who had been leaning backwards, moved closer to the table. He studied her.

'You've got the wrong bloke there,' he said. 'You mean criminals, I take it? But I'm a loner, see? In terms of criminality, I don't have friends. I've found they . . . in my experience . . . well, they fuck things up, excuse the language.'

He stopped, and Janis did not speak. There was definitely a tension in him. She waited.

His face cleared. He leaned further back.

'Anyway, I told you last week when you came. I'm finished with all that. Something to do with Eileen, maybe. Did you speak to her again? When I get out of here this time, I've finished.'

Janis licked her lips once more.

'Eileen did mention friends, actually. She said she used to listen to you planning things. Mickie somebody?'

She saw it strike him, she saw it in his eyes. Ronnie shrugged his shoulders, angled his face away.

'Did she now? Well well.' He turned back to face her, shaking his head. 'Little Eileen earwigging, eh? Wonders will never cease.'

'These friends, though. This Mickie chap, for instance. Could you . . . ?'

'I think he's dead,' he said. 'He ought to be, anyway. Piss

215

artist. Hopeless case. I haven't seen him for . . . oh, a long while.'

Janis gazed in fascination. She'd heard of Mickie from the Conservative Club, not from Eileen. She'd paid twenty pounds in buying drinks, trying not to be too conspicuous and failing miserably. She had not got a surname, nor a date, but Ronnie had had a drink there with Mickie, definitely, in the last couple of months. Mickie who? Mickie the roofer, the pisshead that did tiles.

'Pity,' she said, at last. 'Is there anybody else?'

This time, he pretended to give it some thought. While he pretended, Janis ran her own mind over options. He would be out soon. Maybe he'd never speak to her again. But maybe she had a duty, too, to chuck it in the water and see what sort of a splash it made. Then to go to the police, that dumbcluck Arthur Patten, and try to persuade him that a murderer was about to go off on the loose. If she still thought one was.

'You see, Janis,' said Ronnie, 'you've got the wrong end of the stick, you're barking up the wrong tree, still. You want to understand a criminal, you'll have to take me as I come, listen to me even if it sounds like bullshitting. See, I'm not into all that petty crap, that's a different world. At the risk of sounding swollen-headed, I'm a different class of criminal, we're talking different ballgames. The blokes I used to mix with . . . well . . .'

'Eileen told me where you used to work.' Chuck it in the water, see what sort of splash it made. 'Brook Bank.'

To her astonishment, Ronnie chucked back his head and emitted a bark of laughter, hoarse, explosive. He raised a hand and banged the table, loudly. He stared at her, his face creased with amusement, his eyes as hard as black ball-bearings.

'Go on,' he said. 'Say that again. Are you suggesting what I think you are, you naughty woman? Say that again.'

It was not a threat, his tone was calm, a trifle joshing. He leaned towards her, closer, and the glittering of his eyes was mesmerising.

'You said you knew me, didn't you? I thought about it all over Saturday and Sunday. You were the one that drove into the ditch, you were, weren't you? Good God, and now you think the Good Samaritan's a fucking murderer!'

It was a natural for another burst of laughter, but she noticed he had brought the loudness down, maybe those hard black eyes had strayed slightly in memory of the open door. Now he relaxed, leaned back once more, took up his favourite stance.

'I'm surprised at you,' he chided gently. 'Is that what you really think? Is that what you reckon is a different class of criminal? Is that what Eileen thinks?'

Key question. Of course it wasn't, absolutely no way. She was leading with a lie, and who knows what trouble she was storing up for Eileen? She backtracked fast.

'No it isn't, that's absurd. It's not what I think, either, did I suggest it? I mentioned it because Eileen agreed with what you said. She told me that you had a different view of crime, that you . . . I don't know, you saw things differently, you wanted to break out of it, somehow. Yes, it was me in the ditch! Isn't that extraordinary! I knew I'd seen you somewhere! And you *were* a Good Samaritan!'

'It was a fucking tragedy, the Wilmott thing,' said Ronnie, thoughtfully. 'D'you know, you meet all sorts in this place, all sorts of crazy, vicious bastards. But there's no one I know in here who'd do a thing like that. Animals. Just fucking animals. They ought to bring back hanging, didn't they? At the very least. Hanging's too good for animals like that.'

There was a quiet air to it, a reverential air. Janis dared to say 'So you didn't do it, then?' A bright, defensive smile.

'Thank you,' said Ronnie, quietly sarcastic. 'You shouldn't make a joke of things like that. I knew them, hasn't that occurred to you? I worked for them.'

You got the sack. She did not say it, though. Ronnie sighed.

'We fell out in the end,' he said. 'It was a pity, though, they were a nice old gang. Old Peter in particular, I couldn't believe it when I heard it on the radio. I was in here, you know.' He stopped. He was working something out. His face was puzzled.

'D'you come from down there, then? Maude said you were London. My brief. You're from the *Sunday Times*?'

'I'm a freelance. I get around all over. I was doing some work in the area that week, that's all. Something in Leicester, as I remember. It's just an amazing coincidence, that's all.'

'How did you choose me, then? Where did my name come from? Out of a fucking hat?'

Janis kept her nerve. Neither her eyes nor her voice faltered.

'You'd have to ask the *Sunday Times* that. I think they used the local press agencies, probably going through the files. Probably they were working off the courts and your case came up in Oldham when they were looking for a northern ... connection. When was your case?'

He dismissed it with a gesture. He had brought cigarettes today, and a lighter, which he fiddled with. But he did not smoke.

'Anyway,' he said, 'it was a fucking tragedy. Not meeting you, I mean the Wilmotts. And Eileen's right, it was a way of breaking out of it. I thought we could escape, sort of. You know, get into the country, start up fresh. We could've done it, too, it nearly worked. Maybe next time.'

He flicked the lighter. He seemed slightly down.

'I suppose there won't be a next time with you, though, will there? I suppose you'll drop me, too, when I get out? You'll finish your notes, you'll write up your little article, and you'll bugger off into the wide blue yonder. Goodbye Ronnie, nice to know you, pity you're a bleeding con. Ah well.'

'Not necessarily. I mean ... well, it is pretty much in depth, what I'm doing. There's just a chance it could lead further. You said yourself that I could write a book!'

The smile was back. Questioning, expanding, strangely shrewd.

'I'll be out on Thursday week,' he said.

Their time was up. The prison officer came in, nodding at her, exchanging grins with Ronnie. Ronnie was taken first, then she was escorted down the corridors, through the weird electric 'airlocks' that had replaced some of the huge, old-fashioned doors after the riots, into the open air of Salford. It was drizzling and muggy as she went to see if anyone had vandalised her car.

She had a slight euphoria on her, a sensation that things were going well. Hilary had predicted that he'd call them animals, and he had. It was a queer thing to be elated by, but she was. She dropped the car in the hotel car park and took the lift, whistling under her breath.

As soon as she stepped into her room she knew something was wrong. Someone was in there. As she turned back to get out into the corridor, she heard the cistern flush, followed by footsteps.

'Hallo? Are you back?' called a voice.

It was Buster Crabbe.

THIRTY-FOUR

Janis was coldly furious, and Crabbe just did not understand. He opened the connecting door and stood there smiling while her face went red with anger. She asked him almost incoherently how – and why – he had entered her room, and his smile broadened. He thought that he had been quite smart, and he let her know it. There was an element of fear in Janis's anger that she did not even bother to express: an awareness of how big he was, how tall and strong, how small and weak was she. In the end she turned away and hid it all. But she hated and despised him.

Which from Buster Crabbe's view was a pity. He was in a bold, expansive mood, and fully expected Janis to respond to it. He had brought champagne (it was in the fridge), and there was a bunch of cut flowers waiting for a vase. He had talked to his money men, he said, and they'd come up with a deal for her. He'd thought it time to move the whole thing on, to put some money on the table, then chuck a squib or two into the tale. The only thing he did completely right, in this, was to keep his distance. He was as darkly vigorous as ever, as immaculately turned out, but he did not use his physicality in an oppressive way. Janis found her own space and retreated to it to regroup. For quite a long while, there was silence.

'Well? Doesn't even the money sound attractive? Your month is nearly up, you know. I bet the *Clarion* aren't granting an extension!'

She made a face, but he was right on that score. Her mortgage, Bren or no, was still enormous.

'What do you mean by "chuck a squib", though? The thing's at a critical stage, Donald. I don't want you going in with hobnail boots.'

'There's gratitude. So far I've been the very soul of tact. Aren't you going to ask how much I'm offering? If all goes well, you could be very rich. They'll have the contract done within the week, when there'll be another bottle of champagne. Don't you seriously want to know?'

She was beginning to feel like a sulky schoolgirl, and look like one, no doubt. Janis made a noise of vexation at his face, which was long, duplicitous and keen. What a bastard, what a cheeky man.

'Fifteen K on signature. Just to sign your name. How does that grab you?'

Oh shit. Her legs might just give way. Fifteen *thousand*!

'Fifteen more on delivery of the manuscript, fifteen on hardback publication, fifteen on paperback. And as many dinners with the chairman as you can eat. That's my perk! Janis?'

'That's not six figures. That's sixty thousand. You're a cheapskate.'

If she'd meant it, she'd have impressed herself. Crabbe was not fooled, either.

'Times are harder than I thought. I've argued with the money men, and this time they've won. Accountants rule the world these days, you know. If it goes well you'll make a hundred easily. That's up to you. Publicity, projection, profile.'

'Quality,' she added, faintly. They smiled, together. 'Sorry, how naive!'

'It would be a bonus. Anyway, I'm sure you'll do a marvellous job in that department. The rest can safely be left to me. We're very, very strong in the areas that count. Well, do you accept? Champagne in order now?'

Christ, she thought, as he walked boldly to her fridge. Sixty thousand quid. Before he popped it, Crabbe opened a huge black briefcase and took out two crystal flutes, wrapped in tissue paper. Jesus Christ.

'To guilt,' he said. They were standing, both holding foaming glasses. 'And exploration of a twisted mind. Have you got a title yet? I thought *The Twisted Maze* was rather good.'

She would not say 'to guilt'. She clinked her glass with his, felt hunted, said 'to us, the future' hurriedly, and drank. 'Yes, *The Twisted Maze*. Yes, I like that, I'll think that over.'

'Janis, relax. This is your moment, this is great. Take a mouthful, swallow it, chuck it down.'

'Quaff,' said Janis. 'To quote my Uncle Norman. I'm sorry, it's . . . well, sixty thousand pounds. Are you sure!'

'Never surer. A snip at twice the price. I take it you are, by the way? Sure about the guilt aspect? No more worries on that score?'

'Well, as far as one can be.' She laughed. 'No, I'm pretty confident, which sounds even worse!'

'What about the alibis? I take it you've been digging? Has anything else collapsed underneath the strain?'

'Not yet. I've taken it quite slowly, Ronnie Keegan first. Like I said, two sentences from him might have screwed the whole thing up. I'm sure the police will get there in the end, it can't be much longer before they finally admit they're up the creek with Hegarty and his band of loyal gipsies. I can only push but when they start, they'll shove.'

'I don't have your faith in their intelligence,' said Crabbe. 'In fact, I think it's time we helped them on a bit. One of the squibs I mentioned. I'm going to name him in the House.'

He said it so casually that it did not register at first.

'What?' asked Janis. 'How do you mean?'

'You're a journalist, you've heard of Parliamentary privilege. I'm going to name your Ronnie as the Brook Bank murderer. In jail already for receiving, while the police play games as usual. That should concentrate their minds.'

She was aghast.

'But why? Donald, you can't! It will blow me and my book right out of the water!'

'How do you make that out? If your theory is correct? Maybe I'm testing it to destruction, Janis – before I part with fifteen thousand pounds!'

She drank champagne now not for celebration but for the mental jolt. She drained the glass.

'OK,' she said, 'but listen. If you do that, I'm telling you what will happen. In the short term his house and girlfriend will be mobbed, besieged. Other members of his gang, assuming he's got one, will go to ground. I'm following up one, now. You name him in the House and that's that, isn't it?'

Crabbe, with deliberation, refilled his glass. He offered the bottle but she shrugged rejection, angrily.

'Much more seriously,' she went on, 'as soon as Ronnie hears it, that's me out. All my subterfuge, all my lies – do you think he's completely stupid? At the moment he still thinks I live in

London and I came on him by some lucky accident. I *think* that's what he thinks, although I'm not so sure. The moment you tell the truth I'm finished. With him, with Eileen, with Maude Wimlock, all of them. They'll never say another *word* to me!'

Infuriatingly, he was smiling at her, through hooded eyes.

'I don't see why not. If you're right he'll want to talk about it, these people always do. You've read the books, Janis, the bum-boys boiled down for dogfood, the serial disembowellers, the weird brigade, your most likely problem will be the size of cut he's after. And if you're wrong he'll be even keener to spill the beans, he'll want to give me a bloody nose because he couldn't get me in the libel courts, he'll want to put the record straight.'

'But he'll go to someone else! He'll think I've betrayed his trust!'

'Betrayed his trust! He's a bloody monster! So talk him round, you know him, you've got some sort of relationship already, haven't you? Flash those lovely thighs at him!'

Before she could express her fury, Buster Crabbe held up his hand, laughing to take the sting away from it.

'OK, OK, bad joke! But there's a much more serious point behind all this. Assuming Keegan is your man, what happens when he gets outside in ten days time, or whenever? If you know he's the murderer, or you've got damned good grounds to think he is, what does it make you if you let him out without warning anyone? What if he kills again? I'm a politician, Janis, I've got to bear these things in mind. One of the filthiest and most unpleasant murderers of recent years free to rape and murder more old ladies, free to target his next victims and I don't mention it to anyone? You're on safer ground because at least you tried to tell them weeks ago, before you'd spoken to the man, but now you have, and you've done your level best to convince me that you're right. They'd have my guts for garters. They'd finish me.'

'But would they know you were involved? How would they?' God, that sounded cynical, more cynical than Crabbe. 'Donald,' she went on, slightly changing tack, 'we don't know that he's guilty, do we? I'm confident I'm right but I don't *know*. What if he isn't, what happens to him then? If you name him in Parliament he's got no redress. Surely we can't ruin him until we're sure?'

Crabbe was losing patience.

'Are you worried for him or for your project?' he asked, cruelly. 'If you think he didn't do it, what *is* your part in this? You know he's guilty, Janis, and the main thing is to get it shifting, change into another gear, before he's on the street again. The police are in limbo, they've got to get on track. Think of the publicity! I'll make sure that everybody knows it's you who's done the groundwork, and it'll be an even bigger selling point when the book comes out. Articles as well, the papers will be fighting to sign you up. Believe me, Janis—'

'Believe *me*, Buster, if you do this there won't be a book. No book, no articles – no me, probably! If you name Keegan he'll never speak to me again. I'm there on trust, don't you understand? You're going to ruin it.'

Metaphorically, they both retrenched. They were three feet apart and they both moved back slightly. Crabbe rested one buttock on a sofa-back.

'It's a lot you're asking me,' he said. 'Think of all those lovely headlines I won't get. "MP names the guilty man". "Police in dock over Brook Bank delay". You're a hard woman, Janis Sanderson.'

It was a joke to him, a bloody joke. Despite herself, she almost had to laugh.

'It's not a lot to ask. I just want to let it bubble on a bit, until I've got everything I want and need from Ronnie. I just don't want a spanner chucking in the works.'

'I'll tell you what I'll do,' he said. 'I don't think you entirely appreciate the point I'm making about going public before the lunatic kills someone else, but I won't get up on my back legs and throw his name around in Parliament. I'm going to arrange a meeting with the Home Office, though, and tip them off in private. Also with a strong hint that it isn't going to be a secret very long because there's someone with more nous than our useless police force working on it, although naturally I won't mention you by name. That way we kill two birds, we get it moving and we cover our own backs if he comes out and murders someone else. That way, we stay in the clear.'

'Except that if he ever finds out, I'll be the one he murders. I'm beginning to wonder if fifteen K's enough.'

So she could see the funny side as well. He raised his glass, as if in acknowledgement.

'Fifteen's only the beginning. Where shall we eat tonight? Have you found the best places in this dismal city yet?'

They were alone in a hotel bedroom, with a king-size bed. They were talking big money and drinking good champagne. In Crabbe's bright eye, there was hope and expectation.

'Donald,' she said, 'you can eat wherever you damn well like. I don't take kindly to men who trick their way into my hotel room, however many thousand pounds they're talking. I don't get bought.'

He chuckled.

'You mean, I should have brought the contract, I suppose . . .'

The second weapon turned up in a ditch beside a minor road that ran past an empty field. It was found by a policeman almost at the end of a shift that had consisted, mainly, of grovelling in filth. At first he thought it was a piece of wood, and he'd already formed a curse to utter. Then, even through his gloves, he recognised its smoothness and jerked it from the mud. A gun butt, then the action, then two barrels, sawn short and not quite even. He wiped the slime off carefully. Not very rusty, still slightly oiled in places.

At the laboratory, the gun man told Lance Rosser it was a Spanish 12-bore, mass produced, about twelve to twenty years old. Rather a cheap gun, he thought, the sort of thing bought by a man who was not a serious sport, more a dabbler after rabbits and other suchlike pests. For once, such speculation did not interest Rosser, because he already had its serial number, and its make, even its date of purchase, on one of the computers in the incident room, there remained no doubts. Whatever Peter Wilmott's chosen targets may have been, this had been his gun. Unfortunately, it bore no useful fingerprints, nor signs of recent firings, nothing to excite the scientists. Francis Brady, the firearms expert, wanted to show interest, though, to be polite.

'You must be pleased,' he said. 'Where did they find it?'

Lance Rosser glanced at the docket in his hand. He shook his head.

'It's a bit obscure,' he said.

THIRTY-FIVE

Professor Swale laughed like a drain when Janis told her of her hotel duel with Buster Crabbe. She gave her half marks for not knowing it was coming, and full marks for surviving it intact. The next fight would be harder, she reckoned – actually to get her hands on any cash.

Janis, on her hotel telephone, was taken aback by this.

'Are you joking? Oh for God's sake, Hilary, he's not a crook as well, is he? Next you'll be telling me he's not a publisher at all!'

Another gurgle up the line from London.

'The very opposite. He is a publisher, ergo a rogue. He'll pay up in the end, I expect, but you'll have some hoops to jump through yet. He didn't have the contract with him, did he? Although he said, no doubt, that everything is set? He'll want his pound of flesh, Janis. Do I have to spell out which pound that might be?'

Joking aside, though, they agreed that it was quite a deal, in fact. Janis, naturally, had cold feet about her ability to deliver, but Hilary did not. She should treat it as an exercise in journalism, she said, abnormally extended. Chop it into interesting sections, then elucidate each one in plain and simple language.

'That's what I did,' she insisted, 'and look at me. It's the subject that matters, and you've got a dilly. Has our Ronnie shown any signs of cracking, yet?'

They talked about his, and Janis's, reactions for an hour or more, during which she was well aware that she was holding back. She told Hilary that Ronnie had asked her twice if they would meet up after his release, and that she had demurred, but she could not admit that there was some other element, some fascination that both made her want to, and made her want to run a mile. The nearest she got to admitting anything

227

was expressing her surprise at his charisma and his self-image as a special sort of criminal.

'That's interesting,' said Hilary, 'but it's really not a great surprise. Most murderers I've met have had a lot about them, as they say where I come from. That's the oddball ones, not the ones who've beaned the wife a bit too vigorously. I think they spend a lot of time going over things once the guilt gets to them. They either accept that they've done something unacceptable, or they rationalise it away. Both routes tend to make them seem quite bright. Which way is Ronnie going, do you think?'

'Well he's not eaten with remorse, whatever else! Sometimes I get a shiver down my spine, in case I'm completely wrong. If he doesn't *think* he's innocent, he's a damn good actor. Does that mean that he is?'

The question was unanswerable, and anyway she was sure, deep down, however far away he was from feeling guilt. Professor Swale exhorted her to 'keep the faith', and to definitely agree to meet him after his release – if the police did not rearrest him on the spot. She warned, too, that Buster Crabbe was almost guaranteed to blow the gaffe quite soon, and would do his utmost to take all the credit – 'therefore, march on!' Janis told her she was expecting to be given an address next morning, a key address, and would keep her well informed. Suddenly, and instantly regretting it, she added: 'I find him rather sexy, Hilary. I mean . . .'

There was a tiny pause.

'My dear, I rather gathered that. Be careful, won't you, Janis? Please?'

In some strange way, her meeting with Mick Renwick and his wife was a relief. She came away from it shaken, but with something confirmed that was very important and very basic. She came away feeling that she had at last met people in the case who fitted everything she had expected all along. Most importantly, she had recognised a rage, a hatred, that seemed so yawningly lacking in Ronnie Keegan, a rage that could sustain a human being through the bloody violence that must have taken place the night the Wilmott household died. She sat in the Renault afterwards, buffeted by a gale-force northeaster full of stinging rain, and thought she understood.

Noonsun, for summertime, had put on a classic for her. Bill Stift, her Oldham contact, had come good with the address in the morning, warning her not to leave her car on the estate if it was half-decent. Janis had driven from Manchester in moderate wind and rain, but was in a downpour by the time she crawled under Mumps railway bridge, and down to fifteen miles an hour on the straight as she began the long climb out of the town. When she reached Noonsun there was no question of leaving the car on the main road and walking into the estate, as she had planned to do, because the rain was blowing off the moors in horizontal sheets, the gutters and even the roads running like troubled rivers. There were no people about, few lights in any of the dull windows that were not boarded up, and she did not think that anyone would bother risking getting drowned to scratch her paint or see if she had a radio worth nicking. In fact, she did not care. With her A to Z she found the street and house, stopping fifty yards short to have a study. It was a depressing prospect in every way.

Janis killed her lights and thought. The drumming of the rain and tearing howl of the wind increased her sense of lonely isolation until it was almost fear. Hers was the only vehicle in the street except for two derelicts, one burnt out, which in itself she found amazing. She guessed that in a street of maybe twenty houses, maybe thirty, only about six were occupied, although judging was difficult because they might have been maisonettes. Some had upstairs windows missing, frames and all, while two within her sight had been fired and abandoned. It was the sort of estate that she only knew existed from the TV news, part of the economic miracle, and she knew from the same source that there might be danger here.

She looked over the moorland, down the long, shallow valley that was startlingly enlightened by a large patch of sunshine breaking through the cloud and rain, a patch that rushed towards her. It was as if she were in a ship, on a wild and wasted sea, facing a devastating squall. The mean, sodden houses crouched before the onslaught. What lunatic had put them there?

Janis changed her mind, even about the fifty yards. When

the sun gave way to dark again, she drove slowly along to stop outside the house. Giving herself no time for thought or panic, she pushed open her door, slammed and locked it, and scurried up the pathway, through the empty gatehole in the sagging fence, to the faded red front door. There was no knocker and no bell so she hammered with the heel of her hand, the rain flooding through her lightweight raincoat and pouring down her neck and legs. A catch turned instantly and the door burst backwards in the wind, bowling a small boy along the passage-way where he banged into a pushchair. He stood upright, face crumpling, as the wind roared through, pushing a wave of water a yard into the house from where it had gathered in a puddle behind the door. The boy was wearing a tee shirt, nothing else.

Inside the house, a woman shouted something, let out a squawk of incomprehensible anger. Another door burst open and she came out like a large white animal from its lair, she scuttled with amazing speed. Janis saw a hand raised, heard a bang, watched the boy fall tangled in the buggy then bounce up and disappear behind this woman's legs, almost as fast as she had come. To Janis, it was like a show, a silent film, a comedy. Except there were no laughs in it, remotely. The woman's face now turned to her, then flushed and paled and crumpled like her son's had done, all in a brief moment. She gaped.

'What do you want? Who are you? Oh Christ.'

Another gust, more violent and sustained, was blowing solid rain into the passage, almost blowing Janis along it like a piece of rubbish. Through the open inner door there was a wail of babies, the booming of TV. Janis stepped through the front door and fought it closed behind her, until the catch clicked. The woman watched, sulky and defeated. It occurred to Janis that she was probably used to such invasions, from the middle classes.

'You a social worker, are you? Where's Andrea? Seanie's got a cold, he couldn't go to school. I told Andrea he was coming down with it, you ask her.'

'I'm not a social worker, you needn't worry, I've never heard of Andrea. I'm from the *Sunday Times*.'

'I don't worry,' said Fat Marie, a verbal gesture of routine defiance. 'They can fuck theirselves for all I care. What d'you mean, the *Sunday Times*?'

The question was so bizarre that Janis was at a loss. She became aware of cold water on her back, her legs chilling. She became aware of a smell in the house, and a dirtiness. She took in the sight of the woman properly for the first time, and felt some satisfaction. This was it, the bottom rung, the pits. The woman was not like Eileen Thorpe, and she could bet that Mick Renwick was not like Ronnie. She had found the real thing, and she could believe. It was a brief insight of pure prejudice, but she took advantage of it. She knew how the police must feel, when they met such people, had to deal with them. The dregs.

'I'm from the press,' she said. 'The newspapers. I've been doing something on Ronnie Keegan and he mentioned your husband's name. You are Mrs Renwick, aren't you?'

Fat Marie, to Janis Sanderson, looked like a nightmare. She was five feet three, weighed at a guess twelve stone, and had on a short green skirt that did not fully cover her white thighs. She stood splay-legged, her knees encased in fat above grotesquely enlarged calves. Her feet were like two shaven pugs jammed into fluffy mules, the toes bulbous and deformed by pointed shoes. Above the waist she could have been pregnant, massively, her belly and enormous breasts pushing at the front of a lemon blouse. Her arms were bare, covered with pale bruises where they disappeared into the tight armholes. On one of the thighs, peeping out from the uneven skirt hem, Janis had seen a newer mark, black and violent. To her surprise, she felt no sympathy. In fact, she felt intense dislike.

The face was worst. It was like a pudding, white and puffed and stupid, framed in lank black hair. There were emotions showing on it, fighting for the upper hand. Fear, confusion, possibly aggression. Marie, quite clearly, did not know what she should say.

Janis did. She said crisply: 'I've been talking to Ronnie inside Strangeways. He said he and your husband did some jobs together. He said they did a job the night before he went to prison this last time. Is that correct?'

There was adrenalin pumping inside her, making her almost dizzy. Her daring made her breathless, the speed and distance she had gone out on a limb. She had gone to the house in hope, but little expectation. She had hoped to have a general conversation, from which to draw hypotheses. She felt now she might overwhelm this dreadful woman into a confession, a revelation that would be shattering.

Fat Marie, indeed, was quivering, her eyes closed, her hands outstretched and open, a look of anguish on the pale, fat face.

'Get out,' she said. 'You've got to go. Get out. Get out. Get out.'

'It's true, isn't it?' Janis demanded. 'Ronnie and Mick went out that night, didn't they? How was he when he came back home? Tell me!'

Suddenly, Fat Marie threw back her head and screamed: 'Fuck off! Fuck off! Fuck off, you stupid cow! Fuck off!'

The noise level in the house was already extraordinary. Behind the door the little boy had disappeared through, the television was bellowing, with childish shouts and screams punctuating it occasionally. But Janis stepped backwards at the force of Marie's yell, actually afraid. Fat Marie then came towards her, eyes open and glaring, both hands raised in fists.

'You fucking mad?' she screeched. 'You want to fucking get me killed, you bitch? Fuck off! Fuck off! Fuck off!'

Above them, up the stairs, a man's voice was raised, angry but inarticulate. Marie stopped coming forward, the colour draining from her face. Her hands dropped to her sides.

'Now look,' she said, hopelessly.

'Marie! What's going on down there?' The note rose, in rage. 'What's fucking going on?'

'Get out,' she whispered urgently. She shouted up the stairs: 'Nothing, it's the social! You get back to sleep!'

She forged towards Janis, who backed off almost frantically, horrified at the prospect of being touched. Upstairs there was a crash, the sound of feet.

'I'll fucking kill you! What's fucking going on!'

Mick Renwick appeared on the landing, tiny and brown, emanating waves of violent anger Janis could almost feel. She was fascinated, frightened, but able to note that he wore only a pair of underpants. He sleeps in underpants, she thought, just like they do in TV plays.

'She's just going!' Fat Marie's voice had risen to a thin, high squawk. She knocked Janis to the wall, reaching past her. The door flew open on the wind, a cold, wet gust burst upon them, soaking them, the walls, the floor.

Mick was halfway down the stairs, swaying as he held the banister. His eyes were glaring, in contorted features. Fat Marie was shoving at her, pushing her against the wind and rain.

'Fuck off,' she said, over and over again. 'Fuck off, fuck off, fuck off, fuck off.' Before Janis was out, the door began to close on her, Marie's fat body driving it against the wind. Over her shoulder she could see Mick descending, his face insane with rage. 'Fuck off, fuck off, fuck off.'

The voice was low, almost gibbering, and what she could see of Fat Marie's face was closed in terror now. When the door slammed, Janis stood in the driving, freezing rain, wondering what would happen to her. Inappropriately, she was engulfed by a wave of sympathy, followed by self-disgust. Too late, she thought, too late.

Behind the door, despite the raging wind, she heard the first blow land, but did not dare to knock. After half a minute she turned and went back to her car, already soaked right through to the flesh in every part. She sat for another minute before starting the engine. She put the heater up to full, the booster fan as well.

Oh Christ, thought Janis. How the other half lives. The poor, appalling, bitch.

But the relief came not much later, because at last she had recognised in Mick Renwick's rage something she could under-stand, something that cut through the mystery she had found in Ronnie Keegan. It was a rage engendered by a position on the scale, maybe, but it was a rage that was murderous. She had recognised class hatred in herself inside the house, but Mick's was different. Mick Renwick's rage was murderous.

Janis, because she was so sure now, decided to go home. She returned to her hotel to have a bath and change her clothes, then she sat on her bed sipping a whisky and ginger for some few minutes, looking at the telephone. She wanted to ring Clive, quite simply (she told herself) to ask him what to do. She was sure, she was as certain as she could ever be, that she knew the murderers. And she did not have the foggiest where to move.

It was Crabbe, of all people, who had wakened her to her dilemma. His talk of public duty was quite spurious, she guessed – although she might have been doing him wrong, at that – but the expression of it had lodged somewhere in her mind. Now that she had no doubts left, she knew she had to convince other people, to make the police break out of their predetermined path, to get Mick Renwick safely arrested, at the very least. But not Crabbe's way, that was completely wrong. An announcement in the House, naming Ronnie Keegan, would . . . what? Quite honestly, she could not imagine, but it could not be good. She had met Mick now, she had seen and heard him. He must not be warned, and primed.

Patten then, or Rosser? Perhaps she should ring them first, and try to organise a meeting? She could picture the superintendent's eyes, cold and peculiar, and his sergeant's hotter, crueller ones. Neither of them liked her, neither of them would listen without prejudice, whyever should they? From the start she had got up their noses, and she had no doubt at all that Crabbe's latest moves, however 'secret', would be easily traced to her, possibly already were being. However they reacted, it would not be with an open mind.

In the end, though, she decided it was better to approach the police directly than to try through Clive. Even if he came up with something not involving her, he was the *Clarion* – specific, concrete, with an axe to grind. Like all authority, Arthur Patten and his cohorts wanted to use the media, not to trust them or be helped by them. She had to phone them as an individual, a 'citizen', and make them understand her new disinterest. Even as she dialled the number, she did not believe that it would work.

But Superintendent Patten was not there. She assumed at first that she was being fobbed off by the switchboard, but Lance Rosser was also absent. Put through to the incident room she explained a little, and said she had vital information for the super or his sergeant, but no one else. There was an attitude of 'suit yourself' discernible down the line, and what sounded like a party going on. When she persisted, the voice got rapidly impatient.

'Listen, duck,' it said, 'you're flogging a dead horse. The Boss has gone to Wales, and so has Sergeant Rosser. Who are you, anyway?'

'Wales? What for?'

'On his bloody holidays, you cheeky bitch! Why don't you ring back in the morning?' He gave a loud guffaw. 'Or watch the TV news!'

The phone went down, and Janis then rang Clive. He was not at his desk, but he was in the building somewhere, should they find him? Developments? In the Brook Bank case? Nobody knew of anything.

She put the phone down and finished off her whisky. She was going back.

THIRTY-SIX

The foul weather in the north of England spread southwards throughout the morning, and reached its nadir in the mid-Wales mountains. Patten and Rosser, who had set off in their powerful unmarked car in sunshine, were caught up by light rain near the border, and within half an hour were driving in torrents of wind-blown water. To make it worse, the roads deteriorated the farther on they went, the farther away they got from England, centre of the universe. Both being English they failed to see the irony, and cursed the Welsh, instead, for their appalling roads. Only by sharing the driving, resting eyes fatigued by headlight glare and wipers permanently on top speed, could they keep up an average that almost suited them. For this, and other reasons, they did not talk a lot.

The pressure that had come down on Arthur Patten since Crabbe had turned the heat up had been harsh and quite specific. This time the Home Secretary had been less inclined to shrug it off, because of the unsettling suggestion that subordinates may have left his back uncovered to a missile of enormous power that was airborne and accelerating. Crabbe named the name, outlined the story, and gave the strongest recommendation – short of guaranteeing it personally – that it should be taken as the truth. He also hinted that certain newspapers were on to it, and would not wait long before going public with some garbled stuff or other. Which was true, in part, because he had spoken to his favoured contacts with a promise of something in the air ('exclusive!') that he'd give them in detail when the time was ripe. The Home Secretary, recognising potential scandal, acted quickly to speed responsibility down the line, while letting it be known that somebody had blundered and he wanted blood. It said much for Patten's strength of character that he responded with pure anger when the buck reached him, rather than with fear or doubt.

'It's bollocks, that's why!' he shouted. 'I beg your pardon sir,

I'm a policeman, not a politician, you'll have to put up with the language. It's a load of bollocks!'

His face was white with fury, while the face across the desk was brick red. Cyril Hetherington had been shouted at in his turn by Sir Kenneth Baily, Regional Inspector of Constabulary.

'How is it bollocks?' he roared. 'Have you got anybody else? What have you come up with? Nothing!'

'You know we have! We've come up with names, locations, weapons! I know who's been fostering this Keegan nonsense and I've wasted dozens of man hours just to shoot it down! The man's in prison, and he's in the clear! It's moonshine, sir!'

The vehemence of his response calmed Hetherington to some extent. He knew from his contacts that Crabbe was behind all this, and Crabbe was said to be a liar and a fool. More calming still, he knew he had a scapegoat in his sights – indeed, he had him in his office. If he was wrong, Patten's head would roll.

More reasonably, he said: 'Patten, I don't want a fight on this, believe you me. I hate outside interference in your work even more than you do. I'll back you all the way, as you well know. But we must look into every possibility, don't you see? We've got to guard our backs.'

Patten's grey eyes were glittering with contempt. He saw the man opposite him as a lump of lard, huge, self-satisfied, self-serving. You'll guard mine while it's safe, and then you'll stab me in it, he thought. You smug bastard.

'We can't,' he said. 'Beyond a certain point there's nothing we can do. I tell you Keegan's in the clear, and you'll just have to take my word for it. I tell you we've got good, solid evidence pointing to one man, and you'll have to trust me there as well.'

'Where is he, then?' cried Hetherington, passionately. 'Where is your bloody man? And what about the others you picked up? We can't leave them to rot in jail forever, we've got to move!'

They stared at each other, both breathing hard, as if they had stepped across a hidden boundary line. Patten's voice was firm and quiet.

'I think when we get Bernie Smith they'll tumble like a house of cards,' he said. 'It's just a waiting game.'

Hetherington flapped a large, soft hand, a gesture of frustrated irritation. He doesn't want to drop me, Patten thought – but of course, if necessary . . .

Hetherington told him brusquely: 'You'll have to reinvestigate the Keegan angle. I do trust your judgement, Patten, but some things are unavoidable. Can you do that for me?'

Some request! It flashed through Patten's mind simply to refuse, an instant way of getting off the hook. Off the case and off the favoured list, as well. They wouldn't kick him out, but they might as well do, for the future.

'If it's an order, sir. I don't have any alternative, do I? But I have to tell you that I haven't got the men to do it right away. At the moment—'

Hetherington's colour rose dangerously. He interrupted, hot with anger.

'At the moment, Mr Patten, your head is on the block, just think about it, will you? You can leave me now to work out the logistics. If you still decide you haven't got the men, just pick up the phone and let me know. I will give you half an hour after that to clear your desk. Do you understand?'

Five minutes later, as Patten was reaching for his own phone to call in Rosser and send him off to Manchester, it rang. It was a Chief Inspector Williams in South Wales, a town Patten had heard of but did not know. A town called Fishguard, a ferry port to southern Ireland, as the officer explained. Ten minutes after that, Patten had a second interview with Hetherington, to obtain twelve hours grace. He would go to Manchester himself, he said, if this lead dwindled out, but he had high hopes of it, high hopes indeed. Hetherington, determined only to end up on the winning side, gave him his blessing.

It was mid-afternoon when they reached Fishguard, having been held up for two hours in the mountains by flash floods, but Elfed Williams might have been looking out of the window for them given the speed at which he turned up in the HQ yard. He was a big, fat smiling man, who seemed to have no malice in him, not even the routine malice policemen usually bring to bear on interlopers to their patch.

'D'you want a piss, boys?' he cried, shaking Patten's hand and nodding to the sergeant. 'Oh you'll enjoy this bastard I've got lined up for you! Mine's a double brandy, sir, when the time comes!'

Patten decided to be amused by the lack of deference to his rank, and let the fat inspector hustle him back into the car, while a Panda backed out of a parking slot to take up station in front of them, as guide.

'That's Evans, sergeant, follow him, OK? It's about five miles, we've put him in a lock-up near the campsite, just in case. Fucking gipsies, deh? Slippery as a bag of jellied eels!'

The roads were wet, but clear of water, and bathed in harsh bands of fleeting sunshine now. Elfed Williams – 'pronounce it with a V, boys, we're a queer lot down yer' – explained that one of his brighter men had spotted their target coming off the Rosslare boat.

'That's what I call clever, see? Anyone could have picked up someone on his *way* to Ireland, but my lad worked it out the other way. He had gippo writ all over him, he said – a gippo without wheels! Well, that's suspicious, isn't it? Fucking genius, fair play!'

Patten did not suppress a grin, which the big Welshman appreciated. His excitement was infectious if you let it be, and even Rosser, tired and a little grumpy, could feel his mounting, helped by the cracking pace that Evans kept up on the narrow country roads. As they passed a small and ragged gipsy site, Williams pointed to it.

'That's where my boy trailed him to,' he said, 'then he came back for a conflab with the local bobby and they kept an eye on things until we decided to move in. Six o'clock this morning, we hit the button! Oh, real police work, sergeant, you'd have enjoyed that, deh! We cracked some bloody skulls!'

At the next village there was a police house with a secure room, a relic of the days of slow communication in the wilderness behind the coast. Rosser, his temper forgotten, held the car door open for Williams with a tense grin of anticipation, and all three of them stood for a moment, unspeaking but communing, before going in. A thin constable opened the front door as they approached, his face hiding his curiosity rather badly. Williams touched his arm.

'Superintendent Patten, this is Constable Rhys Lloyd. He's the cunt you'll have to kick if he got it wrong, OK?' He squeezed the young man's arm. 'Well done, boy, well done!'

They walked quickly down a passageway to a heavy wooden

door with studs and a protruding iron key, which the constable seized and turned. Inside, the room was dim and bare, lighted only by a square barred window with heavy frosted glass. On a chair sat a small and skinny man, his face sharp as a rat's, his clothes, his hair, his colouring yelling Irish tinker at the new arrivals. The policemen – Patten and Rosser, Elfed Williams and the nervous Lloyd – moved into a line around him, staring. He glanced up at them once, then down to the wooden floor, uninterested, stoical. He had dried blood on his mouth and a blackened eye.

Patten cleared his throat.

'Are you Bernie Smith? You know what I'm here for, don't you?'

'And if I am him,' replied the rat-faced man, 'I didn't do no murders, sir, and that's the dear God's truth.'

Lance Rosser walked across and punched him in the face. The man fell to the floor and lay there, looking up at them. He did not make a sound.

'He needs a fucking good kicking, sir,' said Rosser. 'Anybody want a go?'

'Leave it,' said Patten. 'Don't dirty your hands.'

There was an odd look on his face. He felt elated, wonderfully elated. Relieved.

'I'd like a cup of tea,' he said to PC Lloyd. 'I'd just absolutely love a cup of tea.'

Now that he was certain, Patten did not hang about. The first news of the new arrests was on the radio by six o'clock, and Janis, flying down the M1 at eighty-five, almost left the carriageway in her attempt to slew across three lanes into a services. She tried Clive at the Granby first, but the *Clarion* crew had gone back to the office, she was told. Mary Faircloth answered on the newsdesk, and they swapped the basic facts in high excitement: Bernie Smith arrested in South Wales, and two more gipsies picked up in Northamptonshire, some hours later, on information received. The place was popping, they were going to work all night to do a special in the morning, was she on her way?

'What are the charges?' shrieked Janis. 'For God's sake, Mary!'

But it was Clive now on the line.

'Where are you? Get your arse back here immediately, if not sooner! Oh baby, is Patten ever going to make you eat his shit!'

'Fuck off!' she shouted. 'Please Clive, don't be an arsehole, just for once! What are the charges, it can't be true, it can't!'

'Not yet announced! But it'll be murder, count on it! Tony's got some great stuff on the side, although we can't confirm it officially. They've got the shotguns, Janis! Two of them! From Brook Bank!'

Oh no, she thought. Oh no, it can't be true.

'Get this!' said Clive. 'Know where they found them? In the fucking caravan! Bernie Smith, this Mick itinerant! Oh babe . . .'

Janis stared out across the service area, crammed with cars and lorries, caravans and coaches, and it all seemed almost monochrome.

'But you've got to laugh, though, haven't you?' he said.

There was humour and elation in his voice, but at the story, really, not her discomfiture. On top of all, he was impatient.

'We need you, love,' he said. 'Where are you now, I need you on the team. It's only coming out now, the TV news will just be factual, the dailies won't get their troops in action properly till tomorrow. We're going to slay 'em in the morning, we're going to do a special that'll sweep the fucking board. Janis – come!'

But Janis was not going. She watched the unit indicator on her phone card flicking rapidly to zero, and she told Clive she would ring him later on. He pleaded and he threatened, but she did not answer. She pushed out of the phone kiosk feeling lower than she'd ever felt before.

You bastard, Ronnie Keegan, she told herself. I know you did it, I just bloody know.

She wondered if these services had a road bridge that would take her to the other side, to get back on the northern carriageway.

I know you did it, Ronnie, she repeated in her head. I'm going to bloody ask you, aren't I?

I wonder if they'll let me in, first thing?

THIRTY-SEVEN

It took Donald Crabbe, MP, until seven twenty-five next morning to cajole or intimidate the switchboard at Janis's hotel to put him through to her. The jangling bell caught her in the middle of a deep, untroubled sleep that had come after a night of dreams and bouts of twitching fear. Time after time she had dozed off, exhausted, to be woken by the presence of Ronnie Keegan, unseen but very real, who had come at her smiling in her nightmares. His face was wide and innocent, hurt, beseeching – and twisted with deceitful triumph. It took her several seconds to adjust to Crabbe's insistent voice.

'It's Crabbe, yes Crabbe,' he repeated, angrily. 'I've been trying to get you since eight o'clock last night. What's going on, Janis? You owe me an explanation, fast.'

Janis, cushioned by her tiredness, felt dull contempt and nothing more.

'I was out. Checking up on things. Look, it's seven thirty, Donald.'

'Yes, and in half an hour or so people are going to be on at me for explanations. You've dropped me in it, haven't you? I've been humiliated, totally exposed.'

How did he think she felt, for God's sake? She'd kill the switchboard, she'd told them no calls, nothing under any circumstances. She moved in the big bed, noting that the sheets were damp. What a night.

'Forgive me laughing,' she replied, 'but you're not back at your public school, you know. I'm not your fag, or something. If you want to talk to me, you can damn well be polite, or I'll put the fucking phone down. Got it?'

She could hear him breathing down the line. Fast, uneven.

'And anyway, how dare you say that I exposed you? What to? Have they been charged yet? What are their names?'

'Of course they've been charged, they were charged last night. Haven't you even been following the news?'

Too well I have. Too well.

'Have they been charged with murder? If not, stop going on at me. I'm not interested in possessing firearms, or burglary, or any other crap, have they been charged with murder?'

'Later today, is my information. There's a press conference and they'll probably announce it then. Confessions too, they've practically admitted it already. They will have done by ten o'clock, won't they? Or tea time? Or tomorrow morning? How long do you think it takes?'

'What are you saying, that they'll beat it out of them? Is that inside information, too?'

'Let's just say they know they have their men,' snapped Crabbe. She could tell that she had needled him. 'My information is that the case is watertight, and it'll be cast iron before it goes to court. Quite frankly, Janis, it hardly matters any more who's right, does it? They will be charged with murder, and my detractors will be beside themselves with glee. If you have a taste for bathetic understatement, I trusted you, I backed you, and you've dropped me in the shit, headfirst.'

'So it's a good job I never got the contract, isn't it?'

There was a pause. She tried to picture Crabbe's hawklike face. Head on one side, the raptor's beady gaze.

'Where is it, Donald, eh? And tell me why I should give a toss for you and your humiliation.'

'It's waiting in my office, actually.'

'Hah!'

'The simple truth. I tried to ring you yesterday before this hit the fan. A little signing party, *tête à tête*. We could still talk. I think we've got to.'

It was her turn to switch on the thoughtful silence. There was only one thing she could imagine Buster would still want from her, but she doubted if he'd pay sixty thousand pounds for it.

'Are you bemused, my dear? Like most reputations, mine is ill-deserved. I'm a man of my word, in fact. Within reason.'

Janis snorted. She liked that.

'I sense,' he said, 'that you really do believe the police have got it wrong, still, despite what's happened in the last twenty-four hours. Now if they have, it won't stop them going down their chosen road, it never has before. But they still might hit

243

the buffers, mightn't they? Collide head-on with truth? If the only British crime is to be found out, the police in recent years are criminals, QED. What can you offer me?'

She wondered if he was serious. More likely it was to keep open a route. But she needed one as well, to a different destination. She needed to go on, and she needed money to finance herself. Excitement and a little terror stirred in her.

'I'm going to carry on at Ronnie Keegan, I'm going to try and see him some time today. I've also spoken to some other people. Cronies. Donald, I am totally convinced that he's the man.' She realised suddenly that that might not be true. How could it be? Surely Arthur Patten would not deliberately . . . what? She crushed the thought. 'It's all too glib,' she said. 'Gipsies, travellers. You know.'

'I agree. I've always been on your side, from the first. At the very least, Janis, there's something fishy going on. The trouble is, you know, they're not so bright, these boys, it's very easy to get their knickers in a twist. Because they're powerful they think they must be smart, but it doesn't always follow. Most members of the Cabinet suffer from the same delusion.'

And why should I assume, thought Janis, that Patten would not do *anything* deliberately? Has he ever tried to do anything but harm to me? For all I know he fits up people for the hell of it.

'Janis? Are you still there? Look, how soon can you come up with something, do you think? Silly question! Come down and talk, come down to London for that *tête à tête*.'

'The contract?'

'We'll see. Yes, obviously the contract, but the money might be different. Not radically, I'm not a backslider, even where cash is concerned. But we'll have to know what we might get, assess how many copies we might sell.'

'The money men,' she said. 'Donald, look I'm sorry about the stick you're going to get. I doubt if we'll be able to slay them in the short term, quite honestly, but when we do, we'll knock 'em dead.'

Crabbe chuckled.

'One grows thick-skinned,' he said. 'To tell the Home Secretary to his face who did the job one day and be shot down in flames the next is quite a bastard, isn't it? Luckily, he's so nervous of the so-called justice system these days that I might still be able to scare him by sheer brass neck. I'll go for it.'

Janis went to her shower feeling almost in control again. She had said she'd come to London very quickly, probably the next day, and she'd ring him when she could definitely commit herself.

But as she soaped herself, she had that doubt again. Whatever else she thought of Patten, she could not believe he'd tell that sort of lie. Whatever reasons he had for his actions, they must be very, very strong.

Convictions. He operated on convictions. What, she wondered – at any price?

But the joke did not crowd out the doubt.

If Ronnie was surprised to see her, he covered it quite well. They both knew from the outset that the visit was unusual, and that it had a purpose. Janis went in first to bat, giving him a clear and level eye.

'I wanted to ask you something,' she said. 'I realised that if I didn't make my mind up soon I'd miss you. You're out on Thursday and I've no idea what happens then. For all I know you disappear to a new life. Run away with Eileen. Run away from her. Do you really want to see me afterwards?'

'Eileen's got a little place,' he said. 'A chalet sort of thing in Wales. It's not unfeasible, as it happens.'

Was he lying? Had she been? They sat opposite each other in the unpleasant room.

'Well?' she said. 'Do we make a date? To tell you honestly, it was something that you said. You said it several times. I'm thinking of forgetting the article for the *Sunday Times*, or using that as a starter, sort of like a bait. I think I might do a book about it, more in depth. A book about a criminal and his life.'

'Am I still a criminal when I come out of here?' He grinned, mocking her puzzlement. 'I've paid my debt, you know. To society. We won't get far if you treat me like a guilty man.'

He found he almost had to hold his breath. She was so small, so perfect, sitting there. She was wearing a floral cotton skirt, a pale blouse with the outline of a skimpy little bra etched through it, her light coat on the chairback. And she would make a date with him? Oh God! But all the time he kept his mocking look, self-confident, controlled. Oh God, he'd like to *eat* her!

In Janis, it bred fascination, mixed with horror. His eyes so keen and clear, his candid, mocking eyes. He could not be a murderer, a monster, she was hideously wrong. He'd paid his debt to society! Oh glory be! If he meant that and still had killed the Wilmotts, he was completely mad.

'Talking of which,' she said, 'talking of guilty men, they got them, did you know that? They got the Brook Bank killers.'

'Did they so? I heard they'd got some Micks. Some Paddy tinkers. There's a few Irish in here had a very hollow laugh. One stamped shit out of his radio, in delight.'

Disgust? No, not disgust, delight! Would he say this if he were guilty? Could Ronnie Keegan be so . . . subtle? She had to pull herself together, afraid her face was open as a book. To be sure, he was studying her like one.

'Don't you believe it, then?' Her voice was breathy, low. She gathered her resources, harder, eyed him boldly.

'Do you? It stinks to me. Most tinkers are too thick to do a job like that and get away with it. They're into nicking things left lying round, they're stupid, ignorant. They're like the police, they match each other perfectly I'd say, on a job like this, they were made for each other. Wouldn't you?'

She was in deep water, she could not feel the bottom.

'Oh. So you don't think . . . But I'd've thought . . .' She pulled up sharply on that track. The eyes were narrowed, black and very shrewd. She'd have thought he might be pleased they'd found a scapegoat. 'You don't think they'd've done it, then?'

Ronnie had a gold chain round his neck, which if she had seen before she'd never registered. Did they allow them jewellery? At its bottom, peeping through black hair, was not a gold medallion, a crude lump of frozen cash, but a plain gold cross. Her dislocation grew.

'They might have done,' he said. 'Quite frankly I shouldn't think the truth's out yet. They could've had a part in it, maybe, but there'll be more to it than that. It's just not their style, is it? It was too sophisticated, too . . . too well *planned*. And executed. In some ways it was a perfect crime.'

Momentarily, her feet touched bottom. Only momentarily. Ronnie laughed out loud.

'You should see your face! Of course the gipsies did it, didn't they? It stands to reason. I heard that copper on the box. He was like a dog with two dicks, and quite right, too, he's played a blinder. What does it matter, anyway, as long as they've got someone? Who gives a fucking toss?'

'Do you know?' said Janis. 'Who did it really?' Her heart was in her mouth with daring, but Ronnie hardly paused.

'What? Bloody hell, love, you don't hear *everything* in here. It was the tinkers if the coppers say so, what's wrong with that? They ought to string the bastards up, give us all a laugh. Listen, get serious, they're going to chuck you out of here in fifteen seconds, I know the signs. Are you straight about a meeting? I still don't really know what you were on about, about a book, but I'm game. Anything for a giggle, eh? There's a pub called the Ducie Bridge just up the road. By Ducie Bridge, in fact, would you believe, near the station. Twelve o'clock in there on Thursday? Dinnertime?'

The prison officer had opened the door. Janis stood, made a gesture, flustered.

'Yes, OK. Eileen . . .'

'She might tear your eyes out, mightn't she? We'll talk to Eileen after. After we've sorted it out. Yeah?'

Thus it had to be. Thus it was. Five minutes later she was outside the awful, massive gates. She felt slightly ill.

THIRTY-EIGHT

Fat Marie turned up at school in the middle of the afternoon with all the children and a suitcase and three plastic bags bulging with clothes and toys and baby's potty. Donna had a bruise across her cheek and Seanie could not move one of his arms without wincing. Billy took up his position against a wall immediately, and started rocking back and forth. Mrs Partington called Mr Hunt, whose anger hid a deep despair. He met her in the door to Billy's classroom and tried to bar her way. Fat Marie did not try to meet his eye, nor did she stop. Not even the class found it comical, the short, enormous mummy pushing the headteacher backwards before her.

'Mrs Conway, please. You can't do this, it's a school.'

Fat Marie continued moving, like a tanker pushing up against a quay. The baby was hanging across her shoulder, fast asleep, its nappy full and reeking.

'Mrs Conway, I shall have to call the social services. Mrs Conway, please, what can we do for you?'

She was in the classroom, and put down the suitcase. The toddler had wandered off and stood by Billy, who was rocking. Sometimes in school he banged his head, monotonously, against the wall. The teachers could do nothing with him.

Mr Hunt abandoned anger, which was just a pose in any case.

'Look, love,' he said, 'you can't stay here. Sonia, get a chair for Mrs Conway, will you? Come on, love, what do you want to do?'

Her eyes were dull and finished, her face was bruised and streaked with tears.

'We was going to run away to my uncle's house. There's too much stuff. I need somewhere to leave the stuff so Mickie doesn't know.'

The class was in an uproar now, but nobody paid much heed.

There were thirty-six of them and Billy was by no means the worst, in general terms, although the rocking and the head-banging were new and horrifying. The teachers, when they'd failed to come to school today, had rather hoped they'd run, they knew that something pretty terrible was going on.

'OK,' said Mr Hunt. 'Come through to my office and we'll sort you out. We'll find a place to put your bags, and you can change the baby in the ladies. You've got some nappies, have you? I expect Dora will find you one, if not. We're used to all sorts here.'

And this was true. They did everything at the school that Mrs Conway's children went to, even teach when they had the space between the crises and there were few enough of the disruptive or disturbed in class. Mr Hunt was worried about the Conway and the Renwick kids but that, he knew full well, was his problem, no one else's. He hoped that he could hold this crisis till it solved itself or crashed into the terminal involvement of the police and social services, and he was glad that she still had the strength to try and run away. Who knew, she might even make it.

Donna had gone into the babies' class and was trying to stab a black boy in the eye with a sharpened pencil. Sean, for all his injured arm, was knocking things off the activities table in the corner. Worst – unknown yet to Mr Hunt – Mick Renwick had just entered the playground by the main gate, staggering, swearing drunk.

Mr Hunt guided Mrs Conway along a corridor, with Mrs Partington and a wide-eyed student trying to keep the children in a herd. When the double door at the end opened to reveal their father, Sean wet himself, a whooshing torrent from beneath his fluorescent Bermuda shorts. Fat Marie dropped the suitcase and two bags and stood in front of them, eyes closed, to hide them. Mr Hunt understood immediately and stepped forward, hissing an instruction to Mrs Partington.

He strode forward boldly, his anger this time no real pose, and faced Mick Renwick in a voice of steel.

'You! Get out of here immediately! Get out of here before I throw you out!'

Mick's eyes ranged down the corridor past the head, and took in two teachers – short, fat and dowdy, tall and thin. Two teacher women and little Seanie, clinging to the short one's leg. Before, he'd seen Fat Marie, for sure he had.

'Where is the bitch? I'm fucking going to kill her.'

Mr Hunt, who was small and neat and light, moved forward like a rugby scrum, the lot of them, sweeping Renwick backwards to the doors. He reached behind him to jerk one open, and pushed him out of it without losing momentum, out into the playground, the cold sharp breeze from off the moorland. Mick went, unresisting, rolling not staggering, blinking at the little man who glared at him so angrily. A man no bigger than himself.

'Tell the bitch,' he started – and the small man waved his arms, a vigorous, flapping dismissal.

'Now go! Before the police arrive! This is private property, there are children here, this is simply not allowed! Now go!'

'I'll be waiting, tell her. I'll . . .'

He was talking to a door. He heard a bolt slam home. He stood there, swaying.

Mr Hunt began to shake, and touched a wall for comfort and support. Mrs Partington was holding Sean, who had bitten her and now was crying noisily.

'All right, Joe?' she asked.

'OK, Sylvia. Dear dear, we don't half get 'em, don't we? We'd better get to Mrs Conway.'

'She's gone,' the student volunteered. She had gone white. 'I saw her through the window. She went through that gate there. Is it always like this?'

At the junction they found the suitcase and one of the plastic bags. Also Billy, sitting rocking by a wall.

'Well, she's got out half the stuff,' said Mr Hunt. 'It's not a bad start. I doubt if he'll be sober enough to understand what's going on, if she manages to stay clear of him tonight.'

Through another window they saw Renwick. He was standing in the playground, staring at the school.

'Should we call the police?' the student asked.

'No point, they wouldn't come for anything less than outright violence. They'd take a half an hour, anyway.'

'But what . . . ?'

Seanie had begun to wail. The noise from down the corridor, from Mrs Partington's classroom, had become terrific.

'Help me with Sean,' Mrs Partington told her. 'He's wet, and watch he doesn't bite. Joe, can you take care of Billy while I pacify the class?'

The girl tried to grab Sean and he tried to scratch her eyes out. She yelped, then spun him round and pinned him, even remembering his painful arm. The headteacher nodded.

'You'll do,' he said. 'That's excellent, Christine.'

'But we need some help! This is . . . horrible.'

'Welcome to the chalkface. Did anybody tell you it was fun?'

He turned, hauling Billy to his feet with care.

'Come on, you. I've got some biscuits in my office if you're good. We'll put the bags away, shall we? Mum'll come and fetch you after school, don't worry.'

Seanie, seizing his opportunity, elbowed the student in the breast. Luckily for both of them, he missed.

There were no fingerprints, no DNA match-ups from blood or semen, no useful physical clues at all. Hetherington, triumphant but still circumspect, came down on Patten like a bear to 'test the evidence', as he put it. He found the superintendent no longer defensive.

'The lack of specifics doesn't matter, sir,' he said. 'In any case, the forensic boys may still come up with something now there's nine of them in custody. It really doesn't matter all that much.'

He was in Hetherington's office, in an easy chair, and quite relaxed about it. Rosser was in a straightback, but there was not much tentative about his smile, either.

'The point is, sir,' he said, 'this was a gang affair, a simple break-in that went completely wrong. They probably didn't intend a major burglary, even, they knew already that the occupants were all defenceless. They probably just went in to lift what they could lay their hands on, knowing that there was money in the family. Smith has admitted some of this, already.'

'Good,' said Hetherington. 'That's very good. So how did it go wrong?'

'Find the lady,' put in Patten. 'Poor Tessa Wilmott just happened to be there.'

All three men pondered for a while. It hardly needed spelling out. The men had come in while she was undressing, probably. She may have confronted them in just a robe, a nightdress.

'The point is, sir,' repeated Rosser, 'there were quite a few of them. Not all of them lost blood – maybe none of them. Not all of them . . . spilled their semen, either. We've got nine men, but there may have been more. We might even release some of this lot, yet, when other names have come to light. It's highly unlikely that all of them were at the house that night.'

'But some of them were? You can prove that beyond a doubt?'

'I could convict most of them on minor charges, sir,' said Superintendent Patten. 'We're well beyond the stage of merely circumstantial evidence. Bernie Smith was there and we'll convict him as a ringleader. I don't know yet who all the murderers were exactly, but he was one of them. It would be nice if his DNA turned up in the gathered semen, but it's not necessary.'

'You see, sir,' added Rosser, eagerly, 'it's scientifically possible, with so much of it . . . ah . . . swilling about, that Smith's might not be detected. Or it's possible he didn't . . . ah . . . have intercourse with any of the victims. That doesn't mean he didn't murder them. We're talking frenzy, right?'

'Then we have the guns,' said Patten. 'Both found in Smith's caravan, one of them with prints, unanswerable. He's been very stubborn about them, Rosser's spent, what, a dozen hours on him, Sergeant? Two? But he's started accepting harsh realities at last. In contrast, he named the other two we picked up after him quite readily, he says they're relatives, they all work as a team. That's Laurence Boswell, sir, and John Lee. By relatives, God knows what they mean, but nobody denies they roam about together. And Damon Hegarty has positively identified John Lee.'

'He has?' Hetherington was galvanised. 'Why didn't you tell me? But that is excellent!'

'This morning, sir,' said Rosser. He was tempted, as the fat man clearly liked the name so much, to mention Hegarty's semen, which he had lately learned would have been among that 'swilling about' at least in his wife's vagina if not his ma-in-law's. But he knew his man too well. 'No time to send it up to you, you had a meeting on. I showed him photos in his office and he remembers him quite clearly as having been around the house begging from old Mr Wilmott. He's close to remembering Lee and Boswell, likewise. He remembers Smith's lorry. Ford Cargo with a white cab. He's very sure of that.'

Rosser wondered if Hetherington would pick up on the use of photographs, a *fait accompli* that the Boss had gone completely fucking spare about. But Hetherington only lumbered to his feet, stretching his shoulders in an expansive gesture, thrusting his paunch across the desk. Good, thought Rosser. No one can say we didn't tell him, can they?

'Gentlemen,' he said, 'you have done me proud. I never doubted that you would, of course, but you have repaid my confidence with interest. I don't mind telling you that people have been snapping at my arse on this one. One . . . person in particular has been causing endless trouble. I'd just like you to know, my friends, that now I'm going to get the bastard. Yes indeed!'

Rosser guffawed loudly, which Hetherington took for his version of 'Bravo!' Patten formed his lips into a smile.

'We've been afflicted by a biting fly as well, sir. I know DS Rosser thinks it's time to settle the account, right Rosser?'

Rosser grinned, but Patten gave him no time to elaborate.

'Just one thing more, sir. The case of Ronald Keegan. I take it you no longer require us to go to Manchester on that?'

Hetherington shook his head.

'Utter waste of time,' he said. 'Not my fault, I assure you, pressure from above. One of the little scores I've got to settle.'

'You and us both,' said Rosser, with a smirk. 'And the best of British luck, sir. If I may say so.'

THIRTY-NINE

There were messages at the hotel for Janis, and they took up time. Her first idea of seeing Crabbe immediately, striking while the iron was still hot, got deferred. Money was money, but there were other propositions that she found more pressing. One name she was given at reception was Bren Hughes, and the other was Clive Smith. Bren had phoned four times, she heard, and sounded anxious. Janis debated for a moment, then rang Clive.

'Ah, the Scarlet Pimpernel. What have you got for me?'

'You called me, remember? And don't give me any shit, Clive, I'm sorry I couldn't come and help but I'm busy on my own work, right? I'm sure you and Mary made a perfect team.'

'Oyoy! What are you insinuating, you mucky bitch? Anyway, you'll need your job now, won't you, now it's all collapsed. Who pays the wages next month? Buster bleeding Crabbe?'

'Come on, I'm busy. What did you want?'

'A chat? Dinner? Another night of love?' He laughed, easily. 'There's a man down here wants to talk to you. He says it's urgent.'

'Go on, I'll buy it.'

'Thin, hard, and handsome. Amazing eyes, the ladies tell me. He's been on the blower twice.'

'Oh God. What, his office, or in person?'

'In person, Mary says. She's jealous. My guess is, it's your blood he's after though, rather than your body. How's it going, by the way – your one woman crusade to prove that he's a lying, cheating bastard?'

Janis felt very lonely. Clive's voice was full of mockery, but there was affection, too. Pisstaking was a way of life, of course. It made her homesick.

'Anyway,' Clive went on, 'give him a buzz, you know the fucking cops. If he wants to see you, don't ignore it or you'll be pulled up every time you drive a hundred yards. Mary told him we weren't in contact regularly but you rang in sometimes and we'd pass it on. Are you coming back?'

'Yeah. Soon. I've got to go to London, probably tonight. Calls to make. I might be back tomorrow.'

'Hey, great. There's plenty to do here if you want to. We've done some wonderful editions, we've put on thousands. Oh, calls – I've got another message here. Hang on. Eileen Thorpe.'

'Eileen Thorpe?'

'That's what it says here. I didn't take it. Oh, it's just clicked. Mr Keegan's wife, so-called. Is this bad news?'

Janis could not imagine. She ended the call quickly, sitting on the bed in silent contemplation. How the hell had Eileen tracked her down? Once, she touched the telephone, then dropped her hand.

'I'd better go,' she said. Ring Patten? Bren? Nah, later, later, let's see Eileen first.

But, responding to a tiny tweak of guilt, she rang her home. She got the answering machine, and put the phone down after the first few words.

Then, faintly startled, she dialled again. This time she listened to the South Wales accent that could so irritate her. Hello, it said, this is Didwell four eight seven one. Janis Sanderson is not available at the moment, so if you have a message, speak after the tone. Leave a name and number and the time. That was it, short, sweet and businesslike.

She put the receiver down and listened to the honking of a tram, rising from the street below her window. She'd heard the message so many times that she could not be sure, it was too familiar. But surely it had changed? Surely, before, it had said 'neither Janis Sanderson nor Bren Hughes'?

Now what the hell was going on?

Eileen Thorpe had tracked her down, it emerged, through Maude Wimlock, the solicitor. It emerged over a gritty twenty minutes, in which Eileen was cold and very nervous, and Janis was embarrassed and uncomfortable. Eileen's attitude to her was much changed.

The house had changed as well, as Janis noticed the moment she was finally let in. She had stopped outside the yellow garage door and walked firmly up the path to ring the bell. Eileen had pulled it open unthinkingly, then frozen in a kind of shock.

'Oh. Oh, it's you.'

Janis smiled.

'I got your call about an hour ago. What's wrong? Has something happened?'

Eileen turned away.

'Look, why don't you sod off and ring me like I wanted you to do? I don't want to talk to you on my own, I don't trust you. Why don't you ring up later?'

'But that's ridiculous!' The figure retreated further. 'No, I don't mean that, of course I'll ring if that's really what you want. But I'm here because *you* rang, not because I've got anything to say. It seems daft if I've got to drive all the way back to Manchester.'

'Manchester? You're still there, are you? Which hotel?'

Why not, thought Janis.

'Crowden. Just off Piccadilly, d'you know it?'

Eileen's hands had dropped down to her sides.

'Oh God,' she said, 'you might as well come in. Is he all right? You've been seeing him, Maude says.'

The pieces started clicking into place. She had, Janis agreed, following Eileen into the front room. And Maude had probably been in touch with him. She wondered if Eileen was going to be in Harding Lane when he returned, or if she still had other plans.

By the look of the front room, the 'other plans' had been abandoned. The room was tidy, clean, devoid of signs of imminent departure. Eileen went towards the kitchen, then turned back to face her, at a loss.

'Why did you do it?' she asked at last. 'Why did you tell me all those lies? You're not just doing little bits about him and other petty criminals, you're trying to pin that Rowsley filth on him. Maude told me not to talk to you till she'd talked to Ronnie, but . . . Why did you *do* it?'

'I'm sorry. I didn't really . . . I didn't lie all that much, and I have come clean with Ronnie. And I do work for the *Sunday Times*, you know. I've had two pieces in about . . .' Oops. '. . . criminals.'

Eileen stated: 'You're a freelance. She phoned the *Sunday Times* and they said to try the *Clarion*. The *Clarion*, I used to read it, I used to live there, if you're so bloody smart and devious. We're not, up here, we trust people, me and Maude Wimlock. I guess you guessed that or you'd not have tried it on. It's disgusting, do you know that? You're daft, you're mental, sick. Do you honestly believe that my Ronnie could be involved in that? In that *filth*? If you'd have told me when you came round here that time, I'd have spat in your face. And you've told him, have you? Well you're a liar, and I don't believe you, you're a bloody liar! Still!'

She was trembling. Janis did not speak. Eileen began again, her anger unabated.

'What do you want him for?' she said. 'That's what I can't just understand, he didn't do it and no one ever thought he did. So what are you after? Some crappy article in the *Sun*? Some shoddy little paperback or something? Criminals I have known and . . .' She stopped, her stare becoming wilder. 'Is that it? Are you after him? Do you think screwing him would be a better story? Well you'll never get the chance, see, because Maude's going to tell him he can sue for libel, she's working on it now. Anyway, I'd run if I was you, while you've got the chance. When Ronnie finds out what you really wanted, when you're forced to tell the truth, he'll tear you into little pieces.'

Janis, ready to respond, spoke fast and earnestly. She began with an apology, mostly for the upset she had caused to Eileen, whom she did not want to hurt in any way. She admitted that she worked for the *Clarion*, or had done, and that the Brook Bank aspect of Ronnie's story had been what first and mainly interested her. At one time – a very short time – she admitted, she had even wondered vaguely if there could possibly have been a connection, however crazy it might have seemed, and she'd said as much to Ronnie, she'd asked him to his face as she, Eileen, could check. And whatever Maude and Eileen thought, at one time the police did have him as a suspect, until they, also, had realised it was impossible. And no, she did not want to sleep with him, and no, she did not envisage dirty stories in the *Sun*, she was a writer looking for a subject for a serious book. Ronnie was unique, she said with vehemence, did Eileen not grasp that yet? He was a small-time criminal, trying to reform, who had become involved in a vile and rotten murder through circumstances outside his control. As a commentator on the action, as an analyst of the sort of mind that could perpetrate such appalling deeds, he was vital to her purposes, he was fascinating – again, he was unique. Maude Wimlock, she said, no doubt from the best of motives, had caused Eileen to get hold of the wrong end of the stick. There would be no libel actions, but with luck, with co-operation, there might be some money in it for all of them. It would not, she finished acidly, be a 'shoddy little paperback'.

At the end of it, Janis was almost panting, unsure of whether she should be triumphant or ashamed. Eileen merely looked uncomfortable.

'I have told him,' Janis said, 'you see? I'm not a bloody liar, after all.' She considered that. 'Look, I have told lies, I'm sorry. I apologise again. But the police have got some other men, and I'm still interested. Don't you see? I'm serious.'

Eileen said: 'Maude was furious when she found out who you were, all those fibs you'd told her. She told me to ask you out here and she'd turn up as well so that we could talk to you together. She's going to talk to Ronnie, say what's been going on.'

'OK, I can handle that. Why not? Tell Ms Wimlock – no, that sounds rude. Tell Maude I apologise to her as well. A necessary deception, that's how I saw it at the time. Tell her Ronnie won't be surprised by anything she says, unless he's misunderstood me, which I don't think he has. No, that's all fine.'

'So do you want to see her? With me? Shall I make a joint appointment?'

She sounded like a secretary, happy but anxious in her role. Janis saw all sorts of opportunities.

'No, I wouldn't bother, thanks. I'll ring her in the morning, tell her that we've met. I'm not sure if she'll be allowed into Strangeways anyway, just like that. Ronnie's out on Thursday, isn't he, it seems a bit unlikely. Are you going to meet him, or will you be at work?'

Eileen was calm now. She shook her head.

'I don't go in for that stuff. Can you imagine what it's like? Anyway, he'll go to the pub and end up pissed. I've seen it all before.'

Janis could imagine very well. Let him just try that on with me, she thought. But she said nothing more to Eileen than goodbye.

Behind the Renault wheel, driving back to Manchester, she told herself it would be easy to talk round Maude, to persuade her out of seeing Ronnie altogether. As she approached the roundabout at Mumps – for the first time in good visibility – she registered that the signwritten railway bridge was welcoming her to Oldham, home of the tubular bandage. Somewhere in her memory, it rang a bell, although she could not precisely place it. It's a bloody funny place, she thought. And a bloody funny notice.

She hoped she would not need a bandage soon, tubular or otherwise. She did not feel too confident at all.

FORTY

Superintendent Patten's attack on Janis was completely different from Eileen Thorpe's. It was cold, forensic, cruel, controlled. He referred to it as a 'character reading', but in effect – and perhaps intention – it was a character assassination. The only plus, from Janis's point of view, was that it was done alone. If there had been a temptation to let Lance Rosser 'sit in', it had been resisted. For that, she was grateful.

Not that she avoided seeing Rosser – he made sure she did. She arrived at HQ at eleven forty-five a.m., by appointment, and the detective sergeant was lurking near the desk where she announced herself. He was in a pale grey suit and white shirt, looking tanned, relaxed and elegant, and treated her to a little sideways nod, a sardonic smile of greeting. She eyed him calmly, but her smile was tight and strained. To her relief, before he had time to make a comment, a uniformed inspector interrupted him.

Janis, like Rosser, was looking cool. She had slept at home – or rather, she had lain in her own bed – and she had showered early and chosen her clothes with care. Court shoes, sheer tights, and a tailored suit over a snowy shirt of doubled silk. As an exercise in power dressing it was fine. Unfortunately, she was tired, drugged, unhappy. At four a.m. she had taken half a sleeping pill – nitrazepam – and had awoken about three hours later with a bad taste in her mouth and a muzzy head. At least the dreams had stayed away, but the man who had set them off had loomed stubbornly in her night thoughts. She did not like Patten, she did not want to talk to him, and she knew that, realistically, she had no choice. Loath as she was to admit it, she was afraid of him, of what he might say or do. No, say. He could do nothing to her, could he? Surely?

She had asked Clive about this the night before, when (rather pathetically, they both felt) she had rung his home to ask if he would meet her. His girlfriend, live-in lover, partner, wife, whatever she was known as, had answered, sounding not a jot suspicious despite the fact that it was after ten o'clock. Clive had come on more grumpily, demanding to know what couldn't wait till morning. Janis told him she had arranged the Patten meeting and was desperate for some backbone stiffening. She also said that Bren had left her, finally, and she was in some kind of shock. Clive, sensitive as ever, had laughed raucously.

'Serves you right! What happened, has he found a nicer person, or has he slunk off home to Mam? Listen, I'm not coming round on that basis, I'd have my balls cut off by Sally.'

Whether Sally was listening to this or not, Janis was jolted. Using men as crutches was against her nature, and certainly against her creed.

'You're a cheeky sod! It's not an open bloody invitation, mate, I meant a pub, not here. I'm not after consolation, least of all from your gross form!'

'Pub's off as well,' he said, not believing her. 'Too late, and we're halfway through the second bottle. The Patten thing's OK, don't worry, just accept your mauling like a man. He only wants to crow, you know. If he roughs you up a bit, so what? You deserve it, don't you?'

She was sitting in her small lounge, and she was hideously lonely. There were cardboard boxes everywhere, that Bren's note had said he'd pick up later, if she didn't mind. Typical of Bren – how could she stop him, short of changing all the locks? The house reminded her appallingly of Eileen Thorpe's when she had first gone there. Why was she lonely? Fuck only knew.

'OK, so he'll have a field day, I can stand that. There's nothing he can actually do, is there? I haven't broken any laws, or anything?'

'Wasting police time? Tampering with witnesses? It would make a great little story! Nah, forget it, he just wants to chew you over. If you want a Bren replacement, why not him? He's divorced, he's good-looking, Mary reckons you must fancy him, you slag him off so much. A fuck at least? Why not ring him now!'

Journalists' jokes. Janis felt suddenly old and sour, tired and pissed off. She wondered if Clive were fucking Mary, now. Now? What did that mean? She and Clive were hardly what

261

the newsroom these days called an item, were they, they'd done it twice, and probably that was that. Certainly that was that, she'd made her mind up! One bad one, one good one, and then goodbye. No more whining gits like Bren around the place.

For much of the rest of the evening, over a bottle of Penfolds Cab-Shiraz, she wondered why Bren had left her, or rather, where he'd got the neck. The note was long and tearful, but boiled down to the fact that he knew she didn't care, and he was not the man to stick around imposing, etc, etc, and her inability to answer simple phone calls and messages over several days when clearly they were urgent, and so on. Fuck him, she thought, recurrently, he's saved me the final job of getting rid. But she was disoriented and rather shocked. He'd had to go, but surely it was her decision? By the end of the bottle Patten was back inside her skull, gnawing like a rat.

So here she sat facing him in his office, tense, tired, nervous and afraid. I've screwed it up, was her overriding thought, I've screwed the whole thing up. She had never been able to believe, in her heart of hearts, that Patten was the sort of man to stoop to things like cooking evidence, downright lies, and looking at him now she still could not believe it. The trouble was, she did not believe it was itinerants either, the men who had been charged. She'd screwed the whole thing up, but she did not know precisely how.

'I suppose you know,' he asked her, 'why I've called you in today? Some people think you should get a rollicking. Lance Rosser, probably, would go even further. I just want to ask you some things, and express an opinion or two about the way I think you've conducted yourself in the past couple of months.'

She made a little shrugging movement. She would have liked a glass of water.

'At first I thought you must have gone on holiday,' he continued. 'When you no longer turned up at HQ, or came on any of the story opportunities. Naive of me. I understand from contacts in the press that you've been busy doing other things.'

An enquiring cast to his features. Janis kept hers neutral. Contacts. She hoped they did not have a mole inside the *Clarion*.

'I understand you've been so far as seeing Ronald Keegan

inside Strangeways. That struck me at first as pretty enterprising of you, until I worked out how you'd done it. The Honourable Donald Crabbe, MP. I assume I'm right?'

His gaze was hard, the eyes extraordinary. Her nod was hardly measurable, entirely involuntary. She could not begin to work out if she should have admitted or denied.

'OK. So the reason, the justification, for my hauling you in here is that. Have you learned anything, anything at all, that might be of any help to me in my enquiries? I suppose I don't have to point out to you your duty in this matter?'

She shook her head, still reacting like a naughty schoolgirl. Although it occurred to her that she had done her best, always. It was the police who had refused to take her seriously.

'I have opinions,' she said. 'As you know, I've always had opinions. I've spoken to him in prison and I've spoken to some . . . associates. I've formed ideas.'

He waited. She wondered if she should mention Mick Renwick and his wife. Even Eileen Thorpe and Maude. She remembered Mick Renwick's awful house, the sounds of beating. Given what she now knew, where was the great significance? She had made an accusation, there had been a lot of noise, the woman had been frightened. And Mick had appeared, a weedy, disgusting, tiny monster. Domestic violence. The only significance was in that Ronnie had said he was dead, maybe. And as to Maude and Eileen . . .

'No,' she said. 'I don't think I've found out anything you don't know. To be quite honest . . .'

'Yes?'

'Well, put it this way. If you thought I was wrong before, you'd still think I was just as wrong today.' She made a face. 'Wronger, probably. You'd probably be right.'

'And on this basis you turned that MP on to our backs? That muckraking playboy? Strange bedfellows, Miss Sanderson, I had you marked down as some kind of feminist.'

The contempt was scarcely hidden. Why don't you just say lesbian? thought Janis. A minor insight: I bet that's what Lance Rosser thinks. Of course. She did not reply.

'So would you say that was fair? A known Parliamentary troublemaker, a known detractor of the police? An opinion that you admit yourself was totally ridiculous? I cannot tell you how much trouble this has caused my men, how much grief. Your friend started at the highest level, you know. His accusations have caused . . . worse, they've seriously hindered us, I feel that you should know that, would you say that that was fair?'

'I didn't say my ideas were totally ridiculous, though.' Her voice was rather faint, but firm. 'I was pursuing what I thought might be the truth. I don't know for certain that it's not the truth. I had every right to follow up a private line of investigation. Now who's being fair?'

'Four people died! You and Crabbe have blundered in without a care for anyone! If our enquiries had been aborted, interrupted for just one day, there might well have been other deaths, don't you understand that? You've risked the guilty people getting off scot-free!'

'All we did . . .' she started. He stopped her with an angry gesture.

'You talked to criminals, as well. Didn't it occur to you that Keegan and his rotten friends would process everything you said to him? Keegan's a fantasist, a small-time crook, but he's got a conman's cunning. He can extrapolate, synthesise, work out what's behind things. Prisons are a grapevine, Miss Sanderson, and anything you said to Keegan about this case, and doubtless things you're not even conscious you were revealing, will be known to every dirty little thug in England. You've acted as an early-warning system.'

'But you've got them!' she snapped back. 'I can't have got it wrong on every count! What does a grapevine matter if you've caught them anyway! Anyway, no one knew what I was after when I talked to Ronnie Keegan, not even him! Nobody!'

Except Buster Bloody Crabbe, MP. Neither of them put it into words, but there it was.

'I have a great distaste for this sort of thing, you know.' There was no anger in his voice, now, sorrow but no satisfaction. 'When I have to give a character reading to one of my men, or women, I find the anger difficult to sustain. Lance Rosser would have done it differently, I think you can imagine that. He did suggest that we might prosecute, or threaten to, and don't think we couldn't make it stick. I'd rather try and get through your shell and make you see yourself as we've been forced to, make you realise a little of the anger you've aroused among my team – quite justified in my view, I'm not ducking that responsibility. Do you know what they call you here? You couldn't even start to guess. You're called The Ghoul. To be quite frank, more usually "that fucking ghoul". You're seen as not just dishonest but as prurient, like some old pervert scratching in the wrecks of human lives, trying to turn it into cash and copy. I'm sorry that I've had to say this, but I believe I owe it to my people. I also honestly believe that you've got no idea. Sometimes since I've known you, I thought you might be capable of learning from it, of taking it on board and finding something out about yourself. I hope that doesn't strike you as too arrogant.'

Sorrow, but no satisfaction, she had thought. But surely this was cruelty, deliberate and sadistic? The quiet, unemphatic words slid like arrows deep into her psyche and as they lodged she felt the barbs engage. The odd thing was, his face showed nothing. He was talking to her quietly, *tête à tête* – oh, shades of Buster Crabbe! He watched her squirm and did not smile with open satisfaction, just weighed the next sentence, the next heavy missile to be gently slung.

But had he finished? Patten leaned away from her, back into his seat, and emitted what could have been a sigh. He picked up a small packet of cigars, then put it down again. Janis kept her internal bleeding as invisible as he kept his intent.

'If I were you,' he said, 'I'd apologise. Not to my team – they'd spit in your eye, they wouldn't talk to you. I'd apologise to Ronnie Keegan, to put it in perspective. Tell the pathetic little no-hoper you thought he was a big, important thug. See how it feels, see how he responds, it might help you get a grip on your own life. Nice thought, but in reality, I suppose you won't be seeing him again.'

The unformed question hung, almost visible, in the room. You're not that stupid, are you? Janis could either fold completely, give in, collapse, or keep up some semblance of good order. She stood up.

'I'm going now,' she said. 'I take it that's all right? As it happens, I will be seeing him again, I'm going to because I said

I would. In fact I thought of ringing you, to ask you. I did ring. When you were down in Wales.'

Truth mixed with lies. She was getting more and more adept. She had rung, but not to tell him she was seeing Ronnie Keegan – nor to ask if it was really safe.

'Interesting. Surely you're not still thinking he's a murderer? You live in a world of make-believe, don't you? Fairy-tale.'

'I might consider apologising, actually. If you can tell me absolutely that he's not. If you can tell me absolutely that it's safe. Can you do that, Mr Patten?'

Patten opened his packet of cigars and took one out. He put the end between his teeth and bit until it crackled slightly. He raised his eyes to hers, and his were filled with cold dislike.

'Please go away,' he said. 'I find your self-aggrandisement very wearing. You fool yourself, Miss Sanderson, nobody's going to hurt you, however much you'd like them to. Just go away.'

Still full of pain, the barbs still deep within her, Janis went.

FORTY-ONE

Janis went to London, but she still failed to get in touch with Crabbe. Before she left Didwell to catch the train at Market Harborough she rang Maude Wimlock in her Oldham office and explained to her what she had done and why. Eileen had already talked to her, and Janis quickly made that right. Then she rang Bren at his mother's home in Cardiff, and mercifully got no reply. Then she rang Professor Swale in her office and told her that they had to meet, that night, to talk. Hilary, down the telephone, picked up the bright, strained tone and named a time and bar. She arrived an hour late, to find Janis toying with a glass of white wine that had gone warm, and picking nervously at her lower lip.

'Janis. My love. You look terrible!'

Janis looked at her somewhere between tears and laughter.

'Hilary, can we get out of here, or are you desperate for a drink? I am terrible, I feel terrible, I might just cry if we don't get away.'

She started talking in the taxi, with Hilary patting her on the knee from time to time. When they walked down the basement steps to the front door, Hilary's presence − large and motherly, in swirling summer robes − had already worked some magic. In the long, untidy room, Janis did not burst into tears, or screech out her frustration and her shame, she went up to the old gas range and put the kettle on. Hilary waved a whisky bottle at her, but she waved it away. Tea and sympathy was what she wanted, but no more blurring at the edges.

'OK,' she said. 'I've told you the bare bones, now I'll fill in the details. Well, the important bits. I've fucked it up, I've lost my confidence, I'm in a mess. Hilary, for the first time in my life, I think, I need an analyst. And that includes my summer afternoon.'

Hilary moved across the floorboards and the rugs, a multi-coloured Arab tent. She took a teapot, emptied and rinsed it at the sink, warmed it with a splash of water from the hissing kettle. She put in three spoonfuls. Disaster tea, strong and serious.

'They're calling me a ghoul,' said Janis. 'The Ghoul, in fact; my nickname. Hilary, I think they're right, for Christ's sake! I'm meeting Ronnie Keegan out of Strangeways, when Arthur Patten insists he's got the men who did it. Hilary, I haven't even told his wife, I'm consumed with guilt, I don't know why I want to meet him, even, what I think I want. I sometimes think it might be even sexual!'

Hilary made the tea. They watched the pot in silence while it drew, as if that were part of some ritual. Hilary got mugs and milk and poured. They sat. They sipped.

'The Ghoul, eh? Who told you that? Your charming superintendent? The one who talked you through the gory details? I think perhaps it's he who needs an analyst, not you.'

'I haven't told you, have I? I've been having awful nightmares. No, fears really. I wake up in the night and think there's someone in the house, or my hotel room. Someone who's going to kill me. It's very real, I feel completely sick with fear, I've never known anything like it. When I'm asleep it's Ronnie Keegan, with a knife.' She took a sip of tea. 'Dracula's meant to be sexual, isn't he? The handsome monster in the dead of night? There's nothing sexual about Ronnie in my dreams. Nothing at all.'

'For a ghoul, my dear,' said Hilary, 'you sound remarkably like a victim. Of a typical policemen's soubriquet, if nothing else. And are you still so sure? That he's a murderer?'

'Of course I'm not. That's the problem, isn't it? That's the ghoulish part, for me.'

It was a very quiet room, silent, indeed, but for the humming of the fridge. Hilary did not interrupt her thoughts.

Janis thought that she must stop all this. She thought that she must give up the struggle, give up the hunt, give up pursuing Ronnie for his truth, give up the ghost. Whatever she'd thought it might lead her to to start with, she now thought she was clinging onto straws.

'I've got promiscuous again,' she said, out of the blue. 'And Bren's run back to mother, I forgot to tell you. I slept with Clive again, the news editor, the works this time. Last night I wanted to again, but he wouldn't. I can't even get the men I want, these days.'

Hilary snorted.

'Two goes and one refusal may be regrettable, but it hardly sounds promiscuous, my love! Is it why the Welsh whinger ran away? No, I can see it isn't. Come on, what is this promiscuity nonsense?'

Janis admitted it was just a form of words. What she had really meant, she said, was that the relationship was like the Ronnie project – dead. Bren had had the guts to kill the one, and she must do the same with Ronnie. No more ghoulishness, no more lies, no more book.

'I quit,' she said. 'Arthur Patten wins. I quit.'

Hilary drank tea, silent, thinking. Her stasis was a reassurance, and Janis became more calm. She studied the plump and placid face, so different from the others she'd been involved with lately.

'Very theatrical,' said Hilary, at last. 'And a classic ballix, I'm afraid. I hear confusion, distress, with a *sauce piquante* of self-pity for good measure. If you were lying on a chaise longue, I'd probably be yawning, I might even be making faces and giving V-signs at you. That's why we do it, you know, sit out of the patient's sight. I knew an analyst who used to masturbate. His analyst told me.'

'So go on. Why is it a "ballix"? Why don't the Irish say bollocks, like the rest of us, by the way?'

'Because they're Irish, naturally. And it's a ballix because it's not just a case of Patten winning. It's a case of you putting yourself on the line, giving your moral sense and sensibilities a hard race across the jumps that's left you with a severely calloused bottom, and facing the imminent prospect of ending up without a job. More seriously, without prestige. More seriously again, without self-regard. You started on a moral crusade, in a quiet sort of way. Quit now, and you end up as a pariah, in your own eyes at least. That's why it's a ballix.'

'But was it a moral crusade or a classic piece of opportunism? Every time someone murders more than three people in a row these days, we're queuing up to explain away their lives, preferably with ghoulish pictures. Ghoulish. The Ghoul. What Patten and his men call me.'

Hilary was nodding.

'It's hard, isn't it? Everybody wants to know, but if you dare to try and tell them, you're a monster, too. It's a conundrum, but I wouldn't let it worry you, my love, the easiest position in the world is being holier than thou. It's like the gutter press – deplored by everyone and bought by most. Explain that away.'

The refrigerator clicked, began to hum.

Hilary added: 'Then there is the book, of course. The actual book, the contract, our dear friend Buster Crabbe. If you don't write it, however it turns out, you won't get the money, will you? Was it sixty thousand? Good God, my darling, how could you risk losing that? Have you had the first slice yet? Have you signed the contract, even? Janis? Janis!'

'Oh, it's all right,' said Janis. 'It's not sixty thousand any more, but it's all right. I'd better ring him, actually, he's been going on about a meeting. I promised him I'd get in touch a couple of days ago but I haven't had the time. He wants dinner, and I suspect a good deal more.'

'But you're not that far down the slope of promiscuity!'

'I am not.' Janis grinned. 'I did make it clear to him that I didn't have any doubts, though, that I was certain the police had got it wrong. God knows how I'll tell him I've changed my mind.'

'If you have.'

'Haven't I? Oh Jesus, I don't know. I have, Hilary, I'm sure I have. That's the only thing I am sure about any more, actually. That and the fact that I'm not sure! Shall I ring him now?'

'Good idea. I know, let's both invite him for a meal, then I can give a helping hand. Until he tries to get you into bed, my love – after which I'm afraid you're on your own, no substitutes!'

They tried all the numbers they had between them for Crabbe, but failed to track him down. Ah well, it was decided – he would keep. Instead they went out for a quiet glass or two.

Sadly for himself, Acting Chief Constable Cyril Hetherington had been unable to blow Donald Crabbe out of the water in person, but he had bowled his googly up the line tremendously effectively. His anger had reverberated round several telephone

270

earpieces, and his sentiments had gained both point and elegance by the time Crabbe received them face-to-face across the largest desk in Queen Anne's Gate. The Home Secretary had used his calm, dry mode, and had dropped in key phrases with a vaguely pained distaste. Crabbe's dark face had gone subtly paler as the catalogue of certitude was rehearsed: confessions, shotguns found in caravans, a lorry recognised, identification by Tessa Wilmott's husband, fingerprints. It was uncrackable.

'Well, Donald,' said his foe at last. 'I think an apology is in order, don't you?'

I do, thought Crabbe. You cow, you useless, stupid cow, Janis. I do.

'But I suppose we will not get one, will we?'

'We probably will not,' agreed Crabbe, sardonically. 'It's a cruel world, isn't it?'

Afterwards he rang Janis's hotel in Manchester, then her Didwell home. When he got Bren's disembodied voice, he improvised a short and bitter message into the machine. Then he wrote a note for his secretary to type up and send by post, which was less sarcastic, but no less terse.

'Janis,' it said, 'you strike me, increasingly, as a fool. In any case, you did not phone, and I am rather tired of waiting. Sadly, I've ripped the contract up. Yours, Donald Crabbe.'

He liked the bit about the contract, particularly.

FORTY-TWO

Mick Renwick knew what she was up to, and sometimes it amused him. Sometimes, when he was soberish, and not too painful in the head, he liked to study her flat, cowlike face, and give her little sneering looks suggesting that he knew her game, that he was only waiting for the best time to jump on her. He liked to watch her efforts to appear innocent; self-conscious, frightened smiles, followed by small patches of blankness, denoting despair or hope, he was not sure. Then he might cock his head, give a suggestion of a wink, renew the leer, enjoy the sight of her confusion grow. He knew what she was up to, and sometimes he thought it might be for the best to let her go, her and the frigging, noisy children. In one way it would be good riddance, no doubt at all of that. But on the other hand . . .

Mick's burden did not sit as lightly on him as he'd thought it would. In actual fact, it had come to him as a big surprise to find there was a burden to be borne at all. He had killed before, although he did not shout about it, and had had no ill effects he could remember, no remorse or guilt or fear. But this time there had been the dreams, and the vivid sensations of taste and colour of the blood, so much blood, and old and withered thighs wrenched open to his eager cock. He had stumbled from the place so drunk that he could hardly stand, full of Doggo's filthy pills as well, and been unconscious for at least a large proportion of the journey back. And Fat Marie knew that he would kill her if she breathed a hint to anyone, but the hatred and the memories made him drink with utter savagery, and he was afraid. Good riddance if she went, but on the other hand . . . what would she tell, to whom?

And she was trying, secretly, to get away. After he'd gone to the school that day he'd found a plastic bag stuffed with children's clothes, that she said she'd got from a jumble down at Watersheddings, a story she'd maintained through thick and thin however much he'd smacked her stupid face. He would have had a go at Seanie, twisted his bad arm, but Seanie did not come back from school that afternoon till late, till after Mick had gone off to the Con Club in fact, taking Donna with him, under protest. Fat Marie wasn't going anywhere without her eldest daughter, that was bottom line. Donna was her favourite.

In bed that night, not completely gone, he had put it to her quite reasonably that she could not get away, however hard she tried. She had no money and no friends, her mother wouldn't talk to her, and he had watchers everywhere. She denied it hotly, swore she never wanted to and never would, rubbing her great fat tits all over him and grabbing his hand and jamming it between her thighs. Mick, interested but unaroused, removed his hand and placed it round her throat to join the other one, and squeezed until her smile of acquiescence began to glaze. Then he got a hard-on, fine, and came all down her leg. Fat Marie seemed satisfied. That time, Mick had been amused.

But he watched her, and became more convinced. He tried to catch her at it – packing clothes and so on – but never could. He tried to catch the children out with questions and with threats, but they acted blank, stared at him with blank and hating eyes. When he was there, and conscious, he wouldn't let her leave the house with all the children, and he warned her that he'd do 'spot checks' in the streets. If he ever caught her with a bag of clothes, except maybe from the launderette, it would be the worse for her. Sometimes, he took the children's shoes away. Fat Marie, behind her dull eyes, despaired. She had to get away before he beat them all to death in one of the drunken crises. But she would not tell on him, that was not the plan. Why would she tell on him? What had stuff like that to do with her?

He caught her out one day as she plodded down towards the school with two blue plastic launderette bags stuffed to bursting. Not with washing, but with clothes for the escape. Mr Hunt, the head, had tried to talk to her about the plan, tried to persuade her that at least she should just drop everything one afternoon and run, that the social would surely clothe the children, even if nobody else could. But Mr Hunt and Mrs

Conway spoke a different language, they did not communicate, it was a normal problem in this school. Fat Marie, as far as possible, was confident the launderette idea (which had been Mick's, after all) would provide the cover that she needed. As to why she had to take the clothes, and risk the lot – well, for that there could be no explanation, not even to herself. She did, that's all.

Today would be the day, she told herself. She had the suit-case she'd got out before, and the plastic bags of stuff, and she had twelve quid. Donna and Billy and Sean were all at school, the buggy had all its wheels in working order, and the toddler had some shoes. Today at the end of school she'd be waiting for a taxi that she knew some teacher would ring for her, and they'd chuck in all the bags and bugger off. Mick had gone out at dinnertime with twenty-seven quid – she'd counted it as he'd snored – so he'd be suited for the afternoon, well pissed, legless. Today would be the day if nothing should go wrong – and if it did, they'd go tomorrow.

Mick spotted them somehow, and yelled across the road. There was a lot of traffic, and she tried to tell herself the voice had not been his. The toddler's crumpled face destroyed the lie, then the yell again, harsh and drunken, thick with hate and rage. Fat Marie dropped one of the bags, and almost pulled the toddler's arm out, throwing her across the baby's lap as the buggy burst forward under maximum acceleration, all her projected weight. The toddler rolled and twisted, pinioned by the arm, but her legs did not fall off and tangle with the wheels. The other bag bounced wildly up and down, a violent blue with yellow plastic handles, banging into people on the busy pavement. As she ran she heard a bang, the loud and character-istic sound a car makes running into someone, and for one wild, joyful second Fat Marie, half-turning, saw Mickie sprawled out in the road, knocked down, dead, there were even screams. Then, before traffic blotted out the sight, he was on his feet, staggering, hands out in front of him like a blind man in a film. Blind drunk man, Fat Marie thought bitterly. Drunk men don't get hurt, drunk men are made of rubber. But it had slowed him down.

She struggled on, the bouncing bag of clothes impeding her, but hooked too firmly across the handle to fall off or be discarded if she'd wanted to. People stared at it, then her frightened, pasty face, sidestepping clumsily or being nudged by it. Further back up the road, after the little man had dodged and darted through the honking traffic, they saw him boot the other bag with absurdist vigour, lifting it high above his head, then jumping at it, kicking again, tearing out the contents with both hands, scattering them and trampling them across the paving stones and gutter. Unrestrained, of course. No one in their right minds would go anywhere near this tiny, roaring dervish, let alone try to restrain him.

The baby was awake and screaming, the toddler was squirming, blue in the face with fright, when Fat Marie blundered into the playground, through the complicated barrier of ironwork that stopped the kiddies hurling themselves out into the traffic. It was too early for the bell by twenty minutes, so there were no other mums around, not even a lollipop lady putting on her coat for duty. As far as it was possible for her to do so, Fat Marie fairly flew across the yard, her face broken open now by the wet gash of her mouth. Her breath was too shallow and too short for screaming, so she let out an awkward, awful, honking noise, punctuated by desperate gasps and gulps for oxygen. No longer looking backwards, she knew that Mick was close behind her, the muscles at the back of her neck, the fat and flesh across her shoulders, already cringing in anticipation of his hands.

Mr Hunt's secretary Dora was the first inside the school to see it happening. She ran helterskelter into his room, her eyes so horror-stricken that he dropped the telephone and jumped straight to the window she was pointing through. Mrs Conway – Fat Marie – was racing straight towards him, mouth open, bag flying, everything about her bouncing up and down. Behind her, smaller, leaner, deadly like a fox or ferret, Mick Renwick ran, also open-mouthed, his teeth visible halfway across the tarmacked yard.

'Call the police! This time they must come!'

As Joe Hunt ran into the corridor, there was uproar starting in classrooms on the playground side of school. Through walls half made of glass, he saw teachers trying to stop stampedes of pupils from rushing to the outer windows. He heard shrieks and shouts of great excitement, mixed with screams and cries of fright. Two doors along, Sylvia Partington abandoned her class and came into the corridor in front of him. Inside the room he caught a fleeting glimpse of Donna. Billy, mercifully, was over at the infants', where he had been transferred to sit in Kath Simpson's class and bang his head against her desk or legs. Mrs Partington's face was white.

'Joe! Have you called—'

He swept past, answering abruptly that he had. Outside, as they barged through the double door, they heard a wrenching scream, the sound of bone on bone. Joe Hunt and Mrs Partington ran into the light aware that Mrs Conway had been knocked onto the ground, and that half the children in the school were cheering lustily. As Mick prepared to spring upon his wife, the head barged into him, running at full speed, sending both men sprawling. Another roar went up, and Hunt heard the doors squeak as – he hoped – more teachers came streaming out. This time, he knew, Renwick was not intimidated by authority, this time his drunkenness was at a different level. He got to his feet as fast as possible to face the danger, but he was already too late. Renwick dropped him with two blows straight to his face, followed by a stomach-kick that caught him as he fell. Sylvia Partington, clinging to Mick's arm, was thrown sideways like a doll, her skirt flaring high above her waist, one shoe skittering off across the playground. This time there were no cheers, at least. For a moment, the children had gone dumb.

A teacher and the student, Christine Meredith, had come into the yard, and they were screaming. Fat Marie, the baby crushed at her enormous breasts, had banged them aside and got into the school, leaving the toddler beside the upturned buggy, silent and bemused. Mick almost trod on her, then got his ankles tangled in the alloy tubing, falling forward in a heap. First Mrs Partington then Mr Hunt tried to prevent him from getting up but were too slow, and possibly too afraid, to hold him back. Christine stepped into his path, bravely, to be smashed up against the wall, then he was in and pounding down the corridor. Mr Hunt led the charge back inside, while Christine ran across the playground to the road, crying for help, towards the group of watchers gathered at the railings, doing nothing.

The corridors were chaos. Half the classrooms had emptied into them, with most of the children crying noisily. The teachers were distracted, frantic, panic-stricken, trying to get along to Mrs Partington's room where Fat Marie had gone to ground, trying to calm the children simultaneously, or restrain them. Mr Hunt was just in time to see Renwick beat a pathway through a knot of screaming children, even trampling a couple under his feet.

'Stop!' he yelled. 'The police are coming! Stop this immediately!'

Mick would stop, he wasn't going on for very long. As he marched through the door, two small children, the last two out, pushed past him in the frame, a squashy logjam of tender flesh, and popped into the corridor, squeaking. The last two except her Donna, the fat cow's champion, the fat cow's favourite, who was standing up in front of her like a fucking pitbull terrier, who was glaring at him with her hands in little claws! Brilliant! Hilarious! Magnificent! Mick was actually laughing as he swiped her with the back side of his fist, knocked her across two tables like something in a Wild West show, laughing as he drove his foot deep into her mother's fat.

The fat cow dropped onto her knees and tried to get underneath the table! A wooden one, with lightweight legs, for tiny little kids! She stuck out of it at every point, it balanced on her bum and wobbled. Mick was laughing so much he almost couldn't kick her! He caught her a good one in the face, and a couple in the tits, but he couldn't get his strength in it! He saw the baby on its back, gob wide open without teeth, and that struck funny, too. Then Fat Marie squirmed, to try and cover it, and the table slipped off sideways and she turned her face to him and he got her a good one in the mouth, he felt her teeth jar on his shoe, and scrape. Dogshit, he thought, I hope there's dogshit on it! He saw Donna coming at him, white and snotty, so he smacked her down again, not very hard, almost with affection. Donna was all right sometimes, it was Sean he really couldn't stand. Donna was all right, sometimes, like Fat Marie.

'You stupid bitch,' he told his wife. 'Why do you make me do these things to you? Get up and wipe your face, for fucksake, you look terrible.'

277

She said something, but blood made a bubble on her lips, which swelled and broke. There were people in the room now, the headmaster and the woman he'd knocked down. Mick felt pity for his wife, but this was not the time for making up, this was the time to scarper.

'Come home now, quick,' he said. He bent close, and said it quietly. 'I know what you've been up to, you daft cow. Get up and come, before I lose my fucking temper.' He put a hand out, and she did not flinch. 'Come.'

The riot in the corridor carried on, but the people in the room were very still. As he turned to face them, the headmaster took a pace forward.

'Mrs Conway . . .'

'Shut your fucking hole,' said Mick. 'She's my fucking wife, she goes with me. Now – out of it!'

'The police,' said Mrs Partington.

'They're on their way,' Mick taunted her. 'They're always on their fucking way, lady.'

Fat Marie was on her feet, the squalling baby muffled in her bosom. Donna walked behind her, stiff with dignity and contempt. In the milling corridor the noise was being hushed, the children forced into order. Mrs Simpson was there with Billy, who was grinning fiercely, while Christine had produced and muffled Sean. Christine was good with Sean, she could control him, sadly for her training as a teacher: she did little else. At the exit stood the toddler, hand-in-hand with a mother who had come to collect her own. The buggy had been righted, the launderette bag still hanging from its grip.

Mr Hunt could only let them go. What else was expected of him, a citizen's arrest? As he said to Sylvia Partington, a grim attempt at humour as they watched them walking in a body across the tarmac that was filling up with parents, they looked just like a family.

'The police are on their way,' she responded, in a similar vein of bitter irony. 'Joe, we've got to do something. We've got to make them understand. We've got to stop that awful man.'

'We have,' agreed Joe Hunt.

*   *   *

But by the time the police did turn up at last, the school was back to normal, which meant, at that time, almost empty. A few kids hung around the playground, shooed off and drifting back again, and a couple of mothers chatted on the pavement. The emergency services – a florid fat policeman with blond hair in his eyes and a skinny black-haired WPC – parked illegally at the kerb and ambled slowly towards the main door, chatting comfortably, amused by the obvious lack of trouble. When he met them, Mr Hunt did not even bother being acid.

'You're too late,' he said. 'It was bloody while it lasted, but they've gone.'

The fat constable was prepared for sympathy, to be diplomatic. In any case, he noted, the head had a cut eye and discoloration to his cheek.

'We did our best,' he said. 'We're very overstretched, you know. Were you involved, sir? Were you actually attacked? Would we find witnesses?'

Hunt shook his head.

'I doubt it. It was total chaos and happened very fast. The point is, though . . .'

The policeman was smiling, holding up his hand. Hunt stopped.

'The point is, sir, in our experience, it's always too late in these matters, whatever time we come. Even if we'd caught them in the act, kicking seven bells of hell out of each other, they'd've denied it, bet your life on it. We know these kind of people.'

'How many kids?' asked the policewoman. 'Four or five?'

There was a kind of knowing sneer on her lips that the headteacher did not relish. He did not reply.

'You might not like it, but you can't deny it, though,' she said. 'We've seen it all before, love. Tear each other's eyes out this afternoon, and tonight they'll be back lovey-dovey, drunk as fools, breeding up some more disasters for us to deal with. And you, of course. I wouldn't have your job, love, believe me.'

Nor I yours, she was inviting him to say – but he did not. To himself, though – as she had guessed – he could not deny the value of her words. In the Waggon afterwards, he and Sylvia Partington discussed it for an hour and both agreed, depressingly, that the outcome would probably be not too far off that. Marie Conway would never get away, and quite possibly, somehow, did not even really want to. It was a tragedy, but that was that.

They were all wrong. That night, as Mick lay snoring drunkenly, Fat Marie got her one sharp kitchen knife, a lean and vicious saw-edged monster called a Kitchen Devil, and went up to their bedroom. She was not sure how to go about it, because the point, the first inch or so, had been broken off ages before when Mick had thrown it at her and stuck it in the wall. He was lying on his back, dressed only in his open shirt, and one bare leg was crooked at the knee, outside the sheet and blanket. At the groin she could see a pulse, and remembered vaguely that that was where the big one lay, the gusher. But his throat seemed much more likely, much more vulnerable, so she suddenly rushed across the room and stabbed downwards, with all her weight and strength, beside his Adam's apple. The flat, broken end met something unyielding, causing the blade to bend and twang, then it sank in deep and completely, sliding down and outwards in her fist, emerging whole in a cascade of blood, bright scarlet, shiny, wonderful. Mick's eyes opened but the second blow hit on the same instant, and they closed again, his face washed invisible under a spray of red. She was not quiet, and the children came to watch.

Something to remember daddy by.

FORTY-THREE

Janis turned up early at the Ducie Bridge, but did not at first go in. It was a lovely morning, and she had a kind of horror of entering the cavern of the pub before midday, and cutting off the sun. In any case, she was less sure than ever that she should be meeting Ronnie, or why she was. She stood beside the wrought-iron walling of the bridge, in dark suit and sunglasses, and decided that she would watch for him, but not fully decide. She had only ever seen him safely in a jail. Perhaps his body would emanate some warning in the open air.

She and Hilary had discussed what she should do for hours, after Crabbe had thrown his hand grenade. Hilary had insisted that she had a duty to 'the remnants of her hunch' to back it to the end, insisted that a book would come of it, however innocent of major crime Keegan should prove to be. The fact that Janis still could not be sure was the aspect she found fascinating, she said – the fact that murderers, monsters, beasts could be so hard to spot. When Janis had said 'because he's not one', she had nodded just as eagerly. Even if he was a petty bumbler, a criminal inadequate, why did he have such presence, sex-appeal, charisma?

'Look,' she said, 'however the truth might turn out, you're going to end up with something valuable, and possibly unique – great insight into one man, one criminal, which few other people have matched or ever can. Even if he's not a murderer he'll be a fascinating book, if only as a starting point to look at others. I'll do a preface, that'll sell it! I'll take it to my own publishers as soon as you've got some words to show them! Balls to Buster Crabbe, you'll make a bomb!'

For the moment, lack of money was not a problem Janis thought about much. At least the collapse of everything had been neatly timed, and she was pretty sure that Clive would have her back unless the local bigwigs ganged up with the cops and put some pressure on the editor. Even if that happened she could get another job, she reckoned, or go to London for a while to do some heavy freelancing – for which a free room at Hilary's would always be available. No, her lack of zest was all to do with Ronnie.

'If I go on believing he might be a murderer,' she said, 'I'm guilty of exactly what I've hated the police for, always. It's mind-set, Hilary, a conviction that I'm right when every bit of evidence points the other way. I've talked to him for ages, I've asked him leading questions, I've tried to trick him, everything. Apart from the time he called them animals, as you predicted, he's behaved exactly like a normal person. Even that, for God's sake! They were animals, these people, they are animals! Why shouldn't he have said it just like anybody else?'

No guilt, remorse, no fear, no nervousness, no quietness or exultation when the gipsies were arrested.

'Perhaps he's just an ordinary bloke,' conceded Hilary, placidly. 'Perhaps that is the point.'

At eighteen minutes past midday, Janis imagined that she might have been stood up. She studied her watch, as if to find an answer there, wondering if prisoners were released at set times or if it were possible he'd been delayed. A second thought took her to the pub door, which she pushed open tentatively. Maybe Ronnie had come early.

He had. He was sitting at a table on the far side of the room like a character from a TV show. His shirt was open almost to the waist, his legs were thrust in front of him in pale, tailored trousers, he held a quite enormous brandy glass in one hand. He was watching her and smiling, and he slowly raised the glass.

There was a woman sitting next to him, who turned her head, although she did not smile at all. Eileen Thorpe.

The sight of Fat Marie standing at a bus stop on the Ripponden Road with all her children round about her was a shocking and confusing one, especially for other people in the queue. It was after nine a.m., but she had washed neither the children nor herself. Her face was white as normal, fixed in the miserable glare of the destroyed, but there were splashes of dried rusty liquid on her cheeks and eyebrows and in her hair. Underneath her anorak she had on a yellow blouse, stiff and

282

horrible with the same rusty stain, and her skirt and legs were caked with it. The baby clutched across one shoulder was also bloodstained, on its clothes and neck, and the two largest of the children had brown blotches. Fat Marie was going to the police.

That was what she said, at least. Before the bus came, a patrol car had pulled up, called by the landlord of the pub across the road who had been alerted by the commotion at the stop. This time the police were quick – however pressed they may have been – because it sounded fascinating. A blood-soaked woman and five kids, waiting for the bus to town! Surely not as a getaway vehicle? Their easy smiles were wiped off when she pulled out the Kitchen Devil, from somewhere underneath the baby. The passengers drew back, terrified, the children grinned, the police prepared to charge. The blood-soaked woman held it out, handle first.

'I killed him with it. Mick. I stabbed him in the neck.'

'When?' said the driver of the car.

'When? Last night sometime. I dunno.'

'Ten past eleven, Mum,' said Donna. She could tell the time.

'Ten past eleven,' repeated Fat Marie.

'Is he dead?' asked the other policeman. 'Where do you live? Last night was this? Ten past eleven last *night*? But . . .'

Momentarily, he ran out of things to say. Fat Marie stood unblinking; ungainly, sad, and fat. The bus appeared, trundling down the hill. The other passengers could not get over it.

'You know the House of Horror thing?' asked Fat Marie. 'Them murders in that house? He done them, him and his mates. He had it coming to him.'

'Can we go in your car?' demanded Sean. 'Hey, copper, let us in your fucking car.'

The driver ducked inside, not to let Sean in, for the moment, but to call the communications room. Probably a nutter, but . . . But within half a minute, everything was happening, at last. Fat Marie, staring stolidly out of the window as Moorside sped past them, covered in the toddler and the baby and the brawling kids, had some satisfaction that she'd saved the bus fares, hadn't she? Her bowels hurt her, and her head. She hadn't got much sleep the night before.

* * *

If Eileen had not been with Ronnie in the pub, Janis would not have gone. After the bright sunshine, the light inside was dim and shadowy, and the tableau that confronted her was disorienting. As she came towards them, Ronnie seemed expansive, smiling, while Eileen struck as dark and bitter. Ronnie behaved as if she were some sort of suitor, some long-lost girlfriend returning to the fold, Eileen as if she thought it too – and was going to fight her corner to the last. Janis was no suitor – with his naked chest and ostentatious gold, she disliked Ronnie now, actively and for the first real time, and obscurely needed him to know it. She nodded at him almost distantly, but turned a face on Eileen that both sought and offered reassurance.

'Eileen. I'm so glad you're here. Ronnie, nice to see you in the world outside, at last. Can I get you both a drink?'

Ronnie stood, the easy smile not quite wiped off, glancing from one to other of them through narrowed eyes.

'My shout. Let me guess, a gin and tonic? A big one, naturally.'

She shook her head, making a driving motion with her hands.

'A small one, thanks. The breath-test never celebrates.'

'Doll?' asked Ronnie, and Eileen shook her head. Both women watched him as he swaggered to the bar.

'I mean that, Eileen. You've no idea how nervous I was about coming here today, I was terrified. Among other things, I thought you might think I was lying to you again.'

'Maude told me, anyway. I did have my suspicions, though.' Eileen lowered her voice, leaning forward. 'He wanted to go away with you. He thinks you're going to make him rich and famous. He wanted me to let him have the key.'

Although she did not fully understand, Janis still felt astonishment.

'He said you had a little place in Wales. But surely he didn't mean . . . What, just him and me? What did you say?'

'He was lying,' stated Eileen, flatly. 'It's not in Wales, it's out in Cheshire, Derbyshire way. He tells lies, you do know that, don't you? All the time. I told him he was mad, I said you wouldn't go. I said I'd ask if we could all go, though, the three of us. You wouldn't have, would you?'

Their eyes met, and Janis shook her head in transparent honesty.

'But for him to think that you'd have let us! That's . . . that's just . . .'

There was a burst of laughter from the bar, from Ronnie and the landlord. It came to Janis that he was not dangerous, he was merely stupid, wonderfully stupid. He was diminishing before her eyes, like the dragon in the fable that shrank before the brave child's steady gaze and disappeared. Ronnie was a fool.

'Anyway,' said Eileen, 'what do you think? I know you want to talk to him, and he went on and on at me. It's not a bad spot, it's really nice, in actual fact. Two bedrooms and a kitchen and a lounge. It's got a fridge, so there'd be ice for your gin and tonics! It's not far from the canal. It's nice.'

Ronnie was coming back, a gin and tonic in one hand, a single glass of brandy in the other. Janis noted with distaste and irritation that he had put the tonic in for her, assuming that he knew the way she liked it. He poured the brandy into his giant glass, assessing them with his eyes, to see if Eileen had broached the subject.

'Big one,' he said, 'sorry, I'm not used to buying little drinks for ladies, I'll change it if you like. Well, here's to the future. Here's to Ronnie Keegan, reformed character. Here's to us.'

It was a strange party, sitting round the small bar table with nothing in common but a brittle awkwardness, but all of them, for different reasons, worked to make it work. Janis, observing Eileen's fear and dislocation, felt guilt for her role in their lives, but had a strong sensation also that Eileen, at the moment, preferred that she was there. For herself, she saw Ronnie stripped of his charisma, oddly glamourless outside the sterile brutalism of the jail, striving to maintain a role of macho superman. She, she realised, was the one who could walk out, with almost nothing sacrificed except perhaps a book, coupled with the discovery, maybe, that she was not a writer after all, but just a journalist. She had come into their lives unasked, and she could get up and go away. That made her think of Hilary, and her couch. She was not sure, at the moment, if there was anything more she wanted to know about Ronnie Keegan, criminal and reformee, or if indeed there were any depths to plumb. She saw a pretty, tired woman, and a vain and shallow man. And herself. How did they see her? How should she?

In the end, with more drink and a little food, some relaxation entered in, some minor pleasure in each other's company. In the end, Janis allowed Ronnie to cajole her, helped by the suspicion that Eileen really wanted her to agree. Maybe Eileen wanted a holiday away from Oldham (and its tubular bandages!) but did not want to go away with Ronnie on his own. Maybe she, herself, wanted to get away from everything and everybody and sit on a canal bank drinking white wine from the famous fridge, free at last of fears of Ronnie both as murderer or potential companion in her bed.

In the end, because it seemed a not unreasonable idea in many ways – she went.

FORTY-FOUR

It was many hours after Fat Marie's arrest before news of her garbled rantings began to seep down to Patten's team, and many hours after that before anyone imagined they might be serious or significant. Lance Rosser took the first call, his superintendent being out, and his response was harshly ribald. As he told it to his friends, he went apeshit, he hit the roof, he laughed it out of court. Some fucking dement, some fat slag of a drunkard's tart, slitting her old man's throat then claiming he was the murderer, not her! Were they daft up there, he demanded, were they mental? He suggested that too much black pudding gobbling was to blame.

The only thing that shook him, although he did not admit as much, was the location. Oldham, Ronnie Keegan's patch. But fortunately, no one had mentioned Keegan, had they? Only a man called Renwick, whom nobody had ever heard of.

Ronnie Keegan's name was not mentioned by Mrs Marie Conway until much later. Mrs Marie Conway – also known as Mrs Marie Renwick, also known as Fat Marie, a snippet she offered without shame or anger – did not volunteer anything of much coherence for several hours, because the police were very hostile, and clearly did not believe a word she told them, and got her utterly confused. One of them – an ugly, overbearing woman – spent forty minutes with her on the children's names alone, reducing stolid Mrs Conway, aka Renwick, aka Fat Marie to stolid, cowlike tears. She hit her once, and pulled her hair, although its dirty feel and texture made her grimace. They would not let her wash, despite a constant stream of references to her state and smell, nor would they let her see the children, after they'd discovered that the baby took a bottle, not the breast. At first, Fat Marie had heard the kids, creating mayhem with their shouts and screaming, but then the sounds had gone away. She asked a lot of times where they were, but no one told her. In fact, the social services had got them –

something of a personal triumph for a girl called Andrea, something of a fulfilled ambition.

Fat Marie had killed her old man, and she'd told them that, so what was all the problem? Why were they so vile to her, what more did they want to hear? Not about Brook Bank, for ages. They just told her she was being stupid.

Superintendent Patten was jolted to his stomach when Rosser told him, and the very violence of his sergeant's rage undermined his natural reaction that it was merely some lurid coincidence, or straight mistake. After listening for some minutes, being invited to agree that anything was possible, up to and including a spoiling operation mounted by the northern force for reasons as yet unclear, he shooed Rosser out and sat behind his desk in silent contemplation. Then he phoned the senior officer involved with Marie Conway and asked some leading questions. Had they known Mick Renwick as a 'client', did they know his wife, what weight were they attaching to the Brook Bank allegations? He did not mention Ronnie Keegan, dearly though he wanted to, in case he should affect their questioning of the woman, give them an angle that might be amplified by a mind steeped in murder fantasy, as they assumed hers was.

The replies he got were bleak enough. Mick Renwick was a drunkard and a batterer, who lived by petty crime as well as roofing, possibly a burglar, probably capable of vicious brutality when in a drunken frenzy. On the plus side, no known means of transport, no record of anything like Brook Bank, no known organisational skills, no known habitual criminal associates of any weight. The biggest plus of all was Fat Marie. Intelligence level barely off the charge-room floor, inarticulate to the point of incomprehensibility, incapable of giving times or dates or places, showing animation and enthusiasm only when asked directly about how she killed her 'husband'. Chaotic, psychotic, psychopathic – the Oldham chief inspector reeled off the jargon with lugubrious pride. They had a nutter, was his feeling, a sicko from a sink estate, but they'd had to pass it on in case Patten and his crew thought different. Co-operation, eh? No sweat. If it developed into anything, they'd be in touch.

Patten then called Rosser back to review at what stage, if any, Acting Chief Constable Cyril Hetherington would have to be informed. Rosser considered it would be a crazy move, giving the 'fat bastard' yet another rod to beat them with for absolutely no reason. Far from vacillating, he said, the time had come to hit the principals with the murder charges, get the bastards into court, and see them sent away to rot in hell. Everybody knew they had the guilty men, the evidence was overwhelming, so they should go for it before they made themselves look total fucking laughing stocks. Patten, assessing just how far around the station this venom had been spat already, just how long, indeed, the news would take to filter upstairs by osmosis, put in a call to Hetherington then and there, making an appointment. This, to Rosser, was just another personal affront.

Cyril Hetherington, although it was not his place to make operational decisions that could undermine the authority of the people on the ground, as he so cutely put it, made no bones about which side of the argument found his favour. He and Patten hit the facts back and forth across his broad, empty desk for more than half an hour, with the fat man becoming so excited that he came dangerously close at times to expressing an opinion. Patten's worry, surely, boiled down to fear of one coincidence, that a low-grade moron had claimed knowledge of the Brook Bank murders in the town where Ronnie Keegan lived. But Oldham was a large town, part of Greater Manchester, with a total population in the catchment of three million souls or more. So where was the connection, what was wrong with that, even Keegan had to live somewhere, didn't he?

By the time that – unprompted and unbidden – the Oldham police came up with Keegan's name late that afternoon, Hetherington and Rosser, separately, could not change their tune. Had the two men spoken to each other, their attitudes would have chimed completely. The country and the county were infested with gipsies and other layabouts, some of whom had not only done it, but had more or less confessed. So there had been coincidences, there always were coincidences, and by coincidence this fat, demented murderess knew Ronnie Keegan's name. She might even know the man, for God's sake, apparently they lived less than a mile apart, and she probably knew that he had worked at Brook Bank not so long ago. It was a grudge, maybe, revenge for some real or imagined trouble he had caused her, but more likely a fantasy, a way of getting even more attention. Let's face it, there weren't many air miles in stabbing your old man, were there? Even the buckets of blood would hardly get your picture in the papers! It was an angle, an inspired gambit, and the truth was that it added not a shred of evidence, real, hard, concrete evidence, linking Keegan with the happenings at Brook Bank.

Even Patten, to whom such thought processes whiffed badly of rationalisation, knew that so far the woman had come up with nothing that was worth a row of beans, in terms of evidence. He was still jolted, out of phase, deeply perturbed, but he knew as well as Rosser did, and Hetherington, that she could repeat Keegan's name a thousand times to no effect at all. Without a peg to hang it on it was just so much hot air, and on balance, every time he forced his reason to a conclusion, he came down on Rosser's side. It was an aberration, a coincidence, one of those bloody things that happened.

Without a peg to hang it on, it was useless. Despite the nagging doubts, he almost prayed that there would be no peg.

The call that smashed it into pieces came at eleven minutes past two the following afternoon, when Oldham police informed him that Fat Marie had at last come up with something that they reckoned must be crucial. Patten, who had hardly slept, responded cautiously, although his chest was hammering with horrified excitement. Faced with the ruin of his case against the gipsies, facing the collapse of everything he had believed in totally and worked so hard to bring to fruition, he was nevertheless surprised by the actual urgency of his desire to deny the value of the information, by the very vehemence with which he told himself it must be explainable away. The man in Oldham, with the scent of something bigger in his nostrils than the sordid little tale of Fat Marie and Mickie, was disappointed by the flat response, but recognised the reason for it and did not push. Patten, having listened twice, said he would get back to him as soon as possible, and slumped back in his chair, feeling drained and physically sick. He allowed himself five minutes, during which time he broke up a cigar, then reached for his Filofax. His first job was to talk to

Hetherington, to face the next instalment of that holocaust, but his first duty lay elsewhere. He looked up Janis Sanderson's home number.

The link with Ronnie Keegan, still, was not conclusive. He told himself this, and his fingers paused above the buttons of the phone. But he remembered with searing clarity the things he'd said to Janis at their final interview, and the intention she'd made plain. When the ringing tone gave way to a metallic silence, preceding the recorded message of an answer-tape, relief that she was absent turned to a deeper stab of shame, and he gathered himself to record, tersely, that she should under no circumstances agree to meet, or even speak to, Ronnie Keegan. Then he paused, facing the implications of his personal disaster. 'Miss Sanderson,' he continued, 'I cannot emphasise too clearly what I have to say. Keegan is probably a very dangerous man, and to meet him would be to court a lot of trouble.' Again he tasted bile, the bitterness of self-disgust. 'Please stay away from him,' he said, 'and contact me immediately you get this message. If you meet him, your life will be in mortal danger.'

He put the phone down with a light sweat on his forehead, which he rubbed off while leafing through for the *Clarion*'s number. The newsdesk told him that she had actually left the paper, which had not occurred to him, and that her whereabouts were unknown to them. Finally, he rang back Oldham, to have confirmed beyond a doubt that Keegan had been released from Strangeways Jail the day before. This time, when he took out a cigar, he lit it, and inhaled deeply. So that is that, he thought.

Fat Marie, allowed a shower at last because they had decided to take her back to Noonsun in a car, had led three detectives to a spot – a 'hidey-hole' – that she'd been mithering about for hours, but which two separate sorties without her had failed to locate. Not surprising, as it was at least a hundred yards from where she'd said, in a maisonette and not a house, and in a back room, not a front. Indeed, they had continued to treat her as a liar and an idiot until the moment she had pointed to the sagging plaster panel behind a broken unit, and a detective constable had gingerly put in his arm and come out with the gun. It was a shotgun, in quite good order except that the barrel had been clumsily sawn off just beyond the magazine, a Remington Wingmaster pump-action, five shot. Also, a plastic bag containing cartridges.

A knowing look had tainted Fat Marie's grin, a triumphant look. She appeared to think that this would get her off.

'See?' she said. 'I'm not so bloody stupid, after all.'

FORTY-FIVE

Ronnie Keegan, comfortably drunk, was bolstered in his love-making with Eileen by the knowledge that Janis would be listening through the thin partition walls of the chalet. From the moment they had rolled into the double bed, Eileen had been aware of it as well, and had been upset and circumspect. The more she had tried to avoid Ronnie's face and hands, the more she had tried to whisper that they must be quiet, the more noisy and insistent he'd become. After a two-month lay-off she could hardly have expected to get away with it, but she may have hoped they'd drunk enough to knock him down and make him lazy. She was wrong.

Throughout the drinking session in the Ducie Bridge, which had lasted late into the afternoon, then working their way through wine and whisky as the sun sank behind the Peak Forest canal outside Marple, the three of them had managed to convert the oddness and the tensions into a sense of simple pleasure at a strange new undertaking. While she was sober enough to keep such complex thoughts in focus, Janis told herself that this was the best, the only, way to break down the barriers of dislike and suspicion she had about Ronnie, to soften them both up for an exchange of the basic truths they were going to have to examine if anything was going to come out of it. It was a journalistic technique, she recognised, and might have been more honestly seen as a desire to get pissed, a desire to abandon her uptightness, and see what would develop. After two big gins she decided also to abandon the red Renault on the demolition lot that had been turned into a makeshift car park, and let whoever had been nominated, do the driving. Eileen that would be, she surmised, correctly. Eileen drank, but not a lot, and continued to appear relieved that Janis was part of the party, while Ronnie drank with a dedication that he attributed, not infrequently, to the fact that he 'had a lot of catching up to do'. In the swing of it, he became fluent and rather amusing, and he and Janis talked a lot about their mutual love of cars and speed. That reminded her, for one brief flash, of Detective Sergeant Rosser, and she acknowledged to herself that Ronnie was a better bet than him, in every way. Eileen, too, liked driving, and she and Ronnie had done some fast cross-country stuff 'in their younger days,' she said. Especially in lay-bys, added Ronnie, with a charming, dirty grin, and Eileen giggled.

They were all quite drunk as they drove to Cheshire out along the A6, although Janis was alert enough to get her overnight bag and spare tapes and batteries from her car, and Ronnie was thirsty enough to stop at the first off-licence to get some bottles. The road was busy and congested, but the merry mood sustained them out into the country, which was new to Janis and different enough from the Oldham Pennines for her to ask Eileen about the landmarks. At a village called Disley they took a bumpy track down into a wood, opened and closed two or three heavy gates, then followed a stony lane that wound along beside the canal, sometimes close and sometimes at a farther distance. The chalet was up a smaller track, in its own copse of broadleaf trees, and hardly visible to Janis until she had it pointed out to her. Behind it, the copse spread into a larger wood running up a steepish hill.

When they stopped, pulled deep under the trees beside the wooden building, Janis was struck by the peaceful silence of it all. The radio went off with the ignition, and the windows had been wound down as they'd bumped along beside the waterway. In the momentary gap before Ronnie and Eileen bustled to get out, she breathed in warm air scented with pine, and heard a peacock calling from not far away. She pulled herself out from the back and filled her lungs.

'Good, isn't it?' said Eileen, proudly. 'I've had it years, I got it for a song when Dad died. We used to come out for parties, in the old days.'

Ronnie, who was pissing behind a bush, called out: 'It's great unless the vandals do it over. Then there's the beetles and the mice! Give me the city any day.'

This time there had been no vandals, although inside there was some sign that small animals had been in. The windows, behind wire stone-guards, were opened wide to the late afternoon sunshine and breeze, while Ronnie checked the water and removed a selection of giant spiders from the lavatory. He also got out folding chairs and placed them on the verandah, plus a folding table, a corkscrew, the bag of bottles, and three glasses. With mock despair he announced that he had forgotten gin, but Janis wanted no more spirits, anyway. Not until her nightcap, maybe. When the fridge had done its stuff, Ronnie promised her, there would be ice in plenty, and chilled wine.

Naturally enough, they touched on the project, but Janis kept it general to a degree. Mostly, she told them about her journalistic life, with Eileen making the connection between the way some of her colleagues lived and drank, and her own man. She was relaxed, however, and seemed fond of him at last, and pleased to have him back. Occasionally Janis caught Ronnie looking at her with something in his eyes she did not care for much, but it was too fleeting – and she too tipsy – for her to pin it down. Something proprietorial, perhaps – conspiratorial more likely? – some hint that he had designs on her, or at least desires that he assumed she ought to share. After a time or two it did not bother her, because she thought she had him now, completely: Ronnie was a show-off and an immature, rather silly man. If he fancied himself enough to think she fancied him, so be it – if it came to it, he'd soon find out. But it wouldn't come to it, because Eileen was here, and they were having fun, and everything was very friendly. All in all, thought Janis, it had turned out exceptionally well.

Once, when Eileen had gone off to the lavatory, he did lean forward as if he might be going to make a pass. Janis leaned forward simultaneously, waving a schoolmarm's finger.

'Now Ronnie, don't do anything that might spoil it!'

He allowed himself to sink back into the chair, nodding.

'No hurry, is there?' He cocked his head, as if to acknowledge that they shared a secret. 'Everything comes to him that waits.'

Janis, feeling slightly flustered, could not think of a suitable reply.

They talked of going to the pub, they talked of going for a meal. But Eileen had brought milk and eggs and bread and ham and butter, and the kitchen was loaded down with tins. In the event they did not light the Calor cooker, but ate makeshift sandwiches in the warm darkness, watching the moon rise above the low hills then sail along majestically as if following the canal. Ronnie was onto the whisky, which made him noisier but less coherent, and both the women less at ease. Janis made the move to go to bed, Eileen coming to help her sort out the sheets and blankets in a quick, anxious way. When it was done, they stood inside her bedroom door for a moment, not quite looking at each other. Then Janis touched her hand, and Eileen went.

Ronnie, when the thought of Janis lying there occurred to him, found it immensely erotic. He had been excited in the first place by her presence in the chalet, then by the largely silent struggle Eileen had put up to make him make love quietly, if at all. That ended with both he and Eileen naked, her rolled backwards across the bed and Ronnie kneeling between her thighs pinning her to the mattress with a hand on each shoulder. He was a strong man, she was small, and by a quick transfer of his hands from shoulders to hips, he lifted her to meet his penis and slid into her like that. Then he threw his body forward, covered her, and folded both his arms close around her neck. It was a struggle, controlled with diamond hardness, but it was somehow tender, too. Eileen still fought for quietness, which involved stopping his mouth with teeth and tongue, her slim body clinging to his to restrict the massive movements that he wanted. Thus glued together, they writhed around the bed, every muscle pitched against its opposite, every sound that escaped from Ronnie's mouth pounced on and smothered as it tried to rise. Despite herself, Eileen became involved, orgasmic, ecstatic even, even while she fought to be polite. She thought of Janis as she came, still in control enough to try and block Ronnie's enormous shout, her release in coming mixed with relief that it was over.

'You noisy sod,' she breathed. 'Oh Christ, I needed that.'

Ronnie had thought of Janis not just while he came, though, nor did he intend the session to be over. Indeed, although his technique (he told himself) had been brilliant, although his shout had been deliberately loud, his orgasm had been more a spasm, possibly not even a full ejaculation. The level of his lust was high, the combination of Eileen's too-familiar flesh and his mental picture of Janis's unknown body fusing into a fantastic composite, but the brandy, wine and whisky had also combined, to deaden the sensation to the point that he could thrust and feel, but not exactly find the spot to touch to tip him over into full release. He pulled out of Eileen joyfully, bounding to his knees again to present her with his hot erection full in the face, sliding his hands around behind her neck.

'That one was for you,' he said. 'Now my turn. Jesus, doll, I've missed you.'

True or false? Over the next hour, Ronnie fucked Eileen in every way he knew, and always in his mind's eye he saw Janis, except when he saw Tessa Wilmott lying there, her face whiter and her eyes more frightened than Eileen's had yet become. Why should Eileen be frightened, anyway – he was not hurting her, and this was nothing new, she knew he could go on for hours when he'd been drinking. He might be fucking Janis in advance, or paying back the dead bitch for all she'd done to him, but it was Eileen who was getting the benefit, wasn't it? She was a better shape than Tessa Wilmott anyway, who had had a tendency to fat, she was more exciting mixed up with Janis, who was slim as a squirrel. Tessa Wilmott had been good to fuck while she was dying, and had been well deserving of her death. A wash and brush up! That bloody Doggo and his jokes! Ronnie laughed, and saw a stain of anguish spread in Eileen's eyes, as if she wondered what could happen next. What happened was he came, unexpectedly and violently, with Eileen, Janis, and Tessa's rumpled form mixed up beneath him, he came explosively, divinely, this time the sound burst out of him, not manufactured, pure joy. A wash and fucking brush up! Oh my God.

Then he lay there, panting into Eileen's face, thinking God Ronnie, what a gash-hound, what a holy terror, what a marvel! Thinking that the difference was, Tessa had turned him down and Janis wouldn't, would she, because Janis was dying for it, for him, for Ronnie Keegan, stud and superstar! Thinking he wouldn't have to rape this one, force her, act like some bleeding animal, because that was what she was there for, wasn't it, that was why she'd been pursuing him like some crazy? Ronnie and Janis, soon. Even sooner since she'd lain there listening, since she'd heard what he could do. An hour! More! Three or four times, or five! What a pity, he thought, gazing at Eileen's swollen eyelids, so close to shedding tears, what a pity that she'd insisted on coming with them, playing gooseberry. What a fucking drag.

In the room next door, Janis was snorting slightly in the sleep that had come to her halfway through the marathon. Her last conscious thoughts had been centred on distaste, and fear that he was putting on a show for her, and a worse one that she had provoked it somehow, if only by her presence. At first she had listened to the vigour and the noise with embarrassed interest – as there was no way at all of avoiding the experience – but later she had felt sorry for, worried for, Eileen. But maybe this was what they always did, maybe Ronnie was the ram he clearly thought he was, and they had been apart for many weeks. Then she remembered drunken sessions of her own, that had gone on joylessly for far too long, then she decided it was a demonstration of his prowess, designed in part to amaze her with his virility. This led her on to Ronnie's expectations, how he saw her part in things, what he thought she might be doing there.

Janis, at least half drunk despite her journalist's capacity, was hardened by these thoughts, and knew that Ronnie figured nowhere in her desires now, if indeed he ever had. She also knew that she had lost the impetus to examine him, to try and get inside his mind, to glorify his little life by article or book. He was, she had come to realise, completely normal, whatever he had done, however he might see himself. As a drinks companion for an evening, perfectly all right, and nothing more. As a criminal, just what Patten said he was – a fiddler-about with a kingsize ego, a nobody. In all, she told herself, as shallow as a plate of piss.

So in the morning, what would she do? She would talk and she would listen, and most of all she'd find out how Eileen felt. She would not dismiss any possibility, but she did not expect that, in the end, she would hang around for long. Really, she supposed, it meant that Patten and his men had been right, and that struck her as rather curious. But, halfway between sleep and waking, she knew she was no longer afraid of Ronnie Keegan, no longer saw him as any kind of monster. When she did sleep, she had no fear that nightmares of violence would come back to haunt her.

She thought of Bren; then – listening to the groanings through the wall – of Clive and his ginger fatness. No, she didn't think she'd hang around for long.

FORTY-SIX

In the morning, Janis had a hangover, and everything seemed a little different. She awoke at eight fifteen, first aware that she was somewhere strange, then that her head hurt, not very badly, but enough. She rolled onto her back, noting the unpleasant sticky sound her mouth made when she opened it, and listened. Outside, birds were singing, and there was the slow thumping that she recognised, from the evening before, as a canal boat engine. The air, despite her state, smelled fresh and sweet, and there were no other sounds but these. Inside the chalet, nobody else had stirred.

He stopped in the end then. Poor Eileen. What a way to end up, with such a pig.

Janis contemplated. She could get up now and go, just walk into the village perhaps a mile away, and get a taxi into Manchester, or she could stay and see it through, see if there was anything to be salvaged of her project. She could imagine Hilary's attitude if she just quit. Her grand obsession, the idea she'd left her job for, her stepping stone to a different sort of life. To quit without the talk to Ronnie, without investigation, would be . . . a ballix. And a girl, in any case, had to make a living, didn't she?

Having slept in a shortish nightie that she'd brought, Janis decided to go into the kitchen and make herself some coffee. Hand upon the latch, though, she thought of Ronnie, and the possibility he might come out and find her there. She rummaged in her bag for cord trousers and a thick red muslin shirt, standing naked for a while before she dressed, enjoying the sensation of the clean, warm country air. When she went into the kitchen, Eileen was there, looking wan and tired with a box of matches in her hand.

'He's still asleep,' she said, towards the bedroom door. 'How was . . . did you sleep all right?'

Their eyes met, and both looked away, embarrassed. A wave of pity washed over Janis.

'Like a log. I went out like a light, before I'd even properly undressed. I've got a headache, though.' She picked up a glass, half filling it with water from the tap. 'Soluble aspirins, in my bag. Reporter's breakfast. Do you want some?'

Eileen lit the gas under the kettle. She shook her head.

'Tired, that's all. I don't get hangovers, or maybe that's how they affect me. I stayed on wine, anyway, Ronnie will be terrible, on the whisky, it has a terrible effect on him. Bad tempered. He snored all night, I thought it might have kept you awake.'

Janis agreed to toast, and went to take her aspirins. She would have liked to have talked it through with Eileen, the sex thing, Ronnie as a person, his personality, but she could not see it happening. They faced each other awkwardly, both knowing that the night had raised the barriers, both aware of the presence behind the flimsy door.

'What will you do?' asked Janis. 'I mean — well, what is there around here? Do you just sit outside and take the sun?'

'I garden, believe it or not. The place is like a jungle, but it would be much worse if I didn't have a go at it now and then. Ronnie doesn't come here very often, he hates it, to be quite honest.' She raised her head, and added quickly: 'For once the isolation was a bonus, I suppose. So that you can talk about . . . you know, work out the project. He's pretty excited about it, underneath it all.'

Her lack of conviction was almost comical. Sipping instant coffee, Janis considered suggesting they should leave, all of them, that she could do it just as well in Manchester, or Harding Lane, even. But it would sort itself out, pretty quickly. As long as Eileen was content to potter while she and Ronnie talked.

'I hope I haven't built his hopes up too much,' she said. 'There's no guarantee that much will come of it. Still, I suppose he's right in one way, there won't be much distraction.'

They were washing up when Ronnie came into the kitchen, and he had the look of a man in the grip of alcoholic suffering. His thin face had a patchy pallor, that was set off by his need to shave. The eyes were deadened by the whisky residue, and his forehead was creased with strain. He raised a smile for Janis, but barely a glance for Eileen.

'Never again. The first day out's always a killer. If we stay here for a week, I promise I won't touch another drop. Give me some coffee, doll, OK?'

With that he walked through another door to the lavatory, where he stayed until the coffee that was made for him was cold. When he tasted it he demanded another cup and took it into the bedroom. Shortly afterwards an electric razor started buzzing.

'I'm going outside,' said Eileen, picking up some gardening gloves. 'Quite honestly, I'm staying out of his way. He'll be all right in a couple of hours, unless he goes back on the booze.' She caught Janis's reaction. 'I don't think he will, because you're here, but it's possible.' The faintest pause. 'You don't have to stay, love. I'll understand if you want to leave.'

Ronnie re-emerged clean-shaven, a pair of dark glasses covering his eyes. He did not comment on Eileen's absence, but complimented Janis on the clothes she wore. For some reason, Janis felt chill fingers touch her spine.

'We'd better talk,' she said. 'We'd better pin down just what it is we hope to do, Ronnie. Do you want to do it here, or shall we go outside?'

'Anywhere you want to do it,' he replied, 'is good enough for me. Aren't you going to take your tape recorder!' Janis, with a sensation of disgust, barged through the kitchen door into the green and fragrant light. She heard it swing behind her, then swing and close once more as Ronnie followed. She walked fast out of the small front garden, not looking back, and down the long slope towards the canalside. On the towpath, she glanced left and right before deciding her direction, then swung along it angrily. Ronnie caught up within a hundred yards, falling in beside her.

'Touchy this morning, aren't we? I didn't mean it that way, you know. It's the booze.'

'I'm here on business,' Janis answered. 'If you remember that, we'll do all right. Otherwise, Mr Keegan, there's nothing to discuss.'

Ronnie formed a tight grin, but kept it to himself. He almost told her that she looked lovely angry, but he had more sense.

I know your game, he thought, you're worried Eileen might have heard, as if that mattered. He became aware that his head was hurting badly, probably from the speed of the walk. He could wait. He wasn't in a hurry to get things moving on.

'I could do with sitting down,' he said. 'I don't know about you, but my brain hurts. I've had enough of country hiking, for one day.'

There was an open field rising to their left, and Janis struck up it beside a dry stone wall. The going was easy, but Ronnie was panting soon so she did not take him far. She sat down on the dry grass, avoiding cowpats, and watched him lowering himself. While he regained his breath she studied the view across the shallow valley, lonely and secluded, dotted with farms and trees, the canal three hundred yards below her. There were no boats visible, although some children were playing at a swing bridge half a mile away, as if they were waiting to open it for one.

'Quite honestly,' he said, 'you don't want to worry about her too much. Eileen. Quite frankly, I don't see us lasting much longer, you know, as a couple. Not her fault, don't get me wrong, she's been . . . well, pretty good to me. In fact, that's probably the problem, I'm not good enough for her, know what I mean? In actual fact, I've been thinking of getting out for quite a while. You know. Going freelance.'

Janis assumed the choice of word was quite deliberate. She thought, poor Eileen; she thought it three times in a row. But not because poor Eileen might be losing him.

'It sounds a shame,' she said. 'Just when you've decided to go straight. I mean, about you not being good enough for her. Surely she ought to be the judge of that?'

'She's too soft. I get away with murder. Even when I'm in Strangeways she thinks the sun shines out of my back passage. Maybe I need a woman with a sort of clearer view. You know.'

'I'd have thought you needed to talk about where you're going to live,' responded Janis brutally. 'And how you're going to pay the rent and buy your food. Isn't it a joint mortgage? Or are you planning to kick her out into the street?'

Ronnie lay back, and put both his hands across his cheeks and eyes. She did not understand the gesture, except that it completely masked his thought processes. When he spoke he sounded both embarrassed and inept.

'OK. So how much do I get? I mean, that's the bottom line, quite frankly. This book. You're not expecting to get my life for nothing, are you? I mean, it's time we got down to brass tacks, isn't it?'

Janis felt like screaming, but she acknowledged a tiny stab of guilt. It was she who'd started it, made this man think he had something saleable. Now she no longer quite believed it she had not yet been straight with him, nor did she want to be, irrevocably. The frustration was obvious in her voice.

'For God's sake, Ronnie! If we're talking enough to live on, enough to split from Eileen with, you've no chance! It doesn't work like that, they don't just hand out sacks of money, be realistic.'

He did not uncover his face or eyes, but she noted that his whole body had tensed. Janis touched him on the arm, and Ronnie jumped.

'Let me explain,' she said. 'Ronnie, I'm not even sure we've got a book here. That's what we're trying to find out. I mean, if you'd been a murderer—'

She stopped, and Ronnie sat up. Inexplicably, she was frightened. His pupils, uncovered, dwindled rapidly in the light, but his expression was not one of anger. It was as if he'd realised something, or some truth were sinking in. Beyond him, on the towpath, Janis saw a figure, waving.

'That's what you wanted, wasn't it?' he said. 'Not just a bit of rough, the whole thing, the special offer package. That's what you wanted me to be.'

It was Eileen. She was carrying a shopping bag. With relief, Janis ignored what he had said.

'There's Eileen.' She stood up, waving too vigorously. 'She must be going shopping, shall we go?'

Ronnie hardly looked.

'If you want a book,' he said, 'you'd better stay and sort it out. You're messing me about, Janis. I don't like that.'

Five minutes later Eileen went off with her list. It was mainly lunchtime food – they thought they'd go up to a pub if they were still there in the evening. The possibility they might be gone was raised by Eileen, nodded at by Janis, and not commented on by Ronnie, who merely added another bottle of Scotch to the list of drink. He did not speak again until Eileen had passed from their sight.

The violence of the trauma that had hit police HQ was belied by the civilisation of the way it was discussed. Police command is structured hierarchically, and protocol extremely rigid. Lance Rosser wanted to tell Patten what a cunt he was, what a mealy-mouthed, back-stabbing, backsliding little gutless shitbag of a traitor to his men, but they faced each other across desks and tables and spoke in normal tones, their faces moulded into some semblance of mutual respect. Patten wanted to tell Cyril Hetherington that to cover up a possible mistake, to pretend there was no reason to suppose that Keegan was a murderer who was possibly murdering Janis Sanderson right now, was immoral, indefensible, and vile. He merely laid out possibilities, worst-case scenarios, that he said might come about unless the danger was acknowledged. Hetherington, in his turn, wanted to crush this stupid, stupid man, whose scruples seemed set fair to destroy his hopes of confirmation as chief constable, who could not see that so far no blame attached to them, nor could it if they played their cards subtly enough. He only hummed and hahed, repeatedly returning to the men in custody, the clearly guilty men, and warning vaguely of the danger inherent in 'muddying the waters'.

Lance Rosser's view was clear. The Boss was going to blow the case against the tinkers, was going to humiliate the lads who'd done the fucking work, was going to chuck a bomb into morale from which they'd probably not recover in ten years, was going to kowtow to the namby-pamby liberals who turned like weathervanes to every breeze that blew, forgetting – like their ilk always did – the suffering of the victims in the desire to be 'fair' to the worthless shits who'd done the damage in the first place. And why? That was the mystery, unless he had the hots for the reporter, which was mooted, certainly, in the detective squad. But surely that could not be true?

Patten knew and understood these feelings, and they caused him genuine distress. He recognised the inability of his team to accept that facts could blind them, that seductive pathways sometimes led to destinations that were simply wrong. Unlike almost all the officers he had ever served with, he did not believe himself infallible, or his judgements writ in stone. But in this case he had been as sure as anyone that they were right, he had believed it to the bone. To tell his men that despite the confessions, despite the guns, despite the weight of probability, he had changed his mind, felt to him, too, like an act of terrible betrayal.

A compromise was necessary, and a compromise emerged. Oldham had got the Keegan bit between their teeth now, so there was no denying that he had disappeared and so had Janis Sanderson. But who was to say that Keegan, and Mick Renwick, too, had not been involved with Bernie Smith and Boswell and the rest? Even if the DNA results from Renwick's body should match some of the samples from Brook Bank – as theirs did not – it would prove little, given the 'buckets of blood and spunk and stuff they'd mopped up around the place', to quote Rosser. And only Smith had so far been charged with murder, fortunately, so if embarrassing clashes looked like arising in the courts, they could quietly drop it by offering no evidence at the trial, and get all nine travellers done for the burglary. What could be fairer than that?

So Oldham, finally, were given the nod, while Hetherington and Patten met the legal men to see about the possibility of naming Keegan, issuing a photograph perhaps, sicking the media onto the fact that a dangerous criminal might be on the loose, and might have a woman hostage. Two women, it rapidly became apparent, when Oldham started swarming over Harding Lane and digging at the council offices where Eileen Thorpe had disappeared from work. Rosser and his cohorts were in deep despair, all this nonsense, this monumental climb-down that must make them look to the black-pudding munchers in the north like a gang of halfwits led by a vacillating prat. For no reason, that was the sickener – there was still nothing in the world directly linking Ronnie Keegan with the Brook Bank thing, except the brainless mouthings of the fat bitch and the cockeyed theories of the thin. Rosser did not have one colleague whom he trusted in the force who did not agree with him that Janis Sanderson deserved whatever she might get.

Oldham went a bundle, and they worked well and hard. Patten, after another tough interview with Hetherington, went north to join them, promising to uphold the honour of his force beyond anything he might personally feel. Rosser, left behind, spat blood and feathers to his friends and drank to Patten's downfall in their favourite bar. The simple truth was, as every policeman knew, they were a marvellous bunch of men (and good old Jenny Venner too, of course) who were let down, always, by the twats in charge. But from any point of view, he felt, the Boss had let them down in spades.

Unluckily for Eileen, the media campaign to save her life had not got under way when she was in the village shopping. She picked up an early copy of the local rag in case they needed the TV guide later, but neither she nor Janis nor Ronnie were featured when she glanced at the front page. After she had done her shopping she went into the Dandy Cock and had a half of shandy, mainly so that she would not interrupt the negotiations on the canal bank. There, leafing through the inside pages, she came across a news item that startled her, then – on reflection – shocked her deeply. She finished her drink, picked up her bags, and hurried down the lane. By the time she neared the garden of the chalet, where she intended to drop her heavy purchases, she was sweating and afraid.

Ronnie was there. As she opened the gate he appeared in the chalet doorway, with a glass of whisky in his hand. From thirty feet she could see that he was drunk again, or at least well on the way. He had an odd look on his face, part grin, part sneer, an aggressive look she recognised too well. Of Janis she could see no sign.

'Ronnie!' she said. 'Something's happened to Mick Renwick! A woman's murdered him! Someone called Conway!'

Ronnie's complexion turned to black, and he made a violent sound to silence her as he leapt forward. Eileen dropped a bag as he tore the folded paper from her hand, hustling her backwards as he did so, forcing her into the trees, hustling her further into the copse beside the wooden house. She opened her mouth to speak again, but saw his eyes and stopped.

'Shut up!' he hissed. 'She'll hear, you fool! Shut up!'

Suddenly, the implications became clear, she knew who Louise Marion Conway was, who had been charged with stabbing Michael Joseph Renwick, 41, a roofer, at his home on

Briar Lane, in Noonsun, Oldham, the day before, stabbing him repeatedly, to death. It was the woman she had heard about, had had pointed out to her, grotesquely fat and with a raft of kids. It was Fat Marie.

Suddenly, more implications flooded in and clarified, popping like fairy lights inside her brain. Janis had been asking questions round the area, she must have known that Ronnie had had things to do with Mick. Mick had rung up that time, drunk, when Ronnie had just got sent off to prison, that was the day after, wasn't it, it must have been. Now Ronnie said that Janis must not know that Mick was dead, now Ronnie had forced her out of the chalet garden, out through the rotten fence, into the wood. Now Eileen had to scream, she had to scream.

Instead she whispered: 'It was Mick and you. She'll tell them won't she, now she's killed him? Janis mustn't know.'

Ronnie's eyes were black and wide. He had dropped the whisky glass, but the newspaper still stuck bizarrely from one hand as he shot it out towards her neck. Eileen's mouth opened for the scream but he drove his strong thumb into the soft front of her neck, crushing it towards his fingers at the back. His left hand released her arm and joined the right, and the bony clamp bit into her with atrocious speed. He squeezed so hard he heard her neck break.

Up until this moment, he had had total confidence that he would get away with it. He had been certain that he had survived Brook Bank.

Ronnie let Eileen's body drop, and tried to spit. But his mouth was dehydrated from the whisky.

FORTY-SEVEN

Janis saw him coming through the garden, saw him white and stumbling, and she knew somehow that everything was lost.

She would have run but there was no way to get past him, and nowhere to hide. Her tongue clove to her palate, her knees began to turn to rubber under her. His face was transfixed with horror, dark and elemental.

'Ronnie. Ronnie. What have you done? What have you done?'

'You knew,' he answered. His voice was strangled. 'It's what you wanted, isn't it? You knew.'

Until that moment, he had known he'd got away with it. It was the knowledge that he couldn't that made him crack. He had a physical sensation of breaking up, his stomach and his organs falling into pieces. From his mouth came a choking noise, harsh and anguished. If Janis had known it, then, she could have got away, pushed past him, knocked him over, walked. But Janis faced him in a not dissimilar state.

'But Eileen? Where's Eileen?'

She threw back her head and screamed, and Ronnie jumped at her like a spider and knocked her backwards into the house. Janis cannoned off the wall into the table, arms and legs and kitchen chairs flying everywhere, screaming as she crashed about. Ronnie was in the doorway, then through the door, then had slammed it after him as she crawled frantically around the floor, hurt and bleeding from the face, crawling like a spider in the bath, a different kind of spider, lost and damaged.

Janis knew fear then that was like her night fears but appallingly different, worse. She was hollowed out by it, her entire mind and spirit cringing at the knowledge that she was going to be destroyed. It was paralysing, although her body moved, she could bring nothing to her mind except that awful knowledge, the anticipation of great pain, annihilation. She could not even look at Ronnie, because the sight could only make it worse. He was the throbbing source of everything, the heart of it, the very agent of her coming death. When she stopped screaming she began to mew, a high, thin noise that broke down into sobs.

Ronnie, flattened up against the door, stared at her, jaws clenched and working slightly. He was going to have to kill her now. Mercifully, he did not see her balled-up body, dark cords and muslin shirt crunched up beneath the draining board, as an object of desire. He saw the whisky bottle rather, almost empty, and his head hurt, splittingly, and his tongue was furred and swollen.

'I didn't want to kill her,' he said. 'She was coming through the garden. I didn't want to kill her, but she . . .'

He moved towards the bottle and Janis began to scream again, muffling it by burying her head between her upper arms, crouched over like a baby in a temper. Ronnie ignored her, neither moved nor angered by the row, and picked the bottle up and drained it. There was not much of it, not enough to make him cough, and he was desolated, lonely, near to collapse. Eileen had dropped one bag in the garden, the other farther out. He had to get them in, in any case, he had to hide them from any passer-by. Oh Christ, he thought, oh fucking Jesus Christ. Oh Christ.

He banged the door behind him, running out into the warm, fresh air, focused only on the shopping bag among the tangled grass. The drink was not in this one, so he ran through the broken fence, glancing at the door that stayed tight shut, stopping when he saw the other bag, open on the loam. Beyond it Eileen lay, crumpled and inert, her face invisible on its twisted neck. He did not know what to do, it was so obvious in the trees, anyone would see it if they came along. But he just snatched up the plastic carrier and ran back to the house. He expected to find she'd put it on the latch, or that she'd run to the back to break a window and escape, but she had done neither. He burst open the door and she was sitting on the floor, beneath the draining board, her face raised as if to see. But her eyes were closed, red and bruised and closed in a white blotched face with blood beneath the nose.

The windows had wire stone-guards, he remembered. That

310

was good. And who would go through the woods? Nobody, they went to the canal to walk their dogs. Nobody, for days on end, for weeks.

'Are you going to kill me, too?' she said. 'Why did you do it, Ronnie? Why did you do it?'

The table, although shifted far across the room when she'd crashed into it, was still standing, so Ronnie set the bag on it and lifted a chair onto its feet. He got a glass and put it on the table, and sat down to unscrew the bottle-cap and pour. He took an enormous mouthful, and this one did make him cough, and almost gag. He did not answer her, he let his pulse slow down, he began to get a grip. Both of them, slowly, became very still. Outside birds sang, and an occasional aircraft flew in or out of Manchester airport, and once they heard a canal boat thumping by. Janis, because she had to, wet herself, easing the urine from her bladder slowly under full control. For a moment, the intense warmth on her thighs was comforting, and she was also comforted by the hope that it would stand her in good stead, perhaps, if it came to rape. Then, quite rapidly, it chilled.

Rape. If Ronnie wants to fuck me, and it will save my life, I'll fuck him. It can't be any worse for me than what he did to Eileen. Maybe he'll be too sore. Christ, he's killed poor Eileen. He killed the others. All the time I thought he'd done it, I was right. Then I changed my mind.

She almost said: 'I've pissed myself,' a flash of anger almost overcame her fear, that in any case had modified quite strangely since he'd gone outside. But she stopped herself, opening her eyes secretly instead. Ronnie's were closed, his head was slumped, almost on the tumbler's rim. He's drinking like a fish, she thought. Excitement welled up inside her, quick, unbearable. Perhaps he'll pass out, drunk!

Ronnie thought: She was just like Tessa Wilmott, down by the canal. She led me on, then she shit on me. What does she fucking want in any case, to put in her fucking book? I don't know what she fucking wants.

He had told her things about his childhood, about how he'd always known he'd be a hood. He'd told her how he and mates had stolen cars from age thirteen, and gone chasing lone women on the motorways, or boxing them into lay-bys and

screwing them. Although he'd said 'seducing', overcome with
the knowledge that she was hating him, and hating him even
more when he'd told her he'd reformed, and the woman thing
was part of it, he'd realised that he'd been 'no good' to women.
Hating him yet more when he'd tried to turn that, clumsily,
into a compliment or a pass, a weird suggestion that he'd
treated Eileen badly but he'd learned, he'd do better with the
next one, and – oh, heavily implied – it could be her. It was
after this that Janis said, courageously, she did not believe what
he was telling her, she'd seen a different version of the story
of his life, and – quite frankly – she did not think that there
would be a book, because ... well, just because. Ronnie,
baffled and enraged, had gone back to the chalet and started
drinking. Janis – from a sense of guilt? – had followed on.

Tessa Wilmott led him on, she tried to humiliate him. She'd
led him on then turned him down, she'd laughed at him and
called him a pathetic little man when he'd suggested something, not even openly to do with sex. She'd sided with Eileen,
too, she'd bawled him out once when there'd been a fight and
Eileen had got a cut eye from falling in their bedroom. Tessa
Wilmott, one day, had got what she'd deserved.

'I did it for the cash,' he said. Janis snapped her head up, as
if shocked. Ronnie, whose own had been drooping, raised it
lugubriously. 'Funny, isn't it? Thirty grand I thought we'd get,
at least. Thirty fucking grand. The mean old fuckpig hardly had
a sprout.'

'But you murdered them. You tortured them. Why did you
do that? How could you?'

Ronnie remembered it. Remembered Doggo's rage, Mick
Renwick's exaggerated, dancing fury. Mickie the Roofer, killed
by Fat Marie. That wasn't possible, that was truly weird. Mick
had smacked the old lady with a fire iron, he'd practically bent
it round her scrawny neck. He'd been screeching like a scalded
cat, money, money, money! They'd all been dancing mad, high
as fucking kites, popped up to the eyeballs, pissed as rats. Only
he'd been relatively normal.

He took another slug of whisky, holding it in his mouth and
letting it go down in liquid packages, looking at her, bleary-
eyed. He noticed that she'd pissed herself, there was a puddle
between her legs where she'd drawn her knees up and put her

arms tightly around them. I wonder if I like that, Ronnie thought, or if I find it disgusting?

'The old lady pissed herself,' he said. 'The other one, the one we done in first. Did you know their names? Joyce. She was getting in to bed when we came in, she had a bedroom on the bottom floor. She tried to fight us, it was funny, it's what set us off. Tessa ran off up the stairs, then ran back down again, screeching like a fucking banshee, it was like one of them farces on the telly. Old Joyce came to her door, then slammed it shut, then banged it open, as if she was planning to attack us. Then Mickie rushed at her and she went over backwards, her legs went in the air. She was screaming, and he was trying to get his trousers down, her old fanny was winking at him like a bloody eye, then she pissed herself. It shot right up in the air, you wouldn't've believed it if you hadn't seen it, right up in a curve, then splashed down on the wall and floor and doorway. Christ, we laughed.'

He stopped, and poured more whisky. This time he sipped it, images crowding his vision, fighting to get out. Janis had gone still again, unmoving, it was as if she was dead as well. Ronnie could see them in the house, all of them, shrieking and wriggling as they were fucked or murdered, but he could not sort it into sequence. He'd pulled the phone wires out – he'd known there were two phones, the old system unchanged since he'd worked there, just the junction in the hall – and he'd found the guns and unlocked the safe with the key that never got moved from its hook beside the pantry door, but he couldn't just remember how or when or where everything had taken place. Tessa had tried to get out and Doggo had knocked her down and torn her dress right off those lovely tits of hers, but they hadn't fucked her then, they'd done that upstairs, he thought, across the double bed after – or was it before? – they'd brained old Pete.

'It's funny,' he said. 'I know she pissed herself, I can see it in my mind's eye, all curved and yellow, and it ponged, but I can't remember if it was then, when Mickie pushed her in, or if it was later, when we had a fuck at her. That's funny, isn't it, young blokes fucking crones? You don't do it because you want to, actually, it's just you get . . . I don't know, sort of carried away. But anyway, I'm telling you. Little Mickie shit

313

himself. Aye, that were it! We were standing round, waiting our turn, so to speak, and she was on the floor and he was in his little shirt and shoes, and he said "Eh fuck, I need a crap," and I said "Not in front of her, you dirty bugger, you'll put her off!" But he did it just the same, just squatted down and did it on the floor. Then he said "I've got no fucking paper, have I?" and he got hold of a sheet, or something, or her nightie or her knickers, I can't remember what, and wiped his bum and chucked it down and then jumped down on top of her and gave her one. What a fucking riot, eh?'

No, that couldn't be right, they couldn't all have been there, who was going to guard the others?

'That was the problem, really,' he told Janis. 'So many of them there, to keep an eye on. It was fucking lucky in a way they were half crippled, most of them. If they'd been able-bodied, so to speak, it would have been a bloody nightmare.'

Had he said that aloud, or had he merely thought it? Doggo can't have been there, he must have rounded up the others, locked them in one room, maybe. Ronnie remembered screams outside the room that Joyce was in, so maybe Boon had been doing Mrs Wilmott in, out in the kitchen. Boon had been the worst about the money, he'd gone holy apeshit, but he'd compensated with the violence, he'd really had a ball. He had a funny prick, Ronnie suddenly recalled, short and bulbous with this thick head, dark blue and purple, almost black. It was so big he couldn't get it in the old crone's mouth, even without her dentures, he had shouted. Which crone was that? he wondered.

Suddenly, Ronnie stood up, so suddenly that Janis gave a little cry, and drove her body back against the woodwork. But he barely glanced at her, he gave a little laugh and went into the room he'd shared with Eileen. Janis could not have got up if she'd wanted to, she was composed of grief and nausea and of shame. Her eyes were open long enough to register that he was shambling, almost shuffling, then they closed to blot out the awful little world. She heard a drawer slide open, and some grunts. She had no idea what it might presage. She had no curiosity.

Ronnie returned and stopped in front of her.

'Look. Open your eyes. Look, photographs.'

She heard paper rustling and had to look. He was tall above her, pulling instant pictures from a folded airmail envelope. The photographs an instant camera makes, lurid and harsh, the colours wildly off. As he fumbled, some dropped towards her, spilled across her drawn-up thighs.

'Mind the piss! Don't drop them in the piss, you dirty cow!'

Her eyes closed on a reflex, instantaneously, like a camera shutter, but presumably because of what they'd snapped. She'd seen a pair of thin white buttocks, tinged with flashbulb blue, marked with bold red spots, hanging above a blurred brown vee that must have been a woman's thighs. She may have seen a scrotum hanging down, a clump of pubic hair burning in the artificial glare, she may have seen a pair of white legs in the foreground, foreshortened oddly, ending in a pair of socks almost at the camera. She felt a hand grab something off her legs and thrust it at her face, the stiff sharp card biting at her chin.

'Look. They're amazing. Look at Doggo's prick. I bet you've never seen a dick like that.'

Her eyes stayed shut, until he banged her full in the face with his open palm, the ball of his hand crushing her nose, crashing the back of her head into the woodwork of the draining board.

'Look, you cow! Look!'

'No,' said Janis. 'No.'

But her eyes were open and she had to focus on the picture held six inches from her face. Too close to focus, mercifully, although she could see it was another fucking shot, someone crouching over an old, half-naked woman with his penis in his hand. Strangely, the other hand was covering his face, exposing only a wildly gaping mouth, presumably a laugh. The man was small and scrawny, she saw that as the photograph was moved away, her focus sharpened. Small and scrawny like a rat.

'Mick Renwick,' said Ronnie, as if identifying characters in a scrapbook. 'Daft cunt covered up his face, as if that made him hard to pick out. Doggo put a basket on his head in one of them.' He shuffled through and thrust one forward. 'Here. What a twat! Anyone would know him by his dick.'

Doggo. Janis looked, taking in the backdrop of a fireplace, the thin leg of what must have been a body protruding at an angle into the frame. A normal-looking man, neither fat nor thin, with a normal-looking penis as far as she could tell, just short and rather thick. A normal-looking photograph except that it was vile, obscene, perverted; a body, and a murderer, and an engorged sex organ. The shopping basket on the head was at a jaunty angle, showing a chin that might have ended in a point and a long thin neck with protruding Adam's apple.

She tried to speak, but the first words jammed up in her mouth. She wet her lips.

'Two of them,' she said. 'So there were three of you. I've never heard of Doggo.'

Ronnie scooped up the pictures – there were six or seven as far as she could see – and dropped heavily onto his kitchen chair. He splayed them out in front of him, gazing intently, while his hand felt for his whisky glass and raised it. He took a mouthful and swallowed it in drops.

Doggo, Janis thought. If I ever get out of here alive, I've got another name. She was able to look at that quite calmly, now. Her eyes snaked round the kitchen, thinking knives, saucepans, breadboards, anything that she might hit him with. He was strong, but he was drunk and getting drunker, he was hung over from last night, exhausted. Doggo, she thought. Why had she never heard of Doggo?

'There were two of us,' he said. 'Look at the pictures, the camera never lies. Two of them. I wasn't there, was I?'

A pause. He seemed pleased, amused by his own brilliant idea.

'You took the pictures, though.'

His smile died. Janis's whole body cringed, inside and out, in case he got violent because of what she'd said. She hated herself, a peculiar, intense dislike of her own half-arsed stupidity. His face relaxed.

'Some of them show Doggo, some of them show Mick. They took them of each other. To be honest, some of them did show me, but I burned them, didn't I? Doggo's a vicious bastard.'

He had switched to introspection towards the end of that. Doggo had gone mad when he'd seen the camera, although Mickie had thought it was a brilliant idea. While Doggo had glowered, he'd chased old Audrey Wilmott out of Joyce's room where they'd shut her in, and posed with his big willie in her

316

hand, ready for anything again once it had seen the camera. He'd put the other hand across his face, and one of her old hanging tits, and he and Ronnie had had such a laugh that Doggo had relented, as long as Ronnie let him take snaps of him as well and they always covered up their faces. It was a definite plus, they all agreed on that. There was something terrifically sexy about posing in some wild position you'd dreamed up, then watching it come rolling out and developing until you could see what you'd done. He'd found it years ago, with Eileen. It could make a shagging session last for yonks. Doggo had checked the pics, but he didn't care much, because his head was covered up completely, always. But Ronnie had planned it all beforehand, and burned the ones of him the next morning.

'I'd've thought you knew by now,' he said. 'You're not dealing with an amateur, Janis. Every move, every detail, every possibility.' He tapped his head, solemnly, with his index finger. 'All up there. We even had a shower after, me and Doggo. Everything. The perfect crime.'

He must have thought the comeback opportunities in that were just too glaring. His eyes narrowed as he waited for a smart remark. Janis, neutral, cold, appalled, neither spoke nor moved a facial muscle. The perfect crime. Boasting again. Ye gods and little fishes.

Ronnie's brain was weary. He was not confessing anything, he wondered if she knew that, but he could not be bothered to point it out. Confessions weren't worth a wank, he'd just deny it all, his word against hers. That pulled him up. The tape recorder. She had a tape recorder. She'd had it in her bag when they'd come back.

He got up and went into her room. He picked up the bag from off the bed and carried it back into the kitchen, upending it onto the table with a clatter. Purse, make-up things, the tape recorder, batteries, a little plastic case that probably held tampons, Eileen had one like it, loose change, some odds and sods. He checked the tape recorder but it wasn't going round.

'Pity, isn't it? You finally get your interview and it's no good to you. Christ, it would've made a cracking book. Christ, I bet not many people have heard a tale like this.'

He clicked the tape recorder on and listened to it hissing. He turned it off, uninterested in such little toys. Janis said quietly: 'Why did you do it, though? It all seems horrible. I don't think you're that horrible a man.'

He looked at her blank-faced. He found it hard to take that in. Was she Mickey-taking? No. What did she mean?

'You should've met Doggo. He's a fucking animal, you wouldn't reckon him at all.'

She never would though, because she'd be dead. He didn't say that, it would have sounded cruel. Doggo was abroad, in any case, as far as Ronnie knew he'd gone off to Amsterdam the morning after. Off to Amsterdam while he'd gone off to court. But Doggo could speak languages and things, or so he said. It all came down to education in the end, like Eileen always told him. He wished he'd gone to Amsterdam.

He said miserably: 'Because it was a fucking laugh, that's why.'

His voice had gone pathetic, and he hated that. He took a heavy drink and coughed. Fags weren't much to him, but he wished he had a fag. Among her jumble there was nothing useful, like cigarettes and lighter. The whisky lit the edges of his mood, but only momentarily.

What was it? How could he explain it, even if he wanted to? It *was* a laugh, it was a terrific buzz, they'd all enjoyed it. Anyway, it was a mighty turn-on, too. Normally, after, you got the droop from too much booze, and pills like Doggo took had never helped him much. That night he'd fucked all three of them, including one who had a walking frame! Not once, but many times! He'd lost count of his comes, but Mick had said he'd had eleven and it had seemed quite possible on the night. It didn't need an explanation, if you looked at it that way. It was a riot, and the worse it got, the better it became. How did she think anyone could *do* it, if it didn't turn them on? Looking back on it, he would admit, some of it had sometimes seemed ... But he'd only admit that to himself, of course. Sometimes, the memory of Joyce Withers' yellow minge ... And the way that Tessa had looked at him once. Between Mick and Doggo having her.

As if she could read what he was thinking, Janis asked 'Weren't you ashamed? Not ever? Once?'

He was pouring whisky as he answered, splashing it into and out of the glass, across the table.

'No fucking way! No chance at all, why should I be? They had it coming don't forget, especially that bitch Tessa! They were so smug, so fucking smug, we'd've done a dozen of them if they'd been there! They asked for it!'

Janis had reawakened him, and reawakened all her fear. She pressed back under the draining board, her chin thrusting down onto her chest. She kept her eyes open, though, whatever good she thought that might do her. His face was getting calmer, oh thank God.

'Tessa was the best,' he said. 'Tessa was the icing on the cake for me. Tessa was a bit like you, you know, a stuck-up bitch who led me on then dropped me. Oh Christ, you should have seen her face! Oh fucking Christ, it was a fucking picture! That's what you deserve, you fucking bitches! That's what you fucking prickteasers all deserve!'

'I didn't pricktease you!' screamed Janis. 'You got me wrong, you got me wrong, I didn't!'

Ronnie was on his feet, his face contorted.

'You should have seen the things we did to her! We got her opened up so far you could have drove a tank up! We stuck a brush in her and cleaned her out! We made her old man watch, we wanked all over him! I'm going to do the fucking same to you!'

He crashed back onto his chair, that squeaked in protest. His eyes were glaring, his fists clenched in front of him. Then he gestured for her to stand, a massive, energetic movement of his arm. Janis, mutely, began to pull herself from off the floor.

'Go and wash yourself,' he said. 'I'm going to do the same to you.'

FORTY-EIGHT

Maude Wimlock saw the headline in the *Oldham Chronicle*, saw the grim official mugshot of her client, and – with a sinking in her stomach that was palpable – bought a copy. Her first reaction was that a vast injustice had been done, that Ronnie Keegan had been set up, libelled, ruined and defamed. Then, reading on, she felt fear grow as she read of Janis's supposed involvement, and the fact that she had disappeared. A detective superintendent leading the Midlands hunt for the House of Horror murderers had come up to aid the northern team, and there was 'grave and growing disquiet' for the safety not of Janis only, but of Eileen Thorpe, Keegan's cohabitee, who was neither at her office in the Civic Centre nor at home in Harding Lane. The police sought information, urgently.

In the incident room, when she got through, there was the usual chaos. Half Oldham seemed to know of Ronnie Keegan, and to have something to say about his whereabouts. The story was in the *Manchester Evening News* as well, of course, and all the local papers in the satellite towns of Greater Manchester. But the system of filtering the calls was well set up, and Maude was persistent. In not many minutes she had told her story twice to detective constables, and shortly after that she spoke to Superintendent Patten himself. He was not in charge, but he had already formed a good relationship with the man who was. Very shortly, Maude was in a car.

Arthur Patten, by now, was sure that time was running out. The enlisting of the press to help flush Keegan out had been inevitable – and had indeed produced Ms Wimlock with exemplary speed – but it was, as always, double-edged. Brook Bank had burst into the forefront of the news again, and the rat-packs would be gathering and swelling even faster than the specialist police teams that had gone on the alert. Wherever Keegan and his hostages were lodged, it was equally inevitable that they would have a radio, or TV, or see a newspaper. How such a killer would respond, Patten could only guess. He tried to keep his guesses very flat.

Maude provided information that was priceless. She knew that Janis had been due to meet Keegan at the Ducie Bridge, and she knew that Eileen had decided to pre-empt her by waiting for him outside the Strangeways gate. She also knew, however, that Eileen had a chalet in Cheshire, somewhere between Marple and Disley. She had not realised at the time why Eileen had mentioned it to her, but now it seemed glaringly significant. It was her suggestion that the police should take her to the house in Harding Lane, to see if there were any deeds or other papers that would reveal the exact location. HQ in Manchester were in on it, of course, and J Division (Stockport) were put on stand-by so that nothing could be accidentally triggered off by a member of the public dialling 999, or some other act of God. Derbyshire Police were warned off from the top, just in case they decided the border area was 'grey' enough to justify them sticking in an oar. Shortly afterwards, Janis's Renault 5 was located three hundred yards from Victoria Station, and the fingers of excitement spread into the very heart of Greater Manchester Police. It was a manhunt, and there were going to be guns. It was a classic.

In Harding Lane, Maude felt like a criminal herself as she hurried through Eileen's and Ronnie's private papers. Despite her noted efficiency at work, Eileen's household files were like almost everybody else's, stuffed with envelopes higgledy-piggledy, spread over two or three areas, with some of the most urgent ones underneath the clock on a corner of the video and CD shelf. In a drawer in the main bedroom, Maude came across a bundle of photographs that made her gasp, and thrust them back into their envelope before the detective constable who was watching her should have a chance to see them. When he held his hand out Maude – blushing to her roots – asked him to call Patten from downstairs, and told him before he opened them what he would find. Patten glanced at two, depicting Ronnie, Eileen and a piece of sheepskin, before deciding they had no immediate relevance, and pushing them back into the envelope. Seeing the look on the young policeman's face, he then put them into his own pocket, showing Maude clearly what he had done. Maude understood.

The information they were seeking took an hour to reveal itself, emerging from a pile of dusty papers underneath a table in the spare room. It was a deed of sale from several years before, which located the chalet within the Disley boundary, in the county of Cheshire, in the curtilage of Knock Bench Farm. Superintendent Patten did not relay the information until he had returned to Oldham Police HQ. As a guest in such a massive operation, he knew only too well how easily he could be left behind.

There were others equally determined not to miss the boat. Secrecy, in any giant organisation, is a slippery commodity, and loyalty as a concept is notoriously difficult to define. Policemen need reporters sometimes, just as vice versa. In Oldham, Stockport and Manchester itself clandestine calls were made, and non-attributable briefings were given to trusted contacts. Armed police squads, in particular, feel that they are generally undervalued, appearing only in the papers to be pilloried for some trifling mistake. As they clambered into their vans to go to Disley, some smiled in quiet anticipation that, for once, they would have a useful audience.

The canal bank had been cleared of fishermen and walkers, the canal itself closed to navigation for a mile on either side of Knock Bench Farm. Despite the enormous difficulties in logistics, the main force, back-up crews, and ambulances had been found spaces at both ends of the pincer movement, the crowds had been dispersed, and the (unexpected) squads of press men and women had been marshalled as far as possible into units that could be watched and bidden. But Arthur Patten, as he joined the groups of senior officers in the trudge down from the Dandy Cock, had a deep foreboding.

That it would all be too much, too late.

Janis, when she returned from the washbasin to the kitchen, was not resigned. Although she had undone the buckle of her belt, staring at her image in the mirror with unseeing eyes, she had undressed no further, and she had not washed. After two minutes she had turned towards the door as if she would go back, then she had turned again and stood unmoving, almost congealed. It was not as if her mind were raging, either, it was – as far as minds can be – in neutral. After a while she became aware that her hands were resting on the basin and that nothing was happening, nothing at all. Nor was there any sound from Ronnie.

Is he unconscious? Is he dead? Has he gone to sleep?

She had no surge of hope with any of these thoughts, indeed, they hardly interested her. She felt light, and hollow, and unreal. She had no fear left, no sense that she would be raped, or murdered, she felt nothing. She did her belt back up and walked over to the door and opened it.

'Ronnie,' she said. 'Why don't you get away? Nobody's after you, you've got the car. Why don't you get away?'

He was sitting as she'd left him, but with all the fury gone. His eyes were dull and his white face was whiter than before. His hand was near the whisky glass and she could see it shaking from twelve feet away. He raised his head, but appeared to have some difficulty focusing.

'You can't stay here,' she said. Her voice was quiet, friendly, reasonable. 'Presumably someone will miss me before too very long. I told people where I was going, you realise that, don't you? I've always been in close contact with the police down there.'

Good old Arthur Patten, she thought. Arthur Patten who told me you were safe. At the moment she felt safe. At the moment.

'Presumably,' she said, 'they'll miss Eileen at the council offices, and I suppose they'll find my car sometime, in Manchester. Someone must know she's got this place, I guess? It can't be very long.'

She could not tell what he was thinking, which way he would jump. But the whisky bottle was a third empty now, perhaps a little more. Perhaps it would be better if she just kept him talking. Perhaps in time he would become incapable.

'I haven't fucked you yet,' said Ronnie.

He smiled at her, the slow smile of a bleary drunk. Janis's bowels clenched in quick revulsion. After a moment, she returned the smile.

'No.'

His breaths were regular, but shallow. He raised his knuckles to his eyes and rubbed. He rubbed his mouth.

'Admit it that you fancied me,' he said. 'Admit it that you started this. Go on, I dare you. Just admit it.'

She was framed in the doorway and she had to touch the wood on either side. She'd admitted in so many words to Hilary that he was right. She'd wanted more than just his story, and she'd hated everything inside herself that had made that true or possible. She would not admit it now.

'Ronnie,' she said. 'You're an attractive man. In any other circumstances—'

'Bollocks!'

He spat the word out, voice heavy with contempt. Panic crushed upwards in her throat.

'But you've killed people! Eileen's body is outside! Oh Ronnie, Ronnie!'

A silence fell, which seemed to come down gradually. They joined in it, each inhabiting some private world of shame. Whether she'd wanted him or not in that sense, Janis had wanted him for her own, had wanted to use his life to profit and to prove something by entering a pact with him. That much she could see, and she found it horrible. Ronnie, sipping whisky, had a mental picture of Eileen, broken in the loam, threatening his life by refusing to be invisible. He had murdered her, and then resented her for bearing witness to it. Now Ronnie did feel shame, it engulfed him.

'I don't know why I told you everything,' he said. 'I don't know what I did tell you, in fact. It's always been like this, you know. It's like I've got a . . . dislocated brain. I wanted to be like Eileen, do you understand, you're not the only classy bird. I used to beat her up, do filthy things to her and I never wanted to, I wanted to treat her like a fucking china doll, a lady. I tried to be like her and I ended up with mad bastards like Mick Renwick and Doggo Boon, a fucking beast, an animal, a weirdo. I'm not a monster, I don't think I am, but there was always something pushing me off the edge. She was cool, good clothes, the car. And fucking Mickie, running round the walls of roofless houses, screaming pissed, shacked up with Fat Marie. She stabbed him, you don't know that, do you? Fat Marie's cut Mickie Renwick's cord, she's topped him. That's what this is all about. I wanted Eileen and I got Mick Renwick, another shit, another worthless shit like me. It's like I'm drowning,

Janis. I've been drowning since the day my fucking mother had me. In a sea of liquid crap.'

The silence grew again. A jet plane came in overhead, low and throbbing in the heavy summer air. The noise appeared to swell, to fill the chalet like a box of sound. But Janis heard only silence.

'You've got to let me go,' she said. 'Please, Ronnie. You can get away in Eileen's car and I won't know where you've gone, I won't be able to tell them anything. You've killed five people now. You've got to let me go.'

'I couldn't get away, you're talking shit. And if I've killed five people, what difference would saving you make, eh? Would you put in a word for me? I promise he's reformed, your honour? Do me a turn, love, do me a fucking favour.' He drew in a sharp breath, with a small, convulsive jerk of his head, like a sigh he'd caught and swallowed. 'I killed Eileen, didn't I? The least I ought to do is kill you, too.'

'But in cold blood? Surely, Ronnie? No.'

The least he ought to do! In her misery, Janis was capable of a muted sort of wonder. She told herself: I don't believe he's going to kill me, I don't believe he will.

'I need you for a hostage when they come,' he said. 'I probably won't even touch you, I probably don't fancy you no more. Can you live with that?' A small sound of amusement. 'Mind you, if they don't come for yonks I might have to stretch a point. We'll both be dying for it, won't we?'

Outside, there was a noise. An electronic cough, a hiccup on a PA system. Janis, shocked herself, saw Ronnie's eyes stretch wide, his features alter almost slowly in fright and amazement. His hand slipped sideways, knocking over his tumblerful of whisky.

'Ronald Keegan.' The voice, through a loudhailer, boomed and scratched. 'Armed police. Come out with your hands placed on your head. Do not attempt to harm anybody. Come out with your hands placed on your head.'

Janis watched his face collapse, as she had watched his personality slowly come unravelled. Given her understanding, she was surprised at the blind fury that arose in her, the searing hatred, as she leapt across the room at him, snatched up the whisky bottle, and swiped it backhanded full into his face.

Blinded by blood, broken glass and whisky, Ronnie crashed backwards off his chair onto the floor, while Janis rushed out of the door into the sunlight. Unaware of any danger from the hidden barrels trained on her, she ran down through the garden, mouth open but not making any sound. She saw policemen waving from behind a bush and went across to them. She was startled when she recognised Arthur Patten. Then she gasped and gave a little moan.

'Are you all right?' he said, and the mad banality of it, the utter inadequacy, almost knocked her into hysteria.

'He hasn't murdered me, if that's what you mean, Arthur! He hasn't even raped me! Is that a failure of poetic justice? At least he should have raped me, shouldn't he? There should have been a sacrifice!'

Her hand was full of blood, she was gripping tightly on long shards of broken glass and one of them had cut into her wrist. Janis noticed this, although she had not felt it, and she fainted, dropping instantly and like a stone. Patten tried to catch her but he missed.

So she did not hear the shots that killed him, and she did not see Ronnie Keegan die. She did not hear the breaking window pane, nor watch the broomstick, so like a shotgun barrel (the experts all agreed) come poking through the wire anti-vandal grille. She came round some seconds later, to the tramping sounds of many feet, and the yells of many voices.

She did not even know for twenty minutes that the animal was dead.

FORTY-NINE

Lance Rosser, left behind like Cinderella, had done well with the new contacts he had made over the course of the Brook Bank investigation. Janis, when she emerged from the first shock of the traumatic afternoon, found herself on the wrong side of the notebook for the first time in her adult life, the wrong side of the cameras and the questions. There were even some in the ranks who had helped to save her who — despite the protection Arthur Patten could provide — would have jammed their knives into her wounds and twisted them. In the evening she saw little news, spending most of it with medicos and answering an endless list of questions from the police, but next day she was the centre of a tabloid storm.

Janis Sanderson, it was implied and almost stated, was a scarlet woman, a gangster's moll, a sort of pervert, some kind of twisted whore. That she had had a relationship with the House of Horror monster was in no doubt, and unnamed prison officers described in detail her demeanour when she had visited him in 'secluded, almost private, prison rooms'. Her link with Rowsley, her 'close friendship' with the murdered Tessa Wilmott, were uncovered as the basis for wild speculation, up to and including the possibility of an affair with Keegan going back for months before the murders. Neighbours in Harding Lane revealed her visits to Eileen Thorpe, and enormous headlines on pages three, four, seven, eight and nine of one paper set up the hare that she had met the couple when Ronnie was released to make a 'sexy threesome in the woods'. It was not merely a 'love-nest,' either, but a 'thieves' kitchen' (police sources believed) for the planning of more lucrative forays on secluded country mansions like Brook Bank. A fellow con who claimed to have spotted Ronnie at the Ducie Bridge described the women who had supped with him as 'a pair of sex-bombs, right little crackers. I can remember thinking that they'd be in bed together before the afternoon was out. I was frankly green with jealousy, I can tell you.'

Rosser's secret briefings (which admittedly were built up out of recognition by the grateful hacks) extended further, to Ms Sanderson's supposed involvement with the case. The legal grounds were far more dicey here than 'harmless gossip-mongering' about the sex life of a woman talked about quite openly by some ex-colleagues as being of unusually progressive outlook in 'matters of the heart', so the hints that did find their way into print were opaque enough to blind all but the most suspicious libel lawyers. But she was derided as a 'gipsies' friend' by one old villager, 'a bit obsessive about proving the investigators wrong', by Monica Pagett, 'landlady of the Rowsley local pub', and 'a woolly-minded do-gooder who doesn't understand the terror such people bring to decent, law-abiding folk' by a prominent Good Neighbour. The most inter-esting distortion in those three (accurately recorded) quotes was what was left out of Monica's. Janis was most obsessed, she'd added, about proving Ronnie Keegan was the culprit, not some hapless travellers. Janis, unaware until this time with what great relish dog would feed on dog, gave a howl of internal pain, and ran away to Hilary, in London. From there she phoned Clive Smith to seek advice on publishing a counter-blast, to set the record straight, but found him thinking purely in terms of interviews, exclusive, written in the *Clarion* by him. A journalist to his toes, and insensitive (he agreed com-placently) as a wagonload of donkey shit, he could not under-stand why she should be so upset. 'You've got a story, Janis, for God's sake,' he spluttered. 'For God's sake *milk* the bastard!'

Buster Crabbe ran her down to earth as well, and was all over her like the proverbial rash. He pooh-poohed the filth the gutter press had ladled (while questioning as delicately as he was able to see if it had a basis in the truth) and told her that the contract was waiting for her signature as if he'd never told her that he'd torn it up. This time there was a contract, too, this time his instincts told him he would have a winner, and he was sure that they could 'wind the money men back up to sixty, quite possibly beyond'. The way he saw it — whatever happened in the little chalet in the woods — she had exclusive knowledge of the working of a killer's mind, a mass killer to boot, and she had been intimate with him, in the sense (*bien entendu*!) that they had faced life and death together and he had spilled the secrets of his inner soul. Janis, sickened by the glibness with which such words were used, not just by Mr Crabbe, told him to . . . told him that she would think about it, but she needed time. When Bren rang, and indicated circumspectly that he was willing, if she thought that it would be a help to her, to 'come home', on any terms, she cried a little and told him the same thing. She was bruised, she said, she was damn nearly broken. But she had to fight alone.

Not quite true, of course. She fought, mainly, with Hilary at her side, with Hilary who knew her mind, it seemed to Janis, precisely as she did herself. Hilary talked with her, endlessly into the night, endlessly through the days, even on the golf course, where, to her amazement, Janis found she actually liked the game. Janis laid all her cards out on the table, cards that went back to her afternoon in Suffolk and beyond, cards that covered sex, and curiosity, and death, and prurience, and disgust both with herself and others. She dug into what still frightened her, and what still fascinated. When the dreams came back, she went and sat with Hilary, drank tea or brandy on her bed, and one night played Cluedo, of all things, until five twenty in the morning.

They talked of evil, naturally. The word so beloved of the press, police and politicians. It was a word they shied away from, although they had to return to it, to pick at it, endlessly. Yes, they solemnly agreed, just because men like Ronnie were abysmal did not mean they could not be attractive, yes, Janis accepted, she'd believed (naively?) that she could get beneath their skins. And do we want aliens, creatures from a horror tale, Hilary had asked, or men slowly overcome by a sea of troubles, people overwhelmed? Ronnie, Janis reported haltingly, had said that he was . . . dislocated. The prurient desire to profit from an awful crime was the parrot cry that haunted her, and sometimes she admitted it was true, and felt that she had learned a lesson of great depth. At other times, she could not remember what the lesson was . . .

What did you learn *about* him? Hilary asked her many times. Only that he was ordinary, and normal, even boring, she replied. Only that the murders genuinely seemed no big deal to him most of the time, nothing to write home about. Except that he appeared to think some aspects of it were funny, especially some of the sex, but then he was appalled, ashamed, when he had killed his girlfriend, Eileen, she was sure of that. That he was sure she had been after him, but did not even want to fuck her, in the end. Had no intention, not rape, not feeling up, not anything. What did she learn about him, that could seriously be set down? *Nothing*.

'Except that I felt sorry for him at the end. I thought he was a human being then, I thought that I could see his suffering, I could almost hold it. And I tried to kill him with a bottle, I wanted to, I could have done, I wasn't strong enough. I hated him.'

Arthur Patten asked her the same question, one night some weeks later when they'd gone out for a drink. Janis was back at home in Didwell, working as a news reporter for Clive, breaking back into real life the hard way, as she saw it. Bernie Smith had been jailed for eight years for burglary – no evidence had been offered on any other count – with six for Lee and Boswell and smaller sentences for some others of the so-called 'gipsies', and the case was well and truly closed. Patten, it was rumoured, had come close to resigning until the murder charge was dropped, but you did not talk to him about that if you had any sense. He had phoned her, out of the blue, and asked if she would come to dinner. She had agreed to drinks, in a city centre pub.

The atmosphere was less strained, from the start, than either of them had expected. Janis had followed the proceedings carefully, and had come to realise that the evidence against the travellers had been very strong, at whatever time that Sunday night they blundered on Brook Bank, and however little she believed they had been there. Patten had explicitly separated the two sets of marauders in his evidence, revealing for the first time how the terrible coincidence had led to an 'unfortunate but real' confusion in the conduct of the investigation. He had also insisted very strenuously that Ms Janis Sanderson had had no interest in, or contact with, Ronald Keegan and his associates except in the course of interviews she was doing with a view to writing it as a book. With a generosity that enraged his fellow officers from the lowest to the very top, he revealed that 'where Ms Sanderson's investigations have led, the police have only followed'. Hetherington, confirmed as full chief constable after the notable success achieved in the Brook Bank affair, let it be known in private and in no uncertain terms that Patten's upward movement in the force was at an end.

Janis did not imagine Patten's invitation could be a sexual overture, but she felt no imperative to scratch his eyes out if she should find it was. Since Bren had left, she'd been with no other man, nor did she have the least desire to, but the pain and rage she'd felt for Patten had dwindled with her raw, cruel memories of the whole grim business. In fact, it became plain quite quickly that he wanted to see if she had come through it intact, to 'test the waters' as he put it, disconcerting her with his clean and penetrating eyes. And then, when they had talked for more than two hours, and had had quite a lot of drink, he asked her what she thought of Ronnie, now.

'I don't think he existed in our world,' replied Janis, instantly. 'I think he was looking for his own world, something to latch hold of. I think he knew he didn't have a hope.'

'You sound as though you sympathise,' he said. 'After all he put you through, one might have thought . . .'

Janis slowly shook her head.

'You and Rosser put me through as much, in some ways. More. You and Rosser invented my existence as The Ghoul, then resurrected it for the world to have a share in. And you still work with him, don't you?'

'I wouldn't say as such, as far as one can have a choice in these things. I could never stand the man, if that's any comfort to you. He likes to make me suffer in any minor way he can.'

'He doesn't suffer, though. He's not the type, is he?'

Patten did not answer straight away. He pulled thoughtfully at his small cigar.

'He suffered because you proved him wrong,' he said. 'He knew that we were right and you upended us. It's a good job Ronnie died, from Rosser's point of view. He might have said that we were wrong out loud, in court. Very awkward.'

'Jesus.'

'I understand your sympathy,' he said. 'I understand why

you had to know. But to Rosser, rightly, Keegan was a monstrous, evil criminal, and to complicate it, what you were doing risked destroying the case against the others, the ones he also *knew* had done it, do you understand? To Rosser you were scum, hellbent on making money from the scrotes and slags and shitbags of this world, and trouble for the good guys. Us. To him, quite genuinely, you were a ghoul.'

There was a truth there somewhere if she could unbury it. Something dark and horrible that she must confront. But the harder she fought to crystallise it, the fuzzier it got. She shook her head for one last try.

'He was a foul, brutal murderer but I felt sympathy. I felt ... maybe there was something else. At the end, I felt ... almost close to him.'

It was as far as she could go. She took a gulp of gin and tonic, and it was a comfort to her.

'You won't believe me, but I understand,' he said. 'It's probably universal, what you felt. Like DPPs who kerb-crawl, like policemen who hate criminals so passionately they turn criminal themselves to nail them to the wall, then not see the contradiction. Like women who stand by their men however vile they are. Like anybody attracted to a monster who's a vibrant human being.'

'But he wasn't!' Janis began. She caught herself, and coloured slightly. She picked out the slice of lemon from her drink and licked at it. 'OK,' she said. 'Vibrant, sad, strange – whatever. You understand. He wasn't vibrant, actually, and I honestly don't think I was attracted. So you understand. Does that mean you forgive me, too?'

She tried a smile, but Patten did it rather better.

'If anyone needs forgiving it isn't you,' he said. 'If it makes you happier, I'll certainly forgive you, though – on condition you forgive me first. Is that a deal?'

'OK.' It was all meaningless, but it didn't matter much. She found the gin more comforting, however.

'I'm not sure we should forgive Ronnie Keegan, though,' said Patten, awkwardly. 'Not, I suppose, that it was ever in your mind.'

It wasn't. Ever. I'd have killed him if I'd had the chance, thought Janis.

'What about Boon?' she asked him, suddenly. 'Did anyone get anywhere with that?'

He shook his head, and gathered up the glasses to get another round. Rather sadly, it seemed to Janis, as she watched.

But then, the thing was full of sadness, wasn't it? Hilary had advised her to draw her horns in, to sit it out until it went away, she had confidence in her courage and her strength, she was certain she'd survive it in the end.

Janis was herself, most of the time. Except every now and then, most often on her own, most often in the silent, early hours. When she felt the fear of night and darkness creeping in.

Other People's Blood
Frank Kippax

To people like Jessica Roberts and Rory Collins, the bloody, unfolding story of their native Northern Ireland is no more than a sombre bass-note to their day-to-day existence. They are young, well-to-do, attractive. When they fall in love, the fact that Jessica is a Protestant and Rory a Catholic is irrelevant – such things are simply not a problem in their world.

But they are wrong. Jessica's father is a powerful figure in the Province, while Rory's – now dead – had the romantic reputation of involvement with the other, Republican, cause. Worse still, Jessica is already involved with a shadowy Englishman called Martin Parr. With appalling speed, their certainties begin to crumble in bigotry and violence . . .

'The tale of two young people whose life is shredded by the Troubles is all too credible. The exposure of lies, betrayals and hypocrisy – personal and political – is challenging.'
Belfast Telegraph

'Kippax writes gutsily and conveys a strong understanding of the divisive passions that are destroying Belfast.'
Sunday Times

'Blood and violence – and sex – there is in plenty, also some fine writing and a genuine feel for the reality of that poor, benighted part of the country.'
Sunday Press

ISBN 0 00 647286 9

The Scar
Frank Kippax

The controversial novel that was made into the BBC TV serial

Underbelly

Violent riots and rooftop demonstrations across the country have brought to light the alarming crisis facing Britain's outdated, overcrowded prisons. How long before the fragile fabric of a crumbling system finally gives way . . . ?

In HM Prison Bowscar, there have already been disturbing rumblings of unrest. But when political bungling brings a mass murderer and a crooked financier together under one roof with a group of dangerous men with deadly connections, a plan is hatched to convert the smouldering discontent into explosive insurrection.

As journalists and others struggle to unravel the tangle of official cover-ups and high-level corruption they have unearthed, inside the Scar there is a time-bomb waiting to explode . . .

'A thundering great novel. What's really amazing is how much he seems to know about so many different things . . . a cracking good read.'   Tony Parker, *New Statesman & Society*

'So topical . . . Kippax develops a complex, ingenious plot at breakneck speed and has a sharp underdog's eye.'
John McVicar, *Time Out*

'Brilliant. I was grossly entertained and thrilled . . . Frank Kippax is a rare talent.'   Jimmy Boyle

ISBN 0 00 617921 5

☐	DUE NORTH Mitchell Smith	0-00-647642-2	£4.99
☐	NIGHTWING Martin Cruz Smith	0-00-647908-1	£4.99
☐	ALONG CAME A SPIDER James Patterson	0-00-647615-5	£4.99
☐	DESTROY THE KENTUCKY Bart Davis	0-00-647639-2	£4.99
☐	THE ICEMAN John Sandford	0-586-21667-7	£4.99
☐	HONOUR AMONG THIEVES Jeffrey Archer	0-00-647606-6	£5.99

All these books are available from your local bookseller or can be ordered direct from the publishers.

To order direct just tick the titles you want and fill in the form below:

Name: _____

Address: _____

_____

Postcode: _____

Send to: HarperCollins Mail Order, Dept 8, HarperCollins *Publishers*, Westerhill Road, Bishopbriggs, Glasgow G64 2QT.

Please enclose a cheque or postal order or your authority to debit your Visa/Access account –

Credit card no: _____

Expiry date: _____

Signature: _____

– to the value of the cover price plus:

UK & BFPO: Add £1.00 for the first and 25p for each additional book ordered.

Overseas orders including Eire, please add £2.95 service charge.

Books will be sent by surface mail but quotes for airmail despatches will be given on request.

24 HOUR TELEPHONE ORDERING SERVICE FOR ACCESS/VISA CARDHOLDERS –

TEL: GLASGOW 041-772 2281 or LONDON 081-307 4052